DEATH COMES BY AMPHORA

DEATH COMES BY AMPHORA

by

Roger Hudson

Published in Great Britain by Twenty First Century Publishers Ltd.

A catalogue record of this book is available from the British Library.

ISBN: 978-1-904433-68-2.

To order further copies of this work or other books published by Twenty First Century Publishers visit our website:
www.twentyfirstcenturypublishers.com

Acknowledgements

I would like to thank Professor Andrew Smith, Head of the School of Classics at University College Dublin, for reading the manuscript from a historical point of view and for his valuable comments. My gratitude to Bernadette Smyth whose eagle eye spotted grammatical errors as well as other anomalies and omissions. Thanks also to the many other friends who have given their support, encouragement and helpful suggestions and not least their enthusiasm for the story – Noelle Barker and John Parker, who read it as it emerged chapter by chapter hot off the keyboard, in Dublin and London respectively. In Drogheda, strong support came from Steve Downes, Maggie Pinder, Tom Winters and other members of Drogheda Creative Writers who have reacted usefully to chapters read at meetings and events. The task of reducing and polishing was aided considerably by Valerie Shortland, my son Simon in Dublin and my oldest and valued friend Marion Thomas in Woodbridge, Suffolk. And mustn't forget Captain 'Bobo' Burns, my classics master at Guildford Royal Grammar School, who intrigued me in the first place.

My gratitude, too, to Fred Piechoczek of Twenty First Century Publishers for picking it up and running with it, and, of course, to my wife Sheila for all the behind the scenes support that kept me going through the cutting and rewriting stages.

Dedication

Dedicated to Marion Thomas,
for our long friendship and
for all her support and encouragement
over the years.

MARKET PLACE
(AGORA 461 BC)

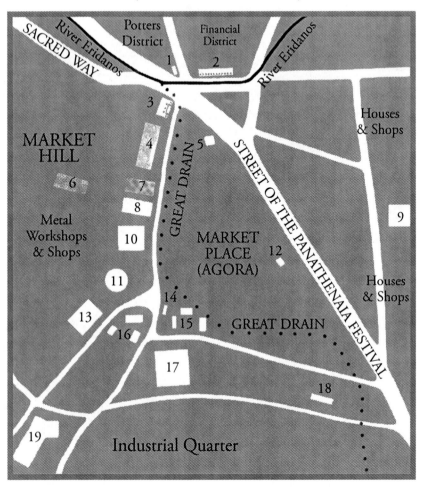

1. Shrine to Aphrodite
2. Painted Colonnade
3. Royal Colonnade
4. Ruins of Sanctuary to Zeus
5. Altar of the Twelve Gods
6. Site of Temple of Hephaistos
7. Ruins of Temple of Apollo
8. Temple of The Mother
9. Temple to Thesios
10. Council Chamber
11. Executive Committee Tholos
12. Tyrant Slayers Statue
13. Board of Generals Office
14. Statues of the Ten Heroes
15. Civic Offices
16. Civic Offices
17. Law Courts
18. Nine-Spout Fountain House
19. City Prison

ATHENS 461 BC

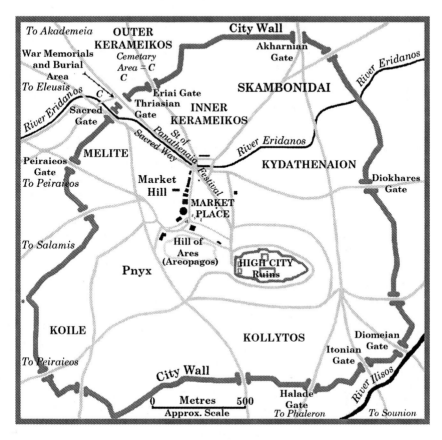

To Akademeia OUTER City Wall
  KERAMEIKOS
War Memorials Cemetery Akharnian
and Burial Area = C Gate
Area C
To Eleusis River Eridanos
  C
  Eriai Gate SKAMBONIDAI
Sacred Thriasian INNER
Gate Gate KERAMEIKOS
River Eridanos Sacred Way St of Panathenaic Festival River Eridanos
Peiraieos MELITE KYDATHENAION
Gate
To Peiraieos Market Diokhares
  Hill Gate
  MARKET
  PLACE
To Salamis Hill of HIGH CITY
  Ares Ruins
  (Areopagos)
  Pnyx
KOILE KOLLYTOS Diomeian
  Itonian Gate
To Peiraieos Gate
  City Wall River Ilisos
  0 Metres 500 Halade
  Approx. Scale Gate To Sounion
  To Phaleron

Knowledge of the ancient city of Athens in 461 BC depends on later written accounts and archaeological evidence, sometimes in conflict.

Much of the road pattern is speculative, but we know that the River Eridanos ran through the city, channelled and covered in places. The Great Drain ran into the Eridanos, and there was also piped water supply, not shown in the maps.

The architecture represents a cultural turning point: rebuilding had recently restarted, which would lead to many of the famous structures that we are familiar with today.

These maps are an assessment of how things may have been in the time of *Death Comes by Amphora.*

LIST OF CHARACTERS
(Real people in italics)

Lysanias (just 18) – an impetuous young man with high hopes, who is in for a few surprises.

Sindron (age 55) – his elderly but opinionated slave with few illusions about his master and not many about himself.

THE FAMILY IN ATHENS AND ITS SLAVES

Klereides (age 43) – Lysanias' uncle, a wealthy aristocratic businessman of dubious morals, recently deceased.

Philia (age 15) – Klereides' pretty wife, chafing against domination by

Makaria (in her late 50s) – Bossy mother of Klereides and of Lysanias' father Leokhares, missing presumed dead. Maybe with a few things to hide.

Hierokles (age 62) – Klereides' insensitive near-bankrupt landowning cousin.

Boiotos (age 31) – Hierokles' boozy bullyboy son, an angry man.

Otanes (age 52) – Klereides' house steward, a know-it-all high-ranking Persian war captive now slave.

Nubis (age 17) – Klereides' dancing girl and maybe something more.

Glykera – plump, bubbly cook-housekeeper with hidden charms.

THE POLITICIANS AND GENERALS

General Kimon (age 46) – top dog in Athens, leader of the aristocrats and victorious commander-in chief of the Delian League in the Great War against the mighty Persian Empire. Now on the skids.

General Ariston (age 44) – Kimon's deputy and hanger-on, addicted to platitudes.

Ephialtes (probably in his 50s) – leader of the democrats and instigator of the new democratic reforms, who needs a push from time to time.

Perikles (age 34) – Ephialtes' deputy. A young (for Athens) politician with ambitions but one with principles – or has he?

Themistokles (age 64) – one-time great war-leader, since disgraced and exiled and risking death by being here. Noted for his cunning.

General Myronides (early 40s) – supporter of Ephialtes, biding his time.

Thoukydides – up-and-coming aristocrat politician with his eye on the leadership of the faction.

THE BUSINESSMEN

Hermon from Syracuse – foreign resident businessman, Klereides' business partner with a knack for being absent at the right time.

Phraston (in his 60s) – very large sweaty banker and prominent backer of Kimon but maybe a little out of his depth.

Lydos (age 48) – slave banker with high hopes. Sindron's friend but that's a long time ago. Phraston's right hand man.

Philebos (age 35) – overseer of Hermon's shipyard, young, on the up.

Hipponikos – slippery smart-talking shipbroker.

THE WORKERS
Stephanos (age 24) – a young stonemason of fierce enmities and strong loyalties, eager supporter of Ephialtes.
Glaukon (age 48) – Stephanos' father, an older stonemason and democrat activist.
Archestratos – Trainer of rowers for Athenian navy, close supporter of Ephialtes.

THE ARTISTS
Strynises (about 38) – satirical poet and news disseminator of the market place. Hated by everyone but they all want to hear him.
Polygnotos from Thasos (age 39) – innovative artist with ulterior motives.
Mikon – well-established Athenian artist not averse to a back-hander.
Aeschylos (age 64) – prominent playwright and supporter of Ephialtes.
Damon – well-known musician and supporter of Ephialtes, ideas man for the democrats, once Perikles' tutor in music and poetry.
Zelias – aggressively radical young sculptor who doesn't care who he offends.

STATE OFFICIALS
Amynias – city naval architect.
Inaros – chief maritime inspector.
Bryaxis – financial scrutineer.

THE WOMEN
Aspasia (about 20) – beautiful top courtesan, more knowledgeable than expected.
Elpinike (44) – Kimon's sister, a mischief-maker bearing grudges, married to Kallias, Athens' richest man and mainstay of the aristocrats, conveniently out of the way on a foreign mission.
Isodike – Kimon's wife, who he loves deeply despite his many affairs.
Phoebe (30) – Ariston's wife, neglected and grief ridden.
High Priestress of Athene – Athens' top female dignitary, and is she angry!
Priestess at Temple of The Mother – not so angry but certainly not docile.

OTHERS
Niko – aged night-watchman at the shipyard with a loyal one-eared dog.
Pythodoros – self-styled philosopher and legal adviser.
Olinthios – king of the thieves and leader of the Athenian underdogs.
Master Barber – owner of barber's shop frequented by aristocrats.
Journeyman Barber – none too efficient at his job, as Lysanias discovers.
Hasdrubal – General Ariston's large Phoenician house steward and slave.

Miscellaneous magistrates, public officials, artists, merchants, shopkeepers, craftsmen, aristocrats, priests, foreign residents, women and slaves.

PRELUDE

Klereides was annoyed. Dragged from a warm bed, away from a playsome wife. Shaken up and chilled by the jolting ride fast through the empty streets of Athens. Downhill on rutted roads to the shipyard in Peiraieos, in the one-horse chariot they had sent for him. He must remember to have that driver sacked!

He shivered as he pulled his cloak tighter round him and rubbed his arms, huddling closer to the watchman's fire, all dignity gone. The flames gleamed on his bald head. Beyond them, the watchman's mangy, one-eared dog growled at him.

"What brings you here this early then, owner Klereides? I don't often have company in the night." The watchman doubtless recognised Klereides' wine-red face and rotund figure from his attendance at launching ceremonies, but he showed scant respect. These democratic reforms! Undermining all the old values. Still, could work in the company's favour if one played it right, Klereides mused.

"That old sun should start rising soon now, but the men won't be here till he's fully up. Can't see to work right, they can't, till he's up." Klereides felt like shouting at the man to be quiet but he was trying to muster his thoughts. "Gets lonely at times, but I'm used to it now. Used to be, I'd hear the creaking of the timbers, as they cooled in the night air, and think the Furies were after me." The fool chuckled, as though it was a big joke. "Doesn't trouble me now, though."

Klereides tried to ignore the scrawny, pock-marked little man with his uneducated accent and turned to warm the back half of his body and limbs at the watchman's fire, but the idiot gabbled on.

"What do you think about these democracy reforms then, citizen-owner?" He didn't wait for an answer, as though hoping his employer wouldn't notice his wary use of the word 'citizen'. "Me, I'm not sure. I always thought that General Kimon did his best for Athens and us ordinary people. They do say he's going to be mighty annoyed. But that Ephialtes, now, he does make it sound as though we could all be better off."

Klereides had to get away from this constant chatter. He had more urgent things to worry about. He needed quiet to think what could be wrong for anyone to summon him at this time of night. The shipbuilding company he and his partner owned had a contract nearing completion, with one of the ships due to be inspected by government officials later in the day. Acceptance, and the next payment, depended on it. And the next big contract.

Klereides tried to summon some dignity and grunted at the watchman, "Meeting at the completed vessel, dawn." That's what the message had said, wasn't it? "Send the others along when they arrive," he ordered.

"Yes, citizen. Will you be all right down there on your own? Here, take this lantern, I'll light another. Only careful if you rest it down. Don't want those timbers catching fire, do we?"

Klereides was impatient. "I know all about safety risks, watchman. Give it here!" He grabbed the lantern, an oil lamp contained within a ram's horn to protect it from winds but allow light through the translucent sides.

The moon was still high with only the faintest hints of daylight appearing in the sky. Klereides was sure he could pick his way safely along the walkways of planks. Fortunately there was a ramp, so he didn't have to climb a ladder. His plump figure didn't take kindly to feats of agility, and, in the morning chill, his old war wound was playing up, making him limp.

Above him, he could sense the tall skeletal shapes of half-built vessels crowding in around him, like dead men's fingers clawing at the dark night sky.

It was such a relief to be away from the watchman's chatter, though he could still hear him talking away to his dog. Klereides felt suddenly very alone. It wasn't the silence. Crickets and cicadas were still chirruping, the birds had just started their dawn chorus, a cock crowed in a not-so-distant farm, a donkey brayed, making him jump. He leant against one of the scaffolding trees to collect his thoughts.

Things had seemed to be going satisfactorily. True, he had panicked not so long ago, with those threats, and sent for his nephew, thinking of adopting him and making sure of an heir. Better than it going to that awful cousin of his. No, he was sure he had smoothed things over, especially after the dinner party last night. If the boy did turn up, he'd just send him back again. Everything was fine. Plenty of time to make his own heir on that frisky young wife.

Only now something really serious must have happened for him to be summoned here at this time. Normally his partner made all the practical business and technical decisions and left him alone. 'To drink and gamble the profits', Klereides joked to himself, smiling. No, I do my bit, he thought. My role is to smooth the way to new business, chat up the politicians who have a say in awarding contracts, entertain foreign buyers. I deserve my slice.

His lamp showed the bulk of the troop carrier looming ahead. Officially, it was a merchant ship but the instructions had been to adapt it to carry a large number of infantry, with storage space for weapons, food and facilities for a long journey. Part of General Kimon's plan for a long-distance strike force, he imagined.

For a moment Klereides thought he heard someone moving on another higher walkway. Odd. He listened – nothing except the insects and birds. As he moved on, something small fell and clattered down, a pebble maybe. Perhaps he had kicked it himself. The planks moved and creaked under his feet. The timbers of ships and scaffolding made strange shapes, silhouetted black against the barely lightening sky, a multi-layered cage all round him, even above where the stars still looked down coldly.

Could the man be here already? He held up the   its light was faint and only cast conflicting shadows.

He called out quietly, "Hello there!" No response. Slightly louder, "Is that you?"

Nothing. Then a slight laugh. Or was it creaking timbers? A cough. Definitely a cough. He headed in the direction of the sound. Thank the gods, they were here. Yes, there, he could see a lamp glowing faintly ahead. Must have taken a quicker route than mine, he thought.

"Coming," he called out confidently. "Why'd you have to drag me out this early, you old rogue?"

Surprisingly, when Klereides reached the lamp, it had been hooked to a scaffold upright. There was no-one there. He was alongside the nearly finished troopship now. Here the walkway, at deck level, widened out to a platform allowing direct access to the vessel. Beside him and above on more scaffolding and platforms were items waiting for outfitting work to commence once the basic structure had been passed by the inspectors. Hatch covers, cleats for tying back ropes, the ropes themselves for all the rigging, the giant amphoras for water storage, the bins and containers for the ship's store of food, and more.

"Where are you?" This was unnerving. There was no sound except the birds and insects and that Hades-rousing donkey. Then, suddenly, the sound of someone clearing their throat. Above him. He looked up. There was a dark shape, beside that big amphora slung on ropes up there.

Klereides stepped back to see more clearly. That laugh again, satisfied. A strange swishing sound and the black shape of the amphora above him seemed to grow suddenly bigger. The gods, it's falling! Must move! But his tired limbs didn't respond quickly enough. He felt a monstrous pain, heard timbers crack beneath him, and then nothing.

The horn lantern he had been carrying broke with the impact, the oil spreading out across the planks, the flame growing with it. In the light from the flames, a dark shape bent over the crushed body. But, at the sound of the approaching watchman, it grabbed the light still slung from the upright, blew it out, and was gone.

"Citizen? Citizen, are you all right?" called the voice of the watchman, alerted by the noise of the crash. The braying of a second donkey joined the first, and the watchman's dog barked and barked, as the firstlight of the sun god Apollo spread through the scaffolding and tried to warm the silent heap of flesh and earthenware that once was man and amphora.

CHAPTER 1

Dawn was the faintest glimmer on the horizon behind the Pride of Attika as the heavy-laden merchant vessel lumbered along the coast, its great sail creaking as it strained against the wind. On the deck, young Lysanias slept soundly, after the recurring nightmare that haunted him since his father's disappearance. Snuggled under a sheep's fur, his precious tool bag beside him, and, surrounded by other passengers, he looked peaceful now.

It was only the familiar sound of carpenters' mallets and hammers ringing across the waters that roused him, with a rush of excitement, to full attention. Eager for his first sight of Athens' massive harbour, he sprang up and ran to the rail.

"Master, where is your modesty? Put this around you, while I fetch your tunic." He grabbed the fur held out by his slave, Sindron, and covered himself. Silly old fool! But he was grateful.

In the cool, clear air that Attika was noted for, everything was sharply outlined, though still distant. There were the stone lions his father had told him about, guarding the mouth of the Great Harbour, whose size more than justified its name. Beyond it, the town of Peiraieos stretched fingers of red-brown roofs, wooden constructions and fire-blackened ruins into the green of farmland and market gardens above, reaching up the hill as though trying to touch the similar fingers of what looked as though they must be hovels, wooden shacks, as well as houses and what might be industrial premises pushing down from the city walls of Athens itself.

Two grey lines like legs stretching down from the city showed where the Long Walls were being built that would protect this area against enemy attack and ensure access to the port, the wall on the left almost complete, the wall on the right little more than foundations it seemed. The city itself was big, bigger than he'd imagined even from his parents' stories, with the sharp-edged, square-topped shape of the High City, the Akropolis, rising above the city walls, and the green and grey of the mountains beyond that.

Only the jagged, fire-blackened pillars of ruined temples broke the hard outline of the High City crag. Lysanias knew the Athenians had vowed not to rebuild them in order to demonstrate the sacrilege committed by the Persians when the invaders had destroyed the temples and burned the city to the ground, but it puzzled him how the Athenians could do honour to the gods without temples. And he was surprised how little of the housing had been rebuilt and how much of the business of the harbour seemed to be done from temporary-looking wooden structures, even though Sindron had explained that every bit of available stone had been commandeered to rebuild the city walls that were the essential defence against the Spartans.

"It's so far away, Sindron, and we can hear it already. There must be hundreds of carpenters at work," he said, with awe in his voice, to the elderly slave who had come up behind him.

They made an ill-matched couple. The smooth-skinned, well-muscled youth and the tall scrawny old man. Lysanias' wavy hair fell to his suntanned shoulders. His light brown eyes and wide, full-lipped mouth held their customary smile, though the eyes revealed a questioning wariness that told of an eagerness to explore, to find out for himself. He put on again the worker's tunic, his usual clothing that he had insisted on wearing for the voyage.

Sindron's beard was long and drew to a point. Like his windblown hair, it was predominantly grey. Below the sharp bone of a nose, the full moustache hung unevenly, hiding the thin-lipped mouth with its humorous twist. The absence of frown lines and the neat homespun cloak he wore suggested that, despite his slavery, this man had not fared too badly in an often-cruel world.

Sindron was horrified that so little had been rebuilt and was wondering what it would be like within the city walls, but he didn't say so. He was painfully aware of the impact of the sea air on his old leg injury that heralded a return of the limp that could slow him down so and lessen his value as a slave.

"That'll be the shipyards, master. Athens rebuilding its war fleet, I expect." Lysanias knew that! Would Sindron never forget he had once been his schoolteacher?

The slave handed Lysanias a piece of bread with a salted herring. Lysanias took one bite and, too excited to eat, tossed the rest to the seabirds noisily circling the ship.

Lysanias knew how timbers could ring as you hammered the nails and wooden spiles home. He had himself worked alongside his father, Leokhares, only on fishing boats and houses, as Leokhares taught him the tricks of the carpenter's trade, but shipbuilding couldn't be much different. He longed to be out there in the early morning sun, with the familiar tools in his hand.

Old Sindron seemed to read his thoughts. "That's all behind you now, young master. Your uncle won't want you involved in a manual trade. You're moving into the upper classes now, boy." The word slipped out and

Sindron regretted it the moment he saw the frown crease Lysanias' brow. But the boy needed his advice. He had promised the lad's mother. Lysanias blushed despite himself. "I can still make things for the household. Anyway, it's none of your business, old man! You do what I say now, not my father or mother!"

Sindron stiffened. It was the same boyish attack but beneath it was the real power the boy now held as his new owner. He decided to try reason, logic. After all, he had always taught the boy to think logically. "Correct, master. But remember that I have more life experience than you and I did live in Athens. I tutored your uncle and your father, before your father emigrated and took me with him." It sounded stiffer, more pompous than he'd intended, and, as a slave, he wasn't at all sure that his experience was that great.

Engrossed and angry, the pair paid little attention to the bustle of rousing passengers around them.

It irritated Sindron that the Athenians cosseted their young men so. Even at eighteen, the boy was so naïve and impulsive. Thank the gods, Lysanias would go straight into two years' military training. That should knock some sense into him. Then whatever business training his uncle might give him before he would have to carry any real responsibility would hopefully mature him further.

Lysanias knew this conflict was going too far. He'd hurt the old man. It was boyish and he was a man now. Eighteen yesterday, even if he hadn't enjoyed celebrating his coming of age away from the family, on board a tossing ship, seasick and lonely.

"I didn't mean it that way, Sindron. You know I value your advice, but you have to admit a lot has happened since then. General Kimon has hammered the Persians in battle after battle till they're not a threat any more. Athens is the top power in the whole Aegean and beyond. It has to be different now."

Sindron saw the humour of Lysanias firing back at him points he had himself enumerated often enough. He relaxed a little.

"It'll all be exciting and new," Lysanias went on. "You won't recognise it." He ventured a smile to cool the temperature, while consoling himself with the thought that he could sell the old slave in Athens, if the man continued to get on his nerves. He wasn't sure he would dare. His mother would be very annoyed, if he did. But he could! He hoped the old man realised that.

The disagreement could not disturb the wonder and satisfaction he felt at coming to the renowned city of his birth.

"We'll see, master. The Athenians can be very conservative."

"And snobs, godsawful snobs." A gaudily dressed, dark-skinned, heavily bearded man, leaning on the rail alongside Lysanias, butted in, his dress and his guttural accent declaring him a foreigner, probably a merchant.

"What do you mean?"

"Oh, not you too! Sorry I spoke. You're one of them, eh?"

"My master was born in Athens, sir." Sindron tried to save Lysanias from further embarrassment. "He is returning to take up his citizenship."

"See what I mean, even the slaves of Athenians are snobs!"

"That's unfair," Lysanias flamed. "He was only trying to give you information, so you wouldn't make a fool of yourself." Sindron found himself in the strange position of being defended by his young master, rather than the other way round.

"Hold on, young man! You've got spirit, anyway. Didn't mean to offend. You've not lived here lately, though, have you? Thought not. I guess it's the wealthy Athenians who are the snobs."

The foreign merchant set off on a tirade against all the taxes that resident businessmen from other cities like himself had to pay to the city and how they were exploited extortionately by the citizen patrons they were obliged to have, giving names and examples. Among them was a name like his uncle's – Klereides – but the accent and speed he talked made it unclear. The foreign merchants were all "from" somewhere – "Hermon from Syracuse," "Isomenes from Kition," Greeks from cities far and wide but all Greeks, although regarded as foreigners in Athens.

The man clearly had a mighty grudge against the city where he made his wealth. Growing angry, Lysanias was about to ask the man why he didn't go back to his home city when a cry interrupted them.

"Look, over there!"

Lysanias joined the rush of passengers to the opposite rail. As their ship turned to enter the harbour, a trireme, a fast war-galley, could be seen approaching from the West, seeming to skim over the water. It was a dazzling sight, the slim tall trireme with all three banks of oars hitting the water in unison.

As it drew closer, he could see the staring eyes painted on either side of the prow to frighten enemies, the fierce figurehead between and, below that, the fearsome lion-headed battering ram repeatedly breaking the surface of the water. A woman screamed nearby, as it appeared to be heading straight toward them.

"That's odd," said the captain's voice behind him. "Warships normally use the military harbour on the other side of the peninsula. They must be in a hurry."

"No, wants the whole town to know he's back, doesn't he? Big-headed bully!" The speaker was one of the stonemasons, the only other passengers wearing workers' tunics. Lysanias had seen them often, a young man and an older one, running round the deck or wrestling together, to keep fit on the voyage. This was the young one speaking, short, broad-shouldered, the bronze colouring of his skin, from long hours working in the sun, a match for Lysanias' own. Both wore their hair and beard cropped in the functional way he knew many workers preferred. As the trireme turned and passed, Lysanias could hear the boatswain setting the time. "Op, O-Op". The cry came over the water and then the piping of the flute-boy to the same beat. Lysanias could make out the detachment of hoplites, the heavy-armed foot soldiers, in full uniform with bronze breastplates and shields polished to perfection. They flashed brightly, in a dazzling tribute to Apollo, as the trireme swung, briefly facing the risen sun.

The warship lined up for its entry into the harbour, the oarsmen all keeping magnificent timing. Then, on the final gruelling spurt, a great unison cry came from the oarsmen. "Rhup, Pa, Pai", they cried. "Rhup, Pa, Pai". It seemed almost a challenge to the silence and dignity of the commander, standing upright in the stern of the ship, the banners of Athens and the Delian League, the confederacy of city states that Athens led, fluttering behind him.

They were so close he could see the anger on the commander's face. Not to be outdone by his own men, he raised the ceremonial trident he held, beat the staff on the boards and the hoplites yelled in unison, "Hail to Athene," in greeting to the city's goddess. Faced with the patriotic cry, the rowers were forced to join in and most of the passengers on the merchantmen echoed them. "Hail to Athene!"

Then it came to him. "Hey, I know who that is. We've got a statue of him in our market square. Look, Sindron! That's Kimon, General Kimon!" and he turned chattily to the man next to him, the older stonemason. "He founded our town, you know, Eion, military colony. It was a Persian army base and he besieged it till they burnt it down and themselves in it. What a commander! See that pennant, Poseidon's trident, that's his symbol."

The stonemason didn't seem as enthusiastic as Lysanias. "Look, son," he confided in a low voice. "I wouldn't shout too much about all that. Out of favour in Athens these days that Kimon is. Democrats in charge now and we think he's been getting too big for his boots. Too Hades keen on war for our liking. Time we enjoyed a bit of peace."

"But he's a great man. Why shouldn't I talk about him?"

The stonemason seemed slightly thrown by this challenge to his honesty. "Well, when you're new in a place, you have to be careful..."

"Too rich by half, that boastful warmonger." The young stonemason was more outspoken than his colleague. "Time us ordinary people had a go, like Ephialtes says."

Lysanias couldn't hold back. "But the rich pay for all the festivals and temples, they know how things work, better to let them run things, isn't it?"

Sindron recognised his own words, coming out of Lysanias' mouth, but knew that was the wrong thing to say. The boy really had so little social experience.

"You're not rich are you, youngster? You wear a worker's tunic. Which side you on?" And he was pushing up close, fists clenched. Though Lysanias was slightly taller, the man's broken nose and swollen ear announced a readiness to fight for his opinions. Reacting angrily, Lysanias was ready to fight too but he realised he didn't really have any opinions yet, certainly not enough to fight over, even though he knew he could give as good as he got.

"No, but..." Lysanias was aware of Sindron hovering nervously at his shoulder, knuckles white where they clenched his staff.

"Then why are you sticking up for them?" The worker was becoming decidedly aggressive. Lysanias tensed. He clenched his fists to be ready. Defend with the left, hit with the right, as his father had taught him. Right.

"Lysanias, I think we'd better get our bags ready to disembark." Sindron was agitated, deliberately avoiding emphasising his own slave status so as not to reveal that his master was no longer the worker he seemed.

"Calm down, Stephanos," the older man butted in. "He's new to Athens. He's got a lot to learn."

"Well, tell him to keep his mouth shut, till he knows what he's talking about." Stephanos turned and shuffled away, muttering to himself. Lysanias was disturbed. He had imagined Athens as somewhere everyone worked together to achieve great things, not a place of argument and hatred. What could justify that? But Sindron seemed to be accepting it.

"He's right, you know," confided the older man, who introduced himself as Glaukon the stonemason. Challenged by Lysanias to say what he had against Kimon, he revealed only that he wanted real democracy and an end of Kimon and his wealthy friends telling everyone else what to do. He and his son had been working in Abdera, when they heard the reforms had gone through, and decided to come back to lend support.

He ended by closing his fists and thumping the right one down on the left, like a hammer hitting an anvil. He looked at Lysanias as though expecting a response but Lysanias pretended he hadn't noticed, wondering if he should know the sign.

"Bit hot-tempered, Stephanos, but his heart's in the right place." He moved off and Lysanias was immediately cornered by a dignified-looking man.

"Don't you listen to them, young man. Fine man, General Kimon, and he's done so much for the people. Opened his orchards to anyone, free dinners at his house for all, however poor, generous gifts to the city. Trouble with this rabble, they don't know who their real friends are." He walked away, a young boy trotting at his heels, holding the man's lyre to his chest. That sounds more like the way people should treat one another, thought Lysanias. His own natural loyalty was to Kimon but now it looked as though there were two opposing sides in Athens. Perhaps he should wait and see where his uncle stood.

"Do you think I could ever achieve as much for Athens as General Kimon has?" he asked his slave. "He had to overcome so many disadvantages too."

"Now lets not run before we can walk," replied Sindron with one of those aphorisms he used that were so irritating. Lysanias fell silent.

Completely surrounded now by the Great Harbour, he marvelled at the shipyards, the timber yards, the warehouses and store sheds for imported goods and the ships from many cities and nations unloading or departing. An Egyptian dhow and a Phoenician vessel gave him a momentary fright. Ships belonging to the enemy! Until he recalled that the ship's captain who had delivered his uncle's message had mentioned the expectations of a truce in the long war. The war must be over. The energy and activity along the docksides declared it.

That strange message summoning him to Athens still puzzled him and he remembered the discussions and arguments with his mother and Sindron. Should he go to join his uncle Klereides in his shipbuilding business or stay to protect his mother, brother and sisters now his father was gone, especially after that big raid had caused so much damage to the town?

Most puzzling of all, why had his uncle scrawled the message on schoolboy's wax tablets, smeared and difficult to read? And those strange phrases he had used.

"What do you think uncle meant by ...?"

"We'll know soon enough, master," his slave responded, busy with their baggage.

As the rowboats turned their ship into position to dock next to the war galley, Lysanias could see that the harbour didn't look as grand as his father's description had painted it. Many buildings, from warehouses on the waterfront to structures up the hill behind, seemed to have been re-built in a hurry and there were still burnt-out plots amongst them, though the sounds from shipyards and sawmills, foundries and forges, confirmed that this was a thriving town.

As they waited to disembark, Sindron registered, among the portside bustle of stevedores and customs officials, General Kimon talking agitatedly with a cavalry officer, another general to go by his helmet, and his horse nearby, as the hoplites lined up in parade formation beside them. The level of social conflict he and Lysanias were encountering was disturbing but he wanted to know more about it before he worried Lysanias with it. He pointed out to Lysanias a small wiry man who seemed to be darting around gathering information from the sailors.

"Who is he?" asked Lysanias.

"Market place poet and news-teller, name of Strynises. Sells news to the highest bidder before making it public. Satire a speciality."

Before he could explain more, they were distracted by the shouts of sailors to enquiring dockworkers as to why Kimon, who had set off at double-pace at the head of his troops towards the city, was in such a hurry.

"Rushing to get his version to the magistrates before rumour gets in before him. He's worried this time. "

It seemed that the Spartans, having originally invited Athens to send troops to help them put down a revolt of their serfs, had become scared by the radical changes in Athens, and asked Kimon, who had always been a friend of Sparta, to leave and take his elite hoplites with him. It sounded as though talk among the rowers to the effect that they should be supporting the revolt rather than suppressing it may have had something to do with it. And the man who said it laughed and winked and was cheered by his fellow rowers.

The citizens will find that rejection humiliating if not an outright insult, thought Sindron, as he checked again that they had everything with them.

Lysanias wanted to ask Sindron what was going on here, what these reforms could be that they caused so much fear and anger, how Athenian rowers, who were also citizen-soldiers, could work against their leader and presumably the policy of their city. He wanted to but he wasn't prepared to give the old bore an opportunity for another lecture. Time to replace the slave with one who would treat him like a master, not a pupil, he thought to himself semi-seriously as they disembarked.

On the quay, their captain was informing the news-teller that the big raid on Eion had been less disastrous than at first appeared though the colony had lost a lot of people. Lysanias was shocked to realise that the brief phrase included his father killed or captured but anyway lost to him.

"That's news," replied Strynises. "Last we heard they were almost wiped out." Lysanias hoped there hadn't been another raid and that his family were all right.

Philia pushed the shuttle through the loom with force, worked the loom and pushed the shuttle back. She was still angry. Klereides hadn't come back, hadn't talked with Makaria. He never kept his promises!

She had used all her wiles the previous night when, after his dinner party, Curly – what a nickname for a balding man! – had paid one of his infrequent visits to her bed. Finally, despite all his flattering and smooth-talk, she had wrung from him a promise that he would speak to his mother Makaria about allowing Philia to share in the running of the household as a young wife should, even if she was very young.

Then, just as she was about to reward him with the sex she herself so desperately wanted in the hope of providing him with an heir, the slave-boy had knocked at the door with that message and Klereides had left her bed and gone out and hadn't come back. So much for his promises!

So here she was at the same old routine, working in the weaving room with Nubis her personal slave and the two other slave-girls, while Makaria rattled on with the same old stories, the same old moans about her sons and her dead husband and how they had let her down, especially Klereides for going into business and darkening the family's name, over-spending like his father. This morning though she seemed strangely agitated, pausing from her sewing and looking towards the door, as though expecting something.

"Philia, you're slowing down! No day-dreaming!" came the old crow's voice. "Pay attention to your work!"

Philia swore a mild curse as she pricked her finger and realised she would have to undo her work and start again. She would make Klereides suffer when she saw him again.

Suddenly there was a loud banging at the front door. "Mistress, mistress, come quickly," the steward's voice called. As the black shape swayed out, Philia fumed at the thought that it was she who should be called "mistress" here.

Then Philia heard Makaria scream and knew something very bad had happened.

CHAPTER 2

"That's it, master, at the top of this rise. You won't remember but that's your uncle's house." Sindron plodded along beside the donkey cart with their luggage.

"Yes I do, yes I do!" shouted Lysanias, running ahead, as old Sindron puffed and panted after him. "There's a lion's head doorknocker."

"Everyone has a lion's head doorknocker," Sindron shouted after him, wishing he had young muscles again.

Lysanias was delighted that his early memories did include that stern frontage with no ground-floor windows and only small casements on the first floor. And blue, he remembered the colour blue.

Sindron felt re-assured too. He knew that the family had intended to rebuild the house the way it was before the invasion, but, even here in the wealthy part of the Inner Kerameikos district, he'd seen houses that only now were being rebuilt to full size and other sites still in ruins. However, compared to the district of Koile they had passed, where people were still living in hovels, this was the land of the gods. Here at least the streets were obviously swept every morning and the household dung collected and taken away. He was pleased to be back, even if his leg was throbbing from the journey and the effort to minimise the impulse to limp.

He wondered what sort of woman the widow Makaria had turned into; she had been tough enough when her husband was still alive, rejecting her younger son's marriage and causing his drastic decision to leave the city.

Lysanias smiled as he imagined how they would welcome him after all these years.

Then, as he looked ahead, he could see that the front door was open. That shouldn't be. Visitors always had to knock on the lion's head knocker. Except when... and he saw that the Herm beside the door, the bust of the god Hermes that protects every Athenian house, was draped with black ribbons, and, yes, there on the other side was the vase of water for mourners to purify themselves on leaving.

And the keening and wailing from inside. How had he missed that? A death in the family! Maybe it was his grandmother; she was the oldest.

He stopped in his tracks, his eager smile fading, as he waited for Sindron and the cart to catch up to discuss what they should do. It struck him that he'd never really had to make a decision without Sindron or his parents there to consult and advise. His panic faded as the reliable old retainer drew closer.

Sindron took over. He roused the porter without causing disturbance. The wrinkled and stooped figure shuffled out, looked closely at them both with his aging short-sighted eyes and grinned broadly in welcome, showing his brown and rotting teeth. He remembered them both, even Lysanias as a very young boy.

"Sindron, welcome! But you've come at a sad time for the household." The old man briefly grasped Sindron's wrist and looked into his face to be sure who it was, then looked closely at Lysanias. "Would this be young Lysanias? Scrawny whelp he was. Used to pull my old dog's tail till the poor beast yelped. What's he dressed like this for, eh? In a play, is it?"

Lysanias suddenly became very self-aware and wished he had taken Sindron's advice to have a bath and change into full cloak and tunic instead of insisting on coming straight here as he was, in his workman's tunic.

Through the big wooden doors, Lysanias could make out a body lying on a funeral couch, feet towards the door, and keening mourners around it. The wailing went on ceaselessly.

"You'll not be welcome to them inside," the porter whispered, startling Lysanias. "Come in, but wait here while I let people know." He gestured to the carter to show him where to unload their luggage and Sindron paid. Had Lysanias heard right? Why wouldn't he be welcome?

They waited in the porter's room, a bare cell of a place that the slave had tried to make homely with a few things that reminded him of his homeland. The porter's latest dog growled at them from his corner, muzzled to prevent him barking and disturbing the mourning. Across the entranceway in the stables, a horse snorted but clearly extra straw had been put down to minimise any noise from the animals.

"Master," Sindron whispered, though Lysanias couldn't think why. With the noise of the wailing, he could have spoken loudly and not been overheard. "Master, dark clothes! You must change into dark clothes for mourning."

"Master." Another voice, softer, sibilant, a distinct foreign accent. He whirled as the steward appeared and introduced himself, giving the ingratiating smile and subservient bow of a slave. Old Manes must be dead, thought Sindron.

"Master." The steward seemed nervous, startled, shifty. "We weren't expecting you. You are welcome but ... We ... The mistress ... Your grandmother thought Eion had been overrun and you were all dead. We heard stories. We thought they were reliable."

He eyed Lysanias' worker's tunic with disdain and Sindron's unkempt beard but, on the word of the porter, accepted that they were who they said they were.

"But uncle wrote for me to come. Didn't he tell you, tell grandmother?"

"No, master. And now he's dead. Accident. Terrible. Unexpected."

Sindron interrupted the flow of unconnected words. "My master has no mourning raiment with him. Can you...?"

"Of course, of course, please come this way. I'll have something brought. Come this way."

He seemed to eye Sindron suspiciously, as he ushered them into a chamber on the other side of the entrance lobby where Lysanias changed clothes. Uncle dead! What would he do now? Why hadn't his uncle told anyone he was coming and why did the steward keep calling him 'master' in that obsequious way? Lysanias wasn't his master. And what was that rumour about everyone in Eion being dead? They must be confusing Eion with somewhere else.

Philia had become hysterical when they'd shown her the body of her dead husband. She screamed and cried, until they threw cold water over her and she calmed down.

Then there was all the rushing to help clean and lay out the body, the funeral cloths and clothing to be taken from the cypress chest, tables with burial goods to be prepared, the household shrine to be draped, and her own mourning clothes to put on.

She didn't like it when they cut off the long dark hair that she was so proud of. That was a shock but it would grow again and she did look distinctive in the mirror, she thought, with her black robes and short, ragged black hair and dark eyes. She really felt important as she crouched by the funeral couch. No, mustn't think that! Poor Klereides! What a way to die!

She let out a wail. She was getting good at this. After being told so many times to "be quiet, Makaria is resting", it was a great way of relieving her feelings. No, mustn't think that way ... Goddess forgive me, she thought.

"Go on, pay your respects to the dead," Sindron urged. "Remember when Eion's chief magistrate died in office? It's just like that," Sindron urged. Lysanias shuffled forward. The glance and the gesture to the family shrine, where the ancestors were honoured; that was first. Then the turn and the gesture to the female figures crouched wailing at either end of the funeral couch, who would be close family. One seemed large and the other tiny, but to Lysanias they were just dark shapes. The paid mourners, further back, continued wailing, beating their breasts, tearing their clothes, in ways family women were forbidden to do.

Beyond them were the tables with the grave-goods that would be buried with his uncle – elegant silver, pewter and ceramic platters, bowls, vases and amphoras to serve him in the afterlife. Beside them, his hoplite armour and weapons, polished and gleaming. The honey-cake was for Kerberos, the three-headed watchdog who guards the gates of Hades, to calm him while Klereides' soul slipped in. In his uncle's mouth would be a silver coin to pay Charon for rowing him across the river Styx. The odours of marjoram and rosemary came up to him from herbs scattered on the bier to disguise the smell of decaying flesh.

By then he was close to the body and it was time to look down and moan, eyes closed, with arms held wide in a gesture of openness in the face of death that comes to all. Then he opened his eyes – and stared. The body wore a mask. But masks were for covering the ravages of extreme old age or the most disfiguring of diseases or ugly facial wounds. And the wreath of flowers round the head, that was more profuse than normal, he was sure. And the shape of Klereides' chest under the embroidered white covering, that didn't seem quite right.

He had to know. On impulse and without thought to the offence he might cause, Lysanias pulled back the cover with one hand and whipped off the mask with the other. There was a startled gasp, as the wailing momentarily stopped, before resuming more loudly.

Lysanias felt sick. What had happened to his uncle? The right side of his chest was completely crushed and the right side of his skull. His arm lay as though broken. The women had done their best to clean up the wounds and build up the chest to make the body look normal, but the damage was too severe.

Lysanias gently replaced mask and cloth. The shock grew into anger. If this was a violent death, if his uncle had been killed in a fight, then it stood to Lysanias to avenge him.

It was difficult to follow through with the ritual gestures, having seen what he had seen. He did his best, then backed away, the picture of his uncle's poor crushed face and crumpled body stuck in his head. Sindron hissed at him and he remembered to gesture again to the black shapes crouched wailing at either end of the bier. The moan he gave now had genuine feeling, as the breath he had been holding escaped and real tears fell.

Then he turned and went back to Sindron and the steward. "Whatever happened?" asked Lysanias, angry, hurt, worried. "Is this a feud? Does uncle have to be avenged?"

"Please calm down, young master. It was an accident. At the shipyard. It seems something heavy fell on him. There was nothing the doctor could do. He lost too much blood."

"This is terrible. Who will look after things now that Uncle has gone? He was going to bring me into the business." Selfish thought! Shouldn't have said that, he realised, and blushed, embarrassed.

The steward glanced across at old Sindron. "Shall I tell him?"

"Perhaps I should." Sindron coughed, and pulled up his shoulders, straightening his cloak. "Master, it seems you are the closest male relative."

"Yes," interrupted the steward, "your father was his only brother."

"And your father is presumed dead after he chased that Scythian and disappeared," added Sindron.

"Yes, but we don't know he's dead for sure," Lysanias responded automatically, still not wanting to believe it. Then, starting to register the broader implications, he felt suddenly cold though his hands were sweaty. He restrained the urge to wipe them in his cloak. "What do you mean?"

"You inherit all this, master." Sindron's lips quivered as he struggled to keep his expression straight, fighting the excitement bubbling inside him. This could solve all the worries of the boy's family in Eion and it totally altered his view of his own future prospects. If only he could improve his relationship with the boy.

"I'm too young. I can't run houses and businesses and..."

Old Sindron was looking sternly at him. Lysanias knew that look. Unmanly! He stopped, took a deep breath.

"I have to learn, right?"

Sindron nodded in assent, his expression still stern and set. This was a solemn time, it said. But he winked. Sindron actually winked at him! Allies, he read it, a truce. They must put on a united front. He calmed down, his heart slowed.

The steward stepped forward obsequiously, bowing yet again. Lysanias looked him over more carefully, suddenly feeling more confident, assured. This slave was well-fed; the spread of his flesh gave testimony to his easy life, as did the round chubby cheeks, the soft, well cared-for hands. The hazel eyes and long, dark brown, braided hair suggested a softness that was deceptive. This man knew how to command, Lysanias decided, and how to deceive. Dark skin colour, Persian name, or was it Phrygian? He'd introduced himself as Otanes. He spoke excellent Greek but with a distinct foreign accent. He must be a Persian! A wave of cold fear swept through him momentarily at being so close to the hated enemy race. But the man was a captive, a slave, nothing to be feared.

Then Lysanias wondered how someone from the hated enemy could function as a slave to any patriotic Athenian but there wasn't time to puzzle over it.

"Master," Otanes began tentatively. "Master, there's no need for that. The old master never bothered much with all that. His mother, your grandmother, looks after household matters ... and the household slaves ... with my help. Hermon, his partner, runs the business side. Your uncle used to get me to visit the offices sometimes to go over the accounts but he rarely went to the offices or the shipyard himself, to my knowledge. There's no need for you to do anything."

"What about the funeral arrangements, and the feast afterwards?" Lysanias realised he should show he was aware of what had to be done.

Sindron decided to leave him to it but there was something about this Otanes that made him uneasy, quite apart from the fact he was Persian.

"Oh, we've got all that organised."

Otanes had seen the look of surprise on Lysanias' face at the phrase 'No need to do anything.' He rushed on. "After the mourning period is over, I can show you, and introduce you. Just leave it to us, master!" Was that a plea or an instruction?

Otanes bowed again and backed away.

"You'll be able to show my master full accounts, of course." Sindron's voice stabbed from the background.

Otanes froze, his head jerked round and he eyed Sindron suspiciously. Sindron realised that perhaps the man saw him as a rival for his position as steward. Maybe he had shown his hand too soon. Then the steward was all smoothness and composure again.

"Of course, after the mourning period. As soon as things are back to normal. Now, can I offer master any refreshment? Well-wishers will arrive soon and you will have to receive them."

"Thank you, Otanes." Lysanias felt a load lifting from his mind, as the thought of all that responsibility receded a little. Something was bothering him, though.

"Doesn't Klereides' wife run the household?" Lysanias suddenly asked.

"No, master, the old mistress feels the young mistress is still too young at fifteen."

"My master would like a short rest now. And we need to cut his hair for mourning. Could you show us where his room will be?" Sindron took over for him, as he didn't continue.

"Yes, that will do fine," Lysanias took his cue. He had forgotten he would have to lose his hair. It would be bound into the funeral wreath to go to the grave with his uncle, he remembered. "We'll talk again later. I must commiserate with grandmother."

Suddenly it flashed into his head and he snapped out. "But, if Uncle rarely went near the shipyard, why was he there this morning when the accident happened?"

"He went to bed, after the dinner party. Then, in the night, it seems there was an urgent message. To meet someone there. I didn't see it. The porter took it in." The steward seemed somewhat embarrassed at the question, though he had his answer ready.

They called in the porter who confirmed it. "Aye, before dawn, master. A long, thin chariot-driver, not a personal slave. Hands me a scroll. The master takes one look, dresses himself and off he goes in the chariot."

The steward interrupted, hurriedly, as though forestalling a question. "He usually takes me on any business visits, master. The boy as well, to run messages. He didn't rouse me, must have been very urgent. At dawn, I went to market to hire a cook for the banquet he was due to give next week."

The steward seemed keen to establish where he was at the time. Perhaps he felt he had neglected his duty in not being with his master.

"Who would have sent such a message?" Lysanias demanded. He had to follow this through, as the new master, and because he owed it to his uncle.

"He had many business acquaintances, master." As a slave, he was clearly not going to be drawn into expressing an opinion about citizens.

"Do they know about the accident?"

"Yes, master. Messengers have gone to all his principal associates, General Ariston, Resident Hermon and others. I understand, though, that Resident Hermon, his business partner, is out of town at the moment. His slaves will surely tell him as soon as he gets back."

The most likely person Klereides would have gone to meet and also out of the way. That seemed a little odd.

"What else has been done?" He could still feel the anger bubbling inside him.

"It happened shortly before sun-up, master, and it was some while before we knew. When they brought the body."

Lysanias realised he was bullying. No way to get co-operation, his father had always said. Unmanly. He allowed Sindron to step in to help him out.

"Presumably you have reported the accident to the authorities," Sindron asked, firmly but in a gentler tone.

"Yes, I sent my assistant to hire the official mourners and report to the authorities – the shipyard will have reported it as well. I've sent messengers off to the family in the country and to local officials down there."

A loud and peremptory knock on the front door interrupted their talk. Who would use the knocker at a house in mourning? Only a very impatient man, not used to waiting.

It seemed familiar to Otanes, who excused himself and went to welcome the visitor, though the proper thing was to allow the porter to deal with whoever it was. Lysanias and Sindron dropped into silence, as they waited. From the lobby they could hear a gruff voice, a voice accustomed to command. "Look after our horses, my man, and see that they and my slave receive some refreshment." Then a brief inaudible exchange between Otanes and the visitor.

"General Ariston desires to pay his respects to the dead and place an offering at the family shrine," announced the porter.

There was a pause that lengthened as the wailing in the background reached a new crescendo and then, with a start, Lysanias realised they were all waiting for him to respond. He was the new master here. Could he really receive this high dignitary?

"General Ariston is welcome," his dry throat just about managed.

The General was above average height, muscular, with gleaming leather armour and bronze buckles, spurs clinking as he strode forward. His face was firm and unlined and his hair and beard full and dark, though he must be in his early to mid-forties, Lysanias guessed. He stood with all the confidence that wealth and power can bring. He was the cavalry officer who had met General Kimon at the harbour, Lysanias was sure. Settled now into the fixed serious expression of bereavement, Lysanias' face gave no sign that he recognised his visitor.

"General Ariston is welcome in our hour of sorrow," Lysanias repeated, memory of another place coming to his assistance.

"In the hour of sorrow, a friend of the deceased is surely a friend of the successor," came the expected reply.

Lysanias and the General faced one another. A straight look into the eyes and the slightest of inclinations of the head – an Athenian citizen would never deign to anything resembling a bow, the gesture of subservience. Lysanias became aware that, behind those penetrating grey eyes, the General was assessing him, the new master of the household, with a great deal of curiosity and maybe a touch of surprise. Could it be because, with the property and interests he was inheriting, he might be a new element in Athenian politics?

Lysanias' heart beat hard. That was an insight that surprised him. Was that really where he was now? Holy Zeus!

Or maybe there was something else? The General clearly hadn't expected to see him here – no-one would – but who had he expected to greet him?

The General dropped his gaze first. He turned away and advanced in military style to the bier. He performed the ritual and Lysanias was relieved to observe that it was not a great deal different from the way he had done it himself.

Sindron indicated that Lysanias should retire to the men's entertaining room. Moving silently into that area, Lysanias discovered that olives and honey cakes, water and wine had been arrayed as a fast offering for well-wishers and realised that he was supposed to take the couch at the head of the room.

Lysanias was slightly surprised to see that the General's slave was already here, seated on a stool, delicately helping himself to morsels - a very attractive fair-haired youth, younger than Lysanias, with tanned, well-muscled, well-oiled limbs gleaming in the lamplight, his tunic belted in the military way but revealing of flesh and muscle. The General joined them.

"Ah, young man. I take it you are the heir. Yes, so I see. But new to Athens? Yes, thought I hadn't seen you at the gymnasium. Well, this is a surprise. Thought I knew all Klereides' menfolk. Have you done your military service yet, young man?"

Lysanias was thrown. "I trained for the defence corps in Eion," he stumbled, before he could stop himself.

"Eion, eh. Certainly roasted those Persians there, didn't we?" He chuckled with delight at the thought of the enemy burning alive in the town they themselves had set fire to, but Lysanias, too, felt that no retribution was too harsh for an empire that had desecrated the temples of Athens and violated the gods. "Before your time, though, I imagine. Plenty of fighting there since, I hear. Great respect for those Thracian horsemen. Still you survived, obviously."

"I didn't see real action yet, sir. Only defensive, as a supply runner when the town was attacked," Lysanias felt obliged to murmur, not quite truthfully. The chaos and panic, shouting and screams, during a major attack, of running backwards and forwards with other boys, slaves and even girls, to keep the defending soldiers on the town's fortress walls supplied with throwing spears and arrows, and stones for slings and catapults, preparing boiling oil and water to be thrown down on the attackers - wasn't that 'real action'?

Strangely, instead of memories of the last fierce attack, which had destroyed much of the town, even their own house narrowly escaping, it was an image of the last time he had seen his father riding away on horseback that flashed into his head, and himself stabbing and stabbing, the reality that fed his nightmares.

"Not yet eighteen, then?"

Lysanias drew himself up. "I was eighteen yesterday, sir."

"Eighteen, eh, a new citizen! We'll have to get you onto the citizen roll then, so you can vote. I'll be pleased to vouch for you, should you need someone."

However, the General's tone was off-hand, as though he was just being polite, and he didn't pause for Lysanias to thank him.

"Knew Curly, hah, your uncle well. Fought in the same battles. Tough man, maybe too tough ... but honest, I used to think. His word was his bond. Can't say fairer than that for any man." Platitudes! Lysanias wondered if he said this about everyone who died. No sense here of a friend gone, though he said Klereides had been his friend, knew his nickname. But there was strain in his voice, as though his mind was elsewhere.

"We were in the same dining club. Golden Trident, hah. Next one's at my place. You must come if your mourning duties allow and perhaps we can talk. Unfinished business, as they say. Sad end this, sad end." Lysanias wondered when the stream of platitudes would end.

As the General talked, his slave had risen and moved slowly forward to stand beside and slightly behind the General, but with a stance not at all slave-like. The look on his face showed total admiration, almost adoration, for the General, as he moved close to touch just slightly at the upper arm, and the General seemed to draw strength from this gentle contact.

Lysanias felt uncomfortably aware of the teenage fluff and stubble on his own chin, his unkempt hair, the body smells of travel. Then Sindron appeared, listened and, with a small gesture, indicated that Lysanias should end the interview.

Again Lysanias surprised himself.

"I'm very pleased to have met you," he came in, just topping the solemn muted tone the General had adopted. "You'll appreciate that I have many matters to catch up on and many kin and friends to meet with. I appreciate your offer of help to ease me into Athenian society and accept your offer to dine as soon as I am free of my familial obligations."

He rushed this out, so that the General had no chance to interrupt. Now he knew why Sindron had always insisted he learn to pronounce his Greek clearly and in an Athenian accent – and learn the formal, polite vocabulary. He wished he had given it a little more attention.

"My thanks and those of the family and tribe for your condolences in this hour of sorrow," Lysanias concluded, immediately wondering why he had spoken so formally and so dismissively. Didn't he trust this man? Immediately he knew the answer was 'no'. It meant he couldn't ask if his uncle had any enemies. But his face retained the fixed expression he had set it in. Behind the General, Sindron looked pleased with him.

Surprisingly, the General did not respond in kind. His manner changed, he leaned forward and his speech dropped into a softer tone that meant his words were meant only for Lysanias.

"Young man, I see you have some of your uncle's toughness. I welcome that. It will aid Athens and the cause." The General's blue eyes had narrowed as he assessed Lysanias and his speech. "We really must talk more closely. These are critical times, times of peril and challenge. Must show these radi..."

Lysanias fought to stop himself showing surprise at the conspiratorial tone the General had used. He glanced across to the General's slave, whose face displayed some concern as his master seemed to grow redder, about to launch on a new topic. He noticed the slave raise a hand to touch the General's arm. Ariston straightened to full military bearing.

"Hah. Enough said. Time of sorrow. Offer of friendship. Steward knows where to contact me. Official duties. Must go now. Time of sorrow. A friend's condolences ... May great Athene guard you."

Still muttering, the General backed through the door and out of the house, though not before Lysanias noticed the General's hand reach as though casually to stroke his slave's shoulder.

Only then did it hit him. His uncle really had moved in the top circles of power and wealth in Athens. A general! One of the ten generals elected each year for the city. The most powerful men in the place. And a close friend of Kimon's.

Then another thought struck him. This general had been the first well-wisher. Kimon, his colleague, only just returned, clearly involved in urgent matters from what Lysanias had seen at the harbour, yet he regarded this as important enough to leave that to come here, possibly as soon as he heard. That must say a lot about his uncle.

In his uncle's sleeping room, as Sindron hacked away handfuls of his hair, Lysanias' glance took in the tapestries and wall-hangings. Great gods, what incredible subjects! Zeus seducing Ariadne, Bacchos disporting with naked bacchantes. And more like them. What sort of man was his uncle?

Clearly a very wealthy one, thought Sindron, and inclined to indulge his own tastes. No Athenian moderation here. The couches, floor tiles, wall hangings, all of the finest quality, looked as though they came from other lands. Despite the long war and austerity rationing, Klereides had obviously managed to obtain foreign luxuries - or perhaps they'd been captured in war.

While Sindron took his shorn hair through to the back of the house, Lysanias glanced round Klereides' sleeping chamber, which now would be his room. This revealed more expenditure and equally sensuous tapestries and decorations. One of the tapestries stirred as though caught by a slight breeze. Curious, Lysanias looked behind. A door! With it's own locking device. Why would his uncle need a secret, private door? When he came back, Sindron could suggest no answer.

Lysanias thought back to his home in Eion where most of the furniture had been made by his father, himself and his younger brother, when they weren't working at their carpenter's trade or tending the family field. Why did anyone need to be this extravagant when, as he had seen on his way up from the harbour, other people were living in poverty and squalor? Hadn't the great lawgiver Solon forbidden such ostentation by the wealthy, to avoid offending the poorer classes? He asked Sindron, who explained that was only the outside of houses, aspects open to the public eye, not inside one's own home where one could do as one wished.

Then his analytical mind started calculating what this might actually mean in real money terms, plus his uncle's evident frequent entertaining, plus what might be deduced of his social habits – and that's before any patronage of the arts or athletics!

Lysanias' thoughts were interrupted by the steward. It was a summons to his grandmother. He half remembered old Makaria, when they had said goodbye before emigrating to Eion. She had tousled his three-year-old head and then berated his father for marrying a lower-class girl and resorting to a manual occupation to support them.

Or did he remember? Was this what his parents had told him? Anyway, the family wisdom was that she had dominated her husband and her sons and been the real power in the household. Would she try to dominate him?

"Come with me, Sindron," he said, feeling suddenly weak at the knees. So much was happening so fast. Sindron decided to adopt a slave-like stance, the pose of the invisible servant, to avoid betraying their close relationship.

Makaria sat grave and dignified, all in black, hair cropped, her veil raised, in one of the guest rooms looking out on the courtyard. The room was lit only by the spill of light through the door from the courtyard, where she could see straight out onto the crumpled body of her dead son. The sharp line of her nose, the curve of her cheeks and chin caught the light but her eyes were barely visible. He could read little of her expressions.

"So you're the new family head. Not a bad-looking boy, but no care for appearances, I see. Just like your father."

The begrudging tone. Had she always had that or did she really hate him because of his father? She'd mentioned his father, her son, but not a word of sympathy, and she must know about his disappearance.

Then, clearly with an effort, she reached out a hand to his and drew him closer, and her voice softened.

"You always were a sharp child, but you're so young. So much responsibility so young."

Abrupt again. "Steward told you he and I can handle most things for you?"

"Yes, grandmother." He found himself dropping into the tone of a young child and was grateful when Sindron gently added.

"Master is a very willing pupil, madam. He'll soon learn to manage things himself."

Despite the gentle and subservient tone, she jerked upright. Maybe this wasn't what she wanted to hear, maybe she hadn't realised Sindron was there in the gloom. There was a cool silence.

Her eyes locked firmly onto Lysanias' as her grip tightened on his hand.

"That's not all, young man. Your uncle married a young wife a year ago but didn't manage to produce any offspring or even get her pregnant.

I imagine that's why he sent for you, to train up an heir just in case. He has looked very worried recently. You have a document from him, you say? Well, you'll have to marry her now. That's what the law says. She's quite attractive. Does her household chores. Too young to manage a household, though, far too young, and inclined to be sulky. You'll need to keep her on a tight rein. You're responsible for the whole household too. I'll do my best to help, but the period of mourning may be difficult. You can go now."

Lysanias was too devastated to speak and he backed out of the room, Sindron silent beside him. He again approached the bier and made the ritual gestures, backing away and going to the entertaining room.

"What does she mean, Sindron? I can't marry! I'm too young! You always told me that, in Athens, men don't get married till they're thirty at least, after their military service, and then they marry young girls of fourteen or so. Tell me I don't have to do this! I don't even know the girl."

"Don't get agitated, master. Sit down. Perhaps you'd like some wine or a honey cake. You've had a long journey and now all this."

"Nonsense, Sindron. Stop fussing. I can do without food for a few hours. Besides I'm chief mourner, I'm supposed to fast. Just tell me what's going on and where I stand. You lived in Athens for a long time, you must know what the customs are."

"Well, do you mind if I have something to eat, master? I'm famished." Sindron felt he needed a little time to think. This was another surprise, but maybe marriage would keep the boy in line, calm him down a little. But all the responsibility! How would the lad deal with that?

"I'm sorry, Sindron, I'm being inconsiderate. I am hungry, too. I wish I could eat as well."

Sindron finally persuaded him that the gods would forgive him if he merely made up for the breakfast he had thrown to the seabirds. Lysanias ate little, feeling guilty and disrespectful, but he was shaking from the release after the nervous tension.

His slave explained that, under Athenian law, if a citizen died without a son, the nearest male relative was obliged to marry the deceased's wife in order to continue the line of inheritance of that family branch.

"But I don't even know what she's like!" Lysanias cried.

"Master, mourning will last for thirty days, but you'll have a chance to see her, get to know her, after that if not sooner, and the wedding can't happen till then, anyway."

Philia screamed shrilly. "I won't! I won't marry him if I don't like him!" She was going to say "I won't marry anyone else I don't like" but you can't speak ill of the dead, even if she hadn't really liked her fat, bald husband all that much. No, that's not fair, he was quite nice sometimes.

"Don't be ridiculous, girl! It's the law! You gave Klereides no children, so you must marry his nearest male relative!" Makaria had just told the girl she would have to marry Lysanias but she hadn't expected this reaction; the girl was usually fairly obedient.

"I don't have to! I can ask for my dowry back and go home to my father!" Philia was finally throwing a tantrum and she could feel it was working.

"Well, wait and see what he's like. You'll get a better chance to look him over at the funeral and I'll arrange for you to talk after that."

Philia screamed again. She was actually quite excited but she wasn't going to show it. She had caught a glimpse of the man as he'd done that terrible thing and exposed poor Klereides' wounds, and he looked quite young. And handsome.

"I'm ... going ... home ... to ... father!" she said slowly and deliberately through clenched teeth.

Makaria's tone became even friendlier. Philia had never known her like this.

"I know I've been hard on you up to now, but you have to learn discipline to keep a household working all year round. From now on we'll see you do more of the ordering of foodstuffs, hm? We'll just ease you in slowly. How's that?"

Yes, thought Philia, it's really working. She screamed again, but not quite so loud this time.

Sindron was looking very serious now as he paused, hesitating to speak.

"And I have to tell you I feel there is something suspicious about the manner of your uncle's death that may mean you should be looking for a culprit," he said at last.

"You think he was murdered?"

"I think it's a possibility."

Lysanias knew this meant he had an obligation to find the killer and avenge his uncle. He found himself tingling with excitement, which didn't seem right if something so terrible really had happened. "There are things that seem odd to me too but he was so important. He knew so many important people. Why would anyone do this?"

"Yes, but consider, master. It looks as though only Klereides knew you were coming back. Maybe someone else thought they would inherit. They thought you and your father were dead, remember."

A thought flashed into Lysanias' head, something his grandmother had said about his uncle being worried.

"Do you think he felt threatened? That's why he wanted me here?" The idea startled him. It carried implications about life in Athens that he didn't want to believe.

"Remember your uncle's message," said Sindron. " 'Need someone close I can trust.' That implies he didn't trust anyone around him."

"Yes. And 'perils', remember? 'Political developments bring perils and possibilities.' That's what he said, isn't it?" But then Lysanias remembered that Sindron had disputed the word 'perils', feeling that Homer had used the same word to mean 'challenge' and the poet Simonides something similar for 'struggle against overwhelming odds.'

In fact, in Eion, they had debated the message for ages, not least the fact that a man who could afford parchment and a scribe had chosen to scratch the message on wax tablets with his thumb-nail, like a schoolboy, and then packed the tablets so hurriedly that the wax had smudged the lettering, making it difficult to read. Also the ship's captain who brought it had confirmed that it had been given to him by Klereides himself, not a slave or messenger.

"Yes, but none of that means he thought someone was out to kill him." Lysanias didn't want to believe where this was leading.

"No, but it's possible." Sindron sounded like the voice of reason itself in the midst of a world that suddenly seemed devoid of all logic. "I can't think why either. Politics, business rivalry, personal enemies. We just don't know what your uncle was involved in. The General used some of those words too, or something very close, you notice."

"What can we do?"

"First, we must find out what the law is now – there have been so many changes lately – and keep our eyes and ears open to become familiar with how things are done in Athens, so we don't upset people."

"Sindron, this is all very sudden. I'm not sure I can handle it."

Lysanias slumped on his couch, feeling tired and alone – except for Sindron, of course – thank the gods for Sindron – and he'd never expected to think that! He was going to need all Sindron's knowledge and rational thinking and more.

"We can't rest yet, master. The law lays down thirty days of mourning when the close relatives don't leave the house, except for the funeral and visits to the tomb."

"So I don't need to go out then."

"Yes you do. If you can't go out, you can't register your citizenship and you can't start taking charge of your uncle's affairs and you can't look into his death, so you can't avenge him. In thirty days time, your uncle's killer will have covered his traces. Where will you be then?"

Lysanias was thrown. He opened his mouth to reply and shut it again. He was stuck. Then a glimmer, maybe...

"You're not a relative, Sindron. You could go out and see people." He realised the flaw in that, even before Sindron replied.

"I'm a slave, master," Sindron said patiently. "Even with my knowledge of Athens, I can't go where a citizen can. People won't answer my questions."

"What can we do, then?"

"I never thought I'd have to say this, master, but we may have to break a few rules." Sindron looked so crestfallen that Lysanias started to grin. Sindron, who was always drumming into him the importance of obeying the rules, sticking by the laws, now telling him to break them. He burst out laughing. Sindron smiled wryly, and went on to explain.

"The law says that the body of the deceased must be displayed for a full day before the morning of the funeral. As nearly half of today had gone before the body was back here and ready, the real display day is tomorrow, so there won't be many more well-wishers today. Hardly anyone in Athens knows you, so, if you were to slip out now in ordinary clothes, no-one would be surprised you aren't dressed in mourning. It'll give us a chance to check on the rumour about Eion, but it can't be true. We've only just come from there and there was no trouble then.

"We can tell the household you're resting and not to be disturbed. You could slip out, using that private door in your uncle's room. I'll join you outside. You can have a bath and a shave in the city, while I find out about the law and what officials you need to see to sort out your citizenship and try to obtain a dispensation from mourning of some sort. We'll get back as soon as we can."

To Lysanias, it sounded horrific. Flouting the laws of Athens, offending the gods, neglecting his duties to the dead – he shuddered as he imagined the possible consequences. He knew, though, that he could never live with himself if he did nothing and let his uncle's killer escape, while his uncle's soul wandered in torment for ever. And that could draw down the wrath of the goddess Nemesis on him.

Gods forgive me, he thought, I will make atonement later, but, to Sindron, he said, "Let's do it," stood up and straightened his shoulders.

Sindron breathed a sigh of relief. At least, the boy now seemed to recognise that he needed his slave and that slave's advice. He felt more secure now than he had since leaving Eion but he wasn't even certain that he was giving the right advice. Only time and the gods would decide that.

"And, Sindron, can we do something about these?" Lysanias indicated the wall hangings. Sindron could see that a young man from a simple background could find the explicitness disturbing. He found them disturbing himself. "I'm sure we can, master. Hardly appropriate for a funeral anyway. I'll speak to Otanes."

CHAPTER 3

L ysanias was a strange mixture of emotions. Out of that dark and shady house of death and suspicion, striding along in the afternoon sunshine, he felt suddenly free and like the young man he was, yet the stark realities of his new position buzzed round and round in his head. He gave little attention to the street of two-storey houses, the second storey overhanging the street, and the few people returning from the market.

Keeping a pace behind as befitting a slave, Sindron was worried, though he tried not to show it for the boy's sake. He wanted to find an old friend, who, he hoped, would be able to explain where they stood under the new laws, without fear of their predicament getting back to Klereides' enemies, whoever they might be.

Yet there was a new spring in his step, his slight limp barely noticeable, and his eyes glistened with a fresh alertness. Sindron had always felt that the big advantage of being a household slave was that you have very limited responsibility. Food, clothing and shelter are provided. As long as you perform your tasks adequately, you retain your place. Generally, being a slave meant little mental effort. Now here he was, forced to act and think as though he was Lysanias' father, his guardian and protector, mentor and advisor, all rolled into one – as well as his personal slave. And all in a context where his master's life could be in danger, and conceivably his own. On top of that, he had to let the boy believe that he was making the important decisions himself, or he might decide to sell Sindron to who knew what disreputable master.

Did he want this new life? He knew the answer without really asking the question. Yes, yes, yes. His heart was beating faster, his mind was racing, he hadn't felt so alive in years. But was he up to it? As a slave, he had so little experience of so many areas his master would now be involved in. And Athens had changed so much he hardly recognised the place. But what a challenge!!!

As Lysanias' head turned, Sindron quickly suppressed a smile, re-imposing the dignified expression he had learnt so many years before from watching the other pedagogues when he first supervised young Klereides, and after him Leokhares, Lysanias' father, on his way to and from school as a boy. He thanked the gods for the leg injury that had seen him delegated to that task at a younger age than most.

"I wish you wouldn't carry that staff, Sindron. It makes me look like a schoolboy," said Lysanias in a low voice.

If the boy had time to think about things like that, at least he wasn't letting the worries of his new status get to him, thought Sindron, realising how accustomed he had become to the staff he had acquired long ago as symbol of a pedagogue.

"I'm an Athenian citizen and head of a household now," Lysanias added.

Or maybe he was.

"I want people to know it."

Oh, no! It was going to his head. "May I suggest, master, that we don't get rid of it, not just yet. We have to remain inconspicuous today. People will just think I'm accompanying you to the gardens of the Akademeia to watch the wrestling practice."

Lysanias looked a little sheepish and, after a short pause, replied over his shoulder. "Yes, I know. I don't mean today."

Sindron had to admit the boy had a point. "I've become used to the staff, master, but I'll try to find a shorter stick when I can."

"Thank you, Sindron."

"Many's the time I've walked up and down this road taking your father to school or the gymnasium," Sindron volunteered, in what, for him, was an unusually personal and confiding tone.

"Sindron, now is not the time for reminiscences!" The boy was sounding as pompous as young Klereides sometimes had.

"Education is not to be frowned at, master. I sometimes think I learnt more than your uncle and your father from sitting at the back of the class and from listening to philosophers and poets with them in the public gardens." Sindron thought of all he had learnt and was grateful for.

"Sindron, could it be dangerous?" The slave's musings were abruptly interrupted by hard reality. A one-horse chariot, the driver grasping the reins with one hand, the other round his passenger who needed both of his own to hang onto his market purchases, rattled towards them, forcing them to leap aside smartly. It gave Sindron time to think.

"Could what be dangerous, master?" His tone was innocent. No point in having the boy worried unnecessarily.

"Athens. The political situation. You know, civil war between factions, classes."

Sindron was amazed the boy had deduced so much on so little evidence. He hadn't realised he knew about such things. In Eion, everyone had seemed to work to the same end – survival – and military discipline had dominated everything, so he had assumed the idea would be difficult to grasp. Then he remembered that the family had talked about it at home when such crises had occurred in other Greek cities, sometimes with disastrous results. Here, even from what they had heard so far, it sounded like a revolution and he knew that, elsewhere, such happenings had brought terrible consequences for the populace. But he didn't say that.

"Yes, master, in theory it could become dangerous. But we've seen nothing that serious here yet."

"Sindron, tell me honestly, do you think I'm prepared for all this? I feel so inexperienced."

Great gods, the arrogant brat was looking at himself with open eyes for once! Asking in humility. The boy had stopped and turned, confronting him. Sindron thought quickly.

"You come from outside, so you can see things more objectively than if you'd grown up here," he started. Making a list, ordering his statements, made Sindron feel more comfortable somehow. "Your father and I have done our best to teach you what an Athenian gentleman would learn. In addition, you know how to work the land, and you have acquired a manual skill, so you are more able to understand the lower levels of society. And you've had more military training, and even war experience, than young Athenians of your age."

Lysanias stared at his slave open-mouthed. The thought that activities that he had regarded as such a chore, even an ordeal, could actually be an asset was difficult to embrace, but it was reassuring. The fact that Sindron could see things that clearly and be that open with him put the value of the slave in a new light, too. Even Sindron's suggestion that they keep their ears open for any useful information on how things worked in Athens, so that they could avoid making serious mistakes, seemed rational rather than alarming. He relaxed a little and became absorbed in the new sights, as they passed the pottery workshops that gave the quarter of Inner Kerameikos its name, with their displays of red and black vases and bowls and roof tiles set out to dry in the sun.

Then they could hear the bustle of the agora, the market place, the buzz in the air like a hive of busy bees growing louder and louder as they approached, and suddenly they were out from the narrow street and looking into the dazzling open space of the market place.

Lysanias stopped dead, soaking it all in. This was it, this was it! He was here, part of it. Mighty Athens, hub of the whole Greek world. He wanted to leap and shout in the sheer exhilaration of it but a glance from Sindron and he controlled himself, like a good Athenian.

But Sindron's face broke into a broad smile and his eyes sparkled and they laughed together, knowing they shared the same excitement. Then Sindron's face became serious and he brought Lysanias down with, "We must be wary, master. We're not familiar with the place. We could be easily duped."

Lysanias was surprised that the old man should be this suspicious, and found it difficult to imagine anything unworthy happening in this place dedicated to the great goddess Athene. He nodded but the thought was gone as he wondered at all around them. Sindron named the different features.

Up to their left, the tall hill of the High City, the Akropolis, with its steep cliffs rising above the bustling modern city, dominated everything, and beyond it the city walls with their defensive towers snaked over the hills, protecting them all. To their right, they had just passed the ancient shrine to Aphrodite, left badly damaged by the Persians, but with a new-looking statue of the goddess, her face, shoulders and arms glowing pink against the sea-blue of her gown.

Now, confronting them beside the entryway to the Market square were Herms of various sizes, portrait busts of the god Hermes, on their square pedestals with the god's sexual paraphernalia displayed below. Dominating them were three tall stone Herms with inscriptions praising Kimon's achievement in defeating the Persians at Eion, which Lysanias read with pride. The god of boundaries, travellers, commerce, poets, athletics and trickery was certainly needed in a place like this, Lysanias thought.

"Touch them, master," instructed Sindron, as if Lysanias needed telling. They were travellers, newly arrived, in a situation where they needed all the luck the god of good fortune, with his familiar friendly face, curly hair and bushy beard, could give them and, if Lysanias had to marry Klereides' widow, a bit of fertility would do him no harm. He laid a hand on the two nearest as they passed, already smoothed and polished by countless other touches.

On their left, an elegant and colourful columned building sparkled in the sun, which Sindron named as the new Painted Colonnade. He wasn't too sure whether it was built by one of Kimon's brothers-in-law or built by Kimon and the paintings on the walls inside commissioned by his brother-in-law but it looked a pleasant place to seek shelter from the sun and to stroll and chat. In front of this were more bronze Herms. From the activity around, it looked as though it was a centre of business as well. Lysanias stood amazed. He had never seen anything like this before.

They crossed the River Eridanos that flowed through the city, though now channelled and covered in, burbling beneath them, and saw, to their right, the Royal Colonnade, surprisingly modest for its importance, but smartly renovated after the Persians in impressive blues and reds. This housed the offices of the chief magistrate, "king for a year" as the saying went, and here new magistrates swore loyalty to the city, Sindron explained.

Beyond it came the sad remains of the Sanctuary of Zeus the Freedom Bringer, dominated by its powerful new statue of the god, the line of its old enclosure carefully fenced and obviously well cared for like the altar in front and the nearby smaller altar to Zeus of the Market Place. On rising ground behind, the hill had been cut away and construction started on what would be a big new building, possibly a temple, that Sindron didn't know about. Turning round, Lysanias looked more closely at the flat-topped hill of the High City that his parents had so often described. Yes, there was the famous wooden statue of the goddess and, behind her, the ruins of temples looking strangely out of place.

The sight of those distant ruins didn't stop Lysanias being horrified when Sindron pointed out nearby the rubble-strewn site that had once been the Temple to Apollo, a god he had worshipped in Eion as the god of colonists as well as of healing and the arts. The god must still look favourably on the people of Athens though, if he bestowed this prosperity on them. Next to it, the giant stones of the Temple of The Mother seemed to have deterred even the Persians in their rampage, though they were not without their signs of attempted destruction. Further on, and covering the hill slopes around and also on the far side of the market square, temporary wooden structures seemed to be serving as civic offices and as shops and workshops.

"Remember, it has been a long war," explained Sindron, disappointed, like Lysanias, that this heart of the city wasn't even back to the state it had been before the invasion.

Sindron pointed out some of the key features of the market place. The shrine to the twelve gods; the performance area in the centre; the running track; the route of the famous religious processions in honour of Athene, the Panethenaic Way, running diagonally across the square, which was also used for chariot races; the statue of the heroic tyrant slayers to remind everyone of the dangers to democracy; the great drain running the length of the market square to carry rainwater from winter storms into the Eridanos and away; the leafy plane trees that, once full-grown, would provide welcome shelter from the heat of the sun. "They're new. I believe Kimon had those planted."

By now they had entered the crowds and the stalls with different areas for each type of produce, the street vendors, the smells, the colours, the shouts, the haggling for bargains. Lysanias was fascinated – the market square at Eion had been sedate compared to this.

Having seen the market in past days, Sindron was more amazed at the range of accents denoting Greeks from other cities and the number of non-Greek people, different races, different colour skins. Some, from their costumes, were merchants, foreign residents; many others were slaves. More people seemed to own slaves than he remembered, not just the very wealthy. Even some stallholders had a slave helping them. The war with its captives had certainly enriched the city with slaves. As a slave himself, he didn't find it a pleasant thought, as he wondered what lives these captives might have enjoyed in their home cities in the days of their freedom, before the battles that brought them here. Sindron realised he had been enslaved too young to have any real understanding of what freedom was like, but he knew that was not a thought to dwell on and dismissed it.

Most of the market activity was finishing but there was enough still going on for Lysanias to be caught by the life and bustle all around him, the sounds of conversation, vendors' calls and hammering from workshops off to the sides of the market square. There was a feeling of excitement in the air, of expectation, of tension.

"Why are so many people just standing around, not working?" Lysanias whispered to Sindron.

"There are a lot of wealthy people in Athens," explained Sindron. "Landowners and the like. They don't need to work and don't believe in it. That's the well-dressed ones. The others are probably passing through, going about their business."

Lysanias noticed that there were clear distinctions, marked mainly by costume but also by mannerisms. As well as the calmly pacing figures in fine fabrics with immaculately dressed hair and beards, there were workers in workers' tunics, who seemed to be more excited even agitated, shopkeepers in their aprons, farmers and shepherds in coarse fabrics and furs, foreigners in the costumes of their native lands, slaves in whatever their owners provided.

"There must be a city meeting, an Assembly, on later today, otherwise I can't see why they'd all be here..."

Lysanias realised that, to an observant Athenian, his neat homespun cloak would place him somewhere in the middle of this hierarchy. There were far fewer women around than would have been the case in Eion, or even than they'd seen in Peiraieos. Just a few female stallholders and wandering street vendors.

Sindron was leading the way purposefully through the crowds. Having kept up with artistic developments in Athens, he was able to point out some of Kimon's contributions to the city. The start of work on the new entrance-way to the High City that everyone already called Kimon's wall, the Herms they had passed, the plane trees, the Temple to Theseos, which housed the giant bones of the hero Theseos that Kimon had discovered and brought back to Athens and which Sindron thought was somewhere on the other side of the market square, and, indirectly, the Painted Colonnade. "Incidentally, he also paid for the foundations of the Long Walls we saw," Sindron said.

Fascinated by the paintings he had glimpsed, Lysanias was heading back in that direction when Sindron halted.

"Well, he certainly has come up in the world," Sindron said admiringly.

"Who?" Lysanias wrenched his attention away from the giant paintings.

"Lydos, my friend, that banker there. Look at the quality of that cloak he's wearing!"

Lysanias was confused. He saw a table covered by a dark cloth, with weighing scales, weights, and small piles of coins glistening on it, and behind it a very prosperous-looking banker, soberly-dressed in fine linen with a deep blue embroidered edging, hair and beard smartly trimmed, brimming with self-confidence. How could this man be Sindron's friend?

"But he can't be a slave!"

"Yes, he can! Or he was when I left Athens. We were once sold at the same time in the slave auction in this very market. Belonged to Phraston. He looks busy. I'll come back when we've got you to the baths…"

It felt so good to see an old friend in this city that now seemed so unfamiliar and confusing – though he wouldn't tell Lysanias that – and such a relief that Lydos was still here. Sindron could have hugged the man except that even slaves didn't do that in public in Athens.

Lysanias' had moved off towards a figure whose head stuck up above the crowd, moving his arms in dramatic gestures. Sindron followed, annoyed.

It was the news-teller they had seen at the harbour. "Don't point the finger of scorn at Kimon," he shouted. "It's not as though he sleeps every night with his sister Elpinike. Sometimes he goes to Sparta and guzzles wine with his pals." He went on to suggest that Kimon had been thrown out of Sparta for having an affair with the wife of one of the Spartan leaders. Lysanias felt a twinge of anger that his hero was being made fun of in such a scurrilous way, but it seemed that, in the big city, it was acceptable to poke fun at and even insult the city's leaders. However, not everyone laughed and some looked very stern.

Strynises balanced it by an equally scatological tale about the radical leaders Ephialtes and Perikles, managing to offend the other half of the crowd, despite the laughs from the well-dressed.

The news-teller was going on with news of other cities, but Sindron was giving Lysanias directions to reach the baths and the barber's afterwards, where Sindron promised to find him.

The baths were great. The cool water poured over Lysanias by the bathman was really refreshing. A rub down with powdered wood-ash and clay to remove sweat and grime. Another rinse down. Then the scented oil smoothed and soothed him all over, before the gentle scrape-down with the curved bronze strigil.

The bathman was chatty. "Terrible tragedy that this morning, wasn't it? Who'd have thought a well-born like that could end up crushed to death in his own shipyard? No telling is there? Who knows when the gods'll call us?"

Lysanias kept quiet. It had been a shock to find his uncle the subject of gossip, but he might learn something here, even if the man's grammar was appalling. Sure enough, the bathman went on. "I'm thinking the workers might have had something to do with it, eh? Wasn't a popular man with his workers, so I'm told. But then, mustn't speak ill of the dead, must we, eh? I'm sure he did his best. Don't we all. Us bathmen, now, we've no Fellowship of Hephaistos like those craftsmen down Peiraieos way. Don't need it neither, to my thinking. Customers are generous."

It was all Lysanias could do to stop from bursting out in anger at this stranger talking about his uncle like that. Despite the hint, he didn't tip the bathman. He hadn't any Athenian money yet anyway, and he'd paid the doorkeeper with the piece of silver Sindron had given him.

Lysanias found that Sindron had unpacked his best tunic and cloak, made by his mother from her finest bleached homespun. Lysanias put them on, and his smartest sandals, but he was aware they didn't match up to some of the immaculate clothes he had seen in the square.

Lydos' table was no different from the others. The seated banker behind, the seated client in front. A discreetly waiting client or two. The bulky bodyguard standing by, and the slave-boy ever ready to run messages or errands. The scribe at a smaller table behind with his chest of parchment scrolls recording the state of individual depositors' accounts and loans.

Lydos looked up as the last client departed. Lydos looked puzzled for a moment, then his eyes locked with Sindron's and they both smiled in recognition and friendship.

He beckoned Sindron over and said, "I never expected to see you again, old friend. When did you get back? Some colony in the back of beyond, wasn't it?" The voice had become much more cultured than Sindron remembered and the manner more sophisticated. Lydos had clearly done very well for his master and for himself. He'd also looked after himself. Some years younger than Sindron, the banker's arms were muscular, his figure trim for his age.

Sindron recalled getting to know Lydos as they had sought a good vantage point for seeing or at least hearing the music and drama contests from outside the performance area when escorting their owners' families to the events. The sharing of views on things slaves weren't expected to have opinions about had been a rare pleasure. But no time for reminiscences now.

He explained that he needed to exchange some money but would also welcome his friend's advice.

"Well, I'll change your money," replied Lydos, "but we normally only deal in big sums these days. Since Athens gained control of the seas and put down the pirates, trade and money-lending for trade has gone crazy."

"You mean Kimon."

Lydos started. "What?"

"You mean Kimon gained control of the seas and put down the pirates."

"Yes, for Athens." He dropped his voice. "Look, things are a bit tricky at the moment, so not too loud. Never know which faction may be listening."

"Is it that bad?"

Lydos didn't answer but suggested Sindron sit beside him to avoid the impression he might be a client. His eyes betrayed an element of doubt about being seen with Sindron and he glanced around. There seemed not a little snobbery in the way he eyed Sindron's plain homespun cloak. Perhaps he should tell Lydos his good fortune now thought Sindron, but a different impulse took him.

"You're still a slave then?" Sindron sensed his friend bristle.

"Yes, but I live out now, no restrictions," Lydos retorted. "My own house and a family, two sons learning the business." Lydos glowed with pride now and gestured, indicating that the young scribe was one of his sons. Sindron congratulated Lydos and felt a tinge of envy, though he had always regarded marriage between slaves as a dubious business, with any children liable to be sold off, as he himself had been. "He gives me full responsibility and takes my advice on major decisions."

Lydos leant closer and whispered. "Phraston has no heirs. His son was killed at the Battle of Eurymedon. Only ship we lost too. Tragic." But somehow the tone suggested the man felt no real sympathy. That surprised Sindron.

"So Phraston has promised to free me and leave me the bank on his death." Clearly, the man could hardly contain his excitement. "Depositors and investors prefer banks to be in the hands of citizens, so there's a good chance I'll be given citizenship as well." Though his face retained the dignity of his job, the tone of his words was that of a little boy who has won his first running race at the gymnasium.

"The old man's having the freedom papers prepared now. Just hope these reforms don't rock the boat," Lydos added. A note of genuine worry crept into the bland tone in the immaculate accent.

Sindron explained his new situation – personal adviser to the heir to a business fortune – briefly, and, he hoped, without arrogance.

Lydos' attitude did seem to change subtly. "Well, that is good news! But, if you don't mind a word of advice, old friend, you should be better dressed than this, you know. The slave has to reflect his master's glory in Athens."

Sindron felt obliged to excuse his dress by explaining they had just arrived. He outlined the problem with his master's age, the need to get him registered as a citizen and his uncertainty about the effect of the new reforms. He remembered that Lydos had always prided himself on his knowledge of the way Athens worked.

Sindron soon discovered that the reforms hadn't changed the old citizenship arrangements. It sounded as though it should be straightforward enough. Lydos explained where the relevant offices were but, before Sindron could ask about the political situation, the banker's attention was diverted by a customer with a complex enquiry. Lydos asked Sindron to wait in the Painted Colonnade, where he joined the small group of onlookers watching an artist at work.

Sindron stared at the paintings of great battles on wooden panels on the inside walls of the colonnade, clearly intended to celebrate Athenian military prowess. Painters were still working on the different panels, as though in a competition, and he was fascinated to see that styles seemed to be changing.

"That's Mikon. He's famous, you know," Lydos said as he came up behind Sindron. He explained quietly that there was a propaganda element here, not just because it showed Kimon's father, Miltiades, winning the Battle of Marathon, but also because Theseos, legendary founder of Athens and father of democracy, represented as lending his support to the Athenians, had been made to look similar to Kimon. "Aimed to present Kimon as the best man to lead the city, I believe. Clever, isn't it? Unfortunately, he needs more than that at the moment!" Away from his banking table, Lydos didn't seem so concerned about using Kimon's name, Sindron observed.

The next panel, with a somewhat older artist tackling the detail of a face, was much more exciting. The burning buildings seemed to recede into the background, the heroic figures to thrust forward. He had never seen anything as dramatic as the figures in what he decided must be the sack of Troy, for there were the flames rising behind the ruined city in deep red and ochre, with the Greek heroes and their captives in front. The fear in the eyes of the captives and the triumph worth fearing in those of the victors was disturbing, haunting. Sindron was impressed.

"Polygnotos from Thasos," explained Lydos. "Trojan War. The word around is, that's the face of Kimon's sister Elpinike that he's put on Laodike, the most beautiful of King Priam's daughters. Of course, that's started everyone saying the artist is having an affair with her, and her husband away on a peace mission in Persia too! That's not so helpful to Kimon."

"Strange subject, isn't it, the trial of the hero Ajax for raping Cassandra?" Sindron had worked out what it must be, for there was Ajax, who Athene had made mad to prevent him killing the other Greek leaders and, once again, this hero was looking surprisingly like Kimon. That couldn't be the sort of image the aristocrats would want to present. Could it be taken to imply that the painter thought Kimon was mad enough to try to kill other Athenian leaders?

"Yes, bit of a rebel, Polygnotos. Claims to be painting it at his own expense as a contribution to Athens. So does Mikon publicly but Polygnotos means it, so we couldn't buy him. Phraston's not too happy with it. Neither will Kimon be when he finds out. If we get the Areopagos restored, they'll take action."

This way of impressing people was new to Sindron and clearly it could work both ways. He wondered how this artist, being from Thasos, which Athens, led by Kimon, had treated very badly only a few years ago for trying to leave the Confederacy, how could he bear to live here on familiar terms with its leaders? But, then, maybe this painting said something about his real feelings. Sindron didn't express the thought, as it wasn't at the centre of what he needed to know.

Lydos suddenly smiled and winked at him, referring to the old days. "The plays are better too," he said. "That Aeschylos, what a writer! Even if I don't always agree with his viewpoint."

"You still get to see the contests then."

"Of course, but I see them in comfort now. Phraston takes me as part of his group."

"Don't think I'd be up to all that climbing and scrambling these days," Sindron smiled back and, for a few seconds, a grin of complicity rekindled memories of their old friendship.

As they started walking, Sindron asked the question he had to ask, "But what about the revolution?"

"Don't use that word!" Lydos looked around to make sure no-one was in earshot, lowered his voice. "It's touch and go. I don't think many citizens realised what a big difference the reforms could make when they voted them through. Now the big man's back, there could be trouble."

"So all these people are waiting for something to happen?"

"Yes. Apparently, he's trying to have a special meeting of the Assembly called, so he can attempt to repeal the reforms."

Sindron still couldn't understand what all the fuss was about. "Why? What's so terrible about a bit more democracy?"

"Aah, I forgot how long you've been away. Things have changed a lot."

Lydos explained that, with so many citizens away fighting during the war, there hadn't been enough voters for worthwhile Assembly meetings, so lawmaking and other powers had fallen to the Areopagos, the council of elders, composed of ex-magistrates, the well-born and wealthy.

Kimon dominated the Board of Generals and his faction dominated the Areopagos. When Kimon was away at the war, Kallias, probably the city's richest and most powerful man, had held everything together, giving a strong line on policy. With little opposition, it worked fine, though the Areopagos had offended the rising young intellectuals by clamping down on morals and any kind of artistic experiment, even nosing into individual citizens' personal affairs. The supporters of Themistokles, never as coherent as a faction as the aristocrats who supported Kimon, fell apart when Themistokles was exiled, condemned to death and fled to Persia. Ephialtes, who emerged as the leader of those wanting peace and reform, was ineffective and didn't dare speak out against the war until, with successive victories, the troops started returning.

As Lydos now halted, Sindron realised they had entered an area behind the Painted Colonnade and that this was where financial traders pursued their business.

"Hipponikos. This is a friend of mine. I wondered if you had something tasty for him to dabble in. "

Lydos was introducing him to a swarthy-skinned merchant in a rather flashy robe, with hair and beard neatly curled, standing next to a large white board scrawled with words and figures in charcoal. Sindron looked enquiringly at Lydos.

"A way of increasing your nest egg, old friend, those savings you've been putting away to buy your freedom. Hipponikos deals in cargo loans."

Hipponikos explained how high the interest rates were on short-term loans to finance merchants to hire ships and purchase cargo for trading overseas and how rapidly an investor could double his money. He outlined a specific voyage with Athenian manufactured goods outwards for sale to the Thracians and carrying shipbuilding timber on the return journey. Sindron could see the trap that his friend was innocently getting him into but he could see no way of backing out.

"How much shall I put you down for? A hundred drachmas, eh? Dip your toe in the water? "

Hipponikos chuckled reassuringly, and Lydos assured him that he had invested in cargoes very profitably himself..

It sounded very tempting and how could Sindron explain that he didn't have such a nest egg, that his meagre savings had been contributed to help the family in hard times. Maybe it had prevented him being sold, but he realised how ridiculous that sort of generosity might appear.

He realised also that Lydos knew he had money on him. All his attempts at evasion were brushed aside. Risk? Very slight. Only if the ship sank could he lose his money and that was unlikely in the safe sailing season and with pirates eliminated. Yes, of course, a slave could invest. Not enough money with him?

"Not a problem," Hipponikos dismissed that too. "If Lydos introduces you, you're a good risk. Twenty five drachmas down as deposit, the rest within two days. I'll lend you the rest till then at no interest. How's that?"

"Regard it as testing it out for your master, old friend," added Lydos. "A good slave always anticipates his master's wishes, they say."

With Lydos encouraging him, Sindron had no choice. If he declined, he would appear a coward, who would remain a slave forever. If he did go for it, he'd be risking his master's modest supply of personal money and perhaps drawings on the inheritance as well. It would be leaving him with less cash than he would have liked for whatever they might still need to spend but it should be enough. Sindron decided to accept and come back later, explain his situation and somehow persuade the merchant to cancel the deal, which they swore by placing hands, one over the other, on the curly carved hair of one of the Herms, for Hermes is also the god of merchants – and of good luck, he thought hopefully. He didn't feel comfortable about it and he recalled wryly his warning to Lysanias earlier.

How had he allowed himself to be tricked like that? Was he really that unused to dealing with other people, with situations where he was a player himself? Or was he really worried about his own future? Or, deep inside, was he a risk-taker, a gambler? Or was Athens corrupting him, making him more worried about saving face than about right and wrong? If he could be tricked that easily at his age, how would Lysanias fare?

Though deeply unhappy at his own misuse of his master's money, Sindron was still determined to find out more about the political situation. All Lydos had given him so far was a bit of historical background. He interrupted his friend's boastings about how much he had managed to save and invest, even acquiring control of a dye works, which he wanted to show off to Sindron sometime.

"You were telling me that things changed when the troops came home," he prompted as they strolled back.

Lydos explained that the rowers in particular, drawn from the lower classes, felt the war couldn't have been won but for them. They wanted their reward but what they found was overcrowded housing, what was left of it, and their jobs taken by foreign immigrants and trained slaves. They became disgruntled. The new Cult of Hephaistos, the workers' god, gave them a spiritual champion and Ephialtes, fed radical new ideas by Perikles and other young intellectuals, became their spokesperson. He had proved quite an effective demagogue too.

Sindron's mind raced ahead. "So the radical democrats became a sort of people's party and came up with proposals to reward the veterans, and naturally they jumped at the offer?"

"That's part of it."

Lydos' admirable objectivity became tinged with a note of bitterness as he described how Ephialtes seemed to become cleverer as he changed his tactics. By suing some of the most active members of the Areopagos for corruption and maladministration, he whittled down its strength and weakened public respect for it. By somehow manipulating that Kallias lead the team sent to Persia to negotiate a peace treaty, he got the main financier and thinker behind Kimon and the aristocrats out of the way. By making sure that Kimon personally commanded the four thousand troops sent to help Sparta, all of them from the wealthy classes and Kimon supporters, and himself recruiting supporters from the lower classes by backing the cult of Hephaistos, he built a majority in the Assembly for the radicals and was able to strip the Areopagos of its powers and reduce it to a law court for murder trials.

"Very cunning," remarked Sindron.

"Cunning is the word. If I didn't know that rascal Themistokles was in Persia cosying up to the Great King," said Lydos, "I would have thought he must be back here, thinking up all these tricks."

Sindron remembered how grateful the citizens had been for Themistokles' trickery when it had saved them from conquest by the Persians by fooling the Great King Xerxes into sending his ships into battle at Salamis, where they could be easily defeated. They'd been pleased too when, by trickery, he had delayed the Spartans long enough to rebuild the city's defensive walls before the rival city could take action. Sindron found it impossible to condemn the exiled statesman who had once been so revered.

Lydos put the radicals' new, cunning tactics down to the advice of young Perikles, who many of the rich regarded as a traitor to their class, and of the young intellectuals around him. Perikles had been very close to Themistokles when he was younger and must have learned from him. But it still wasn't clear why there was so much animosity around, an animosity that Lydos seemed to share.

"If the Areopagos only took those powers because so many citizens were away, what's wrong with that?" Sindron asked. It sounded as though he was disputing Lydos' opinion and he could sense the annoyance growing in Lydos' voice when he replied.

"It gave full power over us all to the Assembly of all citizens, that's what's wrong with it. It means the mob, all the men without property or solid incomes, have power over everyone else, and all the property of the wealthy carries very little weight."

"Yes, but surely the people still respect the opinions of the wealthy citizens, with all their experience?" It was starting to sound like an argument. Sindron enjoyed this sort of animated discussion but he could see it unsettled his friend.

"I wouldn't rely on it."

It was now very clear where Lydos' bias lay, or maybe it was his master's bias: in favour of Kimon and the aristocrats.

Lydos turned his head suddenly to the right. "See that over there?" With a flick of his eyes, Lydos indicated the site of the new building going up on the lower slopes of Market Hill, which Sindron remembered as the area of the smiths and metalworkers. "Temple of Hephaistos, I ask you! Hephaistos, the heavenly smith, a nobody among the gods up to now, but suddenly he's the workers' god, the radical democrats' god, and he's going to have the biggest, most modern temple in all Athens and on public funds! It's alright for new temples to be built but the Freedom Lovers for Zeus cult that my master belongs to can't rebuild his sanctuary till the Persians are fully punished for their sacrilege. Doesn't make sense."

By now they had arrived back at the banker's table, and were seated on stools away from it, while Lydos' son looked after customers, a well-built but serious young man, slightly hunched and clearly settling into this sedentary occupation.

"No wonder Kimon is angry," Sindron ventured, knowing he had got to the nub of the conflict.

"All the aristocrats are, and now Kimon's back to lead them, who knows what they'll do to get their power back!"

The urgency and worry behind Lydos' voice was obvious, and Sindron grew worried himself. "Do you think it could be dangerous, real civil conflict?"

Lydos waved an arm, indicating the crowd. He whispered his suspicion that, some at least of those respectable-looking cloaks and tunics concealed knives or sharp tools, even though no-one except Scythian guards was supposed to carry arms in the city. Sindron found it difficult to believe. Surely Lydos was exaggerating.

"But we're slaves, so keep well out of it, that's my motto."

Sindron knew he didn't mean it. A slave's fortunes were tied to his master's, so, if Lysanias' inheritance had put him on the side of the aristocrats, then Lysanias was thrown right into the middle of this political turmoil and so was Sindron.

Then Lydos' master, Phraston, put in a brief appearance, bringing a customer over to the table. A giant of a man, very overweight for an Athenian, jovial and seemingly popular but with sadness deep in his eyes, Sindron noted, as those eyes swept over him and dismissed him as not justifying attention. Lydos said nothing to indicate if these had been Phraston's opinions he had been expressing, though it was clear that everyone around paid Phraston great respect.

It came back to Sindron that Phraston had been a noted wrestler when young, won prizes in the games. All that muscle had gone to… Well, you could see where it had gone.

"And whose side is your master on?" Sindron asked, when Lydos finished with the customer.

That opened a floodgate. The man's remaining reserve disappeared. "Don't ask! It's too gruesome. Everything could collapse, if we're not careful!"

He revealed that Phraston was a close associate of Kimon's, had handled sales of his war booty and persuaded him to build the new Temple to Theseos partly so Phraston could transfer the bank's deposits to its treasury and away from the ruined temple on the High City. Kimon remaining in power was important to him.

This really was getting the inside story. Sindron felt pleased that his friend felt he could trust him so much, but he noticed that Lydos' son was looking agitated, trying to catch his father's attention. "Phraston has always given funds to the political activities of Kimon's 'party of the best' but, now Kallias is away, Phraston has taken over his responsibilities but he hasn't got Kallias' political skills..."

The voice tailed off as Lydos realised what he was saying and to someone he hadn't seen for fourteen years. His eyes narrowed and his mouth set in a thin firm line. Lydos' voice, harder, sharper, stabbed at him. "This master of yours! The 'business heir'! Who is he?"

"I thought you might have guessed. Recent death – Klereides. My master is Lysanias, son of Leokhares and Klereides' nephew and now his heir. We arrived this morning."

"Who? You're sure?" His expression froze and his eyes seemed to look in on himself. Sindron nodded, puzzled at the reaction.

"Of course you're sure. Lysanias, you say. Klereides' heir. Now that's..." Lydos seemed suddenly unsure, worried, looking for time to think. "You'll have to go! I shouldn't have been speaking to you at all."

Sindron was really confused now. "But why? We're friends. You can trust me."

Lydos gave a cynical shrug. "Friendship, eh? You know the old slave motto. Never trust anyone, especially another slave."

"But..." Sindron looked very downcast, his normal dignified expression wiped from his face. If he couldn't talk to Lydos, that meant he had no friends in Athens he could consult. The expression got through to Lydos.

"Very well. Friendship." Lydos seemed to pull himself together, calculating. "If you really need to see me ... Not here ... Not in public..." Lydos thought for a moment, became abrupt, businesslike. "Dawn every day, I'm at the Temple of Theseos, in the treasury behind the altar. That's the best I can do. But not tomorrow. Nor next day. Important meetings. You've the funeral. Four days time. How's that? Now go, please!"

Sindron went, slightly shaken, and confused at his friend's changing attitude to him and the cynicism he displayed. What could Klereides have done to justify such a reaction? He regretted not having asked

about Klereides first. Then he remembered that he could be late to meet
Lysanias.

CHAPTER 4

Leaving the baths, Lysanias had taken a wrong turning and ended up, the only wealthy-looking person in a slum quarter with dirty, ragged children tugging at his cloak and begging for money. Then more of them and two were holding onto his legs and calling to their fathers that they had caught a 'Kimo'. As two villainous-looking men emerged and advanced on him, brandishing knives, Lysanias kicked himself free and fled for his life, fearful yet angry at his own cowardice at not staying to fight. There really were aspects to Athens that he hadn't expected. He had seen no poverty like this back home.

Slipping into the fountain house to clean the muck of the slums from his sandals and feet and, as far as he could, the hem of his cloak, Lysanias found himself enduring the stares of the female slaves and lower class wives filling their amphoras with water to carry home. Maybe the visit to the barber's would help him to calm down, he thought, but it proved something of an ordeal.

As he stared into the bronze mirror, like the gorgon glaring into Perseus' shield, the barber, horrified at his spikey short hair, insisted on tidying it up, trying to make it look like a new hairstyle that was becoming fashionable with younger men the barber said. The shave was worse. The barber scraped away at his tender young skin with that bronze razor till his face felt red and raw. Scented oil eased it, but he could still feel it burn. He wondered if all the barbers in Athens were as barbaric.

It was the conversation of the other customers, though, that disturbed him most. The name of his uncle had cropped up again, this time in talk about athletes and forthcoming games and disappointment at the loss of Klereides' patronage as a sponsor. News of his uncle's death really had spread rapidly. Lysanias strained his ears but the subject changed.

This shop seemed to be a favourite haunt of the idle rich: well-dressed and immaculately-groomed men at their ease, with watered wine and olives there for the taking.

"It's g-got so a r-rich m-man daren't stand for p-public office for fear of being taken to c-court by Ephialtes for negligence or c-corruption or profiteering or s-somesuch," he overheard, from a mellow voice with a slight stutter.

The man spoke quite clearly, sure he was among friends, but the sour grapes and hatred was thick on the air. There was talk of a massive fine on someone called Hierokles, which had nearly forced him to sell his estate, until Kimon had come to his rescue. Most vehement was a particularly angry and slightly drunken voice that sounded personally involved. They all seemed to feel threatened. This must be the sort of background information that Sindron had wanted him to listen out for.

Then the barber cut his cheek.

"Sorry about that, sir," the barber said, dabbing the wound with half a lemon kept handy for the purpose. It stung and took his mind off the conversation, which switched to ways of removing the object of their hatred, Ephialtes, though other radical leaders came in for their share of abuse.

"Why don't you do something about him?" asked the master barber good-humouredly. The innocent remark produced a short loud laugh from the drunken man and a hushed silence from everyone else during which his own barber's request to puff out his cheek sounded strangely loud. Reflected in the mirror, the man, tall and thin with a neatly-trimmed black beard, narrow pointed nose and frown lines, seemed tense, not fully concentrating on his job.

The master barber indicated that he meant that maybe one of them should challenge Ephialtes to a fistfight or wrestling match but the radical politician's age appeared to rule that out. They had evidently looked into ways of suing him for some misdemeanour but his record was clean. Only ostracism was left, which would exile him for ten years, but his majority in the Assembly meant that was unlikely to succeed. They were left with the hope that Kimon would find some way of reversing the reforms or that Ephialtes would have an accident "like that shipbuilder this morning".

That had to be a reference to his uncle and the knowing laughs that followed were disconcerting. But the barber was speaking in his ear, taking his attention. "Will that be all?" The barber slipped the cloth from round his neck and brushed him down.

"Well, let's hope something happens to him soon. This mobocracy can't be allowed to go on," said a deep rich voice. Heads were turned away from him, but the deep brown hair of one man was plaited round his head in a distinctive way that Lysanias felt he would recognise anywhere.

"My slave will pay," said Lysanias, indicating Sindron, who was waiting near the door. He felt every inch the Athenian gentleman he had just seen looking back at him from the mirror. Was he one of these idle gossipers now, whose accent and superior tone he found so offensive? Or did he have more in common with the stonemasons on the ship? His new life wasn't getting any simpler.

Sindron explained to Lysanias what Lydos had told him about how to register as a citizen, and that dispensations from mourning obligations were possible. Sindron didn't mention the cargo loan – time for that later. They tried to obtain a dispensation first but it proved more difficult than Lydos had made it sound. The official for the magistrate responsible for state religions accepted Lysanias' reason for wanting a dispensation and his claim to be Klereides' heir. "Though that is not what was reported to us earlier," he said. However, he would not countenance a dispensation until Lysanias' citizenship was established. It proved a long process.

They located the city office of Lysanias' deme, the region he was born, in the back of a shoemaker's shop, and the shoemaker, an elected official of the deme, accepted the polished wood medallion that proved Lysanias' birth to two citizens and the date. However, he insisted on proof from his clan or phratry of Lysanias' identity. He referred them to an office in a tavern at the end of the road.

After buying the publican a flask of wine, the man agreed to check the records but then made it clear that a generous donation to phratry funds would be needed. With this made, they obtained confirmation of phratry membership scratched on a small square of bronze. This was enough for the shoemaker who gave them a comparable token of deme membership. Though they felt obliged to buy a pair of sandals each that further depleted Sindron's modest store of money.

With the three proofs, they hurried to the Council offices, the steering committee of the Assembly. The official here was a real obstacle. As soon as Lysanias identified himself, the officious slave knew that the young man should be in mourning and refused to consider an application for registration as a citizen from someone contaminated by the unnatural death of a near relative unless there was a dispensation.

Fortunately, when they went back to the religious official, Lysanias mentioned the name of General Ariston as someone who might vouch for him, the arrogant man saw reason and accepted Sindron's suggestion that he might issue a temporary dispensation. He imposed conditions, though, including a donation to the temple rebuilding fund. The dispensation excused Lysanias from mourning duties only every fourth day and required the wearing of a saffron ribbon on the upper arm. He had glanced round quickly and lowered his voice. "If you conceal it a little with your cloak, that will stop the idea getting around too much," he muttered.

Back at the Council offices, this was enough to win provisional citizenship registration, providing a close male relative verified it within four days and that Lysanias registered with his tribe as soon as possible. With a new understanding of the power of money and influence to grease wheels in Athens, they breathed a sigh of relief and headed back

to the market square. Adding to the relief was the officials' dismissal of
the idea that Eion could have been over-run. Lysanias' mother, brother
and sisters were safe. His relations must have been confusing it with that
other colony upriver from Eion whose survivors they had had to take
in.

As they came out of the Council offices, the tension in the air seemed
much greater. The people in smart clothes had drawn into tighter groups,
and so had the workers and traders. The market stalls had closed down
but the square still seemed crowded. Everyone seemed to be waiting for
something to happen.

And something did happen. Sindron had said, "I think we're too late
to check on your military service, but we'll have a look. That's the Office
of the Board of Generals, the War Department, over there. I think they'd
deal with that." They started to cross through the crowds. Lysanias was
getting used to the presence of Scythian archers, the city's police force,
on guard in front of each civic building, though they still reminded him
of what had happened to his father.

Seeing General Ariston ahead and not wanting to be recognized,
Lysanias was about to suggest to Sindron that they should go another
way, when Ariston and, it seemed, everyone else turned to look as Kimon
marched out of a strange circular but impressive building that Lysanias
had been meaning to ask about and stood stiff with military bearing, his
helmet under his arm.

He seemed even taller than Lysanias expected, his dark curly hair and
full bushy beard with neatly trimmed moustache in the Spartan style
framing his powerful face in a striking similarity to some of the entryway
Herms. But that great scar across his cheek, that hadn't been shown by the
sculptor of the statue at Eion, or that one running the length of his upper
arm. The man must be forty-five by now and he looked in the prime of
life, though those purple veins in his nose betrayed a strong liking for the
grape. Maybe the news-teller was right about that, anyway.

The pan-Hellenic bodyguard, bearing the insignia of major cities in
the alliance, fell into place around him, seeming to appear from nowhere.
The banner of the confederacy was raised above his head, its symbol,
the silver bow of Delian Apollo, echoed in Kimon's highly polished
breastplate. In all the panoply of commander-in-chief of the force that
had battled the mighty Persian Empire to its knees, this was the man,
too, who had forged an empire for Athens. Yet he seemed fixed in place,
staring at something behind Lysanias and Sindron.

The buzz of conversation hushed. For a moment the cries of the
wandering street-vendors could be heard, singing their wares, then even
they halted. The tension in the air was tangible. Sindron wondered what
the great general must be feeling. For all his achievements on behalf of

Athens, here he was confronted with rejection by a major part of the citizenry and the possibility of being ostracised like his father before him, the shame of which he had fought so long to erase. He clearly intended to fight back.

A smattering of applause from the wealthy petered out as everyone saw where Kimon was looking, his eyes burning with hatred behind the stiff composure. Lysanias turned, like everyone else, in that direction. By the notices in front of the Council building that Lysanias and Sindron had just come from, two figures stood, their attention given totally to the writings, and apparently explaining them to citizens who approached them.

One was a rather bent, balding, careworn figure, with unkempt brown hair, snub nose, and pock-marked cheeks, dressed in a cloak of rough fabric, perhaps deliberately avoiding the ostentation of the wealthy. The impression he gave was one of complete honesty. The other, tall, much younger, early thirties maybe, standing upright with a strangely shaped head, his cranium higher than most people, despite the evident efforts of his barber to disguise it with his hair arrangement. But his face was extremely handsome, with that fine straight nose and full lips, his hair glistening in the late afternoon sun.

This man's robe, too, was of coarser fabric but immaculately worn. Their simplicity contrasted with the magnificence of Kimon's entourage.

Lysanias realised. These must be the leaders of the radicals: Ephialtes and Perikles. Those notice-boards must be the new laws, and the workers and out-of-towners were crowding round to find out what the reforms meant, how they would change things. The tension grew.

In the quiet, he could just hear Ephialtes explaining to a smallholder up from the country.

"No," he emphasised calmly. "The rich won't have as much say. The Areopagos won't make the laws any more. The Assembly will – all the citizens."

His voice, slightly harsh and husky, not altogether pleasant on the ear but compelling, rose above the words of Perikles to a citizen-worker. "No, taxes won't go up. There's more than enough from taxes on trade and foreign residents. And we've the tribute money from the allies to fall back on."

As the pause held, both men glanced round momentarily. Their eyes met those of Kimon, oh so briefly, then looked back to their task. They had the power now! Lysanias could smell it. So could the crowd.

As Kimon and his bodyguard turned to march away, the silence broke. A group of workers cheered, while some young aristocrats hissed. One grabbed an egg from a street-vendor's basket and went to hurl it at Ephialtes. Others bent to pick up stones. A swift signal and a low whistle from Perikles and a mixed crowd of workers and stall-holders moved into a defensive ring round the two leaders, a sort of unofficial people's guard under Perikles' command, Lysanias guessed. One dashed forward. Great gods, it was Stephanos, the young stonemason from the ship. He grabbed the arm that held the egg, throwing its owner to the ground. The egg fell, broke and seeped into the dust.

They punched and grappled, as clouds of dust rose around them. A major fight seemed about to happen, with the wealthy youths far outnumbered it seemed.

Suddenly Ephialtes broke through the defensive ring and, with no regard for his own safety, stepped into the fray, the experienced public speaker booming out, "This won't do! Democracy means all views can be heard! We don't need violence to prove our point, not any more!"

The fighters paused, awed, and Ephialtes pulled them apart. But the threat was still there, the tension still in the air, the urge to fight it out. Ephialtes glanced across at Kimon. Was this a plea for peace, a truce?

The bodyguard and Kimon had stopped and turned at the first disturbance. The Scythian archers standing guard on official doorways had unslung their bows in case of real trouble, and one of them had blown a short blast on a small flute-like instrument to summon assistance. Kimon stepped forward. "Enough now, citizens! We'll fight them in the right place! In the Assembly!"

Bloody-nosed and covered in dust, the two contenders drew apart and the young bloods backed off, as members of the protective ring inconspicuously placed themselves between them and Ephialtes. Lysanias glanced at Perikles in time to catch a slight nod of approval. He looked every inch the military commander, even in civilian clothes. Ephialtes walked back and, though Perikles seemed to be congratulating him, there were signs of anger on Ephialtes' face, as though heated words were being exchanged.

But only for an instant. Then they were the calm leaders of the people once again, offering explanations of the reforms to anyone who asked. It was as though everyone was trying to pretend a near-riot hadn't actually happened.

When Lysanias looked behind him, Kimon and his bodyguard had gone. Ariston stood, for a moment, regarding the scene, then, with an arm gesture, turned and, as he stepped out in the direction Kimon had gone, a number of well-dressed men fell into step behind him. Lysanias thought he recognised the cloaks and general appearance of two of the men he had overheard in the barber's. They marched off in step, and took up a marching chant, probably a regimental song, that sounded like a bravado challenge to the workers and radicals. Through the crowd, Sindron thought he saw Phraston edging his way in the direction they had gone.

The street-vendors started crying their wares again and life returned to something like normal. For the first time, as Sindron's grip relaxed, Lysanias realised that Sindron had grasped his upper arm, presumably to stop him getting involved in the fight.

"Decided which side you're on yet then, junior new citizen?"

A rough hand clapped Lysanias hard on the shoulder. He spun round and grasped the wrist, as the training instructor in Eion had taught. And it was Stephanos standing there, laughing. "Good grip, youngster," he said, somehow twisting and jerking his arm to break Lysanias' hold. "Could have been a good fight, eh?" as he wiped blood still trickling from his nose with the back of his hand. "But we'll show them when the time comes!"

He looked Lysanias up and down. "You trying to look like one of them, then, and smell like them?" His nose wrinkled in disdain.

"No, just getting smartened up, got a wealthy uncle, just die..." Lysanias started to reply, but Stephanos shrugged.

"Never mind, citizen. Your hands say where your loyalties lie and those are worker's hands." Lysanias felt relief that he wouldn't have to explain, not now anyway, especially as he couldn't be at all certain himself where his loyalties did lie. Then, as Stephanos was about to turn away, Lysanias caught a glint of sunlight on metal just behind him, a knife in the hand of a well-dressed but dusty young man.

Without time to think, Lysanias grabbed Sindron's staff, the only thing that could reach far enough in time, twirled it and thumped it down hard on the young man's wrist. The dagger dropped and a sharp cry was rapidly suppressed, as the man ran off and was lost among the crowd. Thank the gods that, with the shortage of spears in Eion, they had trained and practiced with staves and wielding them. He stood, holding the staff firmly, excited, eager for more.

Stephanos' eyes widened at sight of the dagger, realising what had just happened. "They are getting desperate! I owe you one, citizen! Thanks. See you in the hiring line, eh?" He darted away to join his colleagues, leaving Lysanias aware how little it could take to ignite the tensions into all out civil war.

"Master, everyone's looking at us," Sindron hissed, and took back the staff, secretly glad it had proved useful. "We were supposed to be trying to be inconspicuous!" Sindron was frightened now, but tried not to show it.

One glance told Lysanias the old man was right. These were furtive looks that people were giving him, confused that a wealthy-looking young man, with short hair in the latest style, should side with an active supporter of the radicals. However, once Lysanias and Sindron had gone a few steps among the dispersing crowd, and passed the statues of the ten tribal heroes, they were as anonymous as ever.

"We must be getting back to the house now," Sindron said, like a parent. "I'll check up tomorrow on whether they can put off your military call-up for a while. By the way, I heard that news-teller again on the way to meet you. He seemed to be referring to Klereides."

"If he was as nasty about uncle as he was about Kimon, I'll want a reckoning when I see him."

"Referred to a crushing force from above, implying the gods or someone helping the gods, ending the life of a greedy rat. Suggesting that all who could should go to the funeral feast as the last chance to get back some of the funds the deceased had won for himself out of state coffers."

"I'll definitely have to have words with him," gritted Lysanias, missing Sindron's point that this might be another view of Klereides' character they should pay attention to. Sindron decided not to pursue it.

On the way back through Inner Kermeikos, they heard a crier making an announcement. Windows and doors opened as he cupped his hands to his mouth and shouted. "Hai, hai, hai." A special Assembly meeting had been called for the next day. All citizens were summoned to attend.

So Kimon had failed to achieve the date he wanted to be sure his troops would be back in time.

"Just what do we know for sure, Sindron? So much is happening. I don't know what to think."

Lysanias felt thoroughly confused, as well as hungry, and increasingly depressed. After he had slipped in by the secret door, a somewhat rushed expedition to the bathroom had done something to justify Lysanias clean and sweetly-smelling state and restore his hair to something like the spikey look it had earlier. He had made a libation at the family shrine to appease the gods for the sacrilege he had committed earlier and sat by his uncle's body for a while. This restored his anger and desire to find the culprit but did nothing to ease the confusion.

Then he and Sindron had sat down together in Lysanias' room with the door tight shut and told one another all they had heard in the city. Well, nearly all. Lysanias didn't mention his terrified run from the slums. Sindron still didn't mention the cargo loan. He now felt silly to have allowed himself to be talked into it. He would go into town tomorrow and sort it out, and maybe see Otanes about a supply of spending money, just in case.

"Don't despair, master. Several people seem to feel that this wasn't a straightforward accident, so we could be right in our suspicions. We've organised you a dispensation, so we can do some investigating."

"Only every fourth day!"

"Well, that's more than we thought we'd have."

"But who are we investigating?"

"Hermon, of course!"

"Why? I get the impression quite a few people didn't like Klereides very much."

Sindron stopped himself sighing as though this was obvious, but couldn't stop his eyes saying it. "Lets list the points. One – Hermon controls the shipyard where it happened, so he is in a position to plan it and to pay someone to set it up. Two – He sent the message telling Klereides where to go..."

"We don't know that!" Lysanias interrupted.

"No, but it's not likely that Klereides would have gone there before dawn on a request from anyone else. It has to be an insider and a close one. Who closer than his business partner?"

Lysanias forgot his hunger, as what Sindron was saying started to bring order to the confusion. "But why? Why would he?"

"Remember those foreign merchants you talked to on the ship? I'm sure one of them mentioned Hermon of Syracuse as an example of a foreigner who had been exploited massively by his patron. That has to be him, so Hermon could have a good reason for wanting Klereides out of the way."

"That's three, yes?"

"Yes. Motive. And, four, he arranged to be out of town to provide an alibi. That's suspicious in itself."

"What about the Fellowship of Hephaistos? Couldn't they have done it?"

"Come now, Lysanias! The workers might slow the work down a bit to show their power, but you don't kill your employer! It could close the firm down and everyone would lose their job, quite apart from how the god Hephaistos would feel about something like that done in his name. No, I think that was just gossip. It has to be Hermon."

"But we haven't even met him and how do we prove it? His alibi may be watertight." Lysanias felt like giving up on the whole thing, but Sindron was firm.

"We must take the first opportunity to ask him questions and check out where it happened and how. There may be clues there. Tomorrow I'll see what people in the household know. Meanwhile, you'll have a heavy day, seeing well-wishers, and the funeral the day after. Time for sleep."

Suddenly Lysanias realised just how tired he did feel. He couldn't even produce a retort to the patronising, paternal and over-familiar tone in Sindron's voice. The old man meant well.

Lysanias fell asleep immediately from sheer exhaustion, but he woke when the house was quiet and he tossed and turned.

Everything had seemed so straightforward. His parents and Sindron had told him the way it would be. Between eighteen and twenty, he would do military training and service. Sow a few wild oats maybe. During his twenties, as a full citizen, he would learn uncle's business, go to war with the army when needed, maybe become an officer. About thirty, get married, set about raising sons, get involved in politics, sponsor a drama or an athlete. Later on, maybe stand for public office, spend more time with the philosophers and historians in the shady groves of the Akademeia.

So it went, all mapped out.

Now it was all going wrong! Sweet Apollo, what's happening to me?

Or maybe Apollo wasn't the god he should be calling to. Demeter, goddess of death and fertility, maybe? No, a god who likes a joke, a sick joke. Bacchos maybe. No, not Bacchos, not important enough. Dionysos, he's the one! He always thought it was funny to screw up people's lives. No. I didn't mean that, gods! I'll make an offering to Dionysos tomorrow.

Or maybe I'll wake up and it will all be a bad dream.

Finally he slept, but his sleep was disturbed by the recurring nightmare he had had since it happened. The two Scythian horsemen racing from the trees on flame red stallions to attack his father and himself as they peacefully herded their sheep and goats back into the city. Himself stabbing and stabbing at the one he had unhorsed. His father galloping after the other and the goat he had snatched up.

"Don't go, father!" Don't go!" With a jerk, Lysanias woke in a sweat and in tears. For he knew it was real. His father was gone, ridden out of his life forever. But he wouldn't allow himself to believe Leokhares was dead. Then his more immediate worries flooded back, pushing even that aside.

CHAPTER 5

The next day, mourning requirements and receiving well-wishers tied Lysanias to the house. Still, that was an important place to start building up a picture of what had led to Klereides' death and what members of the household knew. He had to stay alert despite his restless sleep. Sindron was tired too, not just from the sea journey and the events of yesterday but because he had forced himself to get up early to recall what he could of the layout of the house, speculate on the duties of its personnel and think through what he might be called on to do now.

Before anyone arrived, he and Lysanias sat down with Otanes for a formal talk. Otanes had outlined the plans for the funeral and the feast afterwards, and it became clear that he was still very much taking instructions from Makaria. Lysanias was pleased it was all in hand, and Sindron advised that the way Otanes was organising it would not let the family honour down. They did feel surprised at the number of guests invited, the amount of food being prepared, but Makaria and Otanes must know what was right.

Otanes had been none too pleased when Lysanias told him that he wanted Sindron to have a roving brief to examine anything in the house and to talk to all the other slaves, including Otanes, about the circumstances preceding their master's death.

He queried the necessity, claiming that he could inform Lysanias on everything relating to the household. Lysanias stayed firm and Otanes asked, "Is master suggesting that my running of the household is in some way dishonest?"

"No, no, not at all."

"Then could I ask the master, what my status will be in the future?"

Lysanias was firm.

"Otanes, please don't take offence. We are both impressed with the way you have organised everything so rapidly." Otanes had bridled a little at this. Was it the 'both', the thought of being judged by a fellow slave, or was it the 'rapidly'? Sindron couldn't be sure.

"I'm sure I will wish to keep you in the post of steward, if you do such an excellent job normally. And all the signs are that you do."

Tactfully put, thought Sindron, the boy was learning. Lysanias ventured a smile and Otanes visibly relaxed a little.

"However, I am new to Athens, to this household, to my new responsibilities. I am tied up in funeral duties." He had explained to Makaria and Otanes that he had obtained a partial dispensation from mourning – 'to pursue administrative matters', he had put it – but had avoided being more specific. "I need someone who can report to me on the many things I need to know."

"I can do that, master.".

"Ah yes, but Sindron is a trusted personal adviser."

"Is this something to do with the old master's death?" Otanes asked suddenly, but Lysanias continued, "He knows the questions I would wish to ask."

"But, master, everyone is very busy with the preparations. No-one has been alerted to this."

"Precisely. Now please see that he has every co-operation."

Otanes obviously didn't like it but he must know he had no choice. He must also realise that Lysanias had avoided answering his question about suspicions surrounding Klereides' death.

Philia's throat was sore with all the wailing. She decided to ease off and started going through the motions only. Let the professional mourners do the hard work - it's what they were paid for!

It was becoming boring, but it was better than working in the weaving room. She was still one of the centres of interest. The stream of well-wishers all gestured in her direction, but why couldn't she receive the visitors? That young man, Lysanias, he sat in the entertaining room and only appeared at intervals to honour her husband and make a libation to Zeus. That gave her very little opportunity to study what he looked like, though she definitely preferred him with long hair.

For important visitors, her mother-in-law would withdraw from the bier and receive their commiserations along with Lysanias. It really wasn't fair! However, Makaria insisted the widow had to stay by the body or the gods would be offended, so she held her place.

Philia hadn't slept well. She was angry with herself that she hadn't somehow kept Curly from going out that night and that she hadn't managed to get pregnant and give him an heir. Then she wouldn't have to marry this youngster from the colonies. All the young wives had mature husbands; everyone would look down on her. But then, he was a lot better-looking than Klereides, even if Klereides did have his nice side.

No, she shouldn't be thinking like this! She was mourning a husband. Guilt prompted her to rejoin the keening and wailing with full force.

So many loose ends, thought Lysanias, and here he was cooped up in a house of mourning, while whoever had murdered his uncle covered their tracks. How would this stand with the gods, that he was failing to avenge his uncle? Yet maybe there were clues here to the villains; maybe some of these well-wishers had something to hide.

In the event, most of the well-wishers were quite transparent. They were worried that their source of sponsorship had been cut off and wanted to make sure the heir knew what promises they had received, what they were owed. An athlete, a wrestler, two poets, a sculptor, a silversmith, two potters ... he started to lose track. As a craftsman himself, Lysanias understood the importance of being paid for work you have done, and could sympathise. He tried to give them reassurance without promises. After all, he didn't yet know how much money there was in the estate.

In general, Lysanias was amazed at the way Klereides seemed to have thrown his money around, even if such sponsorship did bring honour and prestige.

Later in the morning came a few politicians and businessmen and they were more difficult to fathom. It was unclear which political parties and factions Klereides had supported financially or with his vote in the Assembly. They all seemed to think he was one of theirs, and that included the representative from the radical democrats, who apologised that neither Ephialtes nor one of the other leaders could come in person, due to the Assembly meeting later that day.

One of the aristocratic party, Kimon's party, who did come spoke with a pronounced stammer and Lysanias was sure it was the man he had overheard in the barber's. The brown hair plaited neatly around the head rang a bell as well. Fortunately, there was no indication that he recognised Lysanias. Lysanias thought of them as the aristocrats, the well-born, and they clearly thought of themselves as the 'best', better than the other citizens. 'The party of the best'. The names of individuals ran together and jumbled in his head.

As someone who had learned his trade as a carpenter, Lysanias felt his anger rising at the assumption of superiority of these idlers, yet he knew that his father's family were among the well-born of Attica. His father hadn't made a lot of it, but Sindron had mentioned it whenever he wanted to persuade Lysanias to control his behaviour.

Sindron had given him lectures on the ship to prepare him. Yes, he knew there were four classes of citizen on a basis of wealth. The wealthiest, the big land-owners, formed the cavalry regiments in wartime. The next class, the smaller landowners, they constituted the heavy-armed infantry. So he was from one of the top classes of citizens, the only ones who could serve as generals or magistrates or commanders of war galleys and who fought as cavalry or heavy-armed infantry in wartime. Yet all male citizens, whether shopkeepers or craftsmen or labourers, had a vote in the Assembly and all had to fight in some capacity.

Since then, Sindron had outlined Lydos' interpretation of recent events, though exactly why different classes should be fighting one another for political power rather than co-operating for the common good, he found difficult to understand. The colonists in Eion had seemed able to get on with one another.

In all this, how did one tell where everyone stood? The politicians tended to declare themselves but the well-wishers seemed to relate to Klereides in so many different ways. There were representatives of deme and phratry and tribe, of regiment and dining club, from business and politics. And no way of telling which were friends and which regarded themselves as rivals, whether they were here out of politeness or curiosity, and which had a merely formal relationship with his uncle.

The effusiveness of sympathies and praise of Klereides offered no guide at all. Whether any of these could be actual enemies capable of murder, as Sindron had suggested, was impossible to assess, even if it was plausible that a murderer would come here and risk giving himself away.

And still no sign of Hermon! The man closest to his uncle, the man he most needed to talk to, if he was to get to the bottom of this mystery, and he was still out of Athens – or so the messengers said who had been sent to enquire.

Lysanias' instructions to Otanes didn't produce the results intended. The steward showed Sindron around the house. The layout hadn't changed much from the old days, apart from an upstairs floor with extra rooms for slaves that had been added beyond the courtyard.

As Otanes had warned, the house-slaves were very busy and gave Sindron the briefest of answers or none at all. As far as he could gather, they had all either been in bed or starting on their household duties at the time of their late master's death. Only Otanes had been out of the house, on a legitimate errand he insisted, and Makaria backed him up. The previous day and evening, the slaves had all been involved with the dinner party, which no-one remarked on especially.

The funeral would be before daybreak the next morning and the funeral feast would follow it. The preparations were enormous for one household. Otanes had hired in a chef but he had insisted on all available slaves assisting with fetching and preparing food.

Today, baking the sweetmeats had top priority. Then the fish would be prepared and marinated for baking in herbs and spices. Meat would come from the lambs and goats to be sacrificed before the funeral. It all meant that, in the chaos of the modest-sized kitchen with everyone rushing backwards and forwards, detailed questioning was impossible.

Sindron decided on a more subtle approach. Once he had met everyone, he said to Otanes, "Don't mind the young master. He gets over-enthusiastic, you understand. I'm not really one for questioning people. Perhaps, if you've a few minutes, we could share a flask of wine and discuss how you would like me to help tomorrow."

The florid red tinge to the steward's rather fleshy nose hadn't escaped Sindron's attention, and he was right. It was an offer Otanes wasn't going to refuse. It was an excellent wine, too, though Sindron made sure his was well-watered. Following Lydos' comments, Sindron had trimmed his hair and beard before his master rose and put on a clean, pressed cloak. He found it did help his self-assurance in speaking to Otanes on equal terms.

Sindron was surprised how much effort it took to be natural with the man. After all, the Persians weren't his enemy. But he had been through the Persian invasion, had felt as vulnerable as the Athenians, felt joy with them at all the Greek victories, all of Kimon's victories. And this man Otanes had been a soldier, a commander of killers.

How could one trust a Persian, the hated enemy? The man's very smoothness, his hissing, sibilant speech became unsettling. Otanes had adopted an Athenian style of hair and beard and dress but there was a sleekness, an odour that seemed to express his foreignness, if not his Persianness. Sindron felt hints of fear and hatred creeping into his words and tone on occasion but hoped this wasn't too apparent. How could Sindron behave as though theirs was an ordinary domestic relationship? But he had to.

On top of that, as personal slave to a wealthy Athenian, he had to behave as though he was Otanes' equal, though when he was last in this household, his status had been well below that.

Otanes showed no awareness. Perhaps he was more concerned that his senior status might now be in jeopardy, even that he was at risk of being sold.

The steward's room, he noticed, was decidedly comfortable, with a small shrine to Kybele, the Persian moon-goddess.

The atmosphere relaxed. Efforts on both sides to pump more information out of the other were gentle and gentlemanly, interrupted only by occasional calls by household slaves for decisions by the steward. Otanes is certainly efficient, thought Sindron.

Equally businesslike, Otanes dealt with the matter of spending money. "Your master will be needing cash for small purchases, I'm sure. Can I entrust this to you for him? It's the amount Klereides used to keep handy." The steward handed Sindron a leather wallet of coins. Sindron had meant to ask for a specific sum to be sure he could cover the loan, if necessary. Now he just had to accept it. The thought he was deceiving his master still nagged at him.

"After the funeral," Otanes went on, "we'll have to see about the master's right to draw on the main account."

Sindron started trying to persuade Otanes to talk more freely. While emphasising that Lysanias was strong-willed and decisive, Sindron indicated that the new master wouldn't be able to manage the household without Otanes' experienced guiding hand. He slipped in the inference that Lysanias wasn't very observant, not too fussy over details, willing to leave it to the slaves. He wanted Otanes to relax and hopefully lower his guard a little.

Sindron marvelled, flatteringly but not entirely falsely, at the complexity and bookkeeping involved in running dinner parties on the scale of the funeral feast. Yes, Otanes made sure he handled the accounts himself, couldn't trust a junior slave these days. The hint that it might be appropriate to show Sindron the accounts was ignored.

"How often did Master Klereides check the accounts?"

"Oh, very rarely, he left that to Makaria mostly."

"Ah, so she's familiar with everything. Lysanias doesn't really need to bother his young head?"

"No, he can leave it to Makaria and myself."

That had proved a dead end, but it left one opening.

"You seem very familiar with the mistress's name. Did you call master Klereides by his name too?"

Otanes seemed to realise he had backed himself into a trap, but he quickly escaped it.

"Ah, yes, a steward is a very trusted member of the household. In private, you understand, personal names were ah accepted."

"Yes, just like the family in Eion."

Sindron knew it wasn't just like that. This was a very conventional family in respectable Athens, not a family of social rebels in the birth struggles of a colony. Something wasn't quite right here, though Otanes took the opportunity to confide that Klereides had promised to give him his freedom at some point, though he didn't seem to welcome the prospect of being a free Persian in Athens without a wealthy owner to protect him.

It might be undermining but Sindron had to ask the question that was bothering him.

"How did the Athenians react to a Persian ex-warrior wandering freely around their city?"

Otanes seemed a little taken aback, as though he had forgotten how bad it had been. "Ah, it was, uh, awkward at first. I dressed in the local clothes Klereides provided, you understand, and had to adopt a slave's hair and beard styling. Hurtful but slavery brings such humiliations, as I'm sure you well know. And I accompanied Klereides mainly. He liked to show me off to other citizens as his triumph." The man's eyes reflected the remembered humiliation.

"Yes, but..," started Sindron, but Otanes continued, needing to express it, knowing that a fellow slave would understand.

"There are still jeers, if you really want to know, especially from the lower classes when my people have suffered a major defeat. Sometimes a shopkeeper will refuse to serve me or insist on taunting. My skin colour and accent give me away. Easier now there are so many new slaves, war captives..."

He tailed off receding into himself at thought of his situation. Then pulled himself together. "Klereides treated me well for all that." Was it true? Or had Klereides enjoyed humiliating the man? Did Otanes have reason to hate his master? Sindron found he couldn't feel sorry for him.

He pulled himself back to the task in hand, though he wasn't sure what he was looking for in his questioning. Just anything out of the ordinary that might suggest why anyone would want Klereides out of the way, but that was difficult when one didn't know what was normal in this household. A Persian slave, now, and one holding the important post of steward, that couldn't be very common.

Sindron had observed a large medal of some sort, round and lovingly polished, holding pride of place beside the shrine. On its face was an eagle with wings spread wide. Now, if that was the imperial eagle of Xerxes, then Otanes must have been a Persian officer. He enquired about the medallion.

"Yes, everyone here knows. Junior command, but important, imperial elite. That's the shoulder clasp." The pride in the achievement was still there, Sindron could see, though Otanes frowned slightly. "You're wondering why I wasn't ransomed. Everyone does." His expression implied boredom with the whole matter, a past life gone by. "I disobeyed an order. To prevent the men being slaughtered, you understand, fine squad of brave warriors. Then I surrendered. To Klereides. It would have been suicide to return home after that. I persuaded Klereides to turn down ransom offers and became his steward." The fleshy face was expressionless.

It all sounded very plausible but, surely, a Persian of the ruling classes would have preferred death to slavery? And was it likely that someone as fond of money as Klereides could be persuaded to turn down lucrative ransom offers, if there were any? Otanes must be a very persuasive man, Sindron thought.

Otanes was no less inquisitive and, feeling he should reciprocate, Sindron briefly told Otanes how, when he was a young child, he and his parents had been kidnapped from their home in Etruria by pirates, sold into slavery and separated. However, it was long ago and he preferred not to think about it, so he decided it was time to return to the attack.

"The income side. Did you keep a record of that for the old master as well as expenditure?"

"No, only the housekeeping monies, expenditure. He would make over a lump sum for the year and expenditure would have to stay within that."

"Really, even with all those dinner parties?"

"Well, I could go to him and ask for more for a special occasion."

"And the sponsorship?"

'Oh yes, there was a separate budget for that, but he set a sum for the year."

"And formal documents. Where do you keep official documents? Contracts, that sort of thing?" Sindron finally reached what he realised could prove to be a crucial question.

"Oh, contracts for sponsorship, with artists and sportsmen? I've got them here in this chest, where I keep the accounts scrolls, and ready cash."

Was the man being deliberately naive? These were perfectly straightforward questions yet the answers seemed to be evasive. Was it just reluctance to confide in another slave or had this man something to hide?

"I was thinking more of business contracts, investments, loans, that sort of thing."

Otanes looked genuinely puzzled that he should be asked the question. "Can't help you there. Kept all that stuff to himself. Deposited them with the bank, I imagine."

"No-one has checked with the bank yet, then?"

"No. Respect for the dead. Leave that till after the funeral, you know."

However, he made it clear that the bank had been among those informed of the death.

"And, ah, which bank would that be?" It was difficult to make that sound casual, but clearly it was no secret, for Otanes came straight back with, "Oh, Phraston and Partners. They handle all the family's affairs."

Sindron did his best to hide his surprise. Why hadn't Lydos told him this? Then he recalled that he himself had only revealed his connection with Klereides at the end of their conversation and they hadn't spoken much after that, though it made his friend's reaction even more puzzling.

Otanes did, then, feel obliged to let Sindron have a glance at the household account scrolls. It was enough to show that they were well and neatly kept but, just at that moment, the housekeeper and the chef appeared with problems that needed Otanes' attention urgently.

The steward excused himself, the scrolls went back into the heavy wooden chest in the corner of his room and Sindron found himself ushered out. A lock but no key on the chest, he noticed, which either meant nothing to hide, or someone wanted to give the appearance of nothing to hide. He had the awkward feeling that perhaps the interruption wasn't accidental.

Late in the afternoon, Lysanias' cousins arrived. Hierokles, the son of Klereides' father's brother so Lysanias' second cousin, and his son Boiotos. Lysanias knew of them, of course, the landowning side of the family with a large estate in rural Dekelia, though his father had not often spoken of them.

Otanes had reported that they had called to pay their respects the previous afternoon but, on hearing that Lysanias was resting, had merely done their duty by the deceased and left. So Lysanias had been expecting them.

It appeared they had been at the special Assembly meeting, for, as soon as they were away from the mourning area, they had exploded.

"That turncoat Perikles," roared Boiotos. "How dare he! From a noble family and he backs an ostracism motion against another of the best people! "

Lysanias found the force of the anger disconcerting at close quarters and couldn't help feeling he had heard that angry voice before. Hierokles' ire was more controlled but obviously deep-felt. His was aimed at Ephialtes, convinced that, now he had power, the demagogue would soon use it to make himself rich despite his 'poor and honest' reputation.

They had entered as though they owned the place, speaking at Lysanias rather than to him. Now Boiotos headed straight for the foodstuffs, although relatives were supposed to fast at such times. His father obviously had more respect for tradition and he had clearly taken the trouble to obtain a dispensation to attend the Assembly meeting for there was the saffron ribbon on his arm. Could Hierokles have been the man Ariston would have expected to greet him yesterday afternoon?

It appeared that Kimon's supporters had been outnumbered by his opponents and his motion to repeal the reforms had been defeated. To make matters worse the leaders of the radicals had put forward Kimon's name for ostracism at the ostracism Assembly meeting that was due in a few days time. Kimon's side had naturally countered by nominating Ephialtes for ostracism instead. Their fear was that, if the radicals succeeded, their leader would be lost to them. In exile, Kimon would be outside Athenian politics for ten years.

The greying hair and beard put Hierokles over sixty but maybe not much over and he appeared still fit and upright, clearly a military man. The strong nose, dark receding hair, deep-set eyes, and haughty manner suggested someone who had held command but preferred to stay aloof from mundane matters. The creased brow implied he had his share of worry. There were old war scars, too, on face, shoulders and arms. Lysanias could see a family resemblance to his own father.

"By the way, as close kin, I reported the killing by inanimate objects to the chief magistrate's office," Hierokles said.

"You're certain it was an accident," Lysanias replied carefully, realising he didn't want to alert a possible culprit to his suspicions by challenging this directly.

"Of course. Shipyard says so. No reason to doubt them."

Boiotos was maybe twelve or so years older than Lysanias, he calculated, but the extra flesh suggested he didn't attend the gymnasium as often as a good cavalryman should. The forceful family nose was bent at an angle, indicating he had seen his share of fighting too, though scars were fewer and fresher. But the attitude that seemed haughtiness in the father came across as a sneering smugness in the son.

Gloatingly, Boiotos told how one of the radical supporters had abused an elderly aristocrat for chanting a pro-Kimon slogan and been beaten up, after the meeting, to teach him a lesson. Lysanias expressed disappointment at such violence in democratic Athens and Boiotos rounded on him.

"What do you know about it, youngster? You're not old enough to understand politics, anyway."

As his cousin's eyes turned on him, Lysanias felt some of the hate that lay behind them. He assumed it was hate for the radical democrats.

Hierokles intervened tactfully. "Now then, Boiotos! Our young cousin is new to Athens, but he is one of us, not one of them."

Lysanias thought he heard a muttered and sarcastic, "Like Klereides, I suppose!"

"It's regrettable that he has arrived at such a sad time in the city's growth."

"Very regrettable," muttered Boiotos, turning away moodily.

"I fear it will be anarchy," Hierokles continued. "How can these nothing people with no education, no breeding, govern a city?"

The arrogance was getting on Lysanias' nerves. "Can't we educate them to make sound decisions?" he said.

Boiotos sprang to life and yelled. "You can't educate gutter scum! This colony-boy, he's going the same way as Klereides, father!"

Startled, Lysanias saw that the hate really was for him. For an instant, he thought he saw a similar expression on Hierokles' face, but then it was bland and haughty again, as he hustled Boiotos off to pay his respects to Makaria.

"Young man, we must talk," his cousin said, sounding just like his father. "Please excuse my son. Disappointment, you understand." Lysanias was puzzled but couldn't show it. Disappointment at what? At the reforms not being overturned? He nodded slightly.

What followed was a rather boring but, thankfully, short lecture on why it was right for the well-born families and the wealthier classes to rule and why no-one else should exercise real power even in a democracy. Lysanias found it immensely sensible, but it still left so many questions unanswered.

"Anyway, I take it we can count on your support, eh?" All Lysanias could do was nod.

"Good," said Hierokles and actually smiled at him.

"Cousin, what did Boiotos mean about Klereides?"

"Ah, yes. Shouldn't have said that, should he? Don't speak ill of the dead. Never. But... well, you'd better know. I've every respect for what Klereides achieved for his side of the family, you understand. Not something I'd want to be involved in, business. Wouldn't suit a family of our standing." Hierokles face had reddened and a vein throbbed in his temple, which Lysanias found it difficult to take his eyes off. "However, just lately he did seem to be behaving as though what was good for business was more important than loyalty to his own class, even his own family, if you see my thinking."

Hierokles glanced at Lysanias out of the corner of his eye, as though Lysanias was supposed to understand a whole world of meaning from this. He started pacing. "Good man, though, Curly, good man. Though why he liked to be called by that undignified childhood nickname, I can't imagine. We'll all miss him." It sounded flat.

He advised Lysanias to use Klereides' money to buy land. "Give the family back its dignity, eh boy? I'd be happy to advise."

Lysanias should have found this offensive, he knew, but his cousin's appearance and mannerisms were so like his father's that he found himself wanting to trust this man, to be liked by him. He started to remark on the similarity but, at mention of his father, Hierokles' eyes flared.

"Hah, Leokhares!" For a moment the voice was full of bitterness. "Did let the side down, I always thought..." He tailed off as he saw the hurt on Lysanias face. "Ah, sorry to hear about his death. Mustn't speak ill of the dead, eh? But, well, you ought to know this, if you don't already. You don't mind me speaking honestly, do you?" Lysanias pursed his mouth, struggled to prevent tears coming, and shook his head.

"Good boy! Great disappointment, your father. Fine athlete. Good soldier. Whole family shocked when he insisted on marrying that tradesman's daughter from Peiraieos. Calculating piece, she knew what she was after. Led astray, that young man, that's my view. Wouldn't listen to reason."

Lysanias set his face solid. This was his mother Hierokles was dismissing as beneath contempt.

"I thought the family cut off his allowance. He had no choice but to leave."

"Cut himself off, we thought. Refused to have anything to do with us. We hardly heard anything apart from official reports on the colony until that message saying he was missing, dead. Then that big raid and you were all listed missing. Mistake that, I see. Not sure whether he intended to renounce any inheritance or not, though you say his brother kept in touch."

There was a note of bitterness in his voice and the vein throbbed even more but now it was clear. The family had virtually forced his father to leave Athens. If they felt like that about his mother, they must feel Lysanias was not a full aristocrat. That's why the porter had said he wouldn't be welcome, he realised.

"Best thing he ever did, clearing off out of Athens, taking his shame with him. Ah, sorry, shouldn't have said that. You know what I mean. Best for the family honour, you understand. Now both brothers dead and here you are, Klereides' heir."

Something about the tone reminded Lysanias that, if he himself and his brother had died in that last Thracian attack, Hierokles would be in his place now. "Your chance to make up for your father's behaviour, restore the family honour, eh?" Was the man really that insensitive or did it show they were accepting him?

He forced himself to mutter thanks to Hierokles for his advice, when, to his great relief, Makaria, still dressed in black and veiled, appeared with Boiotos, to show them to the guest rooms. Lysanias thought he heard them all arguing later in a distant room but he couldn't be sure.

The piles of flowers and grave-gifts for the dead were mounting but Philia had lost interest. She had reached the point of blaming herself for her husband's death.

Maybe, if she had been more insistent that Klereides stay in bed, he would still be alive. Who but Curly would dream of wandering round a shipyard in the dark?

It was strange, wasn't it? He'd never gone off that early for meetings before, not that she knew of.

Philia started involuntarily, a shock of fear running through her body, as she remembered phrases muttered in his sleep. "If they want to play it rough..." "Two can play at that game ... " Then there were the occasional startled awakenings, when he would jerk upright and look around him, as though waking from a frightening nightmare.

The way Lysanias had reacted to Klereides' injuries, though! It looked as though he thought there could have been foul play. Oh, poor Curly, what if it was!!!

Should she tell Lysanias about the nightmares? But how could she? They couldn't talk to one another, not till after the funeral, and then they'd be supervised by that old Gorgon.

Perhaps Nubis could take a message, but she wasn't sure she fully trusted Nubis. Lysanias was only a man after all, and Nubis wore very skimpy clothing.

What could she do?

By early evening Lysanias was beginning to feel hungry from the fast and very weary. His head was buzzing from the repeated greetings and responses.

A well-built but slightly overweight man dashed in, sweaty and agitated, in the bright colours of a Syracusan and with the dust of a journey on his cloak, face and sandals.

"Ah, dear boy, dear boy. Just got back. Business trip. Corinth. Heard the news, terrible, terrible. So sorry. My deepest sympathies. Fine man, fine man." Hermon appeared genuinely disturbed. His hands fluttered, he wiped his sweaty forehead. "You're the heir, right? Must talk, eh? Not now. Wrong time. Another time, dear boy, not this sad occasion. Terrible for the business, and for the family, of course. Dreadfully sorry."

If this man is guilty of murder, he's a good actor, thought Lysanias but, before he could formulate more than a routine response, the Syracusan was gone, leaving Lysanias with so many un-asked questions.

Sindron was annoyed that Lysanias hadn't asked more questions. He himself had ventured into the city to check out more aspects of Lysanias' situation, and felt he had done well in the circumstances. At least he had confirmed that they would have to find the murderer themselves. The clerk to the magistrate in charge of the Scythian guards had been quite clear on that. The office of the preliminary magistrate to the court had been even firmer that they would need a definite wrongdoer to accuse and hard evidence against them before an application for a trial would even be considered, unless they were sure the culprit couldn't be found and wanted a trial against 'person unknown' but that meant going to the chief magistrate's office, as would reporting it as a killing by inanimate object, which the official was sure a member of the family must have done by now. 'Persons unknown' would give them another option, Sindron realised, but he wasn't sure that was what they wanted – it would make it clear they had suspicions.

The clerk at the office of the magistrate in charge of youth military training had been more considerate. Lysanias was too late to be registered for this month's swearing-in ceremony at the Temple of Athene, so he would have to wait until the end of the next month. It gave them a little more time to find hard evidence. They had also offered that, if Lysanias was married before the swearing-in, that could be taken into account as well as his military training in Eion in considering a possible reduction in the period of training.

Back at the house, instead of thanks, all he got was a confrontation.

"Why wasn't I told more about the family's attitude to my parent's marriage? I nearly made an idiot of myself!"

Sindron looked confused at the sharp change of subject.

"My talk with Hierokles." Lysanias added impatiently. "He made it clear he doesn't think much of either of them, father or mother."

Sindron realised this was a sensitive area. "You knew that they left Athens under a cloud, didn't you? Did your parents never explain it to you?"

Lysanias had to admit that he had a general impression but they had never gone into detail and he had no idea of the strength of feeling involved. What had stuck in his head were the romantic aspects. How his parents had met during the laughter and jollity of the wine festival to Dionysos. How they had fallen in love. How Leokhares had insisted on marrying Hermione, in the face of the coming Persian invasion, despite his parent's opposition. How Hermione had been evacuated to the island of Salamis with other women and children and had watched, from its heights, in fear and trembling, the fierce naval battle in the straits below, in which Leokhares was fighting. How, wounded in the leg and demobilised, Leokhares had taught himself a skilled craft to support Lysanias and his mother. How they had emigrated to Eion full of hopes for the future.

It had all sounded so romantic and idealistic.

"Tell me what really happened, Sindron," Lysanias asked, determined to know.

"The family was horrified by the marriage, especially Makaria and Hierokles' father. Marrying at only 21 to a lower class woman way beneath him, as they saw it. I argued for them as much as I could, beyond my position. Then Makaria threatened to sell me. Klereides seemed to be dominated by his mother at that time. In the end, they gave me to Leokhares to get rid of me. I'm sure they never forgave him." Sindron paused briefly, then added, "Your inheriting everything from Klereides must be a bitter pill for them to swallow, even more if Hierokles was expecting to be heir."

Lysanias had listened in silence, his face grim. Then, "Good." That was all he said, but it summed up his determination to stand alone if need be.

He thanked Sindron, then he sprang his surprise, switching his mood with the resilience of youth. He revealed that, earlier in the day, investigating behind a wall-hanging featuring Pandora 's Box, he had discovered a cupboard set into the wall. Sindron's eyes lit up.

"It could be where he kept his personal documents. A will, maybe. That could confirm your position. Contracts..."

"Yes. Or valuables. But I can't find how to open it."

Lysanias held back the tapestry, while Sindron tried to find a handle or handhold but, while the edges of the small oblong door were clearly apparent, he could find no way of opening it. Even prising round the edges with a knife did nothing.

"We'll look in daylight, master, before we risk asking Otanes."

Sindron didn't mention his embarrassing attempt to persuade the merchant to release him from his contract. "No, I'm sorry, a contract's a contract," Hipponikos had said, raising his voice unnecessarily high, then lowering it again. "I'm sure your friend Lydos will help you out, if you're short. If you prefer, I'll go to him as your guarantor before I approach your master for the remaining sum. Would that help?" In the face of this gentle blackmail, Sindron had paid over the outstanding amount. "You wouldn't care to increase your stake a little? I still have a little availability…" Sindron had declined.

How had he managed to get himself into this situation? How could he tell his master that he had embezzled money from him, when the one thing the family had always been sure of about Sindron was that he could be trusted?

Makaria had insisted on herself, Hierokles and Otanes running through the arrangements and rituals for the next day with Lysanias and Philia, so that no-one disgraced the family. Philia still wore her veil and remained almost silent, though Makaria had thrown back her veil to reveal a strong, matronly face, with penetrating eyes, a firm nose and high cheekbones. It took quite a long time to rehearse to Makaria's satisfaction, before they could go to bed.

For once, Lysanias slept soundly, exhausted. Until Sindron shook his shoulder to wake him to prepare for the funeral. It was still dark, for it is bad luck for the sun god Apollo to see the dead being buried or cremated. The sounds from outside his room told him the rest of the household was already up and about.

CHAPTER 6

The funeral procession set off slowly along the dark, empty and silent streets, all three qualities disappearing as the full cortege rounded each bend, bringing with it its mourners, its flute-players and its torchbearers, sending shadows bouncing along the walls ahead of them. In front went four elderly but dignified women, hired mourners skilled in the role, carrying the amphoras containing wine, milk, oil and water from which members of the family would make libations at the tomb. After them, the horse-drawn carriage on which Klereides' body was laid head first, surrounded by green myrtle and rosemary, with a seat behind the body for the widow. Philia felt shaky but exhilarated. She knew she was the centre of attention now, not Lysanias, not Makaria. They were walking behind.

Lysanias followed with Hierokles and Boiotos, then close female relatives led by Makaria. Friends came next with General Ariston, the guest of honour, at their head, along with Phraston, who strode out well for a man of his size. After them came friends who were not citizens, such as foreign residents. Hermon took a prominent position in this group. Behind these were the hired mourners, women over sixty to keep within the law of Solon, wailing and crying, beating their breast and tearing their hair. Last came the flute-players and dirge-singers, sounding a plaintive funeral dirge that went on and on.

Out through the mighty Thriasian Gate they went, for they had decided to pass the stone statues of Athene contemplating the tombs and memorials to the fallen victors of famous battles, Marathon and Salamis, Plataea and Eurymedon in recognition of Klereides' war record. Turning off down a side road and crossing onto the well-paved Sacred Way to Eleusis, they branched off along the Street of Tombs. Beyond the city walls was darkness, each new tomb they approached seeming to spring into square white existence from nowhere as the light of the torches struck it. Philia shivered in the cool breezes before dawn.

At the family tomb, Lysanias assisted with the lifting of Klereides' body onto the funeral pyre. The hair-entwined wreaths and floral offerings were placed around the body.

It also fell to Lysanias to make the first libation to the gods and, after Philia and Makaria and Hierokles had followed suit, to apply the torch to the bottom of the pyre. The scents of herbs and perfumes and decaying flesh were replaced by the smells of burning wood and of roasting, then burning flesh. The breeze had dropped, the clouds had cleared and the smoke and sparks rose into a starry sky. That must be a good omen for Klereides' safe crossing to the Underworld, he thought.

General Ariston stepped forward, his tall figure silhouetted against the flaming pyre. Solon's law forbade orations at the tomb but Ariston clearly wasn't going to let slip any opportunity to bring attention to himself. He kept it short though. "Friends, Citizens, we are gathered to wish a safe crossing to an exemplary citizen, a fine soldier and a noble gentleman. Zeus and Hermes of the Dead, grant him an easy passage." He made a final libation and threw Klereides' armour onto the pyre to burn with him. Lysanias glanced to where his grandmother stood, supporting Philia, who looked distraught, repeated sobs shaking her whole body.

As the flames died, Lysanias had the duty of extinguishing the embers with wine and then raking out the ashes and charred bones that were all that remained of his uncle, washing the bones in wine and scooping bones and ashes into the bronze casket provided for the purpose. This he carried above his head, stooping to pass through the low doorway into the family tomb. Flickering oil lamps, reflecting off stone walls and ceiling, revealed the remains of past family members in caskets on ledges around the square earth-floored chamber. Lysanias placed his uncle's remains in the central area, where the gods would see them clearly and favour his soul.

As he stood aside, other family members followed with the items that were to be buried with Klereides. Philia swayed as she came in, looking ready to faint, but instead, she threw herself on the casket. "No, I won't let him go," she cried. "I want to go with him!" She sobbed uncontrollably and Lysanias took her shoulders, gently but firmly, and lifted her up, feeling her cold and shivering flesh below the mourning cloak she was wearing.

Then she went limp and fell against him, and he was forced to put his arms round her and hold her to him to prevent her falling. He found it pleasant, but he glanced up and Makaria was standing in the entranceway, effectively stopping anyone else seeing Philia's behaviour. Reacting to the stern stance of the bulky black figure, he gently pushed Philia away from him to stand on her own. "Are you feeling better now?" he whispered. A barely audible, "Yes, I think so," was all that came back.

Relatives and guests came in briefly, laying down their grave gifts, usually an oil flask or, in some cases, a pottery or carved statuette representing their own kinship or friendship. The more people in this world who remember the deceased, he recalled, the more respect they would receive in the afterlife.

Hermon was one of the last to enter. He made a sign across his chest that Lysanias didn't recognise and laid down a statuette of a bull with a small medallion round its neck. Lysanias was puzzled. What god, what religion did that represent? Not one he had come across.

As Lysanias emerged from the tomb, first light streaked across the sky. The rattle of a cart drew near and stopped. As the carter jumped down, Lysanias' cousins took up post beside the cart, looking rather smug. The carter pulled away a covering and there stood a carved panel, sized to fit the end of the tomb, depicting Klereides at the Battle of Plataea. Lysanias wondered how they got a sculptor to create that in time. It must be a standard design with the face added to suit. That didn't sound very flattering to the deceased. Unless maybe they had expected Klereides to die? The thought surprised him, and Lysanias dismissed it as ungentlemanly.

The return journey was a blur, though it seemed strange walking back through the city in the daylight of early morning, with farmers and market gardeners taking their produce in to the market. Lysanias' responsibilities weighed heavier than ever on his young shoulders, despite the more lively tunes played by the flute-players, intended to ease the departed's spirit across the River Styx and into Hades. But Lysanias knew Klereides' soul would not be able to cross and find rest until the man responsible for his uncle's murder had been brought to justice.

His thoughts drifted to his father and he realised sadly that, if his own father really was dead, his lonely soul could be wandering lost unable to reach the underworld for want of proper burial and funeral rites for which there had been no opportunity. But today was about Kleriedes. He would look to appease his father and the gods when this was settled.

To cater for so many guests, stools and couches had been lined up along the wall, where the family and principal guests would sit with the tables of food placed in front of them. Other guests would have to stand, helping themselves to food and drink from tables or from trays brought round by slaves. Otanes had tactfully concealed Klereides' lurid wall decorations with plainer and more tasteful hangings at Sindron's suggestion.

Having helped with the preparations, Sindron was to assist with ushering people in and with seeing that food kept coming and that goblets were filled. He would have liked to see Klereides off. He had quite liked him as a lad, though he was not at all sure he would have liked the man he had evidently become. Lysanias' father now, Sindron did feel that loss. Leokhares had been more than a good master. But slaves have their duties.

Once the family were seated, and the cooked food placed in front of them, that strange ritual started. The close relations had fasted since

Klereides' death. Now the guests selected tasty morsels and set about persuading them to eat something.

"Let the remains of your beloved son," they would say to Makaria, "rest in peace – your duty now is to live and look after the family. Please eat a morsel."

"You're exhausting yourself with all this grieving," they said to Philia or to Lysanias. "Please eat some food to give you enough strength to keep on with your mourning."

The statements had an oft-repeated, ritual quality, but seemed strangely unnecessary, when Lysanias was so hungry he felt he could eat a whole goat himself. However, he knew that they were expected to refuse with expressions of their deep grief, and only gradually let themselves be persuaded, so he did what was expected, glancing at Makaria to see when to accept.

As soon as they did start eating, the quiet and reserve of all present vanished and conversations started noisily all round, the flute-players played livelier tunes, slaves dashed hither and yon filling goblets from the mixing bowls where wine and water were blended, bearing extra dishes to the tables as soon as those already there were emptied.

As Makaria leaned forward to help herself to a morsel of spiced swordfish, Lysanias glanced across at Philia who had thrown back her veil now in order to eat and drink. She was more beautiful than he had expected, but she looked so pale and drawn from crying that Lysanias felt sorry for her. An urge grew to take her in his arms for a cuddle, as he did with his little sister Ariadne when she fell and hurt herself. Clearly that would not be correct now.

Philia seemed to sense his look and turned. Before he could glance away, her eyes caught his and she gave a wan smile that he returned, trying to look reassuring. Philia blushed and the rush of colour to her cheeks made her look even more beautiful, he thought, and he tore his gaze away as propriety demanded. For the next few minutes, he kept his head bowed over his food, in case Makaria might suspect this impropriety behind her back. Those dark trusting eyes framed by long black lashes stuck in his mind.

The chef had done wonders with the goat that Lysanias had sacrificed only a few hours before, but his favourite was the spiced swordfish cooked the Carian way.

Was it the ginger that left that pleasant tang in his mouth, or another spice he hadn't encountered before, one that his parents wouldn't have been able to afford or that would have been out of place in the much simpler living style of Eion? Strangely, drinking seemed to cool the hot sensation in the mouth, but didn't quench it. Sindron had advised him to sip the wine but a mouthful seemed to be necessary. Maybe just one more...

Sindron was amazed at the number of people present, presumably all friends or business acquaintances of Klereides.

When Klereides' father had died, Sindron recalled, Klereides looked set to fit straight into his shoes. With no great intellect and no strong opinions of his own, he seemed content to seek a comfortable life bowing to his mother's strong will. If Klereides had died in those years, Sindron was sure, hardly anyone in Athens would have noticed. Yet here were many figures from Athens' political, social, sporting and artistic life. All because Klereides had accepted the role of patron of one of the most able foreign resident businessmen and become rich in the process. It must be the money that brought most of these people here.

Sindron remembered that he had advised Lysanias that they should keep their ears open. When would they have a better opportunity than this? It was precisely why they had decided against Lysanias carrying a spear in the funeral procession to announce that he intended to avenge Klereides – that would have put everyone on their guard. Yet he found his efforts to listen repeatedly frustrated by the need to react to some guest's gesture, or to call for more of this or more of that by summoning a slave to serve them.

Most of what he did overhear was individuals boasting about their own achievements or prowess. The usual chatter of people out to impress one another.

Of course, being a funeral feast, people were duty bound to praise the deceased to each fresh person they spoke to. Early on, these were the usual formal platitudes.

"Fine fellow, great loss to the city, so much to live for."

"Ah, that's fate. Will of the gods."

As the wine flowed and the noise level rose, people relaxed. Comments became more honest, despite the law against speaking ill of the dead.

"Hubris, my friend. Getting too big for his riding boots. No wonder the gods struck him down."

"Strictly between you and me, quite a few people are pleased he's out of the way."

And another group.

"Never really felt I could trust him but he treated me well enough ."

"Me too, don't know where I'll turn for those sort of commissions, if his heir doesn't come through."

"Odd tastes, though. Can't say I'd have chosen those subjects myself."

"Don't you find it humiliating having to ingratiate yourself with some colonial teenager?"

"At least you're always sure the wine will be good in this house. Steward! More of that mulled wine here!"

Sindron glanced across at the main table. There were the country cousins, as he thought of them, deep in conversation with the General, and Lysanias not even trying to overhear. He was too occupied with eating and trying to be nice to his grandmother. Oh, well, perhaps that could pay off too! Sindron only hoped Lysanias would stick to his advice to drink sparingly and make sure his wine was well watered.

Turning his head, Lysanias caught the words 'Ephialtes' and 'scoundrel' from his right. When Hierokles reached across to a dish in front of Lysanias, he took the opportunity to ask, delicately. "What's so awful about this man Ephialtes, Uncle?"

Hierokles spluttered, swallowed the wrong way, and coughed to right himself. His face was red, his eyes bulged and a prominent vein pulsed in his temple.

"That scoundrel! Has no-one told you how he hounded me?"

Lysanias' surprised and horrified expression told him the answer. Then things connected in Lysanias' head. The barber's shop. The name Hierokles. Someone nearly bankrupted until Kimon came to his rescue. It must be this Hierokles.

"Are you a member of the Areopagos?"

"Of course, I am ... was. Held several magistracies in my time." There was an element of preening as he said it. "Not any more. Disqualified. And all because that scoundrel claimed in the Assembly that, when I was responsible for street cleaning and dung collection, I'd neglected the poor districts. Everyone neglects the poor districts! No-one from outside is safe in them."

Lysanias wondered if that was the area he had run from.

"Nearly lost our lands, because of that man," burst in Boiotos, half-rising from his seat and leaning towards Lysanias, as though he was accusing Lysanias of complicity.

He was interrupted by the beating of a loud gong as Otanes signalled that it was time for the speeches in praise of Klereides, the main purpose of this, the very last and final banquet at which he was the absent and departed but very generous host. The chatter stopped. Guests crowded in from the other rooms, ushered in by Otanes and Sindron.

General Ariston, as guest of honour, gave the principal eulogy. It was the string of meaningless platitudes that Lysanias would have expected from the General, but somehow so many platitudes piled on top of one another, all praising what one would think had been the noblest Athenian of them all, made one think there must be some substance behind them.

Lysanias was grateful that his was a formal ritual speech that Makaria and Sindron had drilled into him the previous evening. He stumbled once and Hierokles beside him whispered the right word. The man really did remind him of his father. He got through it and everyone applauded. He blushed bright red.

Then Otanes and Sindron together persuaded the guests to move, revealing the table against the far wall. The fabric-covered items on it, Lysanias knew, were a few of Klereides' commissions, which had reached completion in recent days.

A silversmith stepped forward, introduced himself, and pulled away a cloth, revealing a wine-mixing bowl in gold and silver, depicting exploits of Theseos. It was intended as an offering to the Temple of Theseos, he said. Another master craftsman passed around a delightfully engraved lady's hand-mirror with silver handle and mount. Philia couldn't stop herself clapping her hands together when she saw it, assuming it must be for her. She wept a tear at the thought of Klereides giving her nice things even in death, then recalled that this, too, could be intended for a temple. Or, even worse, for another woman! No, mustn't think ill of the dead. Under her breath, she muttered a brief prayer for forgiveness.

Lysanias recognised the silversmith as a well-wisher but the flamboyant personage who next stepped forward he would certainly have remembered, if he had seen him before. In a bright orange cloak, and with silver vine leaves in his henna-stained hair, he offered a startling contrast with the sober citizens around him.

The colourful man seemed to assume everyone must know his name, and simply stated, "For the new Temple of Hephaistos". That alone drew a shocked intake of breath from the watching guests, which changed to a loud gasp as he pulled away the cloth, from what was clearly a sizeable piece of work, to reveal a carved relief wall panel.

It showed a group of blacksmiths beating out a sheet of bronze, their mighty hammers raised over their heads to strike the next blow, their tunics dropped to the waist to reveal bulging muscles. It could have been a scene from any forge in Athens, Sindron realised, the figures looked so lifelike. Where was the stylisation that sculpture was normally expected to show, the simplification and idealisation, the smooth flowing lines? These were angular, abrupt, like real life.

Despite his own strong liking for the traditional style, Sindron found himself excited by the sheer vitality of the piece. And where was the god? There was always a god or hero, yet this sculptor had made no attempt to include the god Hephaistos. That really was a revolutionary departure! Sindron wondered if it was also sacrilege.

Immediately there was a babble of agitated conversation. The silversmith started arguing with the sculptor that he had abandoned all the principles that had made Athenian art respected throughout the Greek world. The sculptor's voice bellowed that the old tired styles must give way to the young and dynamic forces of the new society that was being born. He seemed delighted with the commotion he had caused, a broad smile on his face, his eyes shining.

Other guests jostled forward to look more closely at the sculpture, as though in disbelief. Lysanias found himself penned in behind the table, unable to do anything to quieten a situation he didn't really understand. Philia was staring in wide-eyed wonder. Makaria looked straight ahead with what could have been a satisfied half-smile on her lips.

Sindron saw Ariston, Hierokles and Phraston consult briefly, then Ariston stepped forward to the table and placed the cloth back over the relief panel. Boiotos shouldered his way through the group disputing with the sculptor, pushed him angrily and seemed about to punch him. Ariston reached out an arm to hold Boiotos back, took the young sculptor firmly by the elbow, and with a look that could have spat flames, steered him towards the door.

The sculptor had expected to surprise people but he clearly hadn't expected to be manhandled. As others surged behind Ariston, enforcing the push towards the door, the silver-wreathed head shouted back, "You reject us now, but our time will come. This is the art of tomorrow. All triumph to Hephaistos."

Listening to ordinary citizens near him, Sindron rapidly realised it wasn't the style that had disturbed most of them but the fact that Klereides should have commissioned such a major work for the Temple of Hephaistos, the religious centre of the workers and radicals. It undermined the whole basis of their friendship with him.

Then the gong sounded again, struck, Sindron saw, by Otanes, aiming to pull things back onto a normal footing. That man really is a very good steward, he thought. And manipulator! The animated chatter tailed off as Otanes helped a dignified figure step up onto something that raised him visible to all, a lyre in his elegant, long-fingered hands.

The praise-singer made lyrical poetry of Klereides' war record in various campaigns, his part in helping Kimon recover the giant remains of Theseos, the clear-flowing water that graced his magistracy in charge of the public fountains, and his sponsorship triumphs in a number of games and song contests. However, it was the statue of Poseidon that he had donated to adorn the Temple of Theseos that rang strangest to many ears in light of the new sculpture for Hephaistos they had just seen.

The thought came to Lysanias that the praise clashed fiercely with all the hints that kept reaching him about his uncle's real character and other citizens' actual attitude to him. Suddenly it all turned sour, as Lysanias realised that, in Athens, if one had enough money, one could buy anything. Even praise. Even honour. It is Klereides' money we are honouring, he thought bitterly, not Klereides. And even the money was earned by Hermon not Klereides himself.

It made it very difficult to smile politely when Ariston brought over the praise-singer and introduced him, though he knew that the man, whom he recognised as the dignified-looking man on the ship, was merely doing his job.

Philia started to cry. The song was beautiful but, suddenly, it all seemed so final, for her as well as for poor Curly. She thought of dropping her veil to hide her tears but realised that widows were expected to cry and she wanted to be seen to do her duty.

She had never seen so many men together in one place and found that Lysanias compared well with the other young men, even the athletes with their glistening muscles. Even some of the mature men such as the General were much trimmer and slimmer than her Klereides. Now why couldn't... Oh! Stop it, Philia! Have more respect for the dead! Sorry, Demeter, I'll pour a libation tomorrow...

"...I'm saying he did. He deliberately sabotaged my negotiations. Snapped the contract from under my nose. Bribery, I shouldn't be sur... Ah, here's Ariston now. Hello, General, fine send off for Klereides."

"Yes, indeed, great loss to the city, what? Must talk to old ... uh..."

"You see, no time for me these days. Used to be very different before that Hermon set up here."

"You must admit their workmanship's good."

"Nonsense, we all hire the same craftsmen, buy the same materials. Grease the right palms, I tell you. Ah, steward, a few glazed figs would be appreciated." And Sindron signalled a slave-boy to do his bidding.

As Otanes passed him, Sindron took the opportunity to congratulate him quietly on the way he had handled the problem. Otanes inclined his head in acknowledgement and was moving on, when Ariston tapped his shoulder.

"Steward! Both of you! Why was that man invited?"

Sindron was pleased to see that Otanes was not prepared to be intimidated by a guest of the house. "My deep regrets for the disturbance, General. Sculptor Zelias' name was on the old master's list of sponsored artists and athletes. I had no way of knowing that a mere artwork could offend so many sensibilities." Sindron liked that. Just a hint that the General and other citizens were being childish in their reactions.

"Humph," the General grunted. "Perhaps Klereides was misled. Odd tastes."

"I believe there is to be a companion panel," Otanes slipped in smoothly, "which features the godly blacksmith." He bent at the waist in a slight bow.

That covered the charge of sacrilege, Sindron realised, but served merely to rub salt in the General's wound.

"Cursed unfortunate. Bad omen. Corrupting influence in our midst. Noble traditions defiled." And still mouthing platitudes, the General moved away amongst the other guests.

His hunger well assuaged, Lysanias looked around at the gathering through somewhat more cynical eyes.

He had registered that Hermon had kept to the place allocated to him at the end of the table, chatting amiably to the man next to him, but now he seemed to be edging towards the door before Lysanias had had a chance to make arrangements to meet him. Lysanias tried to catch his attention as Hermon made small thank you gestures in the direction of the family and to Otanes. He caught the man's eye but Hermon merely gestured that he would leave a message with the porter. Tomorrow, Lysanias told himself. I must corner him for a serious talk tomorrow. I can't let him go on evading me.

The wine was having an effect. Lysanias had rarely been allowed to drink in Eion and never wine of such good quality. He thought he had been careful to make sure it was well-watered too. As his head started to swim just a little, he was surprised to see a new face rising above the mass of the guests. That strange-shaped cranium, he recognised that. It couldn't be Perikles himself, could it? Then the figure was lost in the throng and Makaria made a polite enquiry about his mother. Now that was a breakthrough!

A little later, he felt a hand on his shoulder and a face beside his. Lysanias rose and stood back from the table to talk, using the wall to steady himself as Perikles whispered, "My apologies for not making it to the funeral. I had great respect for your uncle. Astute man and a real loss to Athens. I have to go now, but I felt I should say this. I do hope you will feel able to take over as patron of the shipbuilding business from your uncle. The city will need capable shipbuilders in the future. The party has great plans for the city and I do hope you will take a prominent part in them, despite your young age. I wasn't much older when I first started to make an impact, so don't be put off by these old men who try to hold you back. It's young men like you who are the city's future."

A surly Boiotos had ordered Sindron to organise more wine for him. He stared round blearily. "Where's that stupid colonial cousin of mine gone to?" He was evidently even more drunk than he looked. He was standing swaying now. "Where is he? I want to tell him how silly he looked today, pretending to be a gentleman. What, father?"

Hierokles was trying to calm Boiotos down. "No, father, I won't be quiet. He's stolen our inheritance, hasn't he? Silly colonial! Oh, there he is. Who's that he's talking to? It's that hellhound Perikles! What imperti … impertinence to come to this house. Let me get at him!"

Lysanias had heard the shouting and turned to see what was happening. It looked as though Hierokles had his son under control and was leading him away. Lysanias turned back to apologise to Perikles, but the politician had gone, slipping away in the confusion. However, Boiotos had pulled away from his father and was now confronting Philia.

"And this woman, this woman, she should have been mine as well. Come here and give us a cuddle, honeycomb! You must have been through all the positions there are with that dirty old man!" Philia sat petrified with horror.

"Anyway, beautiful, if this oaf turns you down or your old father sees sense, I'll be waiting." He turned to Lysanias, who had come round the table to confront him, and put his wine-reddened face up close to Lysanias' equally red visage. "How about that, colony boy? Eh? How about that?" Furious, Lysanias pushed Boiotos back and hit him square on the jaw. He had expected a fight but the man had drunk so much that, as he staggered to right himself and swung his whole body in a wrestling charge, he lost his balance and fell with a heavy thump to the floor. He struggled to rise, still cursing as Lysanias stood over him, dropping into a none-too-steady wrestling stance himself. But Hierokles dragged his son to his feet and pulled both his arms tight behind his back.

"My apologies, he doesn't usually get like this, apologies to the young widow. We'll leave now to avoid further embarrassment. Quite uncalled for."

He marched Boiotos off through the crowd, which stood watching in amazement, but images were blurring before Lysanias' eyes and he couldn't be sure it had really happened except for his stinging knuckles. He made efforts to get back to his seat. Then Ariston cornered him, holding him firmly up against the wall as he swayed. At this range, Lysanias could see two of the General's face.

"What did that fellow want?" the General demanded.

Who did he mean? Boiotos? No, must be Perikles. Lysanias was finding it difficult to think clearly. "Just giving his condolences, Gen'l, jus' givin' his condolencenses," Lysanias slurred out, too drunk to be really concerned.

The General grabbed him roughly by the shoulders. "Has he spoken to you before?" Lysanias shook his head, dazedly. "Keep away from that man! He's dangerous!" Ariston gave up and relinquished Lysanias to Sindron, who had edged his way round to try to prevent further trouble. "And destroy that accursed sacrilegious panel!" the General hurled as an afterthought.

"Mus' respec' Uncle's intenshuns," slurred Lysanias, but the General had gone. Sindron eased Lysanias back into his seat and, then, a little later, as the guests started to leave, saw him safely to his room.

Philia cried in bed again that night. That was disgraceful! How could they ruin Curly's funeral feast? All men are pigs, even the young handsome ones. At least Lysanias did defend me. He must be stronger than he looks. He'll look after me. Calmer, she slipped into sleep.

CHAPTER 7

Hermon had left a message suggesting Lysanias break his fast with him at his house in Peiraieos shortly after dawn, but the surfeit of wine at the funeral feast meant Lysanias was not easily roused. Hermon was just leaving, accompanied by his large and muscular personal slave or bodyguard, as they reached his house.

The jolting ride to Peiraieos hadn't helped Lysanias' stomach any. In fact, he felt sick again, though the fresh air had cleared his head a little and he tried to convince himself he was up to questioning the businessman. He knew he had let himself down and vowed not to make that mistake again if he could avoid it.

"Well, my boy, you're a fine addition to the family. I was very upset to hear about your uncle. A tragedy, a real tragedy. So much to live for too, just when the business was expanding."

Hermon appeared genuinely sorrowful and sympathetic, though the quality of his cloak and its fine embroidery suggested his mind must be on an important business meeting later that day. Lysanias had opted for a cloak that was simple but elegant. Sindron found himself trying to conceal the small wine-stain on his own cloak, where a guest had spilled some, which he had only just noticed.

"But life goes on. I'm on my way to the shipyard; would you like to come along? I take it you'll be inheriting your uncle's share of the business. He was my patron, you know. Don't know if you'd feel up to taking on that role as well? I imagine you're not very familiar with Athens' personalities and politics, or its law courts. Important factor, so we'll have to talk it through."

Despite a slight ringing in his head, Lysanias knew he had to break into this chatter with the question he had formulated with Sindron. "Sir, I'm worried about the way uncle died. Could I see the place where it happened?"

"Of course, my boy. I'll arrange it. And, please, don't call me 'sir'. We're partners now, you know." He clapped him on the shoulder in a way Lysanias found really too demonstrative. "Call me 'Hermon'. Everyone knows me as 'Hermon from Syracuse'. Fine city, Syracuse, you should visit it sometime."

While he talked, Lysanias struggled to keep pace with Hermon's businesslike step. Sindron had no trouble, and he was getting to like the new stick he had bought the previous day, shorter than the staff but thick and nobly at one end, enough to make it an effective club-like weapon if needed. In the light of the fighting in the market square, Sindron felt that was an important consideration.

Businessmen seemed to have built their homes near where they had set up their factories, foundries and workshops, so they arrived at the shipyard from Hermon's house quite quickly. Many of the workplaces and habitations seemed makeshift and temporary, though others, like the shipyard, looked as though they had survived the Persian invasion or been built or re-built since then. Walls they passed carried the angry tokens of the political turmoil, symbols and slogans, the trident of Kimon's faction and the hammer and anvil of the radicals. Sindron even made out a very faded 'Themistokles is a traitor'. Now that must be a few years old, considering how long ago Themistokles was exiled!

Inside the big gates were workshops, preparation areas and stores where craftsman of various skills could be seen at work, and beyond them towards the harbour the shapes of vessels nearing completion. The sight was putting flesh on Sindron's idea of the size of his master's inheritance. It made Sindron's own worries over one hundred drachmas look insignificant, but it didn't make the worries go away. It also made clear how important it was that his young master step into Klereides' shoes here, even though his age could well be a problem, which Hermon had only hinted at, he noticed. But if Hermon was the murderer, then all this politeness was a farce. Would a murderer behave like this?

"Not bad, eh, for six years' work?" Hermon boasted. He seemed very proud of his achievement, the scale of the business, the large number of workers employed. "I use slaves for the less skilled work, locals and immigrant workers for the more skilled activities." As they passed, different workers would glance across and nod respectfully to Hermon, or call a greeting. No sign here of the bad relationships the bathman had implied, thought Lysanias.

Hermon explained that he had tried hard to take on a reasonable proportion of Athenian citizens as more craftsmen returned from the wars, though he complained at having to allow them so much time off to attend Assembly meetings.

"And I pay the rates the Fellowship asks. Don't want them fighting us, eh?" So much for bad labour relations as the cause of Klereides' death, thought Lysanias.

"Very lucrative business, with the war going on so long." There was a liveliness, a sparkle in his eye as he talked about his obsession, his business, that attracted Lysanias. The sheer enthusiasm was difficult to resist but Lysanias knew he had to. He couldn't allow himself to trust this man who could very well be responsible for the death of his uncle.

Hermon ushered them into what was clearly a working office but also somewhere one could bring important customers. Rugs on the floor, two couches, chairs, a large table laden with papers and scrolls. His tummy still a little queasy, Lysanias was grateful for the cup of very good wine with water that Hermon offered him. It seemed to help pull him together. Insisting that Sindron remain outside and carefully closing the door, Hermon launched in.

"Now, to business. No time to waste." He left no pause for Lysanias to respond. "I'm sorry I couldn't get to you before. We might have been able to prevent more of the harm done to the company by all this." He blamed his delay in getting back on the difficulty of negotiations in Corinth, where the wealthy were scared the revolution in Athens might spread to them, while other citizens hoped it would. "Same in other cities, I gather."

Lysanias got the sense that the transfer of power to the Assembly and the radicals didn't bother Hermon, as it clearly did many other wealthy people in Athens. Why would that be? Lysanias realised he had to ask the crucial question now or the opportunity would be gone, the man was talking so fast.

"Can you tell me who you were seeing?" He thought it was straightforward enough. But the answer came back, sharply, dismissively.

"No, afraid not, not at this stage. Delicate negotiations." And he went on without a pause, leaving Lysanias stunned by the audacity of it. The man wasn't even attempting to verify his alibi!

"Now, our company, our shipyard is working on an order from the state for two war galleys and a troop carrier. Officially it's a merchantman that could be used as a supply ship but it's being outfitted to carry troops. So you'll have guessed we're talking long distance warfare here, Kimon's territory. Ambitious stuff."

The problem was that the company had a tender bid in for two more such ships and success with that depended on the current vessels passing inspection by the state examiners.

"Now that inspection was due to happen the day Klereides had his accident. He really messed that one up."

Hermon seemed to realise immediately how insensitive that statement was. "Apologies, apologies. I owe Klereides a lot. Down to him we got the order in the first place. He was well in with Kimon's crowd."

Lysanias couldn't help seeing the flaw in this argument. "Surely, if Kimon is out of favour, the democrats will cancel any plans he had."

Hermon looked pleased and impressed. "Knew you were a smart lad. Klereides also managed to keep friendly with the radicals. His report was that they promised not to cancel shipbuilding orders.

"Anyway, a death in a shipyard no-one takes lightly. Fortunately, Philebos my overseer took action immediately. Efficient young man, anticipates my wishes, we're lucky to have him. Ambitious too. He'll have learnt all I know soon and be competing with me from his own shipyard, the gods willing." He grinned, amused at the irony of the prospect.

Lysanias had to pin this down. "What sort of action?"

"He had everything cleaned up, called in priests to do what they have to do to propitiate the gods and cleanse the yard of pollution, and sent full details to the officials. Klereides would have been up to their offices straight away, smoothing things over, but he was gone, so we had no-one. However, thank the gods, they accepted Philebos' word and agreed to do the inspection today."

Hermon paused, as though for approval. But Lysanias' mind was stuck on an earlier phrase 'everything was cleaned up'. If there was evidence of foul play, it would all be gone! "You mean you've thrown everything away that might tell us how my uncle was killed?"

"No, no! Philebos is a tidy man. He'll have kept everything neatly in a corner somewhere. Has to anyway, pending a court ruling on whether the object that killed Klereides should be removed from the state. It's just that the vessels have to pass the test today. A stage payment depends on it." Hermon clearly wanted to move on, but Lysanias couldn't let him.

"What's 'everything'?"

"Well, you know what happened. A rope frayed and broke and a big water storage amphora fell on your uncle. You know all that. An accident." It all sounded so simple, so slight, could happen to anyone. Hermon went on. "So, somewhere in the yard, we'll have all the things that had to be cleared away to make everything look normal and placate superstitious minds. We expected trouble from the craftsmen, but the Fellowship of Hephaistos seemed to take it in their stride."

"So when can I see it?" Lysanias asked.

"Well, that's what I'm saying, I'd rather you left it till after the inspectors have been."

"No, I'm sorry, Hermon!" Lysanias was insistent, though he felt like crying. "We have to see it as soon as possible!" He thumped his cup down on the table. "I'm not convinced it was an accident and I want to make sure as quickly as possible."

Hermon swung round. "It was an accident, Lysanias!" Hermon was trying to be persuasive and dismissive at once. It didn't work. "If it was anything else, the company could be in real trouble. Who is going to give orders to a shipyard with an angry lost soul on the loose and the Furies out hunting the culprit? Please don't say these things! I've got enough to worry about."

Lysanias decided on tact rather than confrontation. "But I must see it soon. Maybe it was an accident, I just need to be sure."

"Very well, very well. Just stay out of the way of the inspectors, eh. I should be going over to meet them anyway, see that they're happy."

"Can we go, then?" Lysanias started to rise.

"Yes. No! I haven't finished what I wanted to say. Despite all this argument, we have to keep the politicians sweet. I don't know how Klereides did it but he did it. You're young and inexperienced, but you've inherited a lot of status in this city, so the politicians will be sniffing round soon. They'll make it look like offering their condolences but they'll really be trying to get you on their side. Please, please, at least don't upset them, or any of the important officials."

"I'm not stupid, Hermon."

"No, son, I'm sure you're not."

"Uh, Hermon?"

"Yes, son."

"They've been round already, some of them. I was polite. To everyone. Though I can't say I like them all, and I don't think I'd trust them."

"That's what I like to hear. Good man! That's just what Klereides used to say, 'Don't trust them but don't let them know you don't trust them'. He was a crafty one, that uncle of yours."

After all the excitement, Philia felt flat. She was still in mourning but the funeral was over, so what was going to happen now? Was it back to normal? More slaving for that old Makaria?

She went down to the workroom late. That was one test. Makaria hadn't sent a slave to call her, as she normally did. All the slave-girls were in place and working in silence. Makaria was in her chair but not working, due to mourning. Philia stood by the door watching. She could sense Makaria looking at her from the corner of her eye, waiting to see if she would sit at the loom. She didn't. This was the second test. Would it work?

"Ah, my dear," said Makaria suddenly, as though just realising Philia was there. "We must start you on your other household duties. If you'll just come through to the kitchen with me..." Philia didn't hear the rest for the beating of her heart at the surge of excitement that told her she had won at least this small victory. She heard Nubis stifle a giggle, and felt re-assured that at least one person in this house was on her side.

"I believe it was along here..."

Hermon was urging them along the walkway. Lysanias was fascinated. The activity they had passed was incredible, and he had wanted to stop longer and look. The sea breezes had finally cleared his headache, so he could handle the noise. It seemed deafening, with so many people hammering and sawing at once, and vessels of different sizes at different stages of construction and repair.

However, in the part of the yard they had now reached, all seemed quiet and deserted, though sounds still carried across. Now at deck level of the big ship beside them, two, maybe three times the height of a war-galley, as big as the merchant ship they had travelled on, they seemed a long way from the ground. It gave a magnificent view along the shipyards and out across the Great Harbour and all its comings and goings.

Sindron was unimpressed. He hated heights and the walkway shook, so he stayed near the uprights. Hermon had left his personal slave at the gatehouse but brought his messenger boy with him, who trotted along behind.

"This would be it, just here," announced Hermon. "See that big amphora up there." Hermon pointed upwards. In the ship they had travelled to Athens on, Lysanias had been fascinated by a similar earthenware amphora, holding the ship's drinking water, swinging in its great leather harness twined through loops sticking out around it. This one was supported only by a rope around the top and suddenly the thought of a giant vessel like that falling on Klereides made him feel slightly sick. He held his breath for a moment.

He asked, "Is it safe now?"

"That's not the one that fell," replied Hermon unnecessarily, as the slave-boy sat on the edge of the planking, swinging his legs. "We had to replace everything quickly. Now, as you've seen where it happened, perhaps we can clear the yard, so the inspectors aren't disturbed."

But Lysanias was on his knees examining the planking.

"What's the matter, master?"

Rising, Lysanias muttered to Sindron, "There are no bloodstains."

Despite his low tone, Hermon heard him. "Of course not," he almost shouted. Then, lowering his voice, "The boards have been changed. They were cracked and broken. Can't have too many people knowing where the death occurred, can we? Bad omen in a shipyard, death, especially by a new ship. Workers could refuse to work on it; the client could refuse to accept it. Fear of pollution, even though Philebos has done his best to purify it."

Lysanias was quietly fuming that he couldn't see how things had been after it happened. He understood Hermon's worries, as the man looked nervously around, but Lysanias ignored him, as he tried to get a mental picture of how it might have happened, where his uncle would have had to be standing in view of the injuries he had seen. Sindron drew his attention to the religious symbol, the messenger's staff and serpents of Hermes, hung on one of the uprights to placate the gods but partly concealed by a hank of rope. Of course! Hermon had said the uprights hadn't been changed! Lysanias knelt to examine the nearest ones.

Just then they heard voices inside the hull, red-painted already, Lysanias had noticed, so that wouldn't show bloodstains anyway. The voices were muffled and boomy at first and then clear, as the speaker came out on deck. "As you see, we've gone to a higher standard than specified in the contract for the..." The voice tailed off as the speaker saw them. "What are you people doing there?" An authoritative voice, annoyed.

Lysanias was still kneeling, examining the lower part of an upright, where someone had obviously tried to scrub away bloodstains and not completely succeeded. Sindron was leaning over him and Hermon standing by, all with their backs to the vessel. As they rose and turned, the voice said, "Oh, it's you Resident Hermon." Lysanias deduced this must be Philebos, the overseer of the shipyard. From his pose and neatly styled fair hair, the youngish man obviously thought highly of himself.

"Citizens, I think you may have met Hermon, joint owner of the shipyard."

"Ah, Resident Hermon, I've always dealt with Klereides but I've heard about you. Delighted to meet you. Amynias, city naval architect. This is Inaros, chief maritime inspector. And Bryaxis, our financial scrutineer. I must say, on a cursory examination, everything looks fine, just fine."

"Delighted to meet you," Hermon responded, over-effusive as ever. "Always pleased to meet an official of mighty Athens, the city that has been so hospitable to my meagre talents." The false modesty was sickening, and transparent, thought Lysanias, but the officials seemed impressed. Lysanias was standing now and Sindron had slipped behind him to be inconspicuous as a slave.

Hermon went on, "May I introduce my colleague, Lysanias son of Leokhares of Dekelia. He's Klereides' heir. I'm just showing him the scope of the business, you understand."

While Hermon spoke, Lysanias was aware of four pairs of eyes examining and memorising his face for future reference, but only after they had taken in the yellow band that tokened a dispensation from religious duties, and had registered how young he was. He felt like a nasty boil being examined by a doctor. Several doctors, he thought wryly.

"Ah, yes. Sad business." Amynias made the sign of condolence, but behind him the others made the sign to ward off ill-fortune from themselves. He turned to Philebos. "We must talk about safety standards, too, some time soon. Good record your yard up to now. Don't want to spoil it."

"Yes, of course," responded Philebos blandly. "Now, if we could just go to the offices, I can show your scrutineer the accounts and..."

Lysanias realised he was being ignored, as parents do with young children. But he was a partner here now. He felt he should say something, make his presence felt. "Just getting to know the business. All the things my uncle was involved in." Did he sense a slight stiffening as he said that? "Very complicated but it won't be long before I get to understand it. Anyway, I'm sure Hermon and Philebos will see you're looked after. They seem to have everything in hand."

He was surprised again at the ease with which he could slip into his new role. Then Lysanias noticed how red the faces of Hermon and Philebos had become, and the anger in Hermon's eyes. Even the inspectors seemed put out at a mere youth talking to them like an equal. Then he remembered that in Athens, although one was a citizen at eighteen and obliged to fight in the army and could vote, one couldn't hold any public office and weren't expected even to speak in the Assembly until the age of thirty.

"Aaah, just so. Sorry to hear about your uncle. May Hermes give him a peaceful crossing." Amynias made the sign of condolence again. "Now we really must be moving on."

Lysanias felt himself becoming red and angry in his turn. After all, he was a citizen, Hermon only a foreign resident. Why should Hermon get more respect? But Sindron grasped his upper arm from behind to remind him to hold his patience, so he simply said, "Thank you. May Hephaistos look kindly on your endeavours."

It had come out automatically. Craftsmen said it to one another back home at critical stages of a job but, clearly, from their reaction, it wasn't appropriate to state dignitaries. They turned huffily and hurried down the walkway, leaving their juniors and slaves measuring and checking the vessel and ticking off the outfitting accessories on long lists.

There was a long pause as they receded, and Lysanias could still hear the shipyard overseer explaining the steps he had taken to placate the gods and ensure they would bless the ship and sail with her. He really couldn't share Hermon's view of this arrogant and over-efficient man, who must be no more than thirty-five.

Hermon was angry. "I hope you're satisfied with yourself, young man! Did your father never tell you young men should be seen and not heard? You realise you have just offended the very people the shipyard depends on for its continued prosperity? I shall have to go and try to apologise for your immaturity."

Lysanias bristled. He couldn't allow Hermon to establish that sort of angry father relationship. If Lysanias was to be his patron, the man needed his protection not the other way round. But Sindron stepped in.

"I'm sure they will understand when you tell them that my master is new to Athens and has just suffered a terrible shock with the death of his uncle." Sindron kept finding himself looking on, as slaves are expected to do, but now there was the added fascination of watching the power games people in authority play. It was better than the theatre. He had never been so close to important matters before.

His intervention worked. Clearly Hermon respected his age and experience. "I realise that but this is a critical time for the business ..."

the businessman started, but Sindron continued firmly. "Everyone trying not to talk about it and tidy up, as though it never happened, must seem very inconsiderate to his grief."

"Yes, of course, but you know how superstitious these Athenians are. And he keeps going on about it not being an accident and needing to investigate. That could mean a court case and bad publicity going on for ages. The business might never live it down."

An objectionable, whining, pleading tone had entered Hermon's voice, but that didn't make it any better. Lysanias found his fists clenching, as he tried to suppress his rising anger. Now Hermon was talking to Sindron about him as though he didn't exist. He couldn't remain silent.

"You should have thought of that before, shouldn't you? Before you lured him down here to his death!" He hurled the words like throwing spears.

"What do you mean?" Hermon stiffened, furious, his face reddening. Hearing the angry voices, the slave-boy had sprung up and stood beside his master, as though ready to protect him or run for help. He looked from face to face, nervously.

"That message he had! It must have come from you," Lysanias challenged.

"That's enough, master! We don't know." Sindron tried to intervene, to calm things. Hermon leant down and whispered in the slave-boy's ear and he scampered off along the walkway, his bare feet pattering enough to set it shaking again.

"You young upstart! How dare you accuse me? He was my partner. I was depending on him to bring in a big new state order. Why would I kill him?" There was no trace of pleading or smooth-talking now, but his face was sweating in the full morning sun and he didn't seem to know what to do with his hands.

"Ah, then you admit he could have been killed," Lysanias spat back.

"No, I don't! It was an accident! The rigger used an old rope, it just frayed through with the weight of the amphora, must have been rubbing in the breeze all night and it snapped. Philebos assured me."

"Where is this rope then? Why has everything been taken away and destroyed?" And Lysanias allowed his sheer frustration to show, the frustration, Sindron realised, of someone little more than a boy at the complexity of the situation he found himself in. It communicated to Hermon and he changed his tone.

"I'm sure it hasn't been destroyed. Philebos saw to the cleaning up and preparations for the inspection, the purification. He'll have had the relics placed under safe restraint somewhere to prevent further contamination, pending a decision by the court." Lysanias didn't understand all that and cast a pleading look at Sindron, who realised he hadn't explained it to him fully.

"But you can't speak to Philebos till the inspectors go."

This gave Sindron his opportunity. "I'm sure that's all my master was requesting, a chance to examine the evidence that will prove it was an accident, as you say."

"But..." started Lysanias till Sindron tapped him on the ankle with his foot.

Hermon seemed to have calmed down. Two of the inspection team had been measuring the ship's rail supports to check that they were the regulation thickness and the correct distance apart. They had gradually moved closer along the deck to where they might possibly be able to hear what the argument was about. A sound of scuffling feet above them revealed another slave, checking off the outfitting items against a list in his hands. It came to Lysanias that, if someone had caused the amphora to fall on his uncle, they would have had to do it from up there.

Hermon had been keeping half an eye on the inspection clerks and now he dropped his voice. "Very well. I just don't like being accused on no evidence. When you see the rope, you'll agree it must have been an accident."

"But why was my uncle here at all?" Though it was a challenge, Lysanias adopted the same low voice to avoid being overheard. He could see Hermon's personal slave striding along the walkway towards them, the slave-boy scampering at his heels. Hermon became visibly less agitated with his bodyguard near.

"I don't know! It wasn't unknown for Klereides to make spot checks to be sure everything was ready, before he brought the state inspectors down." Could that be true? wondered Sindron.

"In the middle of the night!"

"It wasn't the middle of the night. It was just before dawn!"

"It was still dark!" Even in this strange, whispered argument, the note of derision in Lysanias' voice was clear. He was determined not to be intimidated by the presence of the muscular slave.

Hermon became more conciliatory. He had started them walking, ushering them, as they talked, to an area away from the inspection team, Hermon's two slaves backing away before them.

"No, I admit he wasn't one for getting up early usually, but he had a dinner party for government officials the night before. Maybe he heard something about where they would be looking for faults and wanted to see for himself." That brought Lysanias up in his tracks. He hadn't known the dinner party was for government officials.

"Our porter says Klereides received a message on a scroll," he insisted.

"Well, if he did, I didn't write it and you don't know it was to do with the shipyard."

"Come on, he went out straight away and came here!" Lysanias' tone was still derisive.

"Well, if this message-scroll exists, I didn't write it and where is it? No-one has seen it, except this porter, one of your slaves. How trustworthy is he?" Hermon was going onto the attack.

"But you must admit it's suspicious, sir," Sindron interrupted, himself feeling insulted at the attack on the truthfulness of slaves. "Klereides comes to the shipyard before dawn, presumably to meet someone, and gets killed."

"Well, I didn't send him a message, and I wasn't meeting him, and I wasn't in Athens!" Hermon's statement sounded final. He wanted to end the discussion. The pause was tense.

Keep quiet, Lysanias told himself, but blurted out, "You could have paid someone else to kill him!"

Hermon's face was purple now, his eyes bulged and he looked about to have a fit. His slave took a step forward, adopting a pose that implied readiness to grab Lysanias and hurl him to the planking, if he tried to attack his master. The slave-boy beside him seemed to imitate the pose, laughably considering his spindly limbs. Sindron grasped his new stick more firmly, hefted it higher in his hand, realising how ridiculous this might look. Hermon took refuge in formality.

"Young man, you really have gone too far! If you dare repeat these accusations to anyone else, I will be forced to take legal action against you. I realise I have no patron at the moment to initiate it for me, but I'm sure I can soon find an Athenian citizen of note willing to join forces with a prosperous businessman. General Ariston, perhaps."

"But you asked me to be your patron." Lysanias felt totally undermined. He had gone too far.

"I can hardly sue my own patron! Besides you haven't agreed and we haven't worked out whether it's practical or even legal at your age."

"I still inherit my uncle's share of the business," Lysanias responded, hesitantly.

"I agree that could make things awkward, but I shall insist on proof that you are the legal heir and that could delay your inheritance for a long long time." And Lysanias sensed the threat was real, just as the physical threat of the bodyguard was real. This man Hermon clearly didn't make idle threats. "Unless, of course, you agree to co-operate and stop spreading rumours that will damage the business."

Hermon and Lysanias stood staring each other out, like enemies on a battlefield who have both lost their swords and shields in the fray and are down to brute strength. And Lysanias definitely wasn't going to be threatened into submission.

It was Sindron who made a move to resolve the impasse. "Master, this really is getting us nowhere. May I suggest you gentlemen call a truce, until we have seen the evidence of the accident?"

"We can do without advice from a slave," they both responded almost in unison, and then laughed, realising how ridiculous this was.

"I'm sorry, young man." "I'm sorry, Hermon," they both started together. Then Lysanias had the good sense to respect age and stay quiet while Hermon spoke. "I really should be able to control my temper better." He motioned to his slave to stand back, that the crisis was over. "I realise this has come as a shock to you. It has come as a shock to me, too. And it really is a critical time for the business. I apologise if I appeared inconsiderate."

"No, my apologies, Hermon." And Lysanias meant it. "Everything has happened so fast since I arrived in Athens. I get very confused as to whether I should be looking to avenge my uncle or, if it really is an accident, surely I should allow his soul to rest in peace."

"You've got spirit, young man, that I will say for you. Long time since I met a youngster who could stand up to his elders as you do. But you won't get far in Athens, if you keep on like that. You'll need to learn tact, if you're going to take over from your uncle."

Hermon was smiling broadly now, in a way that seemed to accept Lysanias into the fold. Somehow the argument seemed to have brought them closer together. Lysanias felt he understood Hermon better, though, when he thought about it later, he realised there was still a lot that Hermon hadn't told him, that nothing had really changed, and that Hermon was still the prime suspect.

"I'm sure my master will learn," said Sindron in that patronising but useful way of his. "Now if we can see this rope and maybe talk to the night-watchman who was the last person to see Klereides alive?"

"I believe the watchman is off duty. Illness, Philebos tells me." Was there an edge in Hermon's voice when he talked about the watchman? Lysanias couldn't be sure. "Don't want anyone bringing fever into the yards, so he's laid off till the danger's over. When he's back maybe."

Odd that the one person who might have seen something was unavailable to be questioned, thought Lysanias. Then something else struck him. "What about the rigger who tied off the amphora?" It made Lysanias heart beat faster, as it brought back a mental picture of a crushing weight falling on his uncle and that poor mutilated body. Pre-occupied, he only half-heard Hermon's reply, so he had to ask, "What did you say?"

"The man's been sacked, of course. Negligence." Hermon called it back over his shoulder, as he led the way to the store yard, so he didn't see the look of suspicion on Lysanias' face as the young man realised yet another key figure had been neatly removed from the scene.

Makaria went through, with Philia, the system for ordering food and cooking materials – olive oil, vinegar, herbs, spices. How to check quantities in store of things that lasted, how to draw up a list and to order, which stall or shop to tell the slave to get which item from for the best quality and price, where they could use their own initiative. The mechanics of all this Philia already knew. Her mother had taught her, but, in the country, many things were done differently. The aspects specific to this household and to the market in Athens, that was new. Here, spices and foodstuffs she had never heard of before arrived at the Peiraieos from all over the known world. She needed to learn their names and what they were used for. Philia's interest was engaged.

Makaria showed her how to draw up an inventory for longlife household goods, pots and pans, linen, clothing. Philia knew all that too, it was very like her mother's system, but she held her tongue.

"Now this afternoon, while I'm consulting with the steward, why don't you draw up your own inventory just to show me that you've learnt how to do it?"

"Yes, Makaria." Test it, test it! "But couldn't I learn more from watching you and the steward?"

Makaria spluttered and had a coughing fit. Philia patted her on the back. That was something she wouldn't have dared do before.

"Thank you, my child." The old woman's eyes were watering, there was almost a glint of sly amusement there. "No, my dear, we must take this tuition in easy stages. That will be enough for today."

CHAPTER 8

While Hermon went to pacify the inspectors, the assistant overseer led Lysanias and Sindron to the storage yard, leaving them to the slave in charge. And there, roped off in a corner, with signs warning people to stay away from the deathbringer, was the giant amphora, cracks ringing it but still substantially intact, with blood stains soaked deep into the earthenware especially around one of the loops, which must have dug deep into Klereides' chest. Beside it, the cracked bloodstained timbers.

The storekeeper was reluctant to let them close for fear of spreading the miasma, the pollution that attaches to bringers of unnatural death, but Sindron explained that Lysanias was the heir and needed to establish the guilt of these inanimate objects. He looked doubtful but, fingering a strange necklace he wore round his neck, left them to it. As he bent in close to look and touch, Lysanias hoped they were right in thinking this was a deliberate murder and that the pollution would attach to the murderer, not the tools he had used.

Around the neck of the amphora were the remains of a thick rope, knotted and with a loose end curled beside it, terminating in frayed strands. Hanging on the wall behind was its twin, presumably the part of the rope that had been tied above, holding it suspended. It looked like the results of wear and tear, though how such a thick rope could have frayed through in one night Lysanias couldn't see, unless they had used a very old frayed rope to start with.

Lysanias examined it more closely. The colour of the hemp suggested it had been in use for some time, faded from constant sun, wind and weather. He recalled that the hemp he had seen tying the scaffolding together had seemed younger. He tested it between his hands, tugging a short length. There were signs of give, but it should have held that load. Then he looked at the frayed ends. Yes, there were freshly broken strands, he could tell by the lighter, yellower colour, but the ends of many of the strands were indistinguishable in colour from the outside of the rope. They had frayed and snapped long before. Would that amount of sound strands have held that weight? Maybe, just maybe.

Yet would a shipyard of this one's reputation use ropes as old and frayed as that? Then, as he pulled on the rope to test it, it actually shifted where it was tied round the amphora. It wasn't tight! Surely, if it had hung all night and part of the previous day, that knot would have been pulled so tight the rope would have to be cut away.

Cut! A knife could have left marks on the neck of the amphora. The thing was heavy but, with Sindron's help, Lysanias managed to turn it round. Yes! There! Those bright scratches, shining lighter through the rich brown of the earthenware surface. Someone had used a knife there and it looked recent! Lysanias looked for anything else out of the ordinary.

The storekeeper had left them to it, while he went about other business, but, on his return, looked agitated that they were pulling things apart, so Sindron engaged him in conversation. Asking questions he drew him further away, while Lysanias pulled out the cracked and broken planks. There was charring as well, he noticed.

Suddenly he was staring at his uncle's blood, so thick there was still a congealed layer on the surface as well as that soaked into the timber. It made him feel queasy for an instant. Then he saw the footprint. And dismissed it. The night-watchman's probably, when he found Klereides' body. But no... this was a bare foot. Was a watchman who had to wander round a shipyard in the dark and could tread on splintered timber or old nails likely not to wear sandals? Could it be the murderer? His heart thumped at the thought.

Lysanias longed to tell Sindron about his discoveries, but his slave was talking with the storekeeper and Lysanias overheard. "Prides himself on running a tight ship, that overseer. Waste not want not. We re-use or sell as scrap. That's why I have to keep a detailed record of everything coming in and going out.

"Now that old rope. If that wasn't commandeered by the court, that would go into the pile of disused rope in the scrap store like other worn ropes the workmen report. Then the rope maker collects them to make fresh ropes. Or the rug maker, if they're too old for that. Mind you, they should have collected by now. Maybe frightened by the death." He touched the necklace round his neck.

"That sounds very economical," interrupted Lysanias, as casually as he could, moving closer. "Could we have a look?"

"We haven't time, master. We must get back." Sindron sounded impatient, but then the expression on Lysanias face told him this wasn't just a whim.

"You really interested?" The storekeeper sounded pleased to find other people with his own fondness for neatness and order. "Come on then!"

In the next yard were piles of timber, old sails, a broken mast, and many other worn and used materials. There was also a heap of ropes from ships' rigging and, hopefully, from shipyard use as well. The slave was proudly explaining the different heaps, as Lysanias whispered to Sindron to keep the man talking while he looked at the ropes.

It wasn't a big pile, but it confirmed the slave's statement that ropes were normally scrapped long before the state of the one on the amphora. He pulled a rope out full length across a clear space in the yard to look at it and another one tumbled down from the top of the pile. It had a cut end! A recently cut end!

Lysanias glanced round. Yes, Sindron was still ensuring that the slave looked the other way. He turned back to the pile. One cut end, yes! Clean, done with a very sharp knife. And near it a knot. A very tight knot! Now on one of these along from the knot, there should be another cut end to match. Another knot. Carry on. There it was! And it did match! Same cut. Put them together, yes, that's about the size of the neck of the amphora. And... he couldn't believe it ... little chips of earthenware among the strands near the cut. This rope had come off the amphora. Firm evidence!

Now what about the other length out from the knot, either knot. Slightly longer this, a bit tangled. And ... another cut end. More ragged this time. A different knife maybe? Or someone in a hurry or nervous? Or cut through in two stages? Could that be it? Yes, that would explain it. Proof positive!

On the other side of the scrapyard, Sindron interrupted the storekeeper's lecture. "Strange thing, the way the shipyard's owner got killed, eh?" Sindron spoke confidentially, almost conspiratorially, slave to slave.

"We've been told not to talk about it, but..." He glanced to see that no overseers had come through the gateway. "Shook us all up it has. Bad luck runs in threes, they say. You wonder who'll be next. Not that I'm superstitious, you understand, but you like to feel you're safe when you come to work." He fingered the thong round his neck. What Sindron had thought was a necklace actually carried a miniature replica of the symbols of every god Sindron could think of and some he couldn't. He was surprised to see that the one singled out was the sword and scales of Nemesis, goddess of retribution.

Then he realised why. Anyone with the excessive wealth of Klereides, with no measure to control it and the arrogance to play on both sides of the political game the way he seemed to have done, could be regarded as asking for the attentions of the vengeful goddess. But how much of this could the storekeeper have known? Was it common knowledge? Fingering the symbols seemed to comfort the man, let him feel he had appeased the relevant god in some way.

"Of course you do," said Sindron. "The gods defend us all!" He edged to the subject that concerned him. "The night-watchman that discovered the body. He took it in his stride, did he?"

"What? Old Niko? You should see him! He's a nervous wreck. Scared for his soul. Reckons he saw the Furies down there. Athene protect us!" His fingers found Athene's owl and raised it to press against his forehead.

"Off sick I heard," Sindron muttered casually.

The storekeeper burst into laughter. "That's a good one. Niko's never had a day's illness in his life! He'll be on a six-day binge down the Seamen's Rest. With a story like that to tell, he could drink free for months."

Over at the rope pile, Lysanias' sense of triumph had slumped into depression. How could they stop the rope from being destroyed? How could they get it away from the yard? If only he had his tool bag with him.

A desperate idea came to him. Lysanias called out.

"Hello there, I think someone is calling you from the store yard!"

The storekeeper turned and his eyes widened as he saw the rope trawled across the ground.

"Here, what you been doing? I had that pile all neat and tidy, ready for collection."

"Don't worry," Lysanias blurted out, "We'll tidy it up, you go and see what they want." He tried for the tone of a boss and, fortunately, the storekeeper believed him.

"Quickly, Sindron, wind this rope round me," he said as soon as the slave was out of sight, pulling off his cloak without regard to what was on display. "Master, really! Is this necessary? Oh!" Sindron's voice tailed off as his eyes took in the cut ends. "I see."

Starting under the arms, Sindron wound the cut rope round and round Lysanias' body and did his best to tuck in the last end. Then they re-draped Lysanias' cloak to look as normal as possible. It made Lysanias a rather funny shape. How was he ever going to walk home like this?

The storekeeper's voice came back to them from the other yard, shouting angrily, "There's no-one here. What you playing at?" Then, recalling who he was speaking to, "Are you sure you heard someone, sir?"

Sindron hurriedly bundled the other rope back onto the pile and the storekeeper inspected it for tidiness. Sindron kept between him and Lysanias, so the change in girth would not be noticed.

Lysanias waddled back to the gate, with Sindron keeping a careful eye behind him for trailing rope ends showing below his cloak. Their pace was slow but they got out of the yard without anyone speaking to them and found a cart willing to take them into the centre of Peiraieos. Here Sindron discovered a shop selling baskets and bought one big enough to take the rope. Lysanias felt greatly relieved, as he sloughed it off in an alley and then slumped exhausted onto a low wall, laughing at the way he knew he must have looked.

"I just hope you're right about the pollution, Sindron."

"It has to be, master, and we're even more certain now that there's a murderer." Not absolutely, he thought, only that someone is covering something up but that's almost as good. But he didn't say it.

"At least, the other objects will be safe there while everyone thinks they're polluted," replied Lysanias.

"Until the court decides to throw them over the border," Sindron said. "But hopefully they won't move that quickly."

"Shouldn't we get it changed to 'killing by person unknown'?"

"And let every one know we're looking for a murderer?"

"No, maybe not," Lysanias conceded, remembering he had promised not to do anything that might damage the shipyard.

After hurriedly recounting what they had each discovered, the obvious next step was to look for the Seamen's Rest. They carried the basket between them, feeling that, in this area, a master assisting a slave would not attract the curious glances it would in the city.

Philia had played five stones with Nubis during the lunch break, chattering about the young man she was to marry, about Makaria suddenly being nice to her.

Nubis joked about what Makaria and the steward got up to together every afternoon, but it was only a joke. Philia knew Makaria wouldn't. Not with a slave!

Philia didn't like it when Nubis said she fancied Lysanias, and offered to bet that she would sleep with him first. "Don't you dare! He's mine!" She went into a sulk that Nubis couldn't get her out of, running off to her room and throwing herself down on the bed. Philia hadn't realised that being married to this handsome young man had become so important to her. After all, she still hardly knew him and Klereides was only a few days dead. It seemed so disloyal but then Curly had been so much older than her and they'd spent so little time together that she hadn't really known him very well. Her father had arranged the marriage after all. It was all very confusing.

Philia pulled herself together enough to go down and start on her inventory, writing with a piece of charcoal on a thin plank of whitewood. Glykera, the cook-housekeeper, with her rosy shining face, plump arms and work-roughened hands, was there to tell her where things were kept and what qualified as long term. Philia had always liked Glykera, a kindly woman with a homely common sense, though, kept away from these areas, Philia wasn't very familiar with her.

One large bronze bin, not as big as the one for charcoal for the stoves, had no markings. Philia asked, "What's in this bin?"

"Oh, that's nothing special, just where I puts things for the burning," replied Glykera. "Bundle them up and take them round the foundry furnace, we do, if we're not having a fire ourselves. Food that's gone off would go in there. Bedding and clothes from people who've been sick, though we gets rid of that sharpish."

"Oh I see." Philia automatically opened the lid and looked in, just as Glykera was saying, "... menstrual cloths..." She didn't complete her list, because Philia had spotted and recognised the decorative edging round the red coloured cloth at the bottom of the bin and screamed, dropping the lid with a clatter.

"Oooooh! It's Klereides' cloak. Ooooh!"

For an instant, Philia felt dizzy. Though she seemed suddenly cold, her hands and face were sweaty.

"I'm sorry, sorry, mistress, little mistress, I thought I'd seen to that." Glykera tried to forestall any rebuke.

"You told everyone you'd burnt it!" Philia challenged.

"I'm sorry, mistress. I really thought it had gone. I told him that kitchen boy. He must have forgot."

"Ooooh, look at that!" Philia was strangely calm now and had re-lifted the lid, reached in and pulled out the cloak. It wasn't like a cloak any more, just a clump of stiff, crumpled material, stuck together with congealed blood in shades of dark red, almost to black. It felt so dry and hard. "It's all right. I'm not scared any more."

"I'm sorry, mistress, let me take it away now." The cook reached gently for the cloak, but Philia turned away, still staring at it, fascinated.

"Not yet! Not yet! Look at it, though! That's Curly's life all run out of him and dried on his best cloak! Trust Curly to put on his best cloak to die in." He must have worn it for the dinner party.

"Mistress, mistress, you mustn't talk like this. Here let me take it away before the old mistress sees it still around." The cook was worried.

Philia was herself again now. Glykera grabbed at the cloak and tried to pull it away, but Philia stepped back out of reach. She was sure Lysanias would want to see this cloak, and, there, stuck in the folds, was a scrap of parchment, but Glykera was still grasping for the cloak. She was calm again after the shock. Time to play act, Philia thought.

"Noooo!" She screamed. "No, it's my Curly's, my husband! I want to do it. It's my last duty to him. I'll see it's dealt with." She grabbed the stiff awkward mass to her and ran out of the kitchen, with a frightened Glykera shouting behind her, "No, mistress, please , I was told..."

Lysanias phrased his question as casually as he could but it still sounded a bit like an accusation. "You must be the last citizen to have seen my uncle before he was killed?"

The watchman had clearly taken quite a few drinks but he was still cautious. "What do you mean 'was killed', sir?" He was evidently wary lest he be tricked into saying something he shouldn't.

"Before that amphora fell on him."

"Yes, sir, that'd be me, if you don't count One-Ear, the old dog."
He gestured to the mangy dog lying beside him on the sawdust-strewn
earthen floor of the tavern. "Sorry, sir. Didn't mean to make light."

There was an awkward pause. A thought struck the watchman.

"But I hadn't been drinking that night! Sober as an owl, sir! It's just
my normal routine. Leave work at sun-up when the workers arrive, go
home and sleep till midday, then a few cups with the boys and that gives
me time to sober up before coming in at dusk. But I was sober that night,
sir! I swear it by Poseidon and Athene and Hephaistos and any other god
you like!"

It hadn't been difficult to find the Seamen's Rest. The first stevedore
they asked had directed them, though he did look a little surprised that
people not in worker's tunics or clearly travellers should want to go
there.

The tavern turned out to be a favourite haunt of merchant seamen
and dockworkers, so it was a mixture of nationalities and languages.
There was a smattering of passengers, just arrived or about to depart, so
they weren't too out of place, they hoped.

The watchman had been easy to identify. He was ensconced in a shady
area under the trellis, surrounded by a group of stevedores spellbound by
his tale of a night of horror. Lysanias and Sindron ate their barley cakes
and olives and herrings at a nearby table, waiting for the stevedores to
go back to work. Even from a distance, they could verify that he wore
sandals, very worn and dusty sandals.

Sindron had taken the opportunity to tell Lysanias that, while
Lysanias was in the shipyard office with Hermon, Sindron had managed
to chat to Hermon's personal slave. It made them even more puzzled
about Hermon's reasons for not giving a detailed alibi. The best brothels
in all Greece were in Corinth and Hermon had gone to visit the best of
them, as he did regularly at the end of every month. He had given money
to his slave to visit another brothel that accepted the custom of slaves,
again as he did regularly. Yet there was no dishonour in visiting a brothel.
Why not admit it? Presumably the prostitute could vouch for him, or the
brothel-keeper. Could the slave be lying to cover up for his master?

At that moment the stevedores left, looking suitably impressed, even
cowed, by the watchman's story. The empty wineskins around him
confirmed the sensation value. Lysanias and Sindron moved in on Niko,
setting down on the table in front of him their own friendship offering
of a fresh flagon of wine and a jug of water. When Lysanias had told him
who they were – for they needed the truthful not the dramatised version
of the story – he tended to freeze up.

"So you can remember it all clearly?" Lysanias' question jerked him
back into their world.

"Oh, yes, sir. You're the new owner, eh?" A nod seemed the best answer. "Thought you must be. You've got that manner, like someone just taking over, wants to know what's what." The watchman was trying to be ingratiating, but it seemed to be leading him into trusting them more, thought Sindron, though all Lysanias saw was that this man had important information and was taking a long time to tell it.

"I'm trying to find out what happened to my uncle, Owner Klereides. Will you stop blabbering on and tell me something useful?"

The watchman's developing trust had been broken and he jerked back alarmed. Sindron interrupted gently.

"My master just wants to ask a few questions about that night. We haven't much time, so if we could stick to the point?"

"Yes, sir, anything you say." Now the fearful expression in his eyes showed he really was worried about whether he should say anything at all. "You won't get old Niko into trouble, will you?" It was a whine now, the hands shaking as he tried to hold his wine cup steady. "It's not easy to get a job at my age, not with all these foreigners and slaves around. That Resident Hermon fires people sometimes for little things. He's changed half the gang on that ship. You don't think he'll mind if I talk to you, do you?"

This was news. Quite different to the impression Hermon had given earlier.

"No, of course not." Lysanias had the sense now to keep his tone gentle and reassuring. "I'm his partner now. If you haven't done anything wrong, you'll be quite all right." He hoped that he would be in a position to protect the man if necessary.

"Oh good, only..." The man mumbled into his wine cup and took another big drink. He clasped the cup firmly in both hands, but the shaking was still evident. The man's nerves were in a terrible state.

In the same tone, Lysanias asked, "Do you mean Hermon actually fires workers himself?"

The man glanced up, decided there was no point in refusing to answer and maybe something to be gained. "Well, no, he gets Overseer Philebos to do it, but we all know who gives the orders, don't we? Mind you, it was kind of Philebos to tell me to take a few days off to recover after seeing what I saw."

So they did want the man out of the way, thought Lysanias, and the fever story really wasn't true. Sindron put in gently, "Can you tell us what happened on the night, Niko? The way it really was?"

The watchman took another drink, then looked up almost eagerly, his eyes flitting between them. It was as though he had been waiting for just this chance to tell the full story to someone and get the horrible experience off his chest, though now he kept his voice down, so other people in the tavern wouldn't hear.

"Well, I was out on my rounds. I walk round about every hour to see that the fence is sound, and no-one's broken in."

"Yes, yes, but what about my uncle?" Lysanias felt Sindron touch his arm in a signal to let the man talk, but it was out.

"I'm coming to that, aren't I?" Now he had started, he seemed a little more confident. "Well, we were on our rounds, old One-Ear and me. You know how quiet it can be in the hour before dawn. Then we hears this chariot clattering down the hill and I says to One-Ear I says, wonder what madman's driving that fast in the dark…"

"This was the chariot my uncle came in? Driving fast?"

"Well, yes sir, I think so, because soon after that the noise stops and then there's this godsawful hammering on the gates and on the gong outside." His bleary, red-rimmed eyes registering the impatient look on their faces, he went on. "So I hurries as fast as I can along they walkways. I sends One-Ear on ahead to bark at them, let them know I'm not on my own. Could be thieves, you know. I remember when…. Oh, yes. So I asks who it is and Owner Klereides he gets impatient but I recognise his voice, so I lets him in and he hops straight over to my fire to warm himself."

In the momentum of telling his story, the man's confidence seemed to have returned, but his left hand fiddled irritatingly with his grizzled beard.

"Did you get a look at the chariot or the driver?" asked Sindron. "He might be able to tell us something, if we could find him."

The man was busy refilling his cup. The amount of water he added seemed to get less with each cupful, but he had heard.

"What? Driver? No, can't say I did…" He paused, thinking. "Ah, now. I did hold up the lamp, as old Klereides slipped in. There's this one-horse chariot. Light-coloured horse, I remember that. Silver grey, that's right. I thought, that's unusual, don't often see many of them in these parts. And this tall, thin man standing there. Wrapped all in black he is, right up over his head, hides his face. Like one of those Semites from the desert. Guess he knew it would be cold out, eh? Can't say I blame him. Mind you, I worked out in the open all my life, so I don't feel it so much as some."

Still impatient, Lysanias started to say, "Look, old man, we haven't got time for all this" but Sindron stopped him, by coming in slightly louder with, "Is that all you remember?"

The watchman had responded to the flash of anger in Lysanias' eyes, and his purple-veined nose was in his wine cup again. Sindron dropped to his reassuring tone. "Klereides came in a one-horse chariot drawn by a silver-grey horse and driven by a tall man cloaked in black and they drove fast? Is that right?"

The man nodded.

"What sort of chariot was it? A racing chariot or one of those that plies for hire?"

"Yes, one of those, sir, like those you see by the market place up in the city. For the wealthy ones who are too lazy to walk."

"You're sure, now? About the type of chariot?"

The crumpled old man looked surprised at the idea it could be anything other than a hired chariot but the bleary eyes stared into space, trying to retrieve that brief visual image. "Ah. Yes. Now you ask. All painted over it was but, under the paint, some sort of pattern, a bit like those reliefs of heroes they have on racing chariots. Couldn't be sure though."

"Did you hear the driver's voice?" Sindron kept the same tone, and Lysanias realised he was better to keep silent, though the afternoon heat, even in the shade here, was making it difficult to concentrate.

Niko thought. "No, sir, not a word. Owner Klereides tells him not to wait, I think. That's right. Then the driver laughs. Funny sort of laugh. Like there isn't anything anyone can do to hurt him. Not like you'd expect a chariot driver to laugh, though I hear some of them can be rude when they want to."

The man was relaxing again. That was good, thought Sindron. He eyed the wine, and saw Lysanias drinking agitatedly to hold his impatience in check, though he noticed the lad seemed to be controlling it by adding copious water. After all the tension, Sindron would have liked to take a decent drink himself, but they had to get the full story. It was terrible wine anyway, he consoled himself.

"What about Klereides? Did he tell you why he was there?"

"Doesn't say much at all. I think he must have still been sleepy. I say to him it's a strange time to be coming to the yard. Then I think I asks him what he thinks about the reforms and he just pulls a scroll out of his cloak and waves it at me..."

"The message, that must be the message!" The words burst excitedly from Lysanias' throat.

"What did he do with the scroll?" Sindron went on doggedly, feeling he was building up a very useful picture.

"Stuffs it back in his cloak, as far as I know. Does it matter?"

"Try to remember." Sindron leant forward, calm, persuasive. "When you found the body, was the scroll there?"

"Wouldn't know, sir. I just catch sight of the body and all that blood and yell for help. Besides I have to put the fire out."

Lysanias blurted out, "What fire?" Then he remembered the charring on the planks, the black marks on the earthenware.

"The oil lamp smashed when that thing fell on him. Starts a blaze across the boards. His cloak, that's smouldering too."

"Oh gods, perhaps the scroll was burnt!" Lysanias was getting a little self-pitying, Sindron observed, but at least he wasn't interfering.

The watchman took it as an accusation. "I got the fire out quickly, sir, I don't think much got burnt. We have leather buckets of water along there, in case of fire. Then the overseer, no, the assistant, no, the overseer, I'm not sure, I was a bit shaky, he orders them to put up new boards and clean up, because the inspectors are coming."

"Before anyone had inspected to find out why the amphora fell?" Lysanias was horrified. It didn't seem right, for a serious accident in mighty Athens.

"I suppose so. I sounds the alarm for death in the yards, then first man in runs for Overseer Philebos and for a doctor. Then, as soon as the body is moved back to the offices, Overseer Philebos, no, the assistant tells all the workers to stop standing round and to get things back to normal."

Lysanias and Sindron looked at one another with stony expressions but it was Sindron who carried on the questioning.

"Did Klereides say why he was there?"

"Like I say, he just waves this scroll and says he's off to a meeting by the new ships and to send the others on when they arrive, and off he goes without saying who 'the others' are."

It was Lysanias, the craftsman, who realised what this implied. "What? In the dark, along those walkways? You didn't show him the way?"

"He didn't want any help, sir. Just grabbed my lamp and went off, he did."

"And that's the last you saw of him till you found the body," Sindron asked.

"That's right, sir."

"What did you do then, after he walked off?"

"Me? I go back in my hut. Those early morning breezes off the sea, they can be a bit cold, so I prefer to sit down in shelter."

He was continually looking away with an occasional sideways glance, or looking down into his wine cup. Was he trying to hide something?

"You were in there when you heard the crash and you went to see what had happened?"

"Something like that." He was still looking into his wine and the answer was muttered and slurred. Niko fell silent and it looked as though he had fallen asleep, his head bowed, motionless. Lysanias nudged him.

"Come on, Niko! We need to know."

"You're sure I won't get into trouble, sir?" He looked at Lysanias through bleary eyes. The man's breath was foul. No wonder, with that mouthful of rotting teeth. Lysanias tried not to feel repelled. The old man had his sympathy, having to plead like this after a full life's work.

"No, citizen. I'll see to that ... You may even get a reward." Lysanias was getting desperate.

Niko brightened up. "Another flagon over here," Sindron called to a tavern slave. That cheered Niko up even more.

"Well, I hear him clumping along the scaffolding at first but, what with the birds and the cocks and the donkeys waking up, I don't hear much after that."

"So what did you do?" Sindron could see Lysanias trying hard to keep his patience. He leant over and pointedly added a good measure of water to both their cups.

"Well, I get to thinking that he's been gone a long time and no-one else has come, so I tell myself I'd better go see how he is. So I sets off with old One-Ear here but, before we get very far, there's this almighty crash and a whoosh of flame with the oil catching light, and it's all over for Owner Kleriedes. Poor old owner! Gods really had it in for him!" He raised his head and looked around, as though playing to a larger audience. Sindron realised that other customers had indeed gathered close to listen.

"All your money doesn't do you any good when the gods decide to drop a massive great amphora on your head. Couldn't have been Dionysos, eh? Wasn't a wine holder, was it? Big water one, wasn't it!" He cackled at his joke. He'd forgotten who he was talking to and gone into one of the jokes he had enlivened the story with for other barflies, who he felt would ignore the sacrilege. "Me, I pray to Hephaistos, like all the shipyard workers, and to Athene, of course, the Athene who looks after all artists and craftsmen not the one for virgins. But then, Klereides, he wasn't a craftsman, was he?" The watchman was mumbling now, to himself, his head sinking lower and lower.

Lysanias shook him awake. "Did you hear anything, man?"

"Don't you call me 'man' in that tone of voice!" Niko was drunk, slurring his words, having difficulty finding the right ones. "You can call me 'cit'zen'," he slurred, trying to stand up as befitted the dignity of the title, but swayed and sank down again, thinking better of it. "I called the owner man 'cit'zen' 'n' he di'n't like it but they all have to get used to it now, don't they?" The watery eyes looked at Lysanias for support.

Lysanias was mellowing with the wine and sympathy for the old worker. Sitting next to him, he put his arm round the man's shoulders in the comradely gesture that would have applied in Eion but was rare in Athens. "Look, citizen, I didn't mean to be rude but do you remember anything else? Did you hear anything before the crash?"

Niko stared blearily at him, his brow creased in an attempt at thought, memories stirred.

"I thought I heard him talking to himself. I sometimes do that myself, it's that lonely. You do it to frighten off evil spirits. But he seemed to be shouting. I never heard of that, shouting to yourself. Maybe he seen a rat or something. I thought at first might be someone with him but no-one had come in the gate or I'd have seen them."

"You didn't see anyone?"

"Of course not. Lots of shadows flickering round from the flames and I think I see his soul rising from his body like a dark shape merging with the other shadows. Then I realise it must be one of those Furies feeding on his entrails, sucking his blood, stealing his soul."

He shuddered at the thought, even though he must have told this climax to his tale many times already. "Turned me over that did. That's why I've been drinking, don't want to remember that bit!" And he burst into tears, shaking with great sobs.

Then suddenly he sniffed to halt his tears, pulled himself together and shouted, shrugging Lysanias' arm off, "Hey, what you doing, you filthy aristocratic pervert. You get your hands off me or I'll..." and he pushed himself upright, aimed a punch at Lysanias, fell backwards onto Sindron, rolled gently to the floor under the table and passed out. One-Ear licked his master's face and lay down beside him on guard.

"Help me get him on his feet," said Sindron, bending to grasp Niko's shoulder. "Then we'd better find out where he lives and get him there."

But Sindron found himself waiting, while the old dog growled at him but thankfully didn't bite. He glanced up. No Lysanias at all. Where was the boy? Across the tavern, he spotted the lad's haircut, the only short haircut in sight.

Grabbing up the basket with the rope, Sindron headed off in pursuit.

Not far beyond Lysanias, an Athenian stevedore was jabbing a finger at the chest of what could only be, from his skin colour and multiple earrings, a Phoenician seaman. A fight was clearly developing and Lysanias seemed to be heading straight for the centre of it, but the boy swerved, pushed through the small group of onlookers that was gathering, and disappeared from Sindron's sight. Hurrying as fast he could, Sindron skirted the crowd just as the first blows were landed and cheers egged on one or the other protagonist.

Lysanias was clearly aiming for a table by the far wall but Sindron's old eyes didn't allow him to make out why. Then he saw Lysanias grab someone by the front of their cloak and pull the man to his feet. Oh, no, Sindron thought, he's going to start a brawl himself!

Now Sindron was close enough to see it was Strynises, the news-teller. How had Lysanias picked him out right across the crowded tavern?

"What have you been saying about my uncle, you maligning word-twister?"

"Let me go, young fellow. I'm quite prepared to listen to your complaint." Strynises hadn't made any effort to resist or fight back but, by the time he finished speaking, he was free again, and Lysanias held off by two heavy-built men the news-teller had been talking to. Strynises' tone made it sound as though being confronted aggressively like this was a normal event for him.

"Please, sit down." Lysanias didn't really have much choice. Though he struggled, the men pushed him down onto a bench. As Sindron reached the group and stood catching his breath, he could see Lysanias was fuming still, though the anger seemed to have countered any effects of the wine.

"Now, young man, please introduce yourself." Strynises made it sound as though he was the epitome of politeness.

"Lysanias, son of Leokhares, heir of Klereides." Lysanias glared at the poet, making it almost a challenge. The man's thin face and sharp, pointed nose reminded Lysanias of a weasel.

The news-teller's eyes opened in surprise and a broad smile developed as he saw advantages for him. "Really? Curly Klereides, eh? I can understand why you're angry, and I can only plead that it's my profession. Gossip is my business. That's what people listen to, what they laugh at, what they pay me for. I can only assure you that I'm equally nasty to everyone whatever their status or political opinion. In fact..." and his tone was almost confiding "... it's the only way I survive. Frankly, if you heard some of the nastiness I pick up, you'd see how much I do censor out. Others would have accused Kimon of selling his sister to old moneybags Kallias to buy himself out of debt and launch his career. I didn't do that. And, if I'd revealed *all* of Kimon's adulteries, I'd have upset his wife even more."

"You didn't censor out much about my uncle, I hear!"

"Ah, well now, you have to admit it was a very good story. 'Exploiter and lecher struck down in his own shipyard.'" Lysanias anger flared and he was on his feet, fists clenched, until he was pushed down again. "Now, young man, I'm sorry, maybe you don't know everything about your uncle. I assure you I didn't use half of what I've heard. I didn't go into detail on his gambling debts now, did I?"

"But ... but ... never speak ill of the dead!" It was somehow the only thing Lysanias could think of to say. Yet Sindron was wondering if maybe this news-teller's network of informants might not have told him more about Klereides' death than he and Lysanias had unearthed with all their questioning.

"My dear sir ... close acquaintances yes, but I didn't even know the man. I can't turn down a story as good as this out of moral scruples now, can I?"

Lysanias realised he was not going to get anywhere with this man. It was amazing no-one had beaten him up in an alleyway before now.

"If you're wondering how I get away with it, well I don't always." He pointed to a scar on his forehead and a broken finger badly mended. "Fortunately most people respect the fact that we satirists are protected by the great god Dionysos but I prefer to give him a little help. That's why my good friends are here."

"You must have some opinion yourself, some standpoint."

"No, no, I can't afford that luxury. Besides all men are foolish or corrupt in some way, and long may they stay so! It puts food on my table."

Lysanias was shocked at this degree of cynicism, but he didn't interrupt.

"Now, young man," Strynises leaned across the table. "It isn't often I get to talk to the subjects of my poems. 'Battle of Love at Funeral of Squashed Boar.' Now that was a good story, drama and laughs, excellent."

Lysanias tried hard to control his anger. Did this mean he had already been ridiculed in the market place, laughed at by all and sundry?

"'Revolutionary Sculptor Shocks Funeral Party.' If you can come up with more stories like those I'll pay well for them."

The man kept a straight face but Lysanias knew he was making fun of him. Sindron half-realised he should find some way of intervening to calm Lysanias down, but he was impressed. This poet's information network was good!

"Perhaps you can tell me how your hunt for the murderer is going, how it feels to find yourself an heir and about to marry your uncle's widow at only eighteen, how you managed to upset so many city officials in so few short days."

The weasel was openly laughing at him now, and his companions were joining in. Lysanias wasn't going to take this any more. He stood up.

"You ... you..." He couldn't find words for his disgust. "You watch out, that's all. I'm here to defend my uncle's honour."

They laughed even louder and he realised how inadequate this was, especially coming from a stripling of his tender years and brief experience in the world.

He stomped away, Sindron running after him with the heavy basket.

"Let me know if you have any more good stories for me. Or want to hear what I know!" The news-teller shouted after him, to further roars of laughter from his colleagues. Sindron wondered if that could be an offer, Strynises' way of making amends.

"Master, master, maybe he does know more than we can find out ourselves. Perhaps we should talk to him some more."

By the time they reached the street, Lysanias had calmed down enough to accept Sindron's argument. They went back. Sindron took the lead this time, apologising for his master's anger. Strynises made more effort this time to be understanding and offered that the least he could do as recompense for any offence caused was to pass on a few snippets of information he had garnered.

"One thing that has puzzled me is all these scurrilous stories about Klereides. Now one of the beauties of satire is that it doesn't have to be true but I do like to base it on something real and it was difficult to see how one man could have done all that. Brothel-hopping both sexes, illicit affairs with other citizens' wives, massive bets that went wrong, investments in cargoes that didn't pay off, extortion." Lysanias found himself getting angry again as the list went on, but Strynises' tone didn't sound as though he was maligning Klereides and he was looking very thoughtful, so Lysanias held it under control. He merely said, "What are you getting at?"

"Let me finish. He was an old rogue, your uncle, no doubt about it, but it was sounding ridiculous, especially as, at one time, people referred to him as Lucky Klereides. So I checked back on some of the stories, and quite a few didn't appear to be true. Now you always find that with gossip, but these all came from the sort of sources I normally use, reliable sources. It looked as though someone was planting false stories to discredit him. Or to confuse. I even suspected he might be doing it himself to conceal what he was really up to, so I put someone onto following him."

Sindron was getting caught up in this. "Did they find anything?" he blurted out.

"A little. It looks as though he was meeting up with representatives of the radicals. Now he wouldn't want that widely known..."

"You didn't use that in your satire?" Lysanias was really agitated now, and Sindron felt concerned.

"No, I was saving it till Kimon returned to throw into the political cauldron. By then, Klereides was dead." The news-teller looked disappointed that a great opportunity for causing uproar had been lost.

"Another thing, that steward of his, he's started making visits to the harbour, especially when there are ships in from Eastern countries, presumably under instruction."

"He is Persian," offered Sindron, "possibly looking for news of home."

"Dangerous. Could give people the wrong idea. And there was something else. Klereides somehow managed to get away from my informant at certain times."

Sindron brought him back to the point. "So you think he was planting stories to hide something else?"

"Yes, possibly, but I also think someone was putting around stories to discredit him. That's what I thought you'd want to know. I never found out who. That's all I can tell you."

The thought came to Lysanias that, if the man had told him this out of a feeling of guilt, he might as well push it a little further. "If you do find out anything that would help me find my uncle's murderer, will you let me know?"

"Don't rely on me to do your work for you, young man!" The news-teller had suddenly changed from the friendly sympathiser back to the rude hater of all men.

"Just one thing," Lysanias pleaded. "Can you leave me out of your poems, at least until I've discovered who murdered my uncle? I'll never find out, if everyone in town knows every step I'm taking."

"You have my word, young man. I normally charge a small fee for such a service but, as you've given me more than your fair share of stories already..."

"Master. Eion!" Sindron whispered. And when Lysanias looked puzzled, out loud he asked, "Any news from Eion."

"No, all normal. At least that's what the last ship in said."

"So that rumour of being…"

"Over-run? A rumour."

"Good." they said together, greatly relieved.

He called them back. "Ah, I'm being less than honest there, but then I usually am. I admit someone did pay me to exaggerate that story a little. As the conquest of Eion was one of Kimon's big achievements, they thought it would help deflate that image. My apologies if it has caused you any difficulties. I have to make a living. It could happen again." The cynical smile gave Lysanias no reassurance.

As they were leaving for the second time, Sindron remembered Niko. The dog growled but allowed Lysanias and Sindron to pick Niko up, and followed when they helped him back to his hovel of a home. Having to carry the basket of rope as well made the watchman a heavy burden but a mule-cart made the journey home easier. Niko's sighting of what they both agreed must have been the actual killer bending over Klereides confirmed their belief that it was indeed a murder and gave Lysanias' mind a new determination.

CHAPTER 9

"You wicked girl! What wife would defy the gods and ruin her husband's chances of reaching the underworld by hiding his death clothes and worshipping them in secret? How could you?" Makaria was in a flaring rage and all Philia could do was stand there and shiver.

"I didn't mean anything wrong by it, mother of my husband," Philia whimpered.

"Wrong? Wrong? You risk bringing the wrath of the gods down on the whole house and you didn't mean anything wrong?"

"I'm sorry, I'll make amends, I'll pray to all the gods, I'll make an offering to Demeter and to Zeus of the Dead, and..."

"You certainly will, my girl, you certainly will and straight away. What's more this slave-girl,..." and she turned to Nubis who was hovering, shivering herself, beside the doorway behind them, "... this slave-girl is a slave of the household, she is not your personal chattel to involve in your devious and sacrilegious schemes."

All Philia had done was ask Nubis to take a message to Lysanias' room. 'I have cloak' Philia had scratched on a flat stone and asked Nubis to leave it there when he was out, so that they wouldn't be alone together. How could it all have gone so wrong? "I shall see that this disobedient slave-girl is sold as soon as possible, unless she learns her place a lot more thoroughly!"

At that Philia burst in. "Oh, no, Makaria, please don't sell Nubis. It wasn't her fault." Makaria stood black and bulky and grim-faced. "It was my offence, mother-in-law. I persuaded Nubis. I will atone." Philia looked down at the floor, not daring to look Makaria in the eye.

She heard a deep sigh and a "Hmm". Then, "Very well. You girl!" Makaria called to Nubis. "Take this reminder of death to the bronze foundry in Armourer's Alley and see it is burned in the furnace. It should have been burned long before this!" Makaria thrust the bloody cloak at Nubis and pushed her out of the room with sharp prods from her long-nailed fingers.

"As for you, independent-woman Philia, remember your promise! Off to the household shrine with you straight away! We'll go to the temple tomorrow. And we will not tell Lysanias about this sacrilege. Agreed?" Philia nodded.

Now she had lost the cloak! What would Lysanias say? Whatever the old woman said, she would have to tell him. She still had the message-scroll, though. Perhaps that was more important, but how could she let him know?

"Where are you going, young lady?" Sindron had intended it as a joke, to try and get on better terms with the slave-girl, but she responded with a start and tried to rush past him. He instinctively put out his right arm with the stick extended to block her. "Let me past, old man! I'm on an errand." The guilty look in her eyes told him he should find out more.

While Lysanias performed mourning rituals at the household shrine, Sindron had gone to the market square to try for another talk with Lydos but his friend was nowhere in sight. Crowds surrounded Strynises as, somehow beating the official herald to it, he announced the dramatic news that Kimon's troops had been refused transit through the territory of Corinth, the only route back to Athens. Everyone realised that it would make a serious difference to the way voting went at the ostracism meeting if they didn't arrive back in time. Neither Phraston nor other senior aristocrats were in sight, doubtless conferring on what they could do. Perhaps that accounted for Lydos' absence as well.

He had sought out the merchant once again. He knew it was a vain hope but felt he had to go through the motions to set his conscience straight. He tried offering that he would influence Lysanias to make major investments in the future, if Hipponikos would release him from this small contract. "Too late, old friend, ship's already sailed." Why did that give him a thrill? His first cargo was now at sea! Surely, he should have been horrified that his embezzlement was now beyond retrieval, vulnerable to pirates, storms, shipwreck. "Shouldn't you be with it?" he asked, suddenly worried for his cargo's safety. "No. No need for that. Trustworthy captain, and I've an agent on board. It's quite safe. Don't you worry." He looked pityingly at Sindron as one would at any fearful novice.

"Your friend's ship has gone down though." He gestured at a board that announced a shipwreck. "He had a lot of money on that cargo. Still you win some, you lose some." The merchant seemed unconcerned but Sindron was sure Lydos would be unhappy about it. It really frightened him for his own investment. All the more reason to tell his master soon before anything drastic happened to it.

He did get Hipponikos to agree, as a goodwill gesture, to have the captain of his next ship to Eion take a hurriedly written message from Lysanias to his mother saying they had arrived safely and were well. They felt he couldn't really say more for fear of worrying her unduly.

Sindron found the place that chariots stand waiting for customers and talked to a few drivers. No-one recalled a driver who used a grey horse or who dressed all in black but, then, no-one they knew worked during the hours of darkness. In fact, no-one did except by prior arrangement when the moon was full. So they thought the driver must be a private one. Sindron realised that, though the driver could be a key to the whole puzzle, there now seemed no way of finding him.

Making his way home through the back alleys, he had seen the usually springy figure of Nubis shuffling towards him, head drooped and frowning, clutching a bundle.

"It can't be that urgent." Sindron now grasped her upper arm in a firm grip.

"No, please let me go, she'll beat me!"

"No, she won't. You've a new master now. And who is 'she'? Philia?"

"No, of course not! Philia's nice."

"Who? The housekeeper? Makaria?" From the way Nubis tensed he knew the answer. And suddenly it all poured out.

"I didn't mean to tell her, honest I didn't! I meant to do what the young mistress said, but Makaria threatens to sell me to a dockside brothel, if I don't tell her everything. I was taking a message. She caught me." She looked up pleadingly, widening her big dark eyes with the long black lashes, the picture of young innocence.

Sindron knew this expression at least must be a studied act. He sighed. "Yes, yes, I understand but what did you tell her? And what's in the bundle?"

"I told her that Philia had found the cloak."

Sindron couldn't believe it. He dropped whatever friendliness and fatherliness had been in his tone. "Right, open the bundle!" She responded, as a slave must to a direct order, placing the bundle down and kneeling to unwrap it. "Klereides' cloak! The actual cloak!" Sindron gasped, trying hard to control his excitement. "Not destroyed! This is marvellous. Quick, open it out. Is there anything in it? A scroll?"

They quickly but carefully pulled the cloak open where it was stuck together with dried blood, but there was no scroll. The droop of his features betrayed his disappointment but he recalled where they were. "Quick, roll it up again."

His heart was thumping as he glanced up and down the alley. Sindron wasn't sure what to do. Perhaps he could slip in through the secret door and lock the cloak in the chest but, if the bundle didn't reach the foundry and get burned, Makaria might find out.

"Keep an eye on that end of the alley, girl! I've got an idea." He turned his back to her facing the other way. He had to remove his cloak to get his tunic off from under it and he didn't want the girl to see that she and the excitement were capable of arousing a man of his sober years.

He blushed as he re-wrapped his cloak around him, just in time as a slave with a basket on his humped back turned the corner towards them.

"Quickly, turn round, give me the bloody cloak, don't let anyone see, and put this tunic in its place." He kept his voice low as he slipped Klereides' cloak inside his own cloak.

With the tunic stuffed inside the cloth bundle, Sindron instructed Nubis to make sure she arranged to throw it into the furnace herself and to make sure they knew where it had come from.

"Oh, they all know me," she said, smiling. "They always make saucy remarks when I go in and I do them my wiggle." She giggled, did the wiggle, and glanced up at Sindron to see if she had succeeded in embarrassing him. She had, but he managed to conceal it.

"You won't tell Makaria, will you?" the girl burst out, mouthing her greatest fear. Sindron seized the opportunity.

"Not if you help us to get messages to Philia."

"I can't. She watches like a hawk, the old mistress."

"There must be some time in the day when the old lady is resting or occupied. Think!" Sindron grasped Nubis' arm tightly.

"Stop it, you're hurting!" Sindron eased his grip. "There is a time," she said. "When Makaria's with the steward in the afternoons, though you can never be sure. That's when she caught me today."

"Good." Sindron knew it was the best arrangement they would get. "Now, get along to the foundry."

Sindron had had a word with Otanes who had a word with Makaria that Lysanias, the master of the house, felt the household should try to get back to normal routines as soon as possible. So it was agreed that the whole family would eat together for the evening meal.

It was a disaster.

They had arranged the couches in the courtyard. Lysanias offered the choicest morsel of each main dish to the household gods, as he had seen his father do hundreds of times, and made the libations. Makaria's expression looked black. Lysanias reclined on his couch with Makaria and Philia on either side. He said the blessings as required. Makaria looked blacker still. Philia sat bowed on her couch, a slim black statue, unmoving, her black veil concealing her expression and so her feelings.

"Throw back your veil, girl," Makaria was abrupt, almost brutal. "He's dead and gone and, if he hasn't reached the underworld, he never will."

Two automatic responses saw Philia throw back her veil with instinctive obedience to an order, and Lysanias say, just as his mother would have, "Now, grandmother, respect for the dead!" He felt actually quite shocked at this attitude of a mother for her son. At the same instant, he realised the problem. Klereides had probably rarely been at home at meal times, so Makaria would have substituted as head of household, which meant

Lysanias was usurping a place she had come to regard as her own. Well, she would just have to get used to it.

Philia had flashed him a brief expression of gratitude, but this had rapidly changed into one that he could only read as guilt, as though his barb had struck as a personal rebuke to her. Her pale face looked as though she had been crying. Again her head was lowered even as she ate, taking few and tiny mouthfuls.

Otanes had insisted on overseeing the serving and he had given Nubis the chore of actually bringing dishes from the kitchen. Her presence made Lysanias edgy for some reason associated with those twinkling brown legs. While, behind Lysanias' couch, Sindron took dishes and placed them in front of him, striving to do everything right in a role as personal slave he had never played before, under the supercilious gaze of Otanes. The atmosphere was icy.

Lysanias tried to break it.

"The squid is excellent, Otanes. Please pass my compliments to the cook."

"Certainly, master."

"Grandmother, congratulations on your household organisation, most efficient."

"Hrrmph."

Lysanias realised his father would never have said anything so stiff and formal, and, from his young lips, it must seem arrogant, but, in this setting of wealth and formality, anything else would seem vulgar. And he had to speak first to Otanes and Makaria to clear the way to speak directly to Philia.

"Philia, any word from your father yet?"

And she burst into tears. It had been the wrong thing to say or the wrong way to say it. Her father's approval would be needed if the wedding was to go ahead, but he was an officer with the main body of Athenian troops marching back from Sparta that Corinth was refusing to allow cross her borders, on the grounds that they hadn't asked permission. Official heralds had toured the streets announcing it and speculation was rife as to whether this might be a ruse, so that Spartan troops could catch up and attack them from behind, or if it implied war with Corinth. So the girl was naturally worried for her father. He should have realised.

Makaria thawed. "Come now, girl," she said in a surprisingly soft and caring tone of voice. "Your father will be safe. He'll be with us soon. Now dry your tears."

Nubis brought a bowl and napkin and a hand-mirror, and Philia wiped her eyes and essayed a sorry smile. Lysanias still felt embarrassed at having been so insensitive. Makaria kept talking to cover it.

"Philia is making excellent progress in learning the tasks of household management, Lysanias. I'm very pleased with her progress."

"Is that so? Which aspect have you found most interesting, Philia?"
This formality was ridiculous.

"Oh, working out the quantities of different foods to order for a dinner party," she said immediately and with enthusiasm. "You really have to think hard to work that out correctly, depending on the number of guests and the different dishes and what you can afford within the budget."

Her face came to life, her eyes lit up and looked straight into his for the first time, and he knew that he would really like to know this young woman a lot better. He noted that Makaria looked relieved that this was all Philia had chosen to talk about from the day's activities. Sindron had told him about the bloodstained robe, so he could understand why.

Lysanias asked the slaves to leave them, including Sindron. With the ice broken, they chatted about the future. The two young people seemed now to accept that it was their duty under the law to be married, as Klereides had died without a son of his own. The fright and tantrums of a few days before had receded and a not-discontented resignation had taken their place.

Makaria adopted a tone of gentle encouragement. Lysanias and Philia suddenly found themselves blushing, casting sidelong glances at one another and then looking away, as Makaria listed possible dates, after the end of the mourning period, when the wedding might take place, provided, of course, Philia's father agreed to the match.

Lysanias decided that now was the time to set out new guidelines for the household. He called Otanes and asked him to summon all the household slaves.

"Lysanias, what is this about?" whispered Makaria, while they were waiting.

"I just want to introduce myself as the new master while everyone's together." he said, half truthfully.

Otanes coughed when everyone was present. Lysanias was a little surprised that it added up to so many. all those mouths to feed! all his responsibility!

Lysanias summoned what adult dignity he could and smiled broadly. Was a smile the right thing? He modified it, and began speaking.

"I just wanted to thank you all for the excellent way you have handled everything during the funeral preparations, and especially the feast. It really went off extremely well. As you know, I am the new master."

He paused. But all faces were stiff and expressionless, with eyes that implied they were worried there might be bad news such as a reduction in the household and slaves to be sold off. Lysanias noticed a sidelong glance between Makaria and Otanes that didn't seem appropriate, but he had no time to puzzle it. He carried on as he had prepared the speech in his head.

"The intention is that I and Philia will marry, subject to her father's approval. Until she has learnt fully the arts of household management from Makaria, I would like the present arrangement to continue, whereby Makaria organises the household with the assistance of Otanes as steward."

From their expressions, some seemed pleased or relieved, some not quite so pleased, others completely stony-faced.

"Sindron, who some of you have already met, will continue as my personal slave and adviser. To fulfil this role he needs to know a great deal about the household and its finances and to some extent will, as it were, shadow Otanes, purely for information purposes, you understand. I would appreciate it if you would give Sindron every assistance in this, and answer his questions as truthfully and fully as you can. Otherwise please continue to perform your current duties. Does everyone understand?"

Nubis immediately stepped forward. She had looked agitated and had probably been planning to ask the question where no-one could prevent her.

"Master, what about me? I help both the old mistress and the young mistress with their toilet and to get dressed, I weave in the workroom, I run errands, I danced to entertain guests at dinner parties for the old master, the gods give him an easy passage, and other duties." She dropped her eyelids and then stared straight at Lysanias, the brazen huzzy. He knew what she meant and blushed. "Must I still do all that?"

Was she asking if he wanted to sleep with her? In public like this? No, surely not! She had put on a demure look now, cunning little minx ... but very pretty. Better take her question seriously.

"Once I have a better idea of the household finances, we will review all tasks to see whether more household staff should be engaged or tasks re-distributed." A non-committal reply but it evidently struck home in some areas. Were there slackers amongst them?

As he paused, Makaria broke in. "Of course, Otanes and myself will be assisting the new master fully in this review." Sindron registered that Makaria wasn't going to let it appear that she hadn't been consulted in all this, even if Lysanias was improvising.

"Now, to still rumours," Lysanias went on. "You know how I reacted to your old master's injuries." There were whispers, a few smiles, a sniffle from Philia. Sindron could see that Makaria and Otanes looked concerned that he should talk like this at all.

"You should know that I still have grave suspicions about the cause of Klereides' death." A small gasp from Philia probably reflected everyone else's suppressed reactions. "I am determined to discover if unknown enemies of his had a hand in it. If any of you know of anything which could point to a possible culprit or noticed anything unusual in Klereides' behaviour in the days before his death or that of any callers, including that last dinner party, I ask you to tell Sindron."

He paused for effect but before he could elaborate Makaria had stepped in. "Or myself or Otanes, of course, if you feel more comfortable talking to someone you have known for a long time."

Otanes added, "Of course, mistress, but I'm sure I would have heard already if there were anything untoward." The meaning 'If you know anything, keep your mouths shut' hung plainly in the air.

Lysanias was obliged to say. "Of course, speak to whoever seems appropriate..." But the slaves were already filing out and Lysanias felt as though his intentions had been foiled, and at a time when he had been feeling so pleased with the progress they had made in their investigations that day. He wondered what information that the slaves might know Makaria and Otanes could be so keen to keep hidden.

Later that evening, Lysanias and Sindron sat down and tried to list what they had achieved. Considering how little time they had had, it made a quite impressive list.

That it was murder was no longer merely a suspicion. There was evidence of a crime and a murderer had been seen, albeit by someone who thought it was one of the Furies.

They had the rope that Lysanias felt sure had supported the fatal amphora and it had been cut above the knot, proving someone had done the deed, but how could they make sure nothing happened to the other paraphernalia surrounding his uncle's death, the amphora itself and the bloodstained planks with the footprint, before they had found the real culprit and taken action? They just had to hope it would be safe under arrest at the shipyard and that the court would not act quickly.

They had Klereides' blood-stained cloak, but there was no sign of the message-scroll that had summoned him to his fatal assignation, though the watchman had verified that it had actually existed. Perhaps the murderer had taken it.

That was it, apart from widely conflicting opinions as to Klereides' character, trustworthiness and loyalties.

Ever logical, Sindron insisted they must consider the negatives as well as the positives, what people had avoided telling them.

At the house, they had been offered no real statement of the household's financial position, given no knowledge of where Klereides had kept contracts or details of investments, though the locked cupboard did seem a possibility.

On the business side, they had seen little financial information and nothing on the contractual relationship with Hermon. On top of that, Hermon flatly refused to say where he was at the time of Klereides death, while the explanation obtained from his slave didn't make sense.

Most puzzling was that Sindron's friend Lydos had omitted to mention that Klereides' account was held by the bank Lydos works for and to offer details. Though that did seem to be related to somewhat exaggerated fears of the general political situation. But where could Klereides fit into that?

And no-one at all had mentioned a will. Sindron had heard they were normal in Athens nowadays among wealthy families.

Lysanias looked petulant. "Why can't I just ask them all outright and insist?" he demanded.

Sindron sighed deeply. "It looks as though you may have to, but that risks giving unnecessary offence and, if you get a flat refusal then, you could be into force or official action which could take ages."

Silence reigned as they reclined on couches, frowns creasing their brows, as they tried to recall significant details of all that had happened, any detail they had overlooked. Lysanias bit into a pomegranate and felt the flesh and juice slide seductively down his throat. "Did you consider," he slurred through another mouthful, before swallowing. "Did you consider the significance of who came and didn't come to pay respects or to the funeral feast?"

"How could I? I wasn't around much of the time, so I never got to know who they were." Sindron was genuinely tired and a little irritable. He had done so much walking lately that his old joints were aching and his bad leg was throbbing. Thank the gods Lysanias seemed to be able to drop the master-slave relationship in private, and he could at least relax on a couch rather than stand all the time.

"Yes, but think about it." Lysanias swallowed the final mouthful. "No magistrates or other city officials came, which means they all stayed away. They can't all have been too busy."

The idea had started Sindron's memory working as well. "Ye-e-es. That naval architect said he had normally dealt with Klereides but he didn't come, did he?"

"That's what made me think of it. And Ariston is the only general who came."

"Ah, but he was in Klereides' old regiment. The others may not have known your uncle so well."

"Yes, but no other senior officers from the regiment came, except Hierokles. Ariston was the only leading politician too."

"Apart from Perikles' brief appearance," Sindron put in smartly, as though he was afraid Lysanias might have been too drunk to remember it.

"Which makes that even more surprising, don't you think?"

Sindron was pleased to see the way Lysanias' mind was developing. All those memory tests, the logic exercises he had given him as a boy hadn't been wasted after all. He helped himself to another fig.

"Not many from the financial community," he added, still chewing, "though it was the day of an important Assembly meeting, but even so…"

Lysanias pushed on to the conclusion to be drawn from his argument. "So, if we disregard token low level representatives, the bulk of them were people who couldn't afford to stay away like artists and athletes keen to hang on to their source of sponsorship."

Sindron completed the thought. "Or people who were tied to him for business reasons, owed him money or he owed them money. Merchants, traders, businessmen. You're right; it does make some sort of picture! The magistrates and army people would have attended the assembly meeting, of course. Even so, that wasn't all day."

Lysanias' expression showed he was pleased at Sindron's approval. Then it changed to one of puzzled disappointment. "But what does it mean?"

"The others don't want to be publicly associated with his name. That's the logical conclusion."

"But why? What has my uncle done to create that reaction? It's almost like ostracism within the city!" Suddenly he started and sat upright, startled by a new thought. "You don't think he was a traitor, do you? Strynises said Otanes was meeting Eastern people at the harbour. Dealing with the Persians? That's what Themistokles was ostracised for."

"You don't believe Themistokles did that, though, do you?"

Oh, no! He had given Sindron the cue for a discussion on history. That was the last thing Lysanias wanted! But automatically he responded.

"No, of course not! How could the victor of Salamis sell out the Greeks to Persia? Mind you, he didn't do much for his claims of innocence by taking refuge in Persia and accepting a princedom from the Great King, did he?" This was Sindron's favourite hobbyhorse and he wasn't going to let the slave have it all his own way.

"What choice did he have? If he'd gone anywhere else, the Athenians would have caught him and executed him, innocent or not."

Lysanias sighed. This wasn't what they should be discussing. "Look, Sindron, I was just giving it as an example. What do you think about Klereides being a traitor?"

The boy was getting irritated now and Sindron reacted rapidly to calm him. "I very much doubt it. If that was the case and they knew it, no-one at all would have come, but it must be something serious, more serious than anything we've heard about so far. Let's try to piece together the bad opinions we've heard."

CHAPTER 10

One thing Lysanias was sure of – he had to check out the scene of the murder for other evidence and to check if the murderer had left any physical signs of his presence apart from the footprint. Also a rigger must have hung the amphora and substituted the frayed rope for the cut one. It would be useful to find him – but, if he did, would the man talk?

If he arranged to visit the shipyard through Hermon, Lysanias knew he would be given an escort to hamper him. Then, as soon as they knew he was after something specific, he felt sure they might try to destroy it.

There could be one way. Lysanias would have to go in as a worker himself and find an opportunity to explore when no-one was looking. Stephanos! He would know how to organise that.

"What, that uncouth yob?" exclaimed Sindron, when Lysanias told him his plan, but he had to admit it made sense.

The next morning at dawn, there Lysanias was, approaching the hiring line on the southern slope of Market Hill, dressed in his worker's tunic, his tool bag slung from his shoulder, his ribbon tucked away inside it, breaking the rules again. Well, it depends whether one counts yesterday or today as the fourth day, he thought wryly. It felt strange to be again in the familiar garb, after the last few days playing the role of a wealthy heir. Now here he was pretending to be what he regarded as his real self, and with no Sindron to fall back on for advice. But it had felt good to be part of the early morning bustle and clatter of workers going to work, shopkeepers setting out their wares, laden mules and carts bringing in supplies from farms outside the city, and early shoppers determined to buy the freshest produce.

"Come on, hurry up, if you want work today," urged a burly, bronzed fellow who seemed to be in charge of the craftsmen's section. Lysanias quickened his pace, looking round for Stephanos, but Stephanos spotted him first and the heavy clap on the shoulder came from behind yet again. "Hi there, youngster. Never did believe that nonsense about a rich uncle. Come to earn an honest obol, eh?"

Lysanias spun round, a grin on his face, and automatically reached with his right hand to grasp Stephanos at the lower bicep as Stephanos did the same to him.

"So, you were in the Fellowship of Hephaistos in Eion then?"

"No, all craftsmen greeted one another that way," responded Lysanias honestly, and asked what the Fellowship was.

"You really don't know? You know who Hephaistos is, don't you?"

"God of smiths and other crafts."

"Patron god of us workers. The Fellowship, that's just those of us who worship Hephaistos at his shrine in Peiraieos. That's the greeting. This is the salute." He struck his clenched right fist down onto the side of the clenched left in the way Lysanias remembered Glaukon doing on the ship. Yes, he saw it now. Hammer and anvil. Symbols of Hephaistos, the heavenly blacksmith.

Stephanos was still explaining. "Only we've got it more organised now. That man in charge, he's one of our officials, not the city's. My father's helping him out today. We know what rates everyone's paying, which employers are trying to get it on the cheap by employing foreigners and slaves below full rate. Soon see about that now the Assembly's got the power."

He gestured to the workers standing round, many looking dispirited, bearing the scars and wounds of recent war service. "Been away so long their jobs have been filled by trained slaves and foreigners. The Fellowship's battling to get them back. Our great god Hephaistos is growing in power too. More followers every day. Foreign workers too. That way we have more chance of enforcing a rate for the job. That's his new temple they're building over there. One more thing we've got to thank Ephialtes for."

It was almost like hero-worship, the way he said Ephialtes' name. "Is it a political faction too, then? I've seen the slogans on the walls."

"No, lots of people think that. Ephialtes is one of our leading priests, a people's priest, and the Fellowship supports him and the radical party, but it's not the same thing. There's other groups support the radicals as well."

Lysanias forced the conversation onto his own concerns. He explained that he wanted to get employed by Hermon's shipyard. As soon as he said "shipyard", Stephanos reacted.

"You've come to the wrong place, citizen. Hiring line for the shipyards is down in the market place in Peiraieos, and anyway there's a surplus of shipyard workers at the moment. Didn't you know that?"

Lysanias looked dumbfounded. He felt defeated. Stephanos misinterpreted his expression.

"Cheer up. I'll get you a day's work with me. I've got a nice one lined up, fancy marble portico in a smart house but I need a carpenter to rig me a timber framework to support it. Falsework. Ever done that before?"

"Of course." His father had told him about the technique, but there really hadn't been much call for it in Eion.

"There you are then. I'll tell you where to go later, if you really want shipyard work."

Then the man in charge called them into line and he found himself standing with the other craftsmen, to be inspected by hirers, asked questions about their previous experience, even have their biceps felt.

A bulbous Phoenician slave waddled up with an affected accent and bangles on each wrist, the dark green and vivid yellow of his cloak clashing in a way no Athenian would have accepted. Glaukon was escorting him and glanced at Stephanos when he recognised Lysanias standing beside him. Somehow he seemed satisfied to see that Lysanias really was a worker. At a surreptitious hand signal from Stephanos, indicating the need for a carpenter, Glaukon changed his patter rapidly, "This here is the team I recommend, Hasdrubal. Ideal for your purposes." And they were hired. Only then did Lysanias realise that the team included a short, older, slightly hunched man with a missing finger on the left hand and crooked elbow, who had been standing the other side of Stephanos. Stephanos introduced him as his assistant, Lampon. "Have to find work for the veterans," he said in explanation.

As they followed the Phoenician into the wealthy quarter, Stephanos explained in worker's argot that it was a ritual. The slave's owner felt that he would save money by hiring fresh workers every day, but Hasdrubal wasn't so stupid as to dispense with reliable craftsmen once they had started a job, so he had to go through with the hiring routine every day. He accepted their opinion on whether extra skills were needed.

Lysanias tried to explain about his uncle's murder and his new-found wealth, but Stephanos wasn't interested. "Look, citizen, as far as I'm concerned, you're a worker, you stood up for me in the square, you're on the right side, you're a friend. Your personal business, that's nothing to do with me. You don't have to spin me these yarns to get me to help you. I owe you one and that's all there is."

While the colourfully-painted green and brown pillars of the eastern end of the Temple of Theseos were beginning to sparkle in the rising sun, the western face, where Sindron had been directed by an angry priest inside, was dark and gloomy. Behind the row of pillars, a small entrance stood open, its iron-barred gate pulled back. Beside it stood two large, muscular temple guards holding tridents with sharp-looking points. Weapons in the guise of religious icons, Sindron thought.

As Sindron approached, the guards crossed their tridents in front of him, barring him from entering. He explained that he was looking for Lydos, and gave his name. One of them called inside. Lydos appeared and ushered him in.

Adjusting to the oil lamps, Sindron saw to one side the temple treasures – gold, silver and bronze vessels for use in religious ceremonies, effigies, relics and ornate vestments for use in processions and festivals. Some of it appeared to be war trophies or booty, presumably donated or stored by Kimon and other generals. Lydos' assistant was bent over a large stone chest, counting coins into leather bags and placing these in a carrying case. The wooden chest of scrolls had already been removed.

Sindron's anger with his friend had accumulated. "Why didn't you tell me your bank held Klereides' account?" he blurted out, abruptly, without even the customary greeting.

Lydos appeared taken aback, but somehow it seemed put on. "My dear old friend, you are unkind. If you remember, there was hardly time, after you told me who your master was."

"That was your fault, not mine!"

"That may be. If so, I apologise. I take it you would like details. I assume you have brought authority from your master?" The eager enthusiasm of their previous meeting was gone. The banker was businesslike, even with a friend, as Sindron had anticipated, though Lydos turned aside for a moment to send the slave-boy off with a message, as though completing something previously under way.

Sindron had intended challenging why Lydos had reacted the way he had to mention of Klereides, but access to the accounts seemed more important now it was on offer. He showed his authority to act on Lysanias' behalf and proof of his master's citizen status.

When unrolled, the account scrolls were a mass of neatly-written figures and notations, but Lydos guided Sindron to the key points. He had to trust that he wasn't being guided away from anything significant. The account showed most of Klereides' funds committed, significant losses on some investments and a number of debts and an overall low balance, but Lydos then referred to a list of assets. This revealed that Klereides owned not only his house in Athens and the farm in the country but also Hermon's shipyard, Hermon's house, a share in a building contractor's company, one hundred slaves leased to the silver mines at Laurion, five cargoes currently at sea, and two merchant ships jointly with their captains – more than enough to cover any losses. It was staggering, and now it was Sindron's own master who owned all this!

Sindron asked if the bank held the contracts and deeds relating to these, and discovered they had only the contracts for cargoes and those with the mine-owners and ship's captains, not the long-term contracts with businessmen or any title deeds.

"I imagine Klereides had a private arrangement with another temple for depositing those and other valuables. It's not uncommon." Lydos made it sound very matter of fact, but surely Klereides would have told someone about it.

"This is the cash account. We top that up directly from the percentage payments from Hermon, and Klereides' steward Otanes has direct access to that for withdrawals for household expenses, to pay sponsorship monies, and so on. Again perfectly normal procedure."

If it was all in order, why had Lydos as good as thrown him out the other day? Sindron began to steel himself to ask.

The light coming in through the doorway had increased as the sun rose higher, but now, suddenly, it was blocked out. Almost filling the doorway, was the giant frame of Phraston.

Without a pause, Phraston stepped forward with the smile of greeting as though Sindron were a citizen rather than a slave. Sindron found he liked the sensation.

"Ah, Sindron, isn't it? Lydos has told me about you and mentioned you might be coming in. I wonder if I might have a word."

Phraston drew him toward the far corner of the room, while Sindron observed that Lydos took up a position by the door, presumably to stall anyone wishing to enter. This must at the least have been anticipated if not planned. That message the slave-boy had taken, maybe.

Still surprised, Sindron muttered, "Of course." Then decided to respond in kind. "Lydos told me much about you, sir." Better keep a tone of respect, he thought. "I was sorry to hear about your son." Then, to try to get off the subject of death, "I was around in the old days and remember your wrestling triumphs well."

"Ah, long, long ago, but thank you." The man looked pleased that someone should remember, when so many years, so many champions had intervened. "Now, to business. I gather you will be principal adviser to Klereides' heir, young Lysanias. I'm sure you will have considerable influence over him. Good that he has someone he can trust so completely." Sindron felt like saying that Lysanias was quite capable of making his own decisions – and of ignoring any advice Sindron might give, but clearly that wasn't what Phraston wanted to hear right now and the reference to trust implied he might know about the cargo loan, throwing Sindron a little. He merely inclined his head, in a way that did not contradict Phraston's statement.

"On the financial front, of course, we would be very pleased, if he were to leave his account with our bank. I would be willing to continue to offer financial advice relating to investments and asset purchases, as I did for Klereides. Perhaps you could let him know that." Something told Sindron this might not be true. After all, significant elements of Klereides' dealings were not here and, surely, a trusted adviser would have been just that, trusted. With everything. For some reason, Klereides had felt safer keeping certain things under his personal control.

Phraston did not wait for a response, perhaps assuming he was stating the obvious. "But, ah, could I offer a few suggestions?" There were beads of sweat on the man's forehead, Sindron observed, yet it was still cool in the treasury. Perhaps Phraston always sweated.

"Death of Klereides. Sad business. But young Lysanias trying to prove it was murder. Going round asking questions. Could cause trouble, you understand? Delicate time politically. Powerful interests at stake. These radicals could find some way of using such a story, allege corruption, you understand? Blacken Klereides' name and his associates. No-one wants that. A man in your position. You could persuade him to accept that it was an accident and stop asking questions, at least until things settle down politically."

His tone had been neutral. Now Phraston's voice mellowed, became friendly again. "Of course, I'd show my gratitude. We'd create a small account in your name. Regular monthly deposits. Assist you to make wise investments. A little security for the future. Something to cover any little, ah, debts you may have incurred recently. Perhaps, in return, you could keep me informed on your master's thinking. Not disloyalty, you understand, just a sharing of confidences, hmm?"

Sindron was appalled. First, something like a veiled threat about the cargo loan, and now he was being offered a bribe to betray his master. The sense of honour that he had always felt came first in Athens, where had that gone? Yet Phraston, and Lydos behind him, clearly saw this as nothing exceptional and anticipated that Sindron would accept. It said a lot about the moral climate of Athens.

He was even more horrified to realise that he found the offer tempting. He was getting old. His master was erratic enough to sell him off in a fit of pique. It would be nice to have that security, maybe even enough to buy his freedom if necessary. But no, his own upbringing would not allow him to consider this.

"I'm afraid that would be impossible, I..."

Phraston was prepared for this. "Quite so, quite so. Lydos told me you were always a man of principle. What I like to see. Loyalty in a trusted slave, too. Only what I expect from Lydos." It didn't stop him pursuing it.

"What if you were no longer in Lysanias' employment? Say I were to offer to buy your freedom. No strings, no strings at all, though I could then offer a good position with the bank."

Lydos took the cue, revealing himself as an active partner in the enterprise. He suggested that they were looking to open a table down by the harbour to expand their business relating to cargoes and would need someone to run it. "Strictly between ourselves at the moment, you understand, don't want to alert the other bankers before we're ready." He smiled, giving the impression Sindron was a trusted colleague already. What was going on?

Sindron tried to maintain his neutral expression. Why had he personally become so important? He had no knowledge of banking. How could he be a useful colleague in a bank? But a senior position, maybe a partnership! Sindron opened his mouth to reply and shut it again, not knowing how to answer.

Lydos read this sign of indecision. "Don't be hasty, old friend. Think about it. After all, you've that cargo loan of yours to think about too. Wouldn't want that to go nasty on you, would we? Or your master to hear about it? Let us know later. Maybe tomorrow morning."

So these two had discussed the offer together. Lydos must have advised Phraston on how to approach him, read the tinge of envy he had felt the other day at Lydos' good news. Sindron felt a little weak at the knees and grasped his stick more firmly for support.

"Yesss." The word almost slithered out of his mouth, like a snake, betraying him. "The offer, it's very generous, but it's ... so sudden, so unexpected. I'll have to think. Thank you."

Then he was out in the bright sunlight, his old eyes blinking and watering. He had seen the glint in their eyes, the quick glance at one another. They thought they had bought him! Now he knew why Lydos had tricked him into making that loan – to have a hold over him, a lever. His one-time friend really did think well ahead and even before he knew who Sindron's master was! Was it possible that, from Lydos' weird point of view, he thought he was looking after Sindron's best interests?

No, he would not be a party to this commercial corruption that seemed to surround him and his master! He would tell his master as soon as he had an opportunity. Lysanias might then increase payments to him to allow him to save to buy his freedom.

He stopped himself. There I go, thinking like them, he thought. All the same, I'd be silly not to see I get something out of all this.

He wondered if Lydos' reference to Sindron's loan was a veiled threat that he would tell Lysanias. His security in being a slave was crumbling around him. He was being asked to make decisions for himself about himself. He had to get back to the safety of the house, where he knew who he was.

I'm not worth that to them, Sindron thought. They must think I'm the only thing that could bring Lysanias success in his investigations. Very flattering! That could mean we are getting close to the truth but could it also mean they have some connection with Klereides' murder? That's inconceivable. No, must just be, as they say, a general wish for no-one to stir up trouble. But why so determined? And how did they know about the questioning? Who had told them? Someone from the shipyard? Or the tavern? Or the house?

The frontage of the house looked fairly plain, very little different from Klereides' house, though Lysanias didn't fancy the pink colour himself, the colour the flesh of statues was painted. Inside was a different story.

Stephanos explained, in sarcastic tones, that the wealthy of Athens kept to the letter of the laws against ostentation that might create jealousy among the poorer classes on all the visible parts of their houses, but inside, where only their friends could see, they pleased themselves. Here, slabs of marble and quartz covered every surface and the crowning glory was to be the portico with fluted stone pillars that Stephanos was erecting at the entrance from the courtyard to the inner apartments.

"Stop goggling, man! They aren't paying us to stand around." Stephanos the gossip became Stephanos the busy craftsman. He explained what he wanted Lysanias to do, which was basically to complete the supporting structure started by another carpenter the previous day. Lysanias hadn't actually done falsework before but his father had explained it, so Lysanias didn't feel intimidated. Just so long as it could hold the weight of the stone.

It felt so good to be back using his brain and his hands in a common task. His hammer sounded loud and clear, with the creaks and pants as Stephanos and Lampon set up the winch.

Lysanias asked Stephanos, "Whose house do you reckon this is, then?"

To his surprise, Stephanos burst out in a raucous belly laugh. His assistant was laughing too. Lysanias blushed bright crimson.

"What did I say that's so funny?"

Stephanos struggled to regain control. "Didn't you notice the statue of Aphrodite by the front door, goddess of rumpty-tumpty? And the house front? Painted pink?

"Well, yes, but..."

"It's a whore's house, Lysanias! High class whore! 'Companion' the rich call them. But they're still whores." Lysanias noticed Stephanos had dropped his voice to avoid being heard by the customer and giving offence. "Never heard of Aspasia from Miletos, the most famous 'companion' in Athens?"

Lysanias hadn't but decided he should look as though he had.

"Her house? Did she buy all this?"

"No, stupid, her 'gentlemen friends' pay. Thank-you gifts for services rendered. This marble portico now, that's a present from General Ariston, Kimon's right-hand man. That was his steward that hired us."

Lysanias was stunned for a moment. "But Ariston detests Ephialtes. How could you work for him?"

"All citizens are equal, citizen! Besides you have to earn a living. Get to being too choosy and you starve. Anyway, you'd be surprised what snippets of information we pick up by keeping our heads down and our ears open." He winked at Lysanias.

"But Ariston knew... He's not likely to come here is he?" Lysanias wasn't sure why he was suddenly so worried. Whether it was the thought of the social disgrace of being found doing a manual job when he was heir to wealth, or of being fully revealed to Stephanos as not really a worker at all.

Stephanos seemed unconcerned. "Not during the day. Too busy playing politics trying to save Kimon. Anyway, no need to worry. These bastards, they don't really see us workers. We all look the same to them!"

Lysanias was relieved. He hammered a brace into position, nailing it firmly. "What's she like then, this 'companion'?"

"Keep your eyes open and you'll probably see her – and she is an eyeful too!" Lysanias had to grin as Stephanos made the gesture with a rising fist that workers in Eion had made when they talked about an attractive woman.

After a spell, while they all worked away in silence, Lysanias started wondering why the other carpenter wasn't here today.

"Oh, he's on guard duty," said Stephanos matter-of-factly. "Looking after Ephialtes."

He explained that Perikles felt that Ephialtes could be in danger, so workers close to the leaders took it in turns to take a day off and keep Ephialtes company in case of trouble, as they had done in the market place.

"Is that really necessary? In Athens of all places? We vote to exile people we think are a danger, don't we?"

"Oh, we will. We'll ostracise Kimon. But he's only one of them and just because assassination hasn't happened often in the past, doesn't mean it's not possible, even if they are frightened of the pollution that attaches to a murderer. Ephialtes has upset a lot of powerful people."

It could be disguised not to look like assassination, Lysanias thought. Was that what had happened to his uncle?

"... difficult though," Stephanos went on. "He refuses to have a bodyguard so we have to fool him. Someone has to walk with him, keep him in conversation, while the others sort of hover in the background, ready to leap in if anyone attacks him. So far, so good. One incident with a runaway chariot but our boys pushed him out of the way, and an unexplained fire at one of the places where the leaders meet."

Lysanias hesitated, then decided he had to ask. "Stephanos?" He tried to make it sound casual. "Stephanos, your uh defence squad. Would that ever take action first? Attack anyone? Kill them?"

Stephanos seemed a little surprised at the question but answered without hesitation.

"No, purely defensive. Have to be ready."

"Not even if you thought someone was a threat?"

"No, not our style. Hasn't happened yet anyway. Hey up! That's the doorknocker. You'll see her now."

It wasn't Aspasia's looks so much as the way she held herself and moved that made Lysanias grab hold of a post to stop himself from falling. She seemed to float without effort across the courtyard. The paleness of her face and arms were set off by the bright but tasteful light blue and green cloak, and the thoughtful features settled into a welcoming softness as she adopted a subtle smile to greet the visitors.

Welcomes were effusive but, though it was difficult to be sure looking down on them from above, these men, in smart, well-draped cloaks, seemed furtive, with glances back towards the doorway, until they were sure it was firmly closed behind them. Aspasia ushered them hurriedly into a room to one side, then came out again and closed the door behind her. One of the men, Lysanias was sure, was General Ariston, though it was the first time he had seen him out of uniform. Another looked as though he could be Hierokles. And that plaited hairstyle was like the one he had seen in the barber's shop.

Lysanias climbed down and whispered to Stephanos. "I must try to hear what they're saying. I think I recognise one of them."

"You and me both! They're all high in Kimon's faction."

"But we can't both stop work, they'll soon notice the hammering has stopped."

"True, citizen. We'll take it in turns. You first, but be careful! I'll try to signal if I hear anyone coming."

Lysanias took a rope measure from his bag, with knots at intervals, and pretended to be measuring the doorway, in case a household slave passed. But the voices inside were low; it was difficult to hear anything. He thought he caught "...only course left..." and "... surprise, that's the thing." That in his cousin's voice, it seemed. And "... t-t-take the bull by the h-horns, I say..." louder, more agitated. Voices he had heard in the barber's, the stammer, the full rich tones, and another, higher and sharper. Then it happened.

"Hello, who's the pretty spy then?" The voice was mellow and tuneful. He looked into twinkling, laughing, very knowing blue eyes. "I really didn't order any work on that doorway, so it's no use pretending."

Aspasia reached out and took his ear between her thumb and forefinger and twisted. He couldn't believe that anyone who looked so gentle could inflict so much pain.

"Come, now, come with me! That's the way!" She deliberately held his head low and at arm's length, so that he was forced to shuffle and couldn't look up or signal to Stephanos. "Your friends are in on the game, I imagine, but I'll deal with them later."

Philia was puzzled. Makaria was resting, so there was no-one that Philia could ask about the ritual complications of her tasks. Maybe if she crept into Makaria's room, the old woman would give her advice on how to polish Apollo's bronze shield and helmet without giving the god the impression the household felt he was tarnished. She tiptoed towards Makaria's door, in the women's quarters upstairs. She had intended to listen for the rhythmic breathing of sleep, in which case she would leave it till later, but the moans and pants and slapping sounds of flesh on flesh were not those of sleep or rest. But who? Then she realised that Otanes hadn't been prowling round in his usual bossy way. She was shocked. So Nubis had been right all along! Philia found herself being coldly calculating. Could this knowledge be a weapon in gaining more say in the running of the household?

Rushing, from the women's section of the house, she was startled to see Sindron watching her through the doorway from the courtyard.

Nubis had told her about her encounter with Sindron. From Nubis' description, the old man sounded a lot less severe than he looked, and Lysanias seemed to trust him. This might be her chance to get rid of that constant fear of Makaria discovering the bloodstained scroll at the bottom of the cypress chest under Philia's best gown. She just hoped there was no pollution attaching to it that might affect her – she had washed her hands to purify herself and hoped that was enough.

Philia could hear the kitchen boy chopping onions and sniffing in the kitchen nearby, so she whispered to Sindron as she passed him, "I'm going back to the shrine room. Come there in a few minutes." She didn't glance back, so she didn't see the look of surprise on Sindron's face.

All was quiet, except for the clack of the looms and the kitchen sounds that filtered through the house. Philia decided she had to risk it. She sped as quietly as she could up to her bedroom, delved deep into the chest for the blood-stained scroll, wrapped it in a shawl, and, looking ahead of her carefully, stepped silently down the stairs. Placing the shawl before her, Philia knelt at the shrine to the ancestors of this family she had married into, asking their forgiveness for treating their shrine in this way, and pleading for their help in finding who had done this to her Curly, their Klereides.

Sindron appeared in the doorway. "What's this, mistress?" he began, dignified but friendly, a smile on his face, but he grew serious, when she raised a finger to her lips.

"Look," she whispered, and, indicating the shawl in front of her, unwrapped it to reveal the crumpled, bloodstained, fire-scorched scroll.

"The message! It still exists!" Sindron had adopted a low tone to match her own, but he was clearly excited. He glanced over his shoulder, aware that they could be interrupted at any moment.

"Take it, hide it, give it to Lysanias, please!" She was urgent, desperate to get rid of the responsibility.

"Yes, of course." Sindron seemed a little dazed. "Can I take the shawl? I'll give it back."

Philia nodded. He re-folded and picked up the slim package delicately, afraid the parchment might crumble. It was small enough to slip inside the front of his cloak.

"What was going on back there?" he asked.

Philia realised it could be useful to her if Lysanias knew.

"Makaria and Otanes, in bed together," she blurted out, blushing and looking down, realising what she was talking about, and to a man! Even if he was a slave. Sindron looked as though he was going to say something. His mouth opened but all that came out was "Oh!" He left, clutching the front of his cloak where the message-scroll was concealed.

Thinking of what Philia had told him, Sindron shuddered at the thought of having an affair with Makaria but everyone to his taste. Amazing what some slaves will do to ensure their status. Lysanias' mother now – he had always admired her and now she was free. But that's a disloyal thought, he told himself, and dismissed it.

Philia busied herself, red-faced with guilt, at the shrines, her hands shaking.

Then Sindron was back. He knelt beside her, apparently joining in the ritual, and returned the shawl. Then he whispered. "Mistress Philia, Lysanias will be very pleased, but maybe you can do more. We need to know what Otanes is hiding from us." He gave her a quick impression of the missing areas in their knowledge. "Just if you get a chance to find out anything. They may be less suspicious of you."

Philia felt very pleased. Someone treating her as an adult, taking her into their confidence, and Lysanias' adviser at that. She listened carefully.

Then Philia heard the pat-pat of Nubis' feet as Glykera sent her out to check on the sundial in the outer courtyard. "They'll be stopping work soon," she interrupted Sindron. He paused listening. The sound of the looms stopped, and voices started to chatter.

"Anything you can find out," whispered Sindron. "Leave it behind the Hestia here."

"I can't ... That would be sacrilege..." Philia started to say, but Sindron had gone through to the kitchen and the outer courtyard to show his presence. Perhaps he also hoped that someone might take the opportunity to give him some information about the night of Klereides' death.

Down a corridor and into a room but all Lysanias found himself looking at was the mosaics on the floors. Then Aspasia released his ear. He slowly raised his head and stared. It was beautiful! The room glowed.

Lighted oil lamps at carefully selected points shone through the gauze and lace draperies round the bed, in delicate shades of white and blue and green, clearly Aspasia's personal colour range.

As she moved round in front of him, the brightness of the colours she wore stood out against their pale relations in a way that made her seem the centre of the universe, like Aphrodite amidst the waves, the subject of the painting on the far wall.

Lysanias realised his eyes were staring and his mouth was hanging open. "It's lovely," he said, almost to himself.

"My, we do have a country innocent here! Never been in a lady's bedchamber before? That's not an Athenian accent is it?"

Lysanias hadn't realised his accent stood out so readily. "No, I've lived in Eion ... for years."

Should he have told her that? He knew he should take the initiative somehow, but nothing would come into his head. He was dazed.

"A Kimon man then. So why would you want to eavesdrop on Kimon's supporters? It's only a political meeting, you know. One of the few places a faction can meet in reasonable secrecy is Aspasia's place, and you set out to ruin my reputation for discretion. Who do you think you are, young man? You've got worker's hands..." and she took his hands in hers and felt the rough skin from constant handling of hammers and saws ... and worker's shoulders ..." and her hand moved to his exposed right shoulder, gently stroking the bronzed skin. The softness and gentleness of her touch sent a thrill through his body and Lysanias pulled away sharply and stepped back.

"But not a worker's voice or way of talking. You've been educated. You'd better talk, my young virgin! You are a virgin, aren't you? Or I'll have to tell the General and he won't be at all pleased." The young woman's self-assurance was threatening.

Lysanias realised the truth was unbelievable but couldn't think of a convincing lie. At least it was a story he knew and, if he could keep her talking, perhaps Stephanos would have a chance to overhear what was really going on in that room.

"It's nothing to do with politics," he blurted out. "I think my uncle, Klereides the shipbuilder, was murdered, and the General was his friend, and I have to suspect everyone, so I thought I might learn something if I could listen in. I must find who did it and avenge my uncle before the gods." He knew, as he said it, that he sounded very naive and inexperienced in the ways of the world, but maybe that was the best way to appear.

"Klereides! Then you're Lysanias, son of Leokhares! That fantastic funeral feast that everyone's talking about! With the drunken brawl and the sacrilegious carving! You really are the talk of the town, young man, and, at a time like this, that's really something."

"You ... you've heard of me?"

"Yes, of course, everyone's heard of you. People laugh but they see that you know how to handle yourself. They'll respect you."

Embarrassed at first, at the thought that all Athens was laughing about him, he looked at her and she smiled in a way that showed acceptance into her charmed circle. Lysanias had to smile back.

"We've got a secret now, haven't we? No-one else knows you're also a skilled carpenter. How delightful, one of the very wealthy of Athens, with aristocrats and well-born fawning all over you, and you work as a day-labourer for little Aspasia. What a grand joke!" He didn't know whether to look pleased or humiliated. "Don't worry, I won't tell anyone. It's our secret," she said.

"Do you know anything?" His voice was urgent.

"I know all that there is to know, young man." Her voice purred with invitation and innuendo. The hair bristled on the back of his neck but was she making fun of him? She reached out and stroked his cheek. "You are a pretty boy, and young and strong and a virgin. I really must do something about your education very soon."

Aspasia's voice suddenly changed and became businesslike. "You are right to trust no-one in this city. I don't know anything about your uncle's death but I do know a lot about the underhand dealings these people are into that could have got your uncle into trouble. I'm not sure why I should help you, but things are changing, new people are taking power, maybe they'll clean things up. Now listen..."

"Mistress, the gentlemen have finished." The Nubian doorkeeper had appeared at the door.

Still businesslike, Aspasia dismissed him. "I'll have to offer them refreshments. Can you come back tomorrow evening? And stay dressed like that, so as not to arouse suspicion," she added. "Now go!"

The slave led the way and Lysanias had enough composure to walk out confidently, though he could feel himself shaking inwardly with the excitement and sexual titillation of the encounter. But no-one was looking.

The door to the room where the Kimon men had met was open and he could hear joking and laughter that sounded just a little strained. Stephanos and his assistant were hauling at the rope to raise a marble slab for the portico. Lysanias stepped forward to help them.

"Thank the gods you're back," Stephanos welcomed him. "Hold this while I go up and steady the slab into position."

As though nothing had happened! Then Stephanos winked at him and pressed a finger to his lips.

"Right! All hands to the winch it is."

It wasn't till they broke off for a snack and rest in the heat of the day in Aspasia's ornamental garden that they had a chance to talk. Lysanias was surprised to find how hungry he was.

Stephanos nudged him. "How'd you get on then? Did she give you a free one?" Lysanias wasn't sure he could match the vulgarity.

"No such luck. Not for the likes of us, is she? She thought I was spying but I talked my way out of it." Better not tell Stephanos what really happened; he'd never believe it. "Did you find out anything?"

"After you were led off, we had to pretend that, whatever you were up to, we didn't know anything about it," recounted Stephanos. "She put that black slave on the door to watch us, so all we could do was walk past close to him occasionally. An aggressive young aristo arrived late, hammering on the door, demanding to join in. Nearly knocked Lampon off his ladder as be barged through.

"Then they started yelling and shouting in there. 'The High City!' 'No, no, they can surround us there, like they did with Kylon back in the old days!'"

Lampon chipped in, "One of them said, 'The Council House and the main city gates, that'd frighten them.'"

Stephanos came back, putting on an educated accent, "'And the arsenal at Munychia, we'll need that.'"

Lampon did the same and added the stutter Lysanias remembered well, "'B-but w-we haven't g-got enough m-men for all that.'"

Then Stephanos, booming in a good imitation of Ariston's deep voice, "'Quiet all of you, I'm the general here.'"

They all laughed. Stephanos went on, serious again. "Those are just the bits we heard. They got quieter after that. Then, a bit later, there was a cheer and someone threw the doors open."

"Doesn't make sense to me," Lysanias said. "What do you make of it?"

"Well, I don't think they're planning the route of a religious procession. Most likely they think they can seize power and force us back under rich man's rule. Well, two can play at that game. Our boys'll put guards on the main buildings and double our protection of Ephialtes and the other leaders. These plotters realise they haven't enough men to grab control of everything. Not till those troops get back from Sparta anyway. That's good news. Have to tell Perikles. He'll think of a way to stop them."

"You make it sound as though you've been expecting it."

"Well ... Perikles has, and some of the other leaders but Ephialtes won't listen. 'We've got the people with us,' he says. 'No reactionary force can stop the march of true democracy now. The people won't allow it.' Well, maybe they won't but it's best to be prepared. That's what Perikles says. Right, let's go!"

"Where?"

"To warn Perikles."

"What about getting me work in the shipyard?"

"You selfish oaf, this is about whether we keep democracy or not. Not about where you work."

"It's just that you said..."

"Tomorrow not today. But I can show you where to go – it's near there. That do?"

Lysanias nodded. His memory had flashed back to the gossip he had overheard in the barber's shop. He told Stephanos how it had suddenly gone silent, when the master barber had asked why they didn't do something about Ephialtes, if they felt he was so terrible. "As though they had been planning just that. One of this lot was there, the one with the plaited hairstyle, I'd swear it. And there was one with a stutter."

"What! And you didn't tell me!" Stephanos looked really annoyed and Lysanias felt embarrassed and guilty.

"Cheer up! We're not beaten yet. All the more reason to tell Perikles."

Stephanos knew that the radical leaders were at a meeting in Peiraieos, so they set off to run there, leaving Lampon to rest in the heat of the day and make excuses if they were late back.

CHAPTER 11

This is silly, Philia thought. The ideal opportunity to search that chest in Otanes' room and Sindron is eating with Glykera and the others in the kitchen and I can't tell him. She'd heard snoring from Makaria's room; they were both still in there.

Perhaps he found Makaria's affair as embarrassing as Philia did. How could she do that? With a slave! Philia stopped the thought process before she became too intrigued about who had seduced whom.

Over lunch in the inner courtyard, playing with the dog, she decided she would have to trust Nubis. With difficulty she persuaded her to join the search.

"But what if we're caught?" Nubis' tone was plaintive. She was clearly worried.

So was Philia. "Lysanias will protect us." Philia sounded more confident than she felt. Let's hope Makaria and Otanes don't suddenly feel hungry and come out, Philia prayed to herself.

Otanes' room was in the male slaves' quarters directly off the inner courtyard. The door opened easily, and Philia posted Nubis by the door to keep watch. She found the chest where Sindron had described it, and still unlocked, but the lid was very heavy. She had to call Nubis over to help lift it. Then she sent her back to the door. There were so many scrolls, where would she start? Philia lifted out one at random, grubby from frequent handling. She didn't have to unroll it far to see it was the basic household accounts, purchases of food and household items. She put it back as she had found it.

The second one proved to be the record of sponsorship payments to artists and athletes. She whistled through her teeth at the amounts. Nubis was at her shoulder. "What is it? What have you found?"

Philia explained. Then she realised no one was on lookout, and persuaded Nubis to return to her post. Philia was getting annoyed and increasingly nervous. Her fingers shook as she unrolled the next scroll.

"Someone's coming," hissed Nubis. "I'm going."

Startled, Philia realised her position. She couldn't run. She had to get the scroll back and the chest closed to look normal. What could she do? Her hands fluttered as she tried to re-tie the scroll.

"Ha! I had you frightened then, didn't I?"

"You little…!" Relieved, Philia joined in Nubis' laughter, though her hands were still shaking and her heart beating madly. "Is it really safe?"

"Yes, no one about. But hurry. I don't like this."

Philia felt like putting the scrolls away and leaving. It wasn't worth this level of constant fright. She nerved herself and unrolled the scroll again. It was the trading account from the workroom, woven material, sold to that man with the donkey who calls. All the sums of money he'd paid. Monthly totals, then yearly totals.

"What's this on the wall?" Nubis away from her watching post again. Annoyed, Philia turned to scold her.

Nubis had lifted a parchment with a drawing of some Persian god, attached to a rod and hanging by a thong from a nail in the wall.

"Just some old … Hey, what's that on the back? "

It was another parchment but with clear, bold lettering in Greek. Nubis held it up while Philia spelled out the wording for herself. Nubis peeped round the side. "What's it say?"

It seemed to be a contract, or no, a lease for the foundry in Armourer's Alley, site and controlling interest in the business, down to Otanes. She knew slaves and foreigners couldn't own property but could they lease it? Philia didn't know. There, that was the purchase price, for the lease and the rent near the bottom. Where had Otanes found all that money?

They heard the sound of sandaled footsteps.

"Nubis, I told you to look out!"

Philia's heart raced. She knew it must be too late. They managed to put the parchment back on the wall, then had to turn it the right way round.

The footsteps had stopped. Whoever it was must have heard them. Philia turned to put the scroll back in the chest, her hands shaking.

"It's only Sindron." Nubis voice was squeaky.

Sindron fell into the conspiracy immediately, though it bothered him that Nubis was involved. He still wasn't sure she could be trusted, but he congratulated them both on their initiative. From the sums involved and the use they had been put to, he could see now that Otanes really did have things to hide, but it didn't seem to have anything to do with Klereides' murder. A degree of embezzlement maybe, but no more. Then Sindron suddenly felt his own guilt. Tarred with the same brush.

"I can hear Otanes' voice in the kitchen," squeaked Nubis. "I'm going."

No trick this time. She really had gone, her feet pattering hurriedly down the passage. Sindron confidently re-rolled and tied the scroll.

"My room is nearby," he said. "Wait in there, till you're sure it's clear." He pointed to the doorway to his room, and was gone as well.

What a pokey little room, Philia thought. I'm glad I'm not a slave. Only a rug hanging to close the doorway. Shared too, two beds. She sat on one of the beds. She would be missed soon if she didn't reappear in the front of the house. At least her hands were steady again.

She looked out. No-one there. She walked casually along the passage towards the yard, as though she was doing nothing unusual. She would be back in the yard soon and could pretend she had been sitting there all along.

"Hello, young lady, we've been looking for you!" It was Makaria in all her fury. "Where do you think you've been?"

This time Philia was ready. She had worked out her story. "You never showed me the slave quarters. I thought I'd explore."

The old woman was clearly startled at this. "That's the male slaves' area. Respectable young women don't go in there."

"Oh, don't they?" Philia asked innocently. "I won't go again. Just boring little rooms." She whispered confidingly, "Don't have many personal ornaments and things, do they?"

"No, of course not! They're slaves."

It had worked. She had caught the old woman up in her tale and made it plausible.

"I'll get back to the shrines. One more to do." Philia strolled off nonchalantly, leaving a frowning and thoughtful Makaria.

"If you want to see more of the house, you have only to ask," Makaria called after her. "I'll be pleased to show you around."

Philia turned her head back. "Oh, I wouldn't dream of disturbing you, mother-in-law, not when you're not feeling well and need to … ah … rest." Despite Philia's efforts to control her expression, Makaria reacted to the tinge of sarcasm. Good, thought Philia. Let her wonder if I know. Let her worry for once!

Lysanias and Stephanos leaned against a tree for a moment, grinning at one another and getting their breath back after the long run from the city. In the space in front of the shrine of Hephaistos at Peiraieos, a stumpy, deep-voiced man with a massively-muscled torso was haranguing a crowd of workers on the dangers of warmongers like Kimon and the benefits of peace, and advocating the use of public money to create work for citizens. Stephanos explained that these workers, many of them from the shipyards, were 'Brothers of Kedalion', named after the mythical helper of Hephaistos, who led prayers to the god in their workplace every morning. They would go back to rouse their fellow workers into attending the Assembly meeting and voting to ostracise Kimon.

"You are all citizens. You are all entitled to a share of this wealth, not just the noble families." Arkhestratos, who had been chief trainer of rowers during the war, was now champion of their interests, Stephanos whispered.

Lysanias was reluctant to accompany Stephanos inside the shrine building to the meeting of the party leaders, fearful that Perikles might recognise him, but Stephanos insisted that he needed Lysanias to back him up.

After a word from Stephanos, the muscular workers standing guard at the door looked alarmed and ushered them inside. Perikles was speaking, stressing the urgency of getting rid of Kimon if they wanted to avoid further efforts to reverse the reforms.

As Lysanias' eyes adjusted from the sunshine outside, he could make out Perikles and Ephialtes. "That's General Myronides, the serious-looking one with the grey temples," Stephanos murmured. "Most senior general after Kimon, good we've got him on our side. That's Aeschylos, the playwright, and Damon, the musician." He grew excited and blurted out, "And that wrinkly old one, dressed like a foreign merchant, that's Themist…" he stopped himself suddenly. Then, from the look of startled surprise on Lysanias' face, realised it was too late. Lysanias knew it was Themistokles, past leader of the radicals and victor of Salamis, who everyone thought was in exile in in Persia.

"But he's under sentence of death!"

"Yes, so you swear not to tell anyone or you may not be allowed to leave." He looked deadly serious now. "I shouldn't have told you."

Lysanias nodded seriously, appreciating the trust placed in him. The guard urged Stephanos forward and he whispered in Perikles' ear. Lysanias heard Stephanos say, "This brother saw and heard them as well." And Perikles' eyes had turned and locked onto his own. He was sure the man recognised him but nothing in the steely gaze betrayed that fact.

Perikles made Stephanos repeat his information out loud and Lysanias was asked to verify it. Then the group was back into deep discussion, talking low. In the urgency of the moment, they seemed to have forgotten he and Stephanos were present.

Ephialtes argued for caution. "We mustn't be provocative," he suggested. "If we organise like an army, we only encourage them to do the same and that ends in civil war."

Themistokles reacted angrily, his forcefulness belying his years. He attacked them for not learning from his experience of allowing the aristocrats enough leeway to undermine him. "If we don't protect ourselves against Kimon's men, we're done for."

"I really must protest. This is most melodramatic." Ephialtes was still not persuaded, but he heard Arkhestratos from outside rounding off his speech and rose from his seat. "Time for me to conclude the event," he said. "Perikles knows my views and can speak for me." Lysanias saw now that he was dressed in a costume similar to representations of the god Hephaistos, presumably for his part in the religious ceremony outside.

The heated debate continued after his departure. Themistokles pushed for striking while citizens were still offended by the Spartan snub of dismissing the Athenian siege force without an explanation before the siege was broken. This prompted Perikles to question Themistokles whether he had anything to do with that. "No, no, purest luck." However, in denying it, he did confide that he had influenced the Corinthian decision to block the return of Kimon's troops. Response from the younger men was amused, but the older ones were angry that he had gone behind their backs in this way. Their resentment glowed.

"You would never have agreed in time," he retorted, displaying the arrogance he was credited with in the old days, thought Lysanias. "Let's hope they can hold them long enough."

Perikles capped him. "There are rumours Kimon has ridden to Corinth to negotiate their passage, so it may be touch and go."

Ephialtes' voice boomed from outside. "Brothers, never doubt, the hammer of Hephaistos will smite the corrupt and decadent rich." "All praise to Hephaistos," came the roar from the crowd. Could that really be Ephialtes who had seemed so docile in discussion?

Inside the group got down to planning, guided by the generals Myronides and Perikles. How they could strengthen Ephialtes' informal bodyguard, take steps to forestall any attempt at a takeover of key points, organise weapons and use of tools as weapons. Themistokles nodded, evidently pleased to see practical minds at work. Worry at the seriousness of the situation was written on all their faces except Myronides'. An ordinary-looking man, not at all like a general, he nonetheless exuded authority and confidence in his ability to deal with it.

Perikles suggested a rota system to cover all hours and a way of keeping watch during the nights. They ran through possible alarm signals to alert everyone whenever Kimon's supporters struck, using factory gate gongs and even kicking household donkeys and dogs to make them bray and bark.

Caught up in the discussion, Lysanias felt the urge to contribute. "Where I come from, if anyone saw a raiding party approaching, we had to put two fingers in our mouths and whistle like this." And he did it, making everyone jump. Two shorts and a long. All eyes turned on him, registering that he was not a regular party activist. Stephanos jumped in, calming their doubts. "It's all right, comrades, he's a friend of mine. He's sound. Remember? He saved my life, in the square."

"I can vouch for him too," said Perikles, simply and finally. Lysanias didn't miss the sudden question in Stephanos' eyes.

As they once more ignored him, he realised the strangeness of his situation, in the middle of discussions aimed to stave off a civil war. Then he recalled his real purpose was to find his uncle's murderer and bring him to justice. So close to the shipyard with shipyard workers all around, he couldn't let this opportunity slip. While Stephanos was pre-occupied, he slipped outside.

Ephialtes was in full flow and the hold he had over the crowd was obvious, both with his political message and his religious fervour. It was difficult to believe it was the same man. Lysanias found himself getting caught up in the fervour and the chants himself, until, as Ephialtes brought down the hammer on the goat's head to sacrifice it to the god, the thought flashed into his head: was that another example of the hammer of Hephaistos striking his enemies, striking the corrupt and decadent rich, like his uncle maybe? He recalled the words of the bathman and shivered that maybe the idea wasn't too far-fetched.

With the ceremony over, the crowd of workers dispersed and he was able to attach himself to a group going in the direction of the shipyard. Busily chatting about the way things were changing and whether it was likely to come to a fight, they paid him little attention as they walked through the gates to Hermon's yard. He was in! He could rejoin Stephanos at Aspasia's later.

Sindron's mind kept going back to bubbling, laughing Glykera as they had chatted at midday. It occurred to him that if he had his freedom and enough money to live on, he could buy himself a comfortable woman like Glykera to keep him company and look after him in his declining years. He told himself to stop thinking along those lines, that it only made Phraston's offer more tempting, but it was difficult not to imagine being held by those plump arms, sinking into that ample rosy flesh.

Sindron was sitting in Lysanias' bedroom, with the bloody scroll laid out in front of him. Much of the writing was obliterated by dark red bloodstains that had soaked deep into the parchment. What was still readable was in an assured hand, in businesslike rather than casual language, clearly an urgent request to attend a meeting. The seal at the bottom, rolled on in black ink, revealed a porpoise riding a wave. It seemed appropriate to a shipbuilder, so it could be Hermon's, but the nautical symbols he recalled seeing most since he arrived were Poseidon and his trident and the sea horse and he wasn't sure which he had seen where. Unless they could discover who owned that seal, possession of the message scroll didn't get them any nearer finding a culprit.

What about the wax message inviting Lysanias back to Athens? They hadn't looked at that in the light of what they had recently discovered. He took it out from the chest of Lysanias' more personal belongings and opened it out.

Philia was pleased with herself. At last she felt she was gaining ground in the struggle against Makaria. Her appeals to the gods must be bearing fruit.

I am the mistress of this house, she thought. I will see what the rest of it is like. Strange that, though she was Klereides' wife, she had never seen inside his personal room.

She entered, stepping quietly despite her new bravado. She had overheard the slaves whispering and sniggering about the wall decorations and what if they hadn't been hidden for the funeral. She was shocked by what she saw when she lifted the respectable hangings to look underneath. Then she realised these outrageous scenes were exactly the sort of thing she would have expected Curly to squander his money on, while her room had only a couple of tapestries and one rug. But maybe she was being unfair to her dead husband. All this had probably been done before Klereides even started negotiating with her father to marry her.

"Mistress," someone whispered, and she spun round. It was only old Sindron, standing in the doorway to the inner room, looking tired and weary. "Mistress, are you familiar with Klereides' writing?" Somehow the mundane question after her adventures of the day made Philia laugh out loud. The bloodstained scroll, spread out in the open, gave her a start, but the wax tablet quickly intrigued her.

Before they married, Klereides had sent her some lovely letters, full of affection and promises of a rosy life in Athens, but that was ink and this was scratches on wax.

"Yes, that could be his writing, but it's difficult to tell; it's all so smudged."

Sindron read out some of the clearest phrases and asked if she knew what Klereides meant by them.

"Well-wishes on success of colony ... exciting challenges in new enterprise ... political developments bring perils and possibilities ... need for support in this dynamic time ... if Lysanias can be spared ... will not regret it ... junior role at first ... someone close I can trust ... urgent need ... passage paid ... Athena and gods of power protect ... brotherly affection ... Klereides."

So Curly had thought he was in danger. Lysanias must be right in suspecting foul play. His love letters had had this same way of making things sound exciting and dramatic. Philia mentioned this to Sindron.

"So it does sound like the way he might have put things. Good. But can you think why he felt he had no one he could trust?"

"Sorry, Sindron. He never confided in me about his business."

Suddenly Philia remembered Klereides' nightmares. She hadn't told Sindron about them yet. She outlined the things she could remember but couldn't suggest what he might have been afraid of.

"Philia! Philia!" The high-pitched but musical female voice startled Sindron. Philia laughed. "Don't panic, Sindron, it's only Nubis."

"Makaria wants to talk to you, Philia." She winked at Philia. "I won't tell her you were in the master's room with this naughty old man."

Sindron actually blushed. "There was one more question, mistress," hastened Sindron, holding back the hangings to reveal the lines of the cupboard door. "You wouldn't know how to open this wall cupboard, would you?"

"Don't be silly, Sindron. He wouldn't tell me anything like that."

"Oh, that," put in Nubis. "You just take this iron rod here in this pocket in the end of the couch, and you slip it in this hole in the wall and press. See, it opens. "

Philia and Sindron stared as she did it. So Nubis' relationship with Klereides had been more than that of serving girl and dancing girl to master, they both thought, though Philia's reflections were more bitter. Nubis actually knew more of Philia's husband's secrets than she did herself.

Nubis realised how much she had given away. "Uh, I saw him open it once. When I was bringing him some food and wine," she muttered, but no one believed her, and the atmosphere between the two young women was icy as they left.

The gods work in mysterious ways, Sindron thought as he eased the cupboard door wide open. Yes, a few scrolls. There was no will, but he found Klereides' contract with Hermon. The terms did look heavily weighted in Klereides' favour, though he had obligations as well and provided much of the capital, but maybe, from the foreign businessman's point of view, they could be regarded as extortionate.

However, what really engaged Sindron's attention was the seal at the bottom, a porpoise riding a wave, exactly the same as the seal on the bloodstained message scroll, alongside another seal with an olive tree and a plough. That must be Klereides' family seal. So it was Hermon who had sent the message summoning Klereides to his death, however good the shipbuilder might be at feigning innocence. Sindron now knew he had been right all along.

CHAPTER 12

Lysanias had realised this was an opportunity he might never have again, to check whether there were any signs of bloodstained feet leaving the scene of his uncle's murder.

He was dressed as a workman; he even still had his carpenter's leather tool strap round his shoulder. He was sure he would look like a shipyard worker going about his business.

He found the ship, though with riggers and labourers busy installing the equipment and accessories it looked very different. The ship must have passed the inspection. The replacement amphora was no longer there, presumably now installed in the vessel but he finally located the Hermes' staff emblem. This must be the spot.

Now how to examine the ground leading to the fence? A quick glance round to ensure no-one was looking in his direction and he ducked under the horizontal pole, grasped the upright and slid down. At least the walkway and platforms cast shadows down here. Hopefully he would be out of sight and not noticed.

Is this what the murderer would have done? Or would he have jumped down? Risky that, in the dark. Presumably he would have taken the quickest route to the fence and climbed over. The soil was baked hard, so no chance of an imprint of a foot, but maybe the sparse, sun-bleached grass would show something.

The specks of red were not big, but to his eager eyes they stood out, at pace-sized intervals, someone striding with long legs towards....

"Hey you down there! What do you think you're doing?"

Lysanias froze, recognising the voice. Discovered by Philebos the overseer! Then his head cleared. He wasn't a worker. His uncle had been murdered here, and Philebos had been responsible for some sort of cover up over the cut ropes. Right, we'll see who's guilty now!

"Coming, overseer! Just relieving myself," he called up, summoning a ready excuse, made his way back. Philebos had turned to supervise the work. Lysanias composed himself and put on his best accent. "Ah, Philebos, the very man I wanted to talk to." The overseer span round.

"Who? What? I didn't ask for any carpenters to work here this afternoon."

Lysanias noted with satisfaction that his costume evidently did provide an effective disguise. Then Philebos studied his face and recognition dawned.

"Lysanias, my dear sir." Lysanias admired the man's self-control. "There really is no need for this subterfuge. Surely you could have come to me directly, if you were seeking more information about the yard. Perhaps I can help you now?"

"Yes, indeed, Philebos. But perhaps not just here, eh?"

Drawing Philebos to a position where they could not be overheard, Lysanias charged straight into the attack with his prepared question. "Why did you substitute a badly frayed old rope for the knife-severed one that actually held the amphora that killed my uncle?"

"That's not true." Philebos tried to bluster it out. "The actual rope is in the store yard. The rigger who took it down will tell you..."

Lysanias allowed himself a knowing smile at the word 'rigger', and a look of awareness, even alarm flashed into the overseer's eyes, and his voice tailed off. He had jumped to the wrong conclusion, as Lysanias had hoped.

"He told you! The rigger told you, didn't he? Why I'll..."

Lysanias held the smile and gave the slightest of nods, as though agreeing that the rigger had told him. This confession was much more substantial than speculation about the ropes.

"I'm sure you will, Philebos. But I don't think it will help now, do you?"

Lysanias wasn't sure how long he could retain this cool, authoritative pose, but he needn't have worried. The stern, officious overseer suddenly melted into a fawning, apologetic suppliant.

"Ah, you see, citizen Lysanias ... You must realise ... Ah, when I explain..." The false starts spoke more than a thousand words."When a death like this occurs in a shipyard ... an unnatural death in mysterious circumstances. Yes, I will admit they were mysterious. Well, ah, a great deal could be at stake. The future of the yard. Hermon must have hinted..."

"Are you saying Hermon was involved in this deception?"

That hit him. "Ah, no, no, not exactly. I, ah, take full responsibility. You see, the yard is my responsibility, safety, the workforce, security from intru..." The overseer rushed on with a flow of words, trying to cover up that near slip. Had he been going to say 'intruders'? Lysanias was sure he had. That could admit to the possibility of a murderous agent.

"I had to do something, you see. To placate the city officials, to avoid upsetting the workmen, to appease the gods and retain their favour for the shipyard and its ships. I saw the cut ends of the rope and realised it must be deliberate but, for the sake of the yard, I had to make it look like an accident, you understand...?" The tone was almost plaintive.

"I understand that a murder may have been committed, a murder of a prominent citizen, and you have personally taken steps to hide this fact from his family, from the authorities and from the city." The overseer seemed to shrink under the onslaught.

Then Lysanias struck again. "Can I ask where you were on the night of the murder?"

"Now, Citizen Lysanias, I really don't think there's anything to be gained by accusing me..." His voice ground to a halt. Lysanias waited. The man pulled himself up and braced his shoulders. "At the time the watchman says the tragic event happened, I was rising and breaking my fast and then making my way to an early meeting in the city offices at the harbour with the naval officials." So he did have an alibi, but one dependent on his family and slaves, presumably.

"But you didn't go to the meeting?"

"Yes, of course I did. However, a messenger came there from the yard, before we had much business completed, and I rushed down here straight away to see if anything could be done for your poor uncle. They lent me a horse so I didn't waste any time."

Lysanias didn't believe that for an instant, but, if a messenger was sent straight away and Philebos was at an office on the other side of the Peiraieos harbour when he arrived, that would make it very difficult for Philebos to have carried out the murder himself, though maybe not impossible. Certainly not impossible for an agent of his to have done it, that 'intruder' he nearly mentioned.

"You claim you don't know who cut the rope?"

"I've no idea." His face was stiff, expressionless, no sign whether this was truth or lie.

"No suspicions?"

"No. Uh, I'm told Klereides had enemies. So rumour says."

"Thank you Philebos. You have been most helpful. I may wish to question you again. Of course, you may be required to vouch for your behaviour in a court of law at the appropriate time."

"Citizen Lysanias, please think about the future of the shipyard, all our livelihoods ... before you do ... anything rash..."

Lysanias paced away along the walkway. He was sure the man was lying but what about? He must be covering up for some other reason, so had he organised it all or was he covering up for Hermon? That seemed much more likely but how could he be sure.

The long trek uphill back to the city was tough after all the excitement, and he was glad to return to where all he had to concentrate on was the manual work in hand, as he helped Stephanos and Lampon get the marble slabs fixed into position.

Philia entered Makaria's room quietly and carefully. Makaria was reclining on a couch. She gestured to Philia to take a stool beside her, so that Philia was aware that, once again, she was being looked down on. The room was even more simply furnished than Philia's own. One tapestry of the goddess Hera, a soft rug on the floor, a cypress chest and cupboard. The scents of herbs, basil and thyme, filled the air.

"My child, I think it is perhaps time to take your training in household management a little further."

"Mother-in-law, I am not a child. I am a wife and widow, and I would be grateful if you would address me by name." Philia tried to be forceful rather than angry but there was a slight quaver in her voice.

"Of course, my dear, a slip of the tongue," Makaria conceded instantly. "You are still very young, and I admit I may have been a trifle over-protective in the past. My son, you understand, was worried about the perils that might assault a young wife, so inexperienced and beautiful, in the turmoil of temple activities and festival preparations."

"Surely that was my sacred duty, Makaria! How dare you keep me from it?"

Makaria was consoling. "Ah, yes, my dear. Perhaps it was an error of judgement, but we will start to correct things after our day at your husband's tomb. I know the priestesses personally." Philia felt only slightly mollified.

Makaria continued, "Now, my dear, I detect from your attitude towards me that you may have jumped to certain conclusions from things you may have seen or heard today. I feel I should put your mind at rest."

"I'm sure I don't know what you mean, Makaria." Philia decided that, for the moment, she would keep this weapon to herself.

"The Persians, they have this technique of flesh manipulation, body massage, hands on flesh, squeezing and pummelling. It is extremely relaxing, does wonders for my headaches. You understand. Otanes, he knows this technique and, when my headaches are really bad, I, ah, take advantage of this ability. Hmmm?"

Philia had listened attentively but allowed a slight smile to remain on her lips, and an expression of partial disbelief to show in her eyes. But she nodded to indicate she understood. She certainly had to hand it to the old crow: it was a magnificent cover story. At least they both knew where they stood now, and Makaria seemed to be asking at least that Philia not tell anyone else. Clearly the inauguration into city ways was the reward. So be it.

"May I ask one question, mother-in-law? Is it true that some women do own property and investments in their own right, even though the laws forbid this?"

Makaria's mouth came open and stayed that way, as Philia completed her speech. Clearly this was a touchy point. Philia's guess had been correct about who really leased that foundry.

"Ah, well, I think that is a matter for talking about when we are away from the house, if you don't mind, Philia. But we will, we will. I must say you are proving a very sharp young thing. Maybe you could handle a husband yet."

Lysanias parted from Stephanos outside Aspasia's front door. He found it easy to brush off Stephanos' suggestion that he work with them tomorrow. "Got to do my duty at my uncle's tomb," he said truthfully. Stephanos looked disappointed. "You really are overdoing this mourning thing," he muttered. Lysanias sensed that Stephanos now valued him as a friend and work colleague, so he lied about attending a meeting of the radicals the following day and acknowledged a rallying point if there was a takeover attempt. He really couldn't manage all these things, not if he was going to get any nearer to prosecuting his uncle's killer. He nearly forgot to ask Stephanos if he would try to locate the rigger for him.

Citizens, slaves and foreigners passed him, going about their business. Lysanias didn't notice them. It was all so complex. The political turmoil. The whole business world of contracts and tenders and loans and investments and gifts – or were they bribes? Who could help him understand it all? Then the thought: Aspasia! She seemed to know a lot and she had said she would tell him. She had said come back another day, but he needed to know now.

His mind made up, Lysanias almost ran back to her house, his tool bag jogging against his side.

"Forgotten some tools, young sir?" The black slave who answered the door looked at him, his big eyes declaring that workers didn't come to this house except to do work.

"No, the mistress asked me to call and see her. Is she available?" Perhaps that was the wrong word, for he immediately felt embarrassed, but it was said now.

"Wait here. I will see." The black face was expressionless again.

Outside in the gathering dusk, Lysanias realised he was in a well-used street, his own house not all that far away, anyone passing might see and recognise him. He huddled in close to the portico, keeping his face turned towards the doorway.

The slave showed him to Aspasia's bedchamber.

"Ah, it's the Adonis of the saw and chisel," Aspasia purred, reclining on the blue bed, fanning herself with a lacy pale green fan. "I thought I told you I had a dinner party this evening."

Her gown was arranged to reveal rather more of her legs than he had seen before, and he glanced away embarrassed and said to the painting of Aphrodite, which revealed even more, "Yes, but I had to know, you see..."

"Of course, you did." She purred, and rose slinkily from the bed in one smooth movement. "All that young virginity burning to get loose, of course you did."

"No, I don't mean that..."

As she approached him, her nose wrinkled and he realised he hadn't bathed after all the sweat of the day. But her smile widened appreciatively, as she sniffed fully. "Now that's what I call a man's smell! They come in here, smelling of scented oils and perfumes, like the owner of a fragrance shop. But this ... aaah!" She had lifted his arm and was actually sniffing the armpit and licking him.

"Aaah, that salty taste of honest toil."

Lysanias was confused. What could he do now? "You don't understand. I want to know about the crooked business you mentioned, and what goes on ... You told me you would..."

"Ah, yes," She was dreamy-eyed now, lost in the sensual pleasure of smelling and tasting and feeling him. She raised his hand and placed it against her cheek. Her eyes closed and she stroked his hand down onto her neck and on down into the top of her gown and onto and round her breast.

Lysanias found himself shivering, though the room was warm. He could feel an erection rising under his tunic. Aspasia's eyes snapped open. "Now let's see what we have under this grimy worker's tunic shall we?" She had unclasped his tunic at the shoulder and it fell to the floor around his feet.

"Now that's what I call a healthy young chisel." She grinned seductively. Before he could protest or say anything, she was on her knees, had it in her hands and was stroking and licking and smelling it. "Mmmm ... Only virgins smell like that." He was getting really excited and it was driving everything else from his head, why he had come, his coming marriage to Philia, everything. He knew his father had wanted to buy him his sexual initiation back in Eion but his mother had objected, till he was eighteen. Well, he was eighteen now.

"I can pay," he said, then realised how incongruous it sounded.

"No, the pleasure's all mine." Aspasia almost hummed as she stood, unclasped her gown and revealed her well-rounded, sensuous, rose-pink body in all its glory, rivalling and surpassing the painting of Aphrodite. He could see why wealthy men vied for her favours.

"Now before we waste that gorgeous first time..." And she led him backwards to the bed, their eyes locked, a silly grin on his face. She lay down and encouraged him into position. Then his education really started.

It was like nothing he'd ever imagined. Why had he put it off so long? While it left him tingling all over, wanting to do no more than lie beside her forever, stroking that silky-smooth skin, he found it had also cleared his mind miraculously. He still didn't have any answers, but the problems, the unanswered questions, stood out sharply.

"What's this crooked business you think is going on?" he asked as gently as he could, for fear of breaking the magic.

"Ah, down to business, eh? I can see you're your uncle's nephew."

"I thought you didn't know him."

"Did I say that? Surely not. Aspasia knows everybody who is anybody. Now let's see what I can tell you." She ran her finger down the line of his nose and along his lips, a subtle smile on her face. Was she teasing him? Then the playful girl became the knowledgeable woman.

"Did he come here?" Lysanias asked.

"Once or twice, but he liked to experiment, take risks. Maybe that's what got him into trouble. Always liked a gamble, using his money to beat other people to things, whether it was the newest whore in town, or the biggest business contract. Winning, beating someone else was the thing. From what I hear, he didn't always play clean. It didn't make him liked. Has no-one told you this?"

She must have read the small expressions of growing horror on his face.

"No, everyone says what a marvellous man he was."

She put on her experienced woman expression. "Mmm, they would. Hypocrites all, these wealthy Athenians, and the rest of us are forced to copy them. Sorry, I know, you're an Athenian too but you grew up somewhere else, you haven't learnt all their bad habits. Yet. Take me, for instance. They call me a 'companion'. Anywhere else, I'd be a high-class whore. Not that I'm complaining. It gives me a status and a freedom of movement I adore. But you see my point. So 'death' is 'crossing over'. 'Taxes' are 'contributions' or 'tributes'..."

Lysanias tried to concentrate but he couldn't see where this was leading and his hand was on her breast and her hand was stroking his leg and his penis had started to stir again. They kissed and only after another lesson in sex, another position explored, did Aspasia continue.

She poured scorn on the Athenian idea of democracy as the plaything of the wealthy, not involving many of the citizens, though she did acknowledge that things seemed to be changing with the new reforms – no suggestion yet of giving the women a say, though. The Confederacy that had beaten the Persians she saw as an Athenian Empire in disguise.

Even his own home colony she saw as a military outpost guaranteeing Athens access to timber for shipbuilding and to dominance over the nearby goldmines.

"It's all about power, boy! Economic power when it's not military."

Lysanias started to feel very disillusioned.

"You're beginning to sound like a radical politician, now," he said.

"Like Perikles? He's just another rich boy building a power base for himself and his hero." She felt that, just as Kimon had welded the wealthier classes together to support him with the farmers and country people, the radicals were lining up the shopkeepers and master craftsmen behind them as well as the workers, the poor and the intellectuals. She sounded as though she was in favour of the reforms but didn't really believe it would happen.

"The wealthy aren't fools. They'll resist with all their might," she crowed.

Lysanias lay there, astounded as much by the fact that a woman had the intellect to grasp all this as by what she was saying. Women just weren't capable of it. Everyone knew that.

"But how?" he began.

"Did I learn to think? In my home city, women aren't shut away as in Athens but allowed a modicum of education."

She had found that, with her status, she could invite the best minds in Athens to her parties and they came, and, as long as she stayed out of sight, she could listen in on the historians and philosophers in the public gardens and even observe Assembly meetings. So her education continued.

Lysanias began to feel uncomfortable with her attitudes. Aspasia clearly knew her power over men and intended to exploit it to the full. Her feeling that all politicians were corrupt was especially disturbing. Then that golden smile flashed and he was lost in admiration of her beauty.

"I'm sorry if I'm being brutal, Lysanias. Eighteen is the time for innocence, but, if you learn in your own time, the vultures will have torn you apart before you know what world you're in."

She couldn't be that much older than him, early twenties at most, and here she was mothering him. Affronted, he made to get up. Aspasia pulled him back.

"I haven't told you anything that will help you with your uncle's death yet, but don't expect too much."

"Anything that will help me find my way through this labyrinth will do, Aspasia." His look of earnest gratitude earned him another of those smiles.

"It's money that brings out their real hypocrisy," she said. "The old land-owning families like to think it grows out of the ground, so they look down on trade and commerce and manual work. A gentleman should just listen to philosophers, take part in politics and public service, and go off to fight in the wars, they think. All very fine, if you've enough money to feed, clothe and house you and to give away in sponsorship. Most of them, their estates don't produce that much.

"So they put their money in trade at a good rate of interest. However, they don't like anyone to know about it. They back manufacturers as well. A few of them really got it together and there are big boys still in the game, who intermarried with the aristocracy and didn't take kindly to your uncle linking up with a Syracusan and grabbing government contracts that they wanted.

"Am I getting through? Your uncle liked taking risks but maybe he risked too much. These people can be ruthless and they have political allies. You're in his place now, so don't make yourself a threat like your uncle did."

Lysanias eyes were wide open. Another whole area of possible suspects. His euphoria evaporated. He wasn't sure but thought he sensed a tinge of fear for herself for telling him, even though she had General Ariston as a protector.

"There. I've told you. You'll have to go now. I've a dinner party to get dressed for and this bedding needs changing after your sweaty body." She smiled approvingly. He smiled back, thanked her as well as he could, took his cloak out of his tool bag and wrapped it round him. He used the back door through the garden and was once more in the alleys of Inner Kermeikos.

"No, Sindron, no discussion tonight. I'm too tired."

"I understand, master, but I've learnt much today, that you should know about." Sindron allowed his annoyance to show. The boy was exasperating. He'd come in starving, smelling of dubious activities, after playing at being a craftsman all day. Now he was refusing even to listen!

"I've learnt a lot as well, Sindron, but I'll tell you in the morning." Sindron couldn't resist a schoolmasterly comment.

"I'm sure you have, master. I can smell it. Just because you've been working with ordinary people doesn't mean you have to behave like them."

"What do you mean 'smell it'?"

Sindron wasn't sure how to put this tactfully. "Sex, master, intercourse, the bodily juices, they have a distinctive smell ... and the perfume as well. Very feminine. Didn't you realise?"

Lysanias hadn't. "I should have a wash down, shouldn't I? Before other people smell it."

"I think that would be advisable, master. I can tell you about the message-scroll in the morning."

That sent new energy coursing through Lysanias' body, and he insisted on hearing the essence of what Sindron and Philia had unearthed. He was impressed with Philia's initiative. Then Lysanias outlined his own discoveries, especially about Philebos. But his exhaustion proved too strong for much detail. His body-cleansing proved very perfunctory before he collapsed onto his couch.

As he made his way back to his own room, Sindron felt a little guilty that he had not taken steps to assist Lysanias to a sexual education by finding a suitable prostitute. He was sure that the boy's father would have preferred that to a slut used by workmen.

He felt guilty too that he hadn't yet made a clean breast of the cargo loan, but he found he was actually more worried about what might have happened to his very own cargo. Was the ship safe, had it sunk, had the crew pilfered the cargo? Then Sindron's thoughts returned to Phraston's offer. Why did that give him a warm glow when he thought of it, rather than a guilt feeling at not having told his master?

Then even that was rapidly submerged in thoughts of Glykera's plump arms and cosy body, and an awareness of just how long it was since he had slept with a woman.

Lysanias was just dropping off to sleep, when he started up suddenly. Someone had come into the room! He was suddenly wary. But no, it was someone with a small shell lamp, shielded by an equally small female hand.

"Master, it's only me." He recognised the gentle but high-pitched voice as Nubis, and relaxed. Then, dozily, he wondered what Nubis was doing in his room?

"I've brought a message from the young mistress. Something about Klereides she thinks you ought to know."

"Oh, Nubis, I'm so tired. Won't it wait until tomorrow?" He was hardly able to keep his eyes open. Nubis had put the lamp down beside the couch and he could see her young breasts silhouetted against the light as they pushed against the tight-drawn tunic that left her shapely brown legs exposed.

"Poor master, you look exhausted. Why don't you just go to sleep now and I can tell you later?"

Gratefully, he felt himself relaxing again into sleep. "I'll just slip in here beside you and make sure you're comfortable." A gentle hand was reaching round him and feeling where Aspasia's hand had played only a few hours before. Oh, no, he couldn't, not again! Yet surprisingly he could, in the hands of another expert. So this was another of the benefits of having slaves! Her trim muscular figure was like a boy's, he thought. Quite unlike the soft yielding flesh of Aspasia.

"That's good, master! See what we've been missing."

She was encouraging, though he could sense that she was disappointed. But what could he say?

"Master, Philia..." He started at the name, feeling guilty. "Philia says that Klereides had bad dreams and talked in his sleep, saying things about enemies and fighting back that sounded like he was afraid. And, ah, I've heard him too."

He was alert and angry now. "Why didn't you tell me?"

"We couldn't get near you, what with the funeral and the old mistress keeping guard on us." Then she slumped, in disappointment at being admonished. Lysanias put his arm round her shoulders comfortingly and kissed her. He found he did feel affection for the girl.

"Don't be upset. You brought me the message as soon as you could. Now off to your bed with you. I must have sleep. Another big day tomorrow." He was being the strong master, he hoped, but, even as he had the thought, he was asleep and Nubis tiptoed out.

CHAPTER 13

"No need to tell Sindron or Lysanias about the nightmares, Nubis," Philia said gaily, as Nubis darkened her eyebrows and whitened her cheeks just a little to make Philia look more widow-like.

"Why's that, mistress?"

"I told Sindron yesterday."

"Oh, I see."

That didn't quite ring as it should, Philia felt. "What does that mean, Nubis?"

"Nothing, mistress."

Now that was Nubis' standard evasion, instantly recognisable. "Nubis!" Philia hit Makaria's tone exactly, the order to a slave to tell the truth. It drew a response.

"I told the young master. Last night." Then hurriedly, "When he was crossing the courtyard. Just after he came in."

Philia wasn't sure if she believed it. Had the slave-girl gone to Lysanias in his room? If she had, what had happened between them? If she was going to have a new husband, Philia wanted one who would not be away from her bed most of the time like Klereides. So, a little more effort would be required to make sure Lysanias found her irresistible.

"I think I will have just a touch of red earth in the cheeks, Nubis. And a little more of that Arabian perfume Klereides bought me."

"Yes, mistress."

Sindron was straightening and brushing out Lysanias' mourning cloak behind him when he said it.

"Would you consider selling me, master?"

Lysanias had been admiring himself in the bronze mirror, its frame inlaid with rare stones. He was imagining, with pleasure, what women might see in his looks, when Sindron's question stopped his day-dreaming dead.

"Why do you ask, Sindron?" Lysanias feigned indifference.

"I thought perhaps master would prefer a personal slave closer to his own age, someone more accustomed to care of body and clothes."

"Is this something to do with the … ah, way I smelled when I came in yesterday?"

"No, no, master, I am no prude." Lysanias wasn't sure he would have agreed. "I may have felt you might have asked my advice on a suitable, ah, person for a first encounter, but..."

Lysanias smiled at the euphemism. "I assure you she was perfectly suitable, Sindron." His grin broadened, as he remembered Aspasia's pink charms.

"I'm sure, master." Sindron at his most obsequious.

"Sindron, are you concealing something?"

"No, uh..." Sindron started and then decided it had to be shared, now or never. "Master, a wealthy gentleman has offered to buy me and give me my freedom..."

"Who?" Lysanias demanded.

"... and a way of providing for my old age..."

"Who?"

"... and I feel that, at my age, I should be thinking seriously about this." He felt relieved to have completed the statement he had prepared, even if it didn't tell the whole story.

"Sindron, who made this ridiculously generous offer and why?" Lysanias doubted whether anyone could be so foolish as to spend good money in order to give freedom to another person's slave, but then he had never known Sindron be this evasive before. He grasped Sindron firmly by the upper arms, feeling the old bones through the flesh, and forced the slave to look straight at him. For a moment, they just looked at one another, disbelief and curiosity mixed on Lysanias' face, uncertainty and wariness on Sindron's.

"Phraston, master. The master of my friend Lydos. The banker. You're right; it is a bribe to attempt to hinder your investigations. I'm sure of it, though I must admit it is a very attractive bribe. For a slave."

"Why do you say it's to hinder our investigations?" Lysanias' tone was controlled and cold, as he emphasised the 'our'. His faith in the one person he felt he could trust was badly shaken, but he couldn't afford to lose his temper. Not yet.

Sindron's eyes moved shamefacedly away from his own and looked over Lysanias' shoulder at nothing. "Their first offer was that I inform them of your plans and discoveries. For money." He looked back into Lysanias' eyes, agitated. "I refused that outright, of course, master." Sindron put as much force and conviction into it as he could. Lysanias' reply amazed him.

"Good, Sindron! Good! You must accept." Lysanias let go his slave's arms and paced the floor, thinking as he sought words. He believed the man; no-one would make up a story like that, and definitely not someone as conventional as Sindron.

"But, master..."

"Accept the first offer. They must have reasons for wanting to halt our investigations. Maybe we're getting close to the truth. Maybe they're involved with Hermon in some way."

"Exactly what I thought, master, but how can you...?"

"Don't you see, Sindron? That way you can give them false information about what we've found out, and, if they trust you, they may let something slip."

"Master, it's dishonest!"

"Sindron, since I've been in Athens, I haven't seen much that can't be classed as dishonest to some extent. Have you?"

That gave Sindron pause, but he still didn't like the idea.

"What about the freedom offer, master?" It really did seem a pity to let that dream go. "And how do I explain the fact that I refused originally?"

"Ah, yes, that's a problem." Lysanias found he was enjoying working out this devious puzzle. "You could say that it will take time to persuade me to sell you and that, in the meantime, you want proof of their sincerity."

"Master!" Was it he or Athens that was corrupting the boy so that he could think this way?

"Yes, well. You must have lied before in your life, Sindron. Or concealed the truth a little, eh?"

That hit Sindron where it hurt. He still hadn't told his master about that little embezzlement that disturbed him so.

"It is attractive, master."

"What? Oh, freedom. Look, Sindron, support me till we've sorted out my uncle's murder and my inheritance and you can have your freedom, if you want it. And a pension. How's that?" Lysanias felt the old man deserved it and, if he had inherited as much money as Sindron had indicated last night, Lysanias could afford it.

Sindron was shaken. All he had had to do was tell the truth! And he had expected Lysanias to feel he was blackmailing him. How wrong can you be? "Most generous, master."

Lysanias detected an element of hesitancy in Sindron. "But...?"

"I have been dishonest over your money, master," Sindron confessed, assured from what had happened so far that Lysanias would understand. He hoped.

"You, Sindron! You couldn't be dishonest without someone like me persuading you! You've just proved it!" Lysanias was almost laughing with disbelief.

Sindron hung his head. "I did have someone persuading me, master," he muttered.

"All right, tell it, but hurry, they'll all be waiting for us."

Sindron explained about the cargo loan and using Lysanias' money for it. "The dealer was very persuasive," he ended. Expecting an admonition, Sindron was surprised when Lysanias laughed.

"How much? A hundred drachmas! Sindron, if you're right about the size of my inheritance, that's a fleabite!" He roared with laughter, making Sindron feel like a naive child. At his age! "Let's say you made a small investment on my behalf. If it proves profitable, I give you authority, as my personal slave, to make more. Within limits, of course." He was almost serious again. "And you shall have a fifth of any profits earned. You can invest that how you will." Sindron wasn't entirely sure whether to believe him, but this was all beginning to feel intoxicating. Was money really of so little value to the rich? "Must show the world I intend to follow in my uncle's footsteps, eh?"

"Ah, perhaps not all of them, master," said Sindron, now smiling broadly with relief, his face creasing along all its wrinkles.

"Now then, Sindron," Lysanias admonished, pulling his face into a serious expression. "This is the day we visit Klereides' tomb. Mustn't joke about death..."

It was the tradition for the whole household, family and slaves, to go to the tomb of the deceased on the third day after burial. It turned into a pleasant, rather mellow family occasion.

The idea was to share a meal with the spirit of the deceased and also to share memories of him with one another, to demonstrate to the gods that he was remembered and, therefore, deserving of benign treatment in the afterlife. After the initial libations and prayers, seated in a group on the grass beside the tomb, Makaria reminisced about playing with Klereides and his brother, when they were babies and toddlers, for once including Leokhares, Lysanias' father. Lysanias found it difficult to imagine her as a fond mother, so severe did she normally look. Now she cried openly.

Blushing engagingly, Philia described Klereides' courtship, the poems he had sent her, the wedding ceremony itself, and the journey to Athens seated between Klereides and General Ariston as his best friend, on the cart on which she and Makaria had travelled to the tomb today. She was so animated as she relived it all, her dark eyes sparkling, her pale skin, framed by the black widow's gown and veil, glowing in the sun, and those red lips never still as she spoke. Lysanias was captivated. He couldn't take his eyes off her. Even comparison with Aspasia didn't lessen the fascination.

Then it was his turn. He talked, though, about his father's tales of his older brother Klereides. How Klereides had persuaded Leokhares to climb for a bird's nest and then left him stranded up the tree, until Sindron had appeared and sandaled his bottom. How Klereides had taught his father to swim and to wrestle, and cheered him on and encouraged him in the competitions he had won as a boy and as a youth. It began to sound more like a celebration of his father than of his uncle.

Hierokles had arrived at the tomb as Lysanias was talking. Without Boiotos, he was glad to see. Sounding pompous, Hierokles talked of military campaigns in which both he and Klereides had served. Somehow Klereides' part in the battles seemed to receive rather scant mention, while Hierokles' role grew in prominence. Lysanias assumed the man meant well.

While the females were singing a paean to Demeter, for her intervention on Klereides' behalf, interspersed with a slow, stately round dance, Lysanias took the opportunity of the concealment offered by the bushes to relieve himself, and to look more openly at Philia through the leaves. Hierokles joined him. "Ah, m'boy, glad to have the chance for a few words," as the flow tinkled on leaves and sundried grass. "You remember what we talked about. Need for us well-born to stick together, see off these upstarts who think they've taken over power?"

"Ummh," Lysanias didn't want to commit himself till he knew what was coming.

"Things are building to a head, m'boy." Hierokles shook himself and let his cloak fall back into place. "Might need your help."

"Always willing to help, uncle." What else could he say? "Within the limits of the requirements of mourning, of course."

Hierokles seemed re-assured that Lysanias was on his side. He bent closer, though there was no danger that anyone was listening.

"Can't really tell you much detail. Need to keep it a secret as long as possible, you understand. A group of us, large group are meeting up at my townhouse at dusk. You know where that is? Good! Instructions then. And weapons. You get the idea?"

He looked for Lysanias' assent, and Lysanias looked him in the eyes and nodded. He did indeed understand. "Yes, uncle, of course. If I can."

"Good man."

Hierokles excused himself shortly after that, and returned to town, but not before Lysanias had reminded him of his promise to go in to the relevant offices and validate Lysanias' identity for citizenship purposes.

For the rest of the day, Lysanias went through the motions, did what was expected of him. He was now thoroughly confused. This must be the seizure of power the radicals were expecting, but whose side was he on? It could determine which side controlled the city in future. It could even be the first slip on the downhill slide to the civil war everyone clearly dreaded.

Despite his enthusiasm for Kimon's achievements, Lysanias didn't trust the people he knew who were Kimon supporters and felt very ill at ease with them.

Did he trust the radicals either? He had seen blatant disagreement among them. Were these people really capable of running a mighty city, and an even mightier confederacy? Stephanos was a good friend, but...

It was friendship that swung it. Sindron had to make contact with Phraston or Lydos today. He would send the slave-boy with a message for Sindron to take to Stephanos. Sindron could find Stephanos at Aspasia's and tell him that the take-over was planned for tonight. He was sure he could phrase it so that only Stephanos would understand it. Then let the two sides fight it out and may the best side win. He hoped Sindron wouldn't feel that was irresponsible but would explain it to his slave later.

Sindron took time to visit the slave cemetery but found no markers with his father's or mother's name, though there were some in the Etruscan style. By one of these he muttered the bits he could remember of the prayers his mother had taught him as a child. Then he whispered the news that it looked as though he might regain his freedom before he died. They would have welcomed that, never having really come to terms with their slavery he suspected, though he could barely remember them. Then he left the cemetery. A slave cannot afford to be sentimental.

He located Lydos and Phraston in the market-place and they retired to a quiet spot behind the Painted Colonnade. Sindron mouthed the statement he had prepared, that he wished to accept Phraston's offer to buy his freedom, but it would take some time to persuade his master to sell. In the meantime, he felt proofs of goodwill were required. If Phraston would start the account he had mentioned, Sindron would supply information.

Phraston chose to interpret this as meaning that he and Lysanias had argued when Sindron had mooted the question of being given his freedom. Let him believe that, if it helps him accept the story, Sindron thought. It appeared to cheer him up, and Lydos seemed to share his pleasure.

Lydos produced a small scroll, unrolled it and showed Sindron that the name at the top was his and the first entry was a deposit that exactly covered his cargo loan. A nice touch, thought Sindron, especially when Lydos was responsible for his getting into that mess, and he wondered if that really had been deliberate.

He kept a straight face, allowing a measure of his happiness at the idea of having back his freedom someday soon to show through. He told them that Lysanias was thoroughly confused at the number of people who seemed to have reasons to hate Klereides, but that he was favouring the thought that it must be the workforce and this Hammer of Hephaistos Fellowship group that must be responsible, but was having great trouble investigating that. He mentioned Hermon as another possible suspect, studying their faces for a reaction, but there was none.

Phraston and Lydos both seemed very pleased that no names from the aristocratic faction were mentioned, but they didn't offer to take him into their confidence. As to why they wanted this information, Phraston volunteered, "Ah, my friend, you know I'm closely involved with Kimon's party?" Sindron nodded. "Young Lysanias, with all he inherits, represents what you might call a rogue element, don't you see? It helps if we can see the way his mind is working. He could unsettle things, if he gets in with the wrong people."

"I see," Sindron answered. After the surprising way Lysanias had reacted to the news of Sindron's dishonesty, he felt he no longer knew how the lad's mind was working himself. Phraston's explanation made a small degree of sense but he was sure there must be something else.

"You've been most helpful, old fellow." Phraston clapped him on the back with a mighty thump, turned and strode swaying back to the market-place.

Sindron had difficulty refraining from shuddering at the man's touch and such ready acceptance of disloyalty. Lydos leaned close. "Well done, old friend, you're learning what it takes to succeed in Athens, even for a slave." He had the audacity to wink at him. Then Sindron remembered he was supposed now to be one of them and forced himself to wink back.

Sindron managed to keep his shoulders up and a firmness in his step as he walked away, but, once round the corner, his shoulders slumped. He might have retained his loyalty to his master in a roundabout way, but he could no longer regard Lydos as a friend, his only friend. The loss was real, more real than the loss of his parents, who he had hardly known.

Philia had felt Lysanias' eyes on her all day. Even when he was talking to another person, they seemed to keep flicking back to her. She would glance down modestly but be sure to put on her most winning smile, the one that made tiny dimples either side of her mouth. He hardly glanced at Nubis. It really had paid off making the slave-girl wear that long dark gown.

Maybe when they rode home, Lysanias would come on the cart and sit between her and Makaria and she could lean against him and make sure he smelt her perfume.

"It was very awkward, master! That Nubian doorman was most offensive but I'm sure Stephanos understood the message."

"I'm sure he did, Sindron. I'm sorry to have embarrassed you like that."

They had waited late at the tomb, until dusk was falling, for the final libations. Lysanias had ridden back, seated between the two black-veiled women, with the slaves walking behind. Makaria had mentioned that she intended taking Philia to the temples for rituals associated with Klereides' death and asked Lysanias' approval of this. One more sign that the family is really accepting me as head of the household, he thought with some satisfaction. He had found Philia's fragrant perfume even more delightful and disturbing than Aspasia's, as he luxuriated in his new knowledge of women. The streets appeared normal. Perhaps nothing will happen, he had told himself.

Another worry surfaced. "Do you think he could do it, Sindron?"

"What's that, master?"

"Do you think Kimon could march back from Corinth with his hoplites and make himself tyrant?"

Again the boy amazed him. But Sindron had sensed that many people were aware of that danger. After all, it was less than fifty years since the city had rid itself of the tyrants. There were men who still remembered that time.

"I doubt it, master. I'm sure Kimon is a convinced democrat even if his opponents are using democracy against him, though that may be what his supporters are hoping." Lysanias didn't look fully convinced but didn't argue, having other things on his mind.

It was dark outside and getting late. Changed out of his black cloak to something more everyday, Lysanias paced the floor as Sindron told him about his encounter with Phraston and Lydos, and they both went into more detail on the happenings of the previous day. Lysanias' feeling that Philebos was covering up for Hermon seemed to support the conclusion Sindron had reached after finding Hermon's seal on the bloody message-scroll, but Lysanias' mind was elsewhere.

"Do you think I should go, Sindron?" he said, forgetting that he still hadn't explained the message. It came out more like a demand than a question.

"Go where, master?"

"I don't know! To join the take-over crowd. Or to stop them! That's the trouble, I don't know! I'm supposed to meet up with Hierokles at his house and I'm supposed to join Stephanos and the workers on the site of the new Temple to Hephaistos. Both of them expect to arm me and give me a role to play. I can't do both."

"Then don't do either, master," Sindron responded reasonably. He was suddenly worried. That was what the strange message had meant that he had carried to Stephanos. But this could lead to civil war! Best keep the lad out of it. "As you say, it's a mourning day."

"That's only an excuse, Sindron! The day runs from sunset to sunset. It won't hold. What do I say to either of them when I next meet them? They'll think I'm a coward."

Then suddenly it was too late. The quiet outside was shattered by the sounds of gongs and whistles spreading outwards from the centre of the city, taken up by dogs barking, and donkeys braying, as it got louder and nearer. That's it, thought Lysanias, and he was on his feet and out of the door and running down the road towards the market-place as fast as he could. He had to be there, or be cursed as a coward forevermore. Sindron made no attempt to stop him or to follow him. In a strange way, he was proud that the boy had gone but found himself praying to Athene that nothing serious would happen to him.

The market-place was almost deserted, but then, the streets had been empty too. The noise had tailed off shortly after he left, even the dogs had barked themselves out now. His running footsteps had echoed back from the walls until, noticing one or two doors and window-shutters opening slightly and rapidly closing, he decided barefoot he would make less noise and attract less attention so took off his sandals. The impetus of his running had carried him well into the square before he stopped. He looked round warily, realising how exposed he was. He slipped on his sandals to keep both hands free.

The moonlight was sufficient to reveal Scythian guards standing stiffly in their positions. Torches in holders on important buildings outlined others, but they made no move and stood stiffly with their spears erect, like the statues in the square. Otherwise it seemed deserted, though no telling what the shadows beside buildings and under the plane trees might conceal.

Lysanias felt his hair rise on the back of his neck. It was eerily quiet for this big city.

He decided to walk down the side of the square towards the city offices and the council chamber. Those must have been on the list for seizure. Perhaps Kimon's men had succeeded and really had taken over but wouldn't reveal the fact till daylight. But why, then, were there no signs of fighting?

Suddenly a voice hissed from the shadows. "Lysanias! Over here!" Stephanos stepped out. "Better late than never, eh? But you've missed it. It's all over." He gave the hammer and anvil salute and added "Praise to Hephaistos!" Lysanias responded appropriately and muttered, "I had to see the women safely home. What happened?"

"Come in here and I'll tell you. Oh, and thanks for the message." Stephanos pulled him into the shadow between two buildings and now he could see there were ten or more burly workers, armed with hammers and cutting blades, chisels and scythes. A few had spears, swords and shields.

"Groups like this all round the square," said Stephanos proudly, grinning. "And at every important building in the city and in Peiraieos. Here take this. Bit stupid wandering around without a weapon." And Stephanos gave him a short-handled, fist-size hammer from a small pile of tools and weapons beside him. He explained that Perikles had persuaded the magistrate in charge of the Scythian archers to instruct them to stay aloof, unless things got out of hand.

"What happened? Has there been fighting?"

Stephanos laughed. "You won't believe this! They were so confident they actually marched down into the square and formed up in ranks. You know their best men are stuck in Corinth? Well, this is what was left over, old men, teenagers, war-wounded, a number of serving officers and men. Then their officers told them off into squads and gave each squad a building to take over. They marched towards the buildings and then we all stepped out, waving our weapons, like Myronides and Perikles had worked out, shouting and whooping, and banging gongs, enough noise to wake the dead.

"And they just turned tail and ran, falling over one another as they went." Those around them in the shadows burst out laughing, but Stephanos hushed them quickly. "Never know when they might come back, brothers!"

"Is that it?"

"Looks like it. That must have happened everywhere else as well. We haven't heard any sounds of fighting from anywhere."

Lysanias decided he should stay and show solidarity. It felt good to be with the gang of joking, sweaty men, young and some not so young, but clearly all in it together.

A low whistle interrupted them. Stephanos whistled back. Myronides and Perikles approached from the side away from the square, both in general's uniform, checking that all was well. They reported that the attempted takeover appeared to have been defeated everywhere.

"Stay on guard, men." said Myronides bluffly. "They may re-group and try again."

"I doubt it," said Perikles. "They know we're strong now."

"Yes, but they can't be sure how many of us there are," countered Myronides, more impressive in uniform. "They could still try something foolish." The more mature and experienced commander seemed determined to make clear his seniority.

Lysanias stayed in the background, out of sight of the leaders. Perikles turned to Stephanos and spoke quietly. "Stephanos, do you know if Ephialtes reached home safely?"

"Should be indoors safe. We sent four of the brothers with him and two of them are to stand guard at his front door all night."

"Good. Keep up the good work, men. Stay alert!"

Myronides gave a few more encouraging words and the two leaders were off to visit the next group.

A short while later, Lysanias asked quietly, "Do you think I'm really needed here?"

Stephanos thought for a moment, then whispered. "Not really, but we don't want our boys getting the idea they can all go home. If you edge your way up the back there and then slip away, I'll say you're running a message for me, if anyone asks. I'd take off that cloak, though, and just wear your tunic, in case you meet another squad and they think you're a Kimo. You know the call sign, your whistle, only soft."

Lysanias did as Stephanos suggested, but it felt even scarier now that he knew that every shadow could hold a squad of armed men. He was pleased that the fighting had been nipped in the bud, that his message had done the trick. But could this angry peace hold? Away from the market square and the important buildings, and into the wealthy quarter, he put his cloak back on. In this area, his tunic would certainly not identify him as a friend.

In the dark, with no torch to light his way and only moonlight to guide him, it proved difficult to find the street and then the house of Hierokles, but he finally managed it. He banged gently on the lion's head doorknocker. Even so, in the silence, the noise startled him. No-one came to the door. He banged again. The door opened the tiniest crack. "Who's that at this time of night?" The voice was trying not to sound frightened. Lysanias gave his name. The door opened, a hand grabbed his cloak and pulled him inside, and the door was slammed and barred hurriedly behind him.

It was Boiotos, angry, and holding a drawn short-sword under Lysanias' chin. Lysanias nearly dropped the hammer he held clutched inside his cloak. He really shouldn't have brought that, it could give him away. He could now see that the lobby, and the passageway and the courtyard beyond were packed with armed men, the few oil lamps glinting off an assortment of helmets and breastplates, faces young and old, scared and bored and tired. All quiet as mice. Evidently under orders.

Only now did Lysanias realise how tricky this could be. They would know he must have walked through the city, which they were aware was full of armed workers, yet he had arrived here unscathed. He pretended to be out of breath.

"Oh, Boiotos, it's good to see you're safe." They must have thought it was their opponents or the Scythian guards banging on the door, come to arrest them. "I thought I'd never make it. There are armed workers everywhere. It took me ages to find my way through the back alleys. What happened?"

It was difficult to speak clearly with the point of a sword pressed against his gullet but he managed it. Gradually Boiotos' grip relaxed.

"They knew we were coming," Boiotos said in a surly voice, sheathing his sword. "Somehow they knew we were coming!"

"Is your father here?" Lysanias realised his voice sounded squeaky.

"Of course, he's here! It's his house! He's through there. Bit late, aren't you? Why didn't you get here before?" He pushed Lysanias along the passage. A depression seemed to hang over everyone that contrasted with the elation of Stephanos' group.

He found Hierokles in the entertaining room with other important-looking men in officer's uniform and some in civilian clothes. His uncle sounded tired and defeated.

"Ah, Lysanias, my boy. Come and sit down."

"Had to see the women home safely, or I'd have been here earlier," he said hurriedly, "and then I couldn't get through."

"Quite all right, my boy. Bit of a fiasco, eh? They've got a better spy system than we imagined. Half the workers in Peiraieos must have been up here in the square. Too many for us. Decided we'd better hole up in different houses and wait till morning to make our way to our homes. Otherwise we could be picked off in ones and twos. No point in that. Maybe we'll try again when the troops get back from Corinth. Outnumber the scoundrels then, eh?"

Clearly the man was trying to cheer himself up in the face of abject defeat, so Lysanias made consoling, supportive noises. But he knew it wouldn't be the end of it. He was grateful for the heat of the room, with so many men packed in together, that made his face red and disguised the guilty blush he couldn't prevent from spreading across it.

They had relied on surprise and that had been taken from them. Lysanias had taken it from them, he realised, and his heart thumped in fear surrounded as he was by men boiling with frustration and failure, knowing they had let the great man down. The suspicious glances he was receiving told Lysanias he needed to say something more.

"Why didn't you use the cavalry?" Those most elite troops hadn't gone to Sparta, were still here. Hierokles and Boiotos themselves were cavalrymen.

"Ah, not in the city, my boy. Horses no use in the city."

The men could have come without their horses, Lysanias thought, but didn't say. And there must be some hoplites still in Athens who hadn't taken part. It looked as though not all leading aristocrats had agreed to this attempt. Maybe some hadn't been informed.

"Just as well Kimon is still in Corinth. He'd have been humiliated, if he'd known. Let's hope he's on his way back with those troops!" Then Hierokles turned back to his colleagues.

Lysanias found a space on the floor, squeezed into it and settled down to spend the rest of the night there, sleep or not. It clearly wouldn't be tactful to try to leave. He wondered which mischievous god could have lured him into this position of being accepted by both sides in a civil conflict that seemed to become more violent every day and looked to have every chance of getting worse.

Was this the dangerous game that Klereides had been playing? Could it be the thing that had earned him his violent death? Lysanias had never felt more fellow-feeling towards his dead uncle. To make matters worse, he was lying on the hammer. It was most uncomfortable, but he daren't move it further from his body for fear someone saw it, or stepped on it and questioned what it was.

Sleep proved impossible. Through half-closed eyes he looked up to see Boiotos, whispering with two colleagues, cast a suspicious glance in his direction as he toyed with a dagger. Lysanias knew the question on everyone's lips must be who had betrayed them. He really shouldn't have come here. Hierokles had entered, a quiet altercation he could barely hear but he thought he heard the words "It must be him. Who else did we tell who's so new to us?"

"Nonsense," the whispered response. "Would he have come here if he had just betrayed us? We'll question the youngsters who didn't turn up." Perhaps he was right to have come. "Humiliating that we have to put our trust in teenagers."

"I still think we should question him now we have him here."

"No, he's family. We may need his friendship ourselves."

"We could finish him…"

"No! Not here! Not now! In the courts." Hierokles was suddenly forceful.

The danger seemed to have receded and Lysanias' eyelids slid shut, too tired even to think about it.

CHAPTER 14

As soon as light started streaking the sky and there were signs of activity on the streets, the rebels, Lysanias among them, started to leave Hierokles' house in small groups of two and three, for mutual protection, leaving their arms and armour. Lysanias left with a curly-headed fourteen-year-old for whom it had been a great adventure. He clearly wanted to talk about it all but Lysanias hushed him into silence, making sporadic small talk, till they reached the vicinity of the boy's parents' house and he ran off. Apart from the first mule-carts and ox-carts trundling in with produce to the market from the direction of the Thriasian Gate and a dung-cart working its way in the opposite direction, the streets seemed strangely hushed, as though waiting for further momentous events.

Back at his own house, Lysanias lay down to rest. Just for a minute, he thought, but no sooner had he done so, it seemed, than Sindron was shaking him to get up. The slave wouldn't listen to arguments about Lysanias' lack of sleep. Otanes had arranged to introduce Lysanias to the bank and the bankers. It was an important matter for the whole family's finances, so it had to be done. Then they had to find that sophist to obtain legal advice, and they should confront Hermon soon, and there was the ostracism meeting of the Assembly that afternoon, Sindron was sure Lysanias would want to attend that...

Why did there seem to be so many different activities to cram into a day in Athens? Lysanias blinked twice and forced his tired eyes open. Why was Sindron such an old fusser? In fact, Sindron was overjoyed the boy was safe but knew it wouldn't do to say that to him. How would he have ever explained to the boy's mother, if anything serious had happened to him?

Outside, there were no signs that anything unusual had happened during the night but there seemed to be far fewer people around this morning and an eerie quiet in the air. Stallholder's cries rang out singly and tailed off. The bustle had been replaced by a wary stride in everyone's step and a sense of uncertainty about what might happen next. If the bankers felt this, they covered it up.

By the time they reached the banker's table in front of the Painted Colonnade, Lysanias was awake enough to play up his youth and inexperience, his willingness to take Phraston's advice on investments.

No, he didn't want to examine the accounts himself at this stage, he was quite happy for Sindron to do that. Better to let them think he relied heavily on Sindron, that the slave was worth bribing, though Phraston and Lydos were so charming, he found the whole idea very difficult to believe.

Yes, he would use Klereides' seal, which Otanes had passed to him, until he had time to have a new one designed.

Sindron stood back and allowed Otanes to make the introductions and add his explanations to those of the bankers. The steward looked appropriately satisfied when Lysanias re-instated Otanes' drawing facility, less so when he asked for another for Sindron to draw on for Lysanias' personal expenses.

While Phraston drew Otanes aside to chat about what he, as a Persian, felt the chances were of Kallias achieving a conclusive peace settlement, Lydos formally changed the headings on all the accounts in Lysanias' presence, striking through Klereides' name with what seemed to Sindron a horrifyingly final gesture, as though crossing out the man's achievements whatever they were. He opened a new scroll in one case, and, in another, a new column on an old scroll with Lysanias' name at the top and the day and month.

All very formal and boring, Lysanias thought, trying hard to suppress an almighty yawn. How could these people find money and accounts at all interesting? That was his main impression of Phraston and Lydos – nice enough people but essentially boring. He couldn't really see them mixed up in politics and plotting as Sindron had suggested. And he found it very difficult to believe that Phraston had once been a top sportsman.

It was only then it occurred to him to look around at the square. Everything looked completely normal, as though nothing at all had happened last night. He could almost believe it had been a dream. Certainly no-one had mentioned it.

From where he was standing, Sindron could see the accounts scrolls spread out on the table alongside one another. That's strange, he thought. On most of the accounts, one could see clearly that entries down the scroll had been written in slightly different shades of ink, or they had faded to differing extents because of the different times they'd been written. Entries even seemed to be in different hands at some points. But, on the main account showing monthly payments from Hermon and the mine-owner and irregular payments from a variety of merchants set against investments in cargoes, transfers to the household and other minor accounts and major drawings by Klereides, the entries were all clear and black and the ink looked the same all the way down. They were all written by the same person and they looked as though they had all been written at the same time, which was very unlikely! And no signs of fading.

Could it be that someone had rewritten the scroll, created a false scroll? To conceal whatever was in the original scroll? Sindron edged closer to make sure it wasn't his old eyes deceiving him, but, no, the sunlight was bright here, unlike the lamplight of the treasury. He couldn't be wrong.

Could that be why they had been stalled from seeing the accounts? By Otanes not telling them who the bankers were earlier? By Lydos not telling him the bank handled Klereides' account?

In the circumstances, no way to point it out to Lysanias. The boy seemed not to have noticed it himself, but then Sindron hadn't noticed when he was first shown the accounts. Must have been too busy examining the detail, he supposed.

Sindron had established that the best person to advise Lysanias on the strength of his case was Pythodoros of Abdera, the sophist, though his real talents would be revealed in writing the speech for Lysanias to present to the jury. The best time to approach him was in the Akademeia Gardens in the morning before his tuition sessions in rhetoric began.

The two-horse chariot they had hired for a very uncomfortable ride dropped them by the military training grounds, which seemed strangely deserted. They paced past the wrestling practice courts, where young men were already exercising and warming up, to the lawns and groves of the gardens, shaded by leafy plane trees, with the dark spikes of cypresses, the grey-green of olive trees, the stately elms and the florid red blooms of oleanders lending variety and colour. Another of Kimon's contributions since Sindron was last in Athens, the aqueduct that, bringing water from the city, had turned the Gardens from a brown and dusty training ground into a green and restful refuge, which looked to be proving a valuable asset to at least the wealthier citizens, even though the trees and shrubs hadn't yet reached full maturity. From the buzz of insects and the birdsong, men were not the only ones to benefit from Kimon's benevolence.

There were other learned men in the Gardens, but Pythodoros was instantly recognisable from the startling scarlet edging to his cloak, his long dark hair in an ornate coiffure and his great beak of a nose.

While Sindron agreed financial terms for the consultation with Pythodoros' clerk, he asked Lysanias for details of his complaints, as they walked in a shady area. "So that I can decide whether it is a case I would wish to have my name connected with," he said, haughtily.

"I thought you sophists argued you could write a speech for any case and to win any argument?" Lysanias retorted, irritated by the man's businesslike concern for money and the fact that Sindron would not be able to hear this.

"Ah, yes, I have said that. However, you will appreciate that Athenians are a volatile people and, with the new powers of the Assembly and the courts, a dubious case could involve me in, aah, shall we say, accusations later that are best avoided if we can."

Lysanias decided he had better be businesslike too. He explained the nature of the suspected murder and how far they had gone in investigating it.

"Hmm. An interesting problem." The sophist seemed to give it genuine consideration. Lysanias found this encouraging, but then came, "I'm not sure I can help. You are new to this city's legal system, so perhaps I should explain what you need to have a chance with such a case." Pythodoros paused for effect. "I can see that you might have a case for murder against the amphora or against the rope that gave way..."

Lysanias spluttered and strangled a laugh. Pythodoros' eyes sparkled for a moment, as he too saw it with a newcomer's eyes, but his voice kept the same detached, analytical tone.

"I understand your surprise. I assure you there are many precedents and that the highly religious citizens of Athens regard unnatural death as a cause of pollution that can have dire results for the community if not purged by execution of the offending person or animal or the ejection of those or the offending object beyond the boundaries of the state.

"In this case, the offending objects might be likened to slaves, slaves being regarded here as merely 'tools that think', so the real target for compensation would be the owner. Since your uncle was the owner and yourself by inheritance, that doesn't seem very fruitful. Hermon, as the surviving owner at this point in time, could have to recompense you, but I'm sure he would prefer a settlement out of court. Have you approached him on this possibility?"

Lysanias was already becoming angry, at the nitpicking and at the pomposity, but he struggled to keep his feelings under control. "It isn't compensation I'm seeking. I have the duty to avenge my uncle's murder by bringing his murderer to justice."

"My dear young man, I think these desires for vengeance are a little primitive for our civilised age, don't you?" Pythodoros betrayed a tetchiness, as though Lysanias had disturbed the man's measured thinking.

"No, I don't! It is an offence before the gods and they demand vengeance. The pollution must be purged."

Lysanias thought he heard a muttered, "Very dramatic," and realised that to a sophisticated city-dweller the clarity of Lysanias' view of his duty might be disturbing, but so be it. Sindron had caught up with them as they walked talking. At least, his slave would be able to hear this nonsense now.

Pythodoros went on in a strong, clear voice. "Very well. To bring a successful case in the courts, what do you need? You need documentary factual evidence. You have the cut rope. The other side will argue that it is not the same rope, but it is something. That and the footprints might be enough if you were going for a finding of 'murder by person unknown'. The court would direct that the person unknown must exile themselves outside Athens and Attika, thus removing the risk of pollution. That could clear things up fairly quickly and leave you free to get on with your life…" He tailed off as he saw the increasing frustration in Lysanias' eyes.

"Right. Vengeance it is. You also have the remains of the message-scroll. The handwriting is inconclusive, I gather, but it has sufficient of the seal left to identify it as Hermon's seal. We can do something with that.

"Unfortunately, we have nothing to connect the accused directly with the actual, ah, killing of the deceased. True, he could have hired someone to do the deed, and the implications of what the night-watchman saw and the distance between the bloodstains on the grass suggest someone of different build from your colleague Hermon. Still, we have no real proof of this nor idea of who that person was."

It felt strange to be discussing murder and retribution in these peaceful surroundings where small birds sang and the scent of scarlet oleanders and azaleas drifted to Lysanias on the slight breeze.

"You need witnesses. Your porter may be admissible as a witness to Klereides having received the message and reacted immediately, but the testimony of slaves is not normally accepted, unless obtained after torture, and I imagine you would not wish to risk the damage to an elderly household slave that could result from torture, unless maybe you feel at his age he retains little resale value." What a strange logic? Lysanias started to feel an alien, here in Athens!

"You have suggested you may be able to persuade the watchman to testify that he saw someone standing over the body. He is a citizen, so his word is acceptable, but my experience is that, where a person's employment is at stake, they become very reluctant." There were no pauses, so evidently no response was expected. The man took large strides, waved his arms at times to emphasize a point. Lysanias had to quicken his own pace to keep up.

"You need something to make a pathetic epilogue to end the speech. The bloodstained cloak, now. We should be able to build something round that to pull a few tears, especially with references to Klereides' patronage and all the statues and so on that he would have given to beautify the city had he lived longer. Yes," Pythodoros was thinking to himself, evidently testing a few ringing phrases he could build around that. "Yes … there's something there. But, but, but…" Pythodoros' tone implied that it might not be sufficient.

"You need enough substance to build a story reconstructing the crime. Yes, well, Klereides being dragged from his marital bed by a mysterious message, driven to the shipyard in the middle of the night by an unknown chariot and driver, lured to a dangerous spot and executed in a way that would make it appear like an accident, the murderer slipping away unseen under cover of darkness. Yes, we can make something out of that. But where did this killer go? How did the accused engage him? Or pay him? All we have is Hermon's absence at the time of the crime, and he will doubtless produce witnesses to his alibi."

Lysanias was floored by all the questions he and Sindron had failed to ask themselves about the murder, and so failed to investigate.

"Most of all you need a motive. Why should a successful foreign resident of several years standing wish to kill his patron and partner? It doesn't make sense. He'll bring character witnesses as well that will show just how implausible it is." Lysanias was growing red now. Sindron grasped his arm briefly in the hope it might assist him to control his anger. "Yes, yes, I know, even if it is true, the other side will make it seem implausible." He paused while Lysanias regained control, then went on.

Pythodoros asserted that the fact that Klereides had enforced a tough financial deal on Hermon in exchange for his patronage would carry little weight with members of the Areopagos many of whom, though they feared the rise of businessmen swamping the traditional landowning classes, now recognised that the city's prosperity depended on its position as a major trading centre.

"I'm afraid they are likely to value Hermon's contribution to Athens at the present time more than your possible contribution in the future."

For all his attempt at detached objective language, the sophist had a singular ability to insult his client, thought Sindron, especially when that client was an impulsive young man like Lysanias. In fact, Lysanias was coming to feel that Pythodoros' attitude to the law and justice seemed based on a disrespect touching on sacrilege for, after all, didn't Apollo and Athene protect and uphold the ancient law and presumably the modern law as well? But Pythodoros pushed on with his argument.

"Murder is still tried before the Areopagos, one of its few surviving powers, even cases against foreign residents. They tend to be old men from the wealthier classes. They can't be swayed by the same sort of argument as the courts of the people. Cases of complicity in murder, which I take it we are talking about, are tried before a subsidiary court consisting of fifty jurors picked from members of the Areopagos.

"Now, if you could bring a case against Hermon for, say, fraud or maligning the gods, it would go before a people's court and they would immediately be against a wealthy foreign resident. We could produce strong arguments against him as an employer who gives work to foreigners instead of to citizens, who by his nature is not loyal to Athens, oh yes, we could sway that very well."

"But he isn't like that," Lysanias blurted out. "I wouldn't want to win a case on that basis. I want to win on the truth!"

"My naive young man!" The sophist's tone made Lysanias bristle, even if, at other times he might have been the first to admit that he was young and naive. "Where did you come up with such an absurd idea? We are talking here about rhetoric, about using language and presenting arguments in such a way that the listeners are influenced to react in the way the speaker wishes them to react. Truth may be an element but only one element. Persuasion can be much more important. Emotion. Prejudice ... Now, my view is that there may be other individuals who may have stood to gain by Klereides' death that you haven't considered. In my opinion..."

Lysanias was becoming increasingly annoyed. This man's philosophy went against all Lysanias had ever been taught. He couldn't listen to any more of this.

"I'm grateful to you for having given me your time, Pythodoros. If I feel I can use your services, I will return and consult you again. Until then I must bid you good-day."

He turned on his heel and marched away briskly, leaving Pythodoros with his mouth half open, ready to continue his oration. Sindron ran to catch up with the rapidly receding Lysanias. Why couldn't the boy control his emotions? Especially after they had paid such a large consultation fee!

As Philia sat on the cart, dressed in black and fully-veiled, she revelled inwardly to be out in the open in the centre of the city and to be able to see the houses and the people, so many people. Going to the temple to make an offering in atonement was no punishment if this went with it.

She felt sure that her one visit with Klereides, shortly after their marriage, to a tragic play during the Festival of Dionysos had been for him to show off his young bride. From the way pregnant wives greatly outnumbered non-pregnant ones like herself, she had guessed that her husband wouldn't take her again until his friends could see that an heir was on the way. They had gone as a family group to one religious procession but how she would have liked to be in one of the groups of girls and women dancing and singing to the glory of the gods. Klereides or Makaria obviously didn't want her to see the city or make friends.

The groom had rigged the framework that on her wedding day had carried garlands and ribbons so that it now supported mourning drapes. They could see out but not be seen. Glykera walked behind as an added support for the ladies.

Then just as they got to the market-place where Philia wanted to see the market stalls and activity, Makaria insisted on talking.

"This atonement business, Philia. Forget about that. The gods aren't going to worry over one little slip." It sounded like a mild sacrilege, but she was more shocked when Makaria went on. "We women have to be strong, take control of our households and our husbands. They've chosen to pen us up in their houses but that doesn't mean we can't still wield power over them. That's what today's about, my girl, the priestesses will teach you a thing or two."

"I'm sure the men don't mean anything bad to us, Makaria," answered Philia, desperately trying to see all that was going on outside. The smells of fish and cooked meats wafted in intriguingly and she longed to be out there looking at it all but doubted if she was ever likely to. But the women's market, surely she should be able to visit that even if the men did the main shopping.

"They may not mean it, my girl, but they achieve it, if we let them. You asked about property. Well, we can't own it but there are ways of enjoying its benefits, though one needs to be cunning." Makaria gave up there. The sights and sounds and smells – they were just passing the herbs and spices section of the market – were too much to compete with for Philia's attention.

Lysanias sat down on a bench in the wrestling courts, still shaking with anger, his fists clenched and white. He stared straight at the sun baked ground before his feet. Sindron eased himself down beside the lad. He hadn't liked the man's attitude himself, but clearly his knowledge of the law and how the courts actually operated was profound.

"Master, I understand your reactions, but you need someone of the calibre of Pythodoros!"

"Sindron, didn't you hear what he said? Hermon hasn't got an adequate motive. We may be barking up the wrong tree." So the boy had been thinking as well as reacting.

"What if Klereides was trying to increase his share of the profits?" Sindron clung onto his view that Hermon must be guilty. The grunts and cries of naked youths and men, knotted together in wrestling holds, as they tried to throw one another, their oiled bodies gleaming, punctuated their conversation.

"Not enough! With Klereides dead, he is out of business."

"There are other citizens who could become his patron, master."

"Not if Klereides' death frightened them off. I imagine anyone would think twice, if that was the fate of his predecessor. Without a citizen patron, Hermon would have to sell out and move to another city."

"Unless he already had an agreement sewn up with someone, an accomplice. He did mention General Ariston." Sindron was aware his arguments were sounding a little desperate.

"We've heard absolutely nothing to suggest that, Sindron. We have to look at who else might have done it."

"But all the evidence, master!"

"Someone wants us to believe Hermon is guilty. They've laid a false trail."

Lysanias wasn't really sure if that was plausible, but it was a possibility. His attention was taken by a wrestler who seemed to have lost his temper and was breaking the rules. Great gods, he could break his opponent's neck with a hold like that. Lysanias started up, but the wrestling instructor was dealing with it, threatening the offender with being banned from the training ground. That calmed things. When the anger left his face, the tall, strong wrestler looked familiar somehow. That long pointy nose. Now where...? Sindron pulled him back to their argument.

"He may still have a reason, master. We just don't know what it is yet."

"Ah. Yes, he could, but you think there are other people we do know would gain from Klereides' being out of the way. My fine country cousins thought they were going to inherit the estate and we know Hierokles was in financial trouble after that fine. And it says something about their relationship that Klereides didn't help him pay his fine. They really can't have liked one another."

"Yes, but they live out in the country, master. They couldn't have done it." Even as he said it, Sindron realised it was unsound.

"They could have hired someone to do it for them, as we thought Hermon must have." Lysanias was insistent.

"But their own blood relation. You might as well accuse his mother."

They both paused as they registered what Sindron had just said.

A shadow fell across the path in front of them. The wrestling instructor was standing there, feet braced. "Gentlemen, if you don't wish either to take part or to observe and encourage, I must ask you to find somewhere else to converse. You are distracting the wrestlers."

The man was clearly controlling his anger. Lysanias apologised profusely. Neither of them had realised how animated their discussion had become. Stupid, when they didn't want too many people to know about their investigations. They got up and found a quiet corner near the changing rooms.

It was Sindron who put it into words. "No, she couldn't. Not her own son!" Yet was he sure? Sindron knew that traditional values were breaking down in other areas in Athens, why not within families as well? After all, she had made sure that her younger son went into exile in Eion.

"She gives the impression she agrees with Hierokles that Klereides let the family reputation down by going into business and she seems to see Hierokles as what a wealthy Athenian should be like." Lysanias was horrified with himself that he could find these arguments. Was it listening to Pythodoros that had made him think this way?

"But women don't have money of their own, master. How would she be able to pay a killer, even if she had a way of finding someone?"

"She has control of the household monies with Otanes," returned Lysanias. "You told me yourself there were dubious aspects to those records. Perhaps they're in it together. I think we really must confront them soon over the household accounts and that lease for the foundry."

"Yes, and they haven't told us where Philia's dowry money is yet." Sindron thought for a moment, while Lysanias looked at him, anxious that they end up with someone to blame for his uncle's death. "But Otanes, master. I find it difficult to believe. Even if he doesn't seem to have taken seriously Klereides' promises of freedom, he did seem to regard Klereides as his security as a Persian in a Greek city. Otanes wouldn't want to risk that, surely!"

"Not unless there was something more pressing."

"Look, master, these aren't motives. They're only suspicions."

"Well, what about other businessmen? That rival firm, now. They'd expect to get more government contracts with Klereides gone." Lysanias told Sindron Aspasia's view of how ruthless Athenian businessmen had become. Sindron found it difficult to believe that a prostitute, even a high-class one, could be that knowledgeable but what she had said made so much sense that he had to admit to himself that he might have misjudged the boy's motives. He would apologise to him later. But he wasn't convinced businessmen would have gone that far.

"Politicians now," he put in. "I never did trust that Ariston."

"Yes. Always a bit too full of praise for my uncle. No-one can be that marvellous! Especially considering the tales we've heard that say he was devious, to say the least."

"Don't talk ill of the dead, master."

"Precisely. It's one thing not speaking ill of him but they didn't need to praise him so much. What if Ariston had found out Klereides was talking with the radicals? He would regard it as treachery to their class, their party. So would Hierokles."

"But master, where do we stop, if all these people have a motive. We've got no evidence on any of them, and we've no way of investigating most of them."

"You're being stupid now, Sindron."

Sindron bristled. "I think not, master. Like the philosophers say, we must apply strict logic. We must assume everyone with a possible motive could be guilty. Then we eliminate those who couldn't have been involved."

"A conspiracy! Now you think there was a conspiracy!"

"I didn't say that, master..." Sindron meant that. Where had the boy come up with that idea from? But was it a possibility?

"This is all getting too confusing." Lysanias looked downcast.

"On the other hand, it could have been more than one of them..."

"But how do we find out?" Lysanias cried, plaintively.

Sindron was silent for a second. Then, "I really don't know, master. I'm sure we'll think of something." They sat dejected.

Lysanias was staring at one of the statues of a wrestler, erected by the proud winner of the wrestling event in one of the major games, when it came to him. "That carving Hierokles and Boiotos gave for Klereides' tomb - Klereides at Plataea. If they ordered that before he died, that would show they knew he was going to be killed."

"Yes. We know who the stonemason is. It ought to be possible to check on that."

"They did arrive very soon after his death, given the time it must take for a messenger to reach Dekelia and for them to get ready and travel here. Could you work that out?"

"I could try, master, but you're the one who is good at measurements, like your father. There is something else I could check."

"What's that?"

"You remember when we were trying to get your citizenship and dispensation sorted out? I'm sure at least one of those officials said that Klereides' death had already been reported with someone else's name given as heir."

"Did they? I don't recall that. Who on earth...?"

"Now, it may not mean anything, especially if the family really thought you'd been killed in Eion, but it would tell us who had most to gain from Klereides' death."

"Sindron, you're a genius."

Then Sindron threw in his latest discovery. "Also I think we have to include Phraston and Lydos as suspects."

"Why? Just because they tried to bribe you?"

"No, not just that. Though with a bribe like freedom, they must have something serious to hide. No, when they were showing you the accounts, I noticed the main scroll had been re-written and recently."

"So you think they've created false accounts to hide the something underhand they were doing on the real one!"

"Precisely. I think they may have been misusing funds in your uncle's accounts without his knowledge. In view of my bribe, it could be quite a large amount. Enough for them to be seriously worried."

"Enough to kill for? Surely they wouldn't kill someone because of that? They seem so respectable."

"Yes, master, but remember what your blue and green courtesan told you about how vicious business can become in Athens. Maybe bankers are as bad as businessmen."

"But Lydos is your friend, Sindron! How do you feel about suspecting your friend?" Lysanias half intended it as a tease. Sindron seemed to want to suspect half the population of Athens.

"Very disillusioned, master, very disillusioned!" Lysanias realised that Sindron certainly looked it. He must mean it.

"Great Zeus, you really do think he could be involved, don't you?"

"I'm afraid so, master, though I hope I'm wrong."

There was a pause while they both thought over all that had been said. Finally Lysanias ventured, "I don't see either of them leaping over the shipyard fence and climbing scaffolding in the dark, do you? Especially Phraston! He'd collapse the whole thing if he tried." At least Lysanias was joking again, Sindron was glad to see, amused himself at the mental image it conjured up. "Frankly, I don't see any of them doing it, even Boiotos, though he's violent enough to kill someone."

"No, master, but any of them could have paid someone or sent a servant. Your cousins have slaves, so does Ariston – we've seen one of them. He has soldiers too. Phraston has slaves: Lydos has his sons."

"Ariston wouldn't trust soldiers in the current atmosphere, would he?"

"I don't know, master. They'd be young aristocrats, so maybe."

Lysanias continued the listing. "Hermon has slaves and foreign workers. He might have someone he can trust to do any dirty job for him. That big personal slave maybe. He would know the shipyard."

"You could say much the same about the rival shipbuilders," said Sindron becoming resigned to going round in circles, not reaching a conclusion.

"We've no way at all of finding out about them. Even if I went to work in their yard, I doubt if I'd find out anything at this stage."

"I still think we should consider this Hammer of Hephaistos crowd you've been knocking around with. Amphora falls on Klereides: hammer beats out metal. The similarity is very close. From the way you say this Ephialtes harangues them, any of them could have picked up the idea and decided to apply it."

As he spoke, Sindron had drawn, in the dust at their feet with the tip of his stick, a crude sketch of a hammer descending on a ball of metal on an anvil and, next to it, a bulbous amphora descending on Klereides' round head. He had even dotted in Klereides' eyes. Seeing the look of pain on Lysanias' face as he glanced at it and realised what it represented, Sindron scrubbed it through with his sandaled foot.

"And I wouldn't put anything past those two ruffian stonemasons we met on the ship," Sindron concluded.

"They were on the ship with us at the time Klereides was killed, Sindron!"

"Yes, well, their friends, then. I'm sure they're as primitive."

"Sindron, everything I have seen about the Fellowship of Hephaistos and about the radicals is that they arm themselves only in defence. I must admit, if I was in charge, I'd be a bit more aggressive but that's the way they are!"

"Hmmm!" In the face of the lad's conviction, Sindron decided to drop that argument – for now.

"Anyway, if Hermon isn't guilty, then Philebos wasn't covering up for him. So there's no harm done in confronting Hermon with the evidence of the message-scroll and of Philebos' cover up and see what he says. I think we should do that now." Setting action to the words, Lysanias sprang up and set off back towards town and the road to Peiraieos.

"Right, master," said Sindron, taking up his stick and following, glad that some decision had been made. "We must do it forcefully, too, and get some real answers."

As Makaria and Philia climbed the steps to the top of the High City, Philia glanced back and saw the market place spread out below her, and around that the whole city of Athens. Beyond that was the road to Peiraieos and its three harbours and the sea, glinting in the morning sun.

At the top, the sound of female chatter was immediately familiar to Philia's ears, just like a sewing circle back home. And so it was, but two big circles. That circle over there, that must be the new cloak for Athene they were embroidering, the brightly-coloured cloak that would be presented to the goddess's ancient wooden statue after being paraded through the streets of the city at the next great Panathenaia Festival.

Philia laughed and clapped her hands, forgetting her mourning. This would be fun – to sit embroidering and gossip while doing it. Then her heart missed a beat. Strolling round the circle was great Athene herself. The goddess had appeared. Philia stopped in wonder, her mouth open in awe.

"Go on, girl, it's only the priestess," and Makaria pushed her forward.

Philia breathed again. The priestess was tall and stately, with helmet and breastplate and flowing gown, every inch a female warrior, so like the statues of the goddess. Yet the woman's manner, as she made suggestions on colours, patterns and stitches, was friendly and feminine.

She turned as they approached and raised her hands above her head in the salute of Athene Victorious. "Athene salutes the widow, all honour to the widow." It sounded like the ritual it was but Philia was impressed, and her knees shook slightly. The priestess knew who she was! Then she saw that Makaria had thrown back her veil, and was immediately recognisable. Philia threw back her veil as well.

"You'll be Philia, widow of Klereides, I've heard about you." Philia bowed her head, as she held out her offerings. The priestess thanked her and waved for an acolyte to take them.

She drew Philia forward, over the grass and rubble and stones of the ruined temples, towards the women seated among the jagged remnants of pillars and walls.

"You see us in a sorry state, my child. Our temple still in ruins eighteen years after it was destroyed, but that is the way the men will have it."

Then Philia came in for a great harangue from the priestess. She was clearly annoyed that the women were obliged to pursue their acts of devotion in the open air, where the sun could bleach their colours and a shower could damage the fabric. Their only refuge was a wooden shack. Even the wooden statue of great Athene was housed in a temporary wooden building. All because the men had decided not to rebuild Athene's temple.

"Mighty Athene is patron of this great city and she is angry," continued the priestess with vehemence. "Such disrespect will bring down nothing but shame on those who have displayed it. I have read the omens and they are not propitious for those who have long been our leaders."

When Philia offered the usual reason, that this was to display the sacrilege done by the Persians, the priestess cited temples built in recent years to male gods and heroes in the lower city by leaders such as Kimon.

"What other reason could they have?" Philia was genuinely puzzled.

"What reason? The only reason! Male power! Economic power!"

The decision, she explained, had allowed them to remove the bulk of the city treasury from the Temple of Athene and several banks had taken their deposits elsewhere as well. All moves that denied wealth and honour to the goddess and dignity to her priestesses.

In the face of such vehemence, Philia felt a little dazed, yet honoured to be taken into the confidence of the highest female dignitary in the city.

The priestess seated her between two wives who were possibly some eight or ten years older than herself. They gave her needles and thread and seemed to approve as her fingers rapidly stitched a design, which, while owing something to ideas in theirs, twisted them into new patterns of Philia's own devising.

From here, she could see straight across to the grey and green mountains stretching to the immaculate blue of the sky. She felt an immediate sense of freedom from all constraints and couldn't keep her eyes from skipping round the other women. That elaborate hairstyle, with the coil to one side and flowing down on the other, looking like natural wavy hair – that was new. She'd love to try that, when her hair grew again. And that unusual way of draping her cloak that woman had on the other side of the circle, that was really nice. And that lovely lavender colour mantle, oh yes!

Philia listened to the chatter of the other women. She was amused and not a little shocked to hear the tales of how they had tricked, cajoled or led their husbands into giving them what they wanted, using sex or withholding sex, how they had extended their control over the household purse-strings, often without their husbands realising it. Were they boasting, she wondered. She had never managed it with Curly. She knew she couldn't match their stories, so was content to listen, while they seemed happy to chatter. These women could be good friends, she thought to herself, full of a new satisfaction.

The young woman on her left started pointing out some of the other women. "That weepy one, that's General Ariston's wife, Phoebe, though what she's got to cry about I don't know." Philia speculated that the woman could be quite attractive if it wasn't for her miserable expression.

The rather older woman on her right chipped in. "You see those two expensively-dressed women near her? The plump, homely-looking one, that's General Kimon's wife Isodike, and the one who puts on the airs, that's his half-sister Elpinike. The men sing dirty songs about her, but I don't believe it. Just because she had to live with her brother when their father died and keep house for him, they said they were committing incest. Don't you think men are awful?"

She whispered some story about how, annoyed with Kimon's adulteries and with his having forced his sister into marriage with rich old Kallias, they had devised a scheme with a painter to discredit Kimon and teach him a lesson. Philia really couldn't believe that.

Then there was the story of the wife who couldn't stand being bossed around by her husband, so she deliberately weakened the straps on his armour before he went into battle so that, under stress, they would break and he would be killed and she could be free again. And he was killed! By a spear thrust through the heart! Oh, dear sweet Athene, protect me, Philia prayed. If a wife could do that, so could a mother!

One thing Lysanias and Sindron were agreed on was that Hermon had to be confronted and as soon as possible. They knew they had to make sure that they place all their charges in front of him before pleasantries and the distractions of his work could interrupt. It was Sindron who suggested the method. He remembered something like it from a comedy he had seen years ago. They agreed it might work.

As luck would have it Hermon was in his office. The slave showed them in and shut the door behind them. Looking up from some accounts,

Hermon started to rise, all charm, saying, "Well, gentlemen, it's very nice to see you. I wondered when you would be able to find time from mourning to come and talk again."

Mindful of the need to be forceful, Lysanias charged straight in.

"You may not have a motive, Hermon, but, if you still don't think it was murder, you explain this."

Sindron jumped in, on cue. "Why was an old frayed rope substituted for the real one that was cut through with a knife?"

Followed immediately by Lysanias. "Why was there a bare footprint in the dried blood on the planking?"

And back to Sindron, as they alternated. "Why was the workman who tied the rope sacked and the watchman sent home with some false excuse about fever in the family, leaving no-one who could be questioned?"

"Why did the watchman think he saw a dark figure bending over Klereides' body?"

"Why can't you tell us who you saw in Corinth?"

"And why does the message that summoned Klereides to the shipyard carry your seal?"

"See, here it is!" Sindron pulled the scroll out from inside his cloak as carefully as he could and unrolled it on the spot, as Lysanias accused:

"Motive or no, Hermon, can you explain all that and still claim you are innocent?"

The expressions flitting across Hermon's face had run the gamut, as they kept up the barrage of questions leaving no gap for a response. They had ranged through surprise, anger, disbelief, cynicism, affront, worry and just plain confusion. When they finished, the silence rang, despite the hammering noises from the yard outside.

Hermon quickly regained his external composure but the broad smile was no longer there and the eyes were narrowed as they switched between the two accusing faces.

"Well, gentlemen, you have been busy and I thought you were in mourning." Could that be intended as a joke? If so, Lysanias found it offensive.

Hermon dropped his gaze and turned away to look down at the dark red ragged shape of the scroll that Sindron had placed on his table.

"Company seal," he muttered. "You're right, it's my seal but we also use it as the company seal. Several people have access to it, use it for official documents." His tone lacked confidence, seemed apologetic.

"Who?" Lysanias spat it out, in evident disbelief.

"The overseer, my naval architect, the clerk who orders materials. It's nothing special."

This information had removed an important link in their chain of evidence, and, in the silence as they thought what this now implied, Hermon added, possibly feeling he had got himself off at least one hook,

"Have you really established that the rope was cut and that someone replaced it to hide the evidence?"

Hermon seemed genuinely to want to know. He was looking straight at them, questioningly.

"Yes, we have the rope," Lysanias said, in a dispirited tone that betrayed his uncertainty about what use it now was. "It even has earthenware fragments where it was cut away from the amphora and you can see the fresh knife mark on the neck of the amphora."

"Master Lysanias confronted Philebos yesterday and he confessed to organising the cover up," added Sindron.

"'For the good of the yard,' he said." Lysanias completed the story.

Hermon looked thoughtful, then angry. "He did, did he? What right has Philebos to take it on himself to cover up a murder of my partner without the least reference to me? Yes, I was out of town, but no mention, not one mention." The businessman looked genuinely annoyed. Could he be acting this? "We must go and see him. Can't leave this hanging around to plague the business. We'll have the authorities down on us, not to mention the gods."

Lysanias pursued the new tack. "Would Klereides have responded to a message from Philebos? Did they meet regularly?"

"If they did, I'd want to know about it. Ambitious man that Philebos. Wouldn't want him influencing the patron behind my back."

"But did they meet?"

"Not to my knowledge but it's possible."

It was Sindron who asked, "But the other questions? What about the other questions?"

"Oh, yes. Who did I see in Corinth? I don't suppose you'll accept that I went all that way to see a prostitute, a high-grade prostitute? No, I didn't think you would. Though it is partly true. I go about once a month, when we're not at war with them. Do a bit of business at the same time, of course, look out for any new developments in their shipbuilding techniques." He paused, held by their demanding eyes, and lowered his voice even more. "I suppose I shall have to take you into my confidence, but I must ask you to keep this very quiet, perhaps for ever. It's very sensitive politically."

He looked straight into Lysanias' eyes, betraying in his own both a trace of real fear and an effort to project trust. He was clearly looking for an answer.

"I'm not sure I can promise that ... If it has no direct relevance to my uncle's death, I give you my word. And, of course, Sindron too."

"Of course," said Sindron, who was even more intrigued than his master.

Hermon stepped closer and lowered his voice. "You know how crucial the votes in the Assembly are for certain people these days?"

They nodded.

"How much difference it could make if Kimon's troops, all likely to vote for him, were delayed on the way back to Athens?" He didn't wait for reactions but went on, "Syracuse was originally a colony of Corinth, both are composed of Dorian Greeks, so I'm in a position to speak to their leaders, where a citizen of Ionian Greek Athens can't. One of the radical leaders here asked me to go and persuade them to find an excuse for holding up the troops for a few days. Klereides had been working to become friendly with the radicals. I thought this would help even more. They would owe us a favour then. There!" He looked relieved to have told someone, but the fear was still there in his eyes. No wonder! If Kimon's men knew, thought Sindron, they would slaughter him and it could mean war with Corinth. Hermon must be much braver than he looked to undertake such a dangerous mission.

"Themist..." uttered Lysanias, then stopped himself.

"You know he's in town?" Hermon hissed it out, in surprise.

Lysanias nodded. "I, uh, met him yesterday."

"Well, you do get around, young man. Very impressive!" Hermon evidently felt reassured now he could believe Lysanias was already trusted within the radical fraternity. "He used to visit Syracuse in the old days, when he was negotiating for our tyrant Gelon's support against the Persians, but then Sicily was invaded by Carthage, so Gelon couldn't help anyway. We were good friends. But no one else must know. Is that agreed?" They nodded.

"Why would the Corinthians agree to do that?" Sindron was genuinely puzzled.

"That's easy. They're the second most powerful city in the Peloponnesian League, which is dominated by Sparta, so they're quite happy to weaken her occasionally. With Kimon out of the way and democrats in control in Athens, they think that will boost Corinth's power. They've no love for Themistokles though."

Lysanias asked it. "What is it you're so afraid of, Hermon?"

"Do I look afraid? Yes, I imagine I do. It's not just fear of Kimon's men finding out about Corinth. It's this."

Hermon reached under a small pile of shield designs on a side table and brought out a panel of wood. On it, scrawled in green paint, "Be warned!" with a rough symbol of a hammer. But the colour for Hephaistos is red, thought Lysanias, though he didn't say it.

"Philebos claims he found it under the scaffolding where Klereides died. Could have been left at the same time and slipped down. I can't help feeling it's aimed at me."

"I understand your fears," said Lysanias. He noticed that Sindron was thoughtful.

"Did Klereides ever talk of receiving threats?"

"Not that I recall. Kept a lot to himself, that man. Solid."

Hermon pulled himself together. He pushed the wooden message out of sight again, and said, "Now let's see about this deceiver Philebos!"

Sindron excused himself and headed back to Athens as they had agreed. It was important that he check certain things out with city officials before all the offices closed down for the Assembly meeting.

As they climbed down towards the market place, Philia could see the men gathering in the sacred central area for the Assembly meeting that Lysanias had spoken about. He must be somewhere among that crowd she thought to herself proudly, despite all the other women had just been saying about men. It gave her a thrill to think that such a young man should be so knowledgeable about the politics of the city. And he was hers. She was sure her father would be impressed with Lysanias, when he arrived. All the stories were that Kimon had ridden to Corinth himself to arrange the passage through of the troops, so her father should be home soon.

From the top, she had spotted the road to Eleusis and then on to Megara and Corinth snaking off in the distance, and, in the clear air, far, far away on the horizon, the High City of Corinth, but, for all her staring, there was no sign of a column of troops marching back.

"Surely all men and all marriages can't be that bad, Makaria, can they?" She asked it almost pleadingly.

"Most of them. My husband was a fool, anyway."

"Did you hate him?"

"Not hate, despise maybe. I'm sorry to be so brutally honest, young lady, but it's time you learnt."

The old woman's statements were as blunt and unfeeling as always, but they gave Philia the cue for the question to which she dreaded the answer.

"Klereides, did you hate Klereides?"

"No, nor did I despise him. I didn't like the way he got involved in business, or some of the gossip about him, but he pulled the family out of the financial mess his father landed us in. I have to be grateful for that, even if he has squandered his money recently." It sounded very grudging. Makaria went on to a statement that sounded almost prepared. "You'll find it's difficult for a woman not to want to mother and protect her sons. Whatever they do. However corrupt and deceitful they become." There was a slight pause. "I'd never have done anything to hurt him, if that's what you mean."

"Thank you, Makaria." Philia couldn't tell whether Makaria was telling the truth or not. She couldn't see into her eyes. It just didn't sound like Makaria to say that sort of thing. She had to feel grateful to her mother-in-law for being so open with her and began to feel a little differently towards her now Makaria was treating her as worthy of respect.

The Temple of The Mother was like nothing Philia had ever seen before. From a distance, it had looked like a rock outcropping from the hill behind. Close to, it was a curving wall of giant rock piled upon giant rock, as though the titans of legend must have placed them here, for no man could surely move great rocks of that size and weight.

Makaria urged Philia to enter through the central opening, where she knew only women were allowed to go. She felt herself quaking, but why should she be afraid? This was a place of women, of the great Mother, protector of women. Here was the home of Gea, the earth spirit, but also of Rhea her daughter, mother of all the gods, of Demeter, her daughter, goddess of the grain and fertility, and of her daughter Kore, of Hera, wife and sister of almighty Zeus, and of Aphrodite, goddess of love and marriage, wife of Hephaistos. Not a vengeful male god among them, so why be afraid? Besides, Makaria was behaving as though entering here was an everyday occurrence.

Ahead of them ran a long wide passage, open to the sky. At its end stood an enormous, bulbous, weather-worn statue of the great earth mother, stolid and dignified as the earth itself.

Makaria introduced Philia to the priestess, who was attired in a flowing gown of earth-brown and gold thread with golden sandals, garlanded with the produce of the earth, vines and olive leaves, corn and barley. She admonished Makaria for not bringing Philia before, then gestured for her to follow.

"Come, my child. I am about to address a gathering below in the underworld."

Makaria excused herself, saying that she had something else to attend to, and went, leaving Glykera with Philia.

Could this really lead to the underworld, Philia wondered, grateful of the comforting figure of Glykera beside her, as she descended the spiral steps, down and down. At the bottom, the great chamber hewn into the rock, itself like an arched temple, with oil lamps glowing and flickering in niches, and statuettes of The Mother in her various guises, mother, wife and maid, in hollows in the walls.

Philia felt totally enclosed, as though in the womb of the Mother, warm and comforted. The priestess' address reinforced what she had heard in the High City.

"The stories of the gods teach us that marriage is a battlefield and that wives must always look out for their own interests and those of their offspring." The opening statement drew a gasp from some of the younger, newer women like herself. The priestess continued.

"Gods and men will always seek to constrain and possess women and, while we may be bound as wives and daughters to serve them, yet we can take steps to ensure..."

Philia realised how confused she was feeling. She had always secretly thought that the behaviour of the gods was rather reprehensible. Now here was a priestess saying it was acceptable to behave as badly as the gods! Were these the rules men go by?

"And this is the natural way of things. It proves that female wisdom and power is greater than the male..."

Philia knew that she had always felt that she, and her mother and sisters had more stability than her brothers, who were always off getting into some scrape or another. Now the priestess was giving a firm religious conclusion to her speech.

"The only true worship must be to the source of all the gods and the source of all humans, men and women, the great earth mother, Gea."

Philia joined in the chants absent-mindedly, lost in thoughts of this whole new way of seeing the world, so contradictory to what she had been led to believe but so rational.

If it was the natural, gods-given order of things for women to conspire against their husbands, then it could be acceptable for Makaria to conspire in the murder of Klereides. Clearly, all women were expected to support and aid one another, so Philia should assist Makaria to conceal this fact. Was that why Makaria had brought her here? To win her support? No, if Makaria had killed Curly, Philia could never forgive her! After all, Klereides had always been kind and gentle towards her; Makaria never had. But she still found it difficult to believe even Makaria could do that.

Philebos had crumbled when Hermon and Lysanias confronted him. He admitted he had loaned one of the company seals to the city naval architect Amynias. Senior naval architects and administrators had a drinking club, Men of Poseidon. They were worried at the way Klereides seemed to be backing the radicals and their peace proposals. Without the constant need for war galleys that continued war brings, the status of shipbuilding would decline and so would that of the Men of Poseidon.

"At that last dinner party of his, he tried to persuade us that wasn't his intention, but he spent so much time smoothing up to the officials in charge of construction, roadways and public works, we didn't believe him, so we didn't cancel the plan."

Lysanias was horrified. "So you killed Klereides for that!"

"No! The plan was to frighten him, to scare him into changing his ways. I suggested the place. There were lots of less heavy things that could be made to fall close by him but big enough so he'd get the point. Something went wrong."

"Wrong!!" Lysanias blurted but Hermon stopped him.

"You'd better tell us the whole story, Philebos."

"Amynias and Inaros were organising someone to do it. So we wouldn't be implicated. That's what they told me. They persuaded me to arrive at the yard shortly after, find Klereides shaken up and calm him. If I could find some way of hinting that maybe someone was warning him, all well and good. I was to claim that I had called him to a meeting to show him…"

The overseer's expression changed. The realisation had hit him.

"By the gods, they set me up to take the blame! And I was stupid enough to agree. No wonder they invited me to join their dining club. They must have meant this all along. I promise I'll tell you everything."

The overseer looked terrified, as well he might. Accomplice to murder. Not a nice charge for a very ordinary administrator of industry to face. At last, though, someone had admitted involvement in Klereides' death and the story sounded plausible, even though the man was clearly trying to rid himself of any direct responsibility. Lysanias felt he was getting closer to the real culprit.

It was Hermon who saw the flaw. "Why didn't you claim to have summoned Klereides to the yard?"

"When I was nearly here, I heard the alarm for a death jangling. I knew he was dead. I realised I could be blamed, or you, Resident Hermon, but you were out of Athens."

"Was it intended that I should be blamed?" Hermon looked very angry.

"No, no, of course not. He shouldn't have been dead. But he was. I had to contact Amynias to arrange an alibi, but we didn't expect so many questions. You were a big shock to us all, Citizen Lysanias. Fortunately, my assistant had taken the right steps by the time I got back, and I got a rigger to switch the ropes, but I couldn't find the scroll. I hoped it had been taken or destroyed."

Hermon made Philebos summon his assistant. The skinny young man confirmed the action he had taken and when Philebos had arrived, but he knew nothing about anyone changing a rope. He'd just ordered the men to carry everything to the store yard, hadn't really examined it himself, and then Philebos had taken over. He looked puzzled and intrigued by their serious expressions but they sent him away without explanation.

Hermon instructed Philebos not to leave town and to report to him the following day for a decision on his future with the company. The man was visibly shaken. Well, he deserved it, fumed Lysanias. He's lucky I didn't break his neck! Hermon had promised to take it up with the naval architect and officials at the first opportunity, which could be as early as that evening at General Ariston's dining club.

He revealed to Lysanias that the new shipbuilding contract had gone to the rival company, and Hermon obviously saw this decision as part of the same conspiracy that had ended in the death of Klereides. However, Lysanias found it difficult to see that as the most urgent concern.

Yet he did ask, "Who owns this company?"

"Oh, it's Isomenes and Partners, fellow from Kition in Cyprus. His patron's that big financier. You may have heard of him. Involved with Kimon's party. Phrasion, Phrastos, something like that."

"Phraston! You mean the banker?"

"Yes, that's him."

Lysanias was dazed. Why did everyone seem to have connections with everyone else? It really was like the labyrinth he had compared it to earlier, but at least Theseos had finally come face to face with his Minotaur. Lysanias was beginning to wonder if he ever would find his monster, the murderer, at the end of this never-ending tunnel. If he ever did, was he capable of finding his way back out of all the deceit and corruption?

CHAPTER 15

Lysanias was still fuming when he arrived back at the market place and walked towards the red-roped enclosure. His head was going over and over what Philebos had said and the irony if Klereides had died only as the result of a silly prank that went wrong.

Increasingly aware that he was having to fit in with people from different social spheres, Lysanias had that day deliberately worn a fairly straightforward cloak, with a simple design embroidered in two lines around the edge in brown. He was grateful for a while to find himself anonymous amongst the crowd.

From the number of farmers, shepherds and fishermen it was evident that the aristocrats had made great efforts to bring in their supporters from the countryside in an attempt to balance out the craftsmen and shopkeepers of Athens and Peiraieos.

From overheard snatches of conversation, Lysanias gathered that tension was still high over the failed attempt to seize power, worry about how the vote would go and whether Kimon's troops would return soon and what result that might have. Though Kimon himself was back from Corinth and had secured their passage, it was now unlikely that his troops would arrive in time but some were still hoping.

Then Lysanias realised he must find Hierokles, so that he could be registered to vote. He needed a family member to introduce him and hoped his cousin had remembered.

He started to move towards the gap in the rope that served as an entrance to the meeting area. Then, there right in front of him were Stephanos and Glaukon talking with Arkhestratos. Lysanias had hoped to avoid significant contact with either faction. It was too exposed. The other side might see and his divided loyalties would really be obvious, but it was too late now.

"Is everything all right?" he asked.

Stephanos pulled away from the others to talk. "We're worried about Ephialtes. No-one's seen him all day. Apparently his slave said he was sleeping soundly when the boys asked this morning."

"Probably preparing his speech."

"That's what we thought earlier but it's not like him. Perikles has gone to fetch him, with a few bodyguards. Can't take any risks!" Tucked in a group of workers, Stephanos obviously felt reasonably confident to speak his mind, but now he lowered his voice. "How'd you know they were going to try to seize power last night?" The question Lysanias had hoped to avoid, but sometime he would have to tell Stephanos the truth, why not now?

"I thought you'd realise when I told you I had a rich uncle..."

"Thought you were telling a tall one, citizen. You've really got rich relations?"

"Yes. My uncle was..."

"And still you told us...?" Stephanos looked amazed, almost admiring.

"Yes, my uncle was Klereides."

"The one who was crushed in the shipyard?" Then Stephanos smiled. "That explains a lot."

"I think he was murdered, that's why I wanted to get work in the shipyard. To check it out."

A light seemed to dawn in Stephanos eyes, taking over from the suspicious look that had lurked there. "You think one of the rich lot did it, don't you? That's why you sided with us, right?"

Lysanias grinned, recognising he had made his decision without realising it. "I think that's because I regard myself as a worker."

"Too right, brother. Soon as I saw you handling those tools, I knew you weren't faking it." Lysanias was obliged to exchange the Fellowship greeting grip with Stephanos, who seemed eager to share the news with his colleagues. Lysanias stopped him, "Could you keep it to yourself for the time being? Till I find the murderer? Just wanted you to know that, if you see me talking to any of Kimon's supporters, it doesn't mean anything."

Reluctantly, Stephanos agreed, and Lysanias managed to move away amongst the crowd, hoping none of the aristocrats he knew had spotted their conversation.

He wasn't sure if he had given the real reason for his siding with the radicals. He couldn't really pretend, even to himself, that he was still a worker. He had no need any more to work to support himself. He was a wealthy Athenian now, and they didn't work. His interests might well lie with the aristocrats. He just didn't feel like one of them. Maybe it was that the wealthy seemed so lazy, selfish and conniving, even corrupt, while the workers like Stephanos were so much more straightforward, said what they meant. But Themistokles, he wasn't at all straightforward, nor some of the other radicals. Lysanias had a feeling he might regret this later.

He noticed Boiotos moving from group to group among the younger well-dressed men, presumably trying to consolidate the pro-Kimon vote.

"Ah, Lysanias, heir of Klereides." Lysanias turned. Had he been noticed talking with Stephanos? No, it was only Strynises. With his system of informants, he must know already about Lysanias' double life. "A little something you may not have heard already, young man," he said, then recited a few lines of verse.

"When a general favours boys,
A lovely wife may stray,
But who's to tell the world
If vengeance is disguised."

His eyes twinkled mischievously. Was this serious? Then the poet gave a gesture of farewell and moved on with his bodyguards. He must need them among this crowd, which was likely to contain many people he had aggrieved. Yet what in Hades was the information he thought he had given in that doggerel? "Call it an inspired guess, if you will," he called back over his shoulder, leaving Lysanias even more puzzled. The man was playing with him!

With the offices closed, Sindron realised he had some time to spare before the Assembly meeting started, which he was eager to watch. Something had urged him to walk round by the rear of the Temple of Theseos, though he wasn't sure why.

He stood for a while in the shadows of an alley on the other side of the street. He had seen Lydos and his subordinates arrive back from the table in the square, carrying the chest and scales and other attributes. The subordinates left after a while but not Lydos. Then shortly afterwards, Otanes had arrived. Instead of going in, he had stood waiting by the portico, looking down the road that led from the square. Then a black-screened cart had come along, driven by the groom from the house, and who should get down and go in but Makaria. Both she and Otanes entered the Treasury.

A woman dealing personally with a bank! As far as Sindron had heard, that just didn't happen, and it suggested connections between her and Lydos that he would never have imagined. What intrigue could this imply?

Sindron had slipped away without the groom noticing him and made his way back to the market place.

Lysanias found Hierokles. His cousin was in a grim mood. He muttered something about things looking bad and did his duty perfunctorily of introducing Lysanias to the officials of the tribe. After the brief swearing-in ceremony at the statue of his tribe's hero, Lysanias found himself an area within his tribe's section occupied by a mix of citizens amongst whom he knew not one face, and hoped he would be inconspicuous. From the conversations he overheard, even people from the country, small farmers

and fishermen, seemed fed up with war and constant preparedness that
they saw as Kimon's policy because of the impact on their farms, families
and livelihood of the menfolk having to be away so often fighting. They
wanted peace now. And not a few seemed to be blaming Kimon for
"bringing all these foreigners into the city."

Then Stephanos was edging towards him through the throng, looking
very serious. "It's bad," he whispered. "They did it. They killed him.
Those aristos we overheard, can you find out who they are? We need
names. "

Lysanias was horrified. The plotters included his cousin Hierokles
and General Ariston.

"But they were plotting that attempt to seize power not…"

"They're the most likely people. And the ones you heard in the
barber's."

Lysanias searched his memory. "I remember only a hairstyle, a way
of speaking, no faces. All these people…" He gestured at the assembled
citizens thinking Stephanos was asking him to look for them here.

"Not now. We have to keep it quiet for now."

"You and Lampon saw them too."

"We're looking too but you talk to these people. You can go where we
can't." He indicated Lysanias' cloak and his own worker's tunic.

"But my uncle's murderer. I have to find him…"

"Could be the same." The idea surprised him. Yes, it could.

"How did they do it?"

"No-one knows. The brothers were outside all night. They saw no-
one enter or leave. No sounds. No traces except Ephialtes dead with a
sacrificial golden trident through the big vein in his neck. Must be from
one of the temples but, if it's meant as a sign, lots of people use a trident
as a symbol, including Kimon."

The words sounded familiar. 'Golden trident.' Then Lysanias
remembered. The dining club. That was its name. Ariston again, and it
was meeting tonight.

He didn't mention it. Too far-fetched. No-one would be so stupid as
to implicate themselves in a murder that clearly. Must be a false clue to
point away from the real culprit.

Suddenly, the herald was uttering his piercing cry and calling the
Assembly to order. Stephanos had to get back to his place, so Lysanias
indicated he would do his best. He had to. As if investigating his uncle's
death wasn't complicated enough!

Stephanos looked back. "Oh, I found the rigger you were looking
for but he won't tell you anything. Drowned in the harbour, during the
takeover attempt. The only death on our side. Watch yourself."

What had he agreed to? Lysanias couldn't take on everyone's problems. He found a place where he recognised no-one to try to think. Maybe the speeches would give some clues.

The chief magistrate was seated on his throne on the wooden platform that had been erected to one side of the square. To either side of him were the eight other principal magistrates. At one end were two chairs. Kimon was already seated on one of them. The other was presumably for Ephialtes, the other citizen named for ostracism in today's debate. One of the tribe officials had given Lysanias a small piece of broken pottery, a potsherd, on which he would write the name of the person he wished to be ostracised at the end of the debate.

Now Perikles had stepped forward to whisper to the herald who whispered to the chief magistrate. Murmurs arose amongst the waiting crowd. The herald called for silence again, and it descended surprisingly quickly on the vast gathering. A quorum was 6,000 for an ostracism vote, and this looked much more. The chief magistrate stood.

"It appears that one of the targets of accusation has died during the night."

There was a sudden mass intake of breath.

"The cause of death has not yet been established. While there is doubt, the meeting will proceed."

The magistrates must have decided to cover up the cause for the sake of a peaceful meeting, but there were cries of disbelief, and a whispered word from many lips that could only be "assassinated". There was anger and fear in the reactions, surprise and horror, though some didn't seem too unhappy that Ephialtes was out of the way.

"The Assembly will proceed with the motion of ostracism against General Kimon."

Lysanias became aware that rumours were spreading, whispered, contradictory, as to the cause of death, some violent, some natural. It confirmed what Stephanos had told him, but was he right? Was it the group who had planned the attempted seizure of power? They had made a mess of that. Or the boasters in the barber's shop? As he recalled, they seemed all talk and no action. It had to be someone much more efficient and determined.

The herald once again called for silence. Pigs were sacrificed on the altar to Zeus of the Market Place and, while the purifiers marked the boundaries of the sacred assembly area with the pigs' blood, formal hymns were sung to the king of the gods to ensure that the people in Assembly would debate wisely and reach just decisions. Then the herald ordered everyone to be seated. Somehow everyone managed to sit or squat, though legs had to be tucked up rather than stretched out.

Among the lesser magistrates and officials grouped round the platform he could make out Amynias and Inaros, and his bile rose. Those were the madmen he had to talk to, but there was no chance in this gathering. To either side of the platform stood a small force of Scythian guards to keep order, but clearly totally inadequate if real trouble arose in this vast crowd, though presumably there were others elsewhere around the square.

As everyone sat, Lysanias could now see that the front area seemed to be almost totally occupied by the very poor and the unemployed, who looked somehow out of place in their rags and dirt. His neighbours had noticed them too.

"Not often that ragged lot bother to turn up."

"At least, if they're here, they're not robbing our shops and homes."

The thought crossed Lysanias' mind that there were far bigger villains among the rich.

Sindron found a place just outside the ropes that he felt would enable him to see and hear the Assembly meeting. Around him was a motley assortment of foreign merchants and businessmen, and a smattering of slaves of a senior grade like himself. Among them he noticed a man in a dark blue cloak with a hood that went forward in front of his face and concealed it completely. He must be very warm in there, thought Sindron, as his eyes moved on. He saw no-one he knew.

While he waited, Sindron puzzled over what he had learnt in the short period before all the offices and workshops closed. The heir who had first been named was, as he would have expected, Hierokles, but that didn't mean anything, if everyone really thought Lysanias' side of the family had been killed off in that last big raid on Eion. He remembered it had been chaotic with the Scythians managing to breach the walls at one point and establish fires before they were ejected, buildings destroyed, people killed. Lysanias missing for a time trying to find his father and only getting back shortly before the main raid, and the younger children trapped by a fallen wall. It was quite possible that an official report had not included their names among the survivors.

The family seemed to have accepted Lysanias. No-one had so far challenged his right to inherit, and Hierokles had kept his promise to vouch for Lysanias with the appropriate authorities, though only Boiotos had referred to the inheritance. Could that mean Hierokles might be planning to challenge Lysanias' claim or merely seeking to avoid ill-feeling?

The tomb carving had led nowhere definite. Sindron had spent some time locating the workshop of the stonemason involved, who had explained that it was a standard design modified so that the face bore some resemblance to the deceased. It could be and was done rapidly. He thought it had been ordered on the day Kimon returned from Sparta by a rather drunken youngish man. That could only be Boiotos, Sindron decided.

In an attempt to confirm this, he chatted with the slave who ran the workshop. The rudeness he described did fit Boiotos but the man thought it had been ordered very early in the morning and volunteered that the customer had made an initial enquiry a few days before. That sounded incriminating but would hardly stand as proof of prior knowledge, though it could mean Boiotos was in Athens at the time of Klereides' death.

Sindron had talked also to two carters and then to some countrymen from rural Attika about the distance from the Dekelia area to Athens and how long the journey would take. It seemed likely that Hierokles and Boiotos would have travelled by horse, being cavalrymen, and in a direct line it couldn't be far. However, the time depended on how slow they might have to go on rough country lanes between their country house and the main route from the town of Dekelia to Athens. Sindron didn't know that nor did the carters.

It seemed likely that Hierokles had started out before the news of Klereides' death reached there from the messenger despatched by Otanes. Hierokles had implied that the messenger calling them to the Special Assembly meeting had met them on the road to Athens. So what had made them start out so early?

The chief magistrate opened the meeting and it was Arkhestratos who answered the herald's call, "Who wants to speak?", to make the first speech, in place of Ephialtes. Behind the officials the row of ten statues of ten heroes of ten tribes looked on in stony silence.

It was a stumbling address to start with, the Peiraieos worker's accent and clumsy grammar of Arkhestratos drawing laughs from the educated and cheers from the workers and poor. He accused Kimon indiscriminately of having too much wealth, being a warmonger, causing the death and the maiming in battle of too many Athenians and wanting to cause more, of being too friendly with Sparta, of giving his sons Spartan names, of causing Athens to be humiliated by Sparta, and of hubris in having his likeness in public paintings alongside gods and heroes.

Then he hit his stride. Looking straight at Kimon, he said: "Your heavy-armed hoplites are on their way back from a shameful and shaming episode in Sparta. Who among them has no home when he returns? Who among them has to wear rags when he returns? Who among them has to scavenge for food when he returns?

"Stand up, my boys the rowers!" he called out to the crowd, in his deep coarse voice. Dotted through the crowd among the workers and, to a surprisingly large extent, among the poor and unemployed, more and more men rose to their feet, some of them displaying noticeable wounds and lost limbs.

"Who among you will say that these men have not fought and bled for Athens and the Greeks? Who will say they have no right to a share in the city's victory, in its prosperity?"

The chief magistrate protested to him about the standing men. Did he think it was a threat, a show of strength by one side in the conflict that seemed still to simmer just below the surface formalities? Arkhestratos gestured for them to be seated again.

"This man says that! This man, if he is not ostracised, will work to deny you these rights, my brothers. We cannot allow that! The great god Hephaistos will not allow it!"

He left the stand, visibly shaking with his own high emotion. A mighty roar went up from the workers and shouts of "Power to Hephaistos" could be clearly heard. Lysanias was impressed with the powerful impact and filled with sympathy for the men.

It occurred to Lysanias that, if he was to follow the lines he and Sindron had taken concerning Klereides' death, then everyone should be suspect of killing Ephialtes, even the demagogue's friends. But the other radical leaders seemed to have so much respect for the man. It wasn't plausible. Arkhestratos, for instance, was totally transparent.

Perikles took the podium, standing tall and erect. His speech and grammar were those of an educated man, but he seemed to take care to use phrases ordinary citizens might understand. He wore a plain, homespun cloak and he reached a hand inside to withdraw a flat, square object.

"Fellow citizens," the voice rang clear, but he seemed not very experienced at public speaking. "Fellow citizens, I hold in my hand the wax tablets that bear the notes of my dear colleague Ephialtes, the notes for the speech he would have made to you today. I will make a humble attempt to create for you the essence of that speech, as he would have wished."

A hush had fallen on the Assembly, and Perikles looked down at the tablets as though he were reading Ephialtes' own words from them. Basically, the speech attacked Kimon as a warmonger, a faction leader, an extremist, and it seemed clear that Ephialtes did not regard himself as an extremist. "There is no need for conflict either within the city or between cities. We radicals are willing to co-operate with all, and that co-operation should include the poor and the rich, the worker and the businessman, the farmer and the farmhand, the ship's captain and the sailor."

That drew a few jeers of disbelief from among Kimon's supporters. From his distant vantage point, Sindron could see the naivety of much of this. The love of war was too much part of the Greek soul for cities to ever co-operate for long. But he could also see the appeal of such a claim at the present time.

"I know of one prominent and wealthy citizen, active in the business community, who saw the logic of co-operation with Ephialtes' policies," Perikles interjected his own comment. "Unfortunately, like Ephialtes, he is no longer with us." It could only be Lysanias' uncle, Klereides. Was Perikles implying that the two deaths were linked?

"Kimon, however, refuses to accept the will of the people, and, in view of recent events, I, Perikles, would say, 'will stop at nothing'..." He was clearly accusing Kimon of causing the death of Ephialtes and of the attempted takeover, though without putting it into words. Could he have evidence of either? More likely this was a political insinuation.

"... so the people must ostracise him for its own protection," he concluded ringingly with the intonation Ephialtes would have given it.

Perikles paused and looked up and round the assembled sea of faces.

"That, my friends, is the last wish of Ephialtes. I bid you all to respect it."

He bowed his head and even the Kimon supporters, the haters of Ephialtes, felt obliged to do the same along with the many who had previously voted for Ephialtes' reforms.

After a few moments of silence, a lone voice uttered the slogan "Power to Hephaistos". Others took it up and it grew louder, till it became a chant. None of them, mused Sindron, seem to realise that it negates all that Ephialtes said about co-operation, which must imply the end of factions.

However, Perikles did not leave the stand. He waited for the chants to lessen, then gave his own dream – that this was the time "to rebuild our homes and streets and trading facilities to make this a city worthy to be the centre of a great Confederacy. This will give full employment and prosperity to all citizens."

If that was the offer of a bribe to the workers and the unemployed, they were certainly eager to accept, for the cheers and shouts were long and loud. Perikles stood there blinking, apparently taken by surprise by the response but emerging clearly as the new leader.

Now there's a thought, speculated Lysanias. Here was a man who had a lot to gain from Ephialtes' death: leadership of the radicals. So he had motive. He was close enough to Ephialtes to administer poison, say, without being noticed but not close enough to kill him while the man was asleep and certainly not with a sacrificial knife. No logic in that, except to mislead. But Perikles also had too much to lose. The killer had to be an aristocrat but how could an aristocrat have got that close without being seen?

"Now he knows what it's like, the handsome bastard." The man next to Sindron was muttering to himself and shaking with elation at every attack on Kimon. Yet, with his foreign-looking cloak and its big hood that covered his head, the man looked like a stranger, not someone involved in Athenian politics.

Then Sindron recalled that Lysanias had said he had met Themistokles in Peiraieos. Could this be the great man beside him, in disguise? Sindron couldn't see the man's face for the hood but then it turned briefly in Sindron's direction and he would have known those eyes anywhere, even after all these years and despite the wrinkles round them. Themistokles clearly realised he had been recognised and put a finger to his lips and winked. Then he calmly turned back to watch the debate. What a risk for someone under sentence of death to take! To mingle with this crowd where any of his enemies might identify him. Sindron was stunned.

After the dramas that Arkhestratos and Perikles had presented, what could Kimon say that would stem the tide of opinion flowing against him? Lysanias had heard that Kimon had always prided himself on his down-to-earth speaking style, but would that be enough?

Kimon was very dignified. Still a general, he was allowed to address the Assembly in full panoply, though without sword or dagger. He looked impressive but Lysanias realised this may have been a mistake. It separated him out.

First, Kimon said that no-one regretted the death of Ephialtes more than he did; an able opponent was always to be respected and political assassination was unthinkable in modern Athens. But the doubt was now in everyone's mind.

Could he have been involved? wondered Lysanias. Not personally but at a distance by asking someone else to organise it, leaving his own hands clean. Lysanias had seen the hatred in his eyes. Kimon clearly viewed Ephialtes as responsible for his current troubles, but would the death produce the desired result for him? The radicals had other capable leaders. It would have been an act of desperation and Kimon had always given the impression of being an honourable man, though, as Lysanias well knew, appearances could be very deceptive in Athens.

Kimon appealed to their patriotism. He presented Persia as still a mighty enemy, one that he had humbled on behalf of Athens and the Greeks. With his long line of battles won, Kimon was Athens' best security.

How must he be feeling now, thought Lysanias. The man had never lost a battle. An elected general, even general-in-chief for as long as Lysanias could remember, yet he would be painfully aware that the citizens were capable of turning on their heroes. They had done it to his father, the cause of much of the difficulties of his own early years.

They had done it to Themistokles. He had probably had a hand in that himself. He knew how much depended on what he said now.

However, every word he uttered led further and further into the yawning abyss of awareness by the ordinary citizens that this man considered himself and his colleagues better than them and that they were inferior, lacking in intelligent judgement. He must have felt it himself, for he stumbled to a halt. A strange silence followed, as though everyone knew that this great man was great no more.

Then Kimon cracked. One could see he knew he'd lost. Up to now, he had been playing politics within his limited powers of oratory. Now it was what he really felt.

"Do you realise what I've done for you, citizens? What I've done for Athens? Athens' leadership, Athens' hegemony extends throughout the Aegean and far beyond. We have driven the Persian wolf back into its lair and it dares not come forth. My friendship with the Spartans has ensured peace with them."

Mention of the Spartans was a serious mistake, in view of the recent snub, though everyone must know Kimon had been spokesperson for Sparta for many years and that his relationship with the Spartans had stopped them intervening while Athens increased its power. Hisses sounded throughout the listening crowd. Kimon struggled on.

"The allies will revolt, the Persian wolf will grow strong again, our rivals in mainland Greece will resist our power!

"Yet you can confirm our power. Let me stay and together we will bring peace and freedom to all the Middle Sea."

What came across though was the arrogance of a man who could claim such powers to himself, the powers of a god, when everyone knew it was they, the citizens of Athens, who had defeated and fought back the foe, who had built the confederacy and led it to triumph, not any one man among them.

Then Lysanias suddenly felt guilty. Had he done this? Brought his hero low? If he hadn't given warning of the takeover, would the aristocrats and Kimon be back in charge and Kimon not in danger of exile? No, he couldn't blame himself, the radicals had been well prepared for trouble. It would have happened this way anyway.

General Ariston spoke on Kimon's behalf but he was no orator and his jagged phrases and empty clichés rang hollow and sounded like a paean to a great man who has had his day.

Hearing Ariston speak again, Lysanias thought of the meeting of plotters at Aspasia's house. If Stephanos was right, this dignified general, in uniform like Kimon, was responsible for Ephialtes' death. Yet they had overheard nothing to suggest this, though, as Kimon's deputy, maybe he could have acted on Kimon's orders or felt he was anticipating his wishes.

Did that mean Ariston had also had something to do with Klereides' murder? Lysanias could understand the political hatred that could have motivated the assassination of Ephialtes but the only motive he and Sindron had been able to come up with connecting Ariston with his uncle's death was his possible disgust with Klereides for aiding the radicals against his own class and faction. Was that really sufficient motive for murder? Lysanias doubted it.

What had Strynises said? 'The General' or was it 'a general'? Could that be Ariston? And 'favours boys'. There had been that pretty slave-boy with him when he had called to give his condolences. But Ariston was Aspasia's patron. That didn't suggest he favoured boys. On the other hand, why would Strynises have told him, unless it was connected with his uncle? What if Klereides was having an affair with Ariston's wife? That would certainly give the General a motive. Yet, according to Sindron, killing a wife's lover was the one form of excusable homicide in Athens. Why didn't Ariston just kill Klereides openly? Then Strynises had said 'vengeance is disguised'. What if it was some other general Lysanias hadn't even met yet? Or Kimon? But Kimon hadn't even been in Athens. Even more opportunity for his wife to take a lover. Yes, but he wouldn't have found out. This was getting too confusing. If only he could talk to Sindron about it.

These thoughts prevented Lysanias from giving much attention to succeeding speakers, though he was aware that Phraston played on the economic gains of Kimon's leadership. Other speakers seemed to feel that Kimon should go to avoid civil conflict.

Now a youngish man, immaculately dressed, was taking a different line.

Though clearly supporting Kimon, he argued that now was a time for compromise and balance. Strong parties were needed on both sides to counteract the excesses of either.

Then he sprang his surprise. Blaming the current unrest on deceit and trickery, he asked, "And who is the prince of trickery? Yes, the great rogue Themistokles. And I have proof that the scoundrel is here now, in Athens, and is behind the schemes of the radical party. Can we discount his hand or that of other radical leaders in the death of Ephialtes." His voice, which sounded very like one he had heard at the barber's, had risen to shout it out, for gasps and hubbub of conversation amongst the crowd made him difficult to hear. Someone near Lysanias identified the man as Thoukydides of Alopeke.

That revelation could make things awkward for the radicals, Lysanias realised. Harbouring such a man was a crime. Now there was a politician who had done some underhand things in his time. Could Themistokles have had Ephialtes killed in the hope of regaining the leadership? He was probably capable of it but he owed his very safety in Athens to Ephialtes.

The next speaker shocked the crowd even more. Despite his flashy clothes and jewellery, he spoke with the uneducated accents of the slums, but his pock-marked face, and bushy beard and hair drew massive cheers from the ragged poor. This was Olinthios, known as King of the Thieves, Lysanias' neighbours informed him.

"... And if we don't get our share of the spoils of war very soon, I tell you, you wealthy citizens in your fine houses and expensive clothes, we'll rise up, the starving, the unclothed, unhoused, we'll rise up and take it. So get rid of Kimon, who cares only for his own, and share some of the city's wealth or your future may be bleak."

There was hushed silence at the audacity of this threat in the citizen assembly. Then the poor and ragged rose to their feet to cheer him and then turned to jeer and scowl and raise angry fists at the better off in the crowd behind them.

As Olinthios stepped down, the Scythian guards stepped forward to suppress any disorder and to tell the demonstrators to be seated.

At the news that the aristocrats knew of his presence in Athens, the man in the merchant's cloak and cowl became very agitated. He grasped Sindron's elbow.

"Old man, I have to get away from here. I imagine I'll be less conspicuous if I appear to have a companion or a slave. I wonder, could I ask you if you would walk along with me? If anything should happen to me, if I'm arrested or set on by the mob, perhaps you would be good enough to report that to one of the radical leaders. On the chance they may be able to help, you understand?"

Sindron nodded his assent. Somehow he felt his duty to protect the aged politician who had once saved Athens. A glance at the skyline in any direction showed the city walls that, with the fleet, were the man's legacy to the city, the defences that had kept it safe – and he'd taken the opportunity to increase the area they surrounded, to enlarge the city. People even called them Themistokles' Walls. Sindron remembered helping, along with all the available men, women, children and slaves, carrying every suitable piece of stone, even tombstones, to rebuild them after the Persians destroyed the old ones.

They started to edge their way through the attentive non-citizens. The soft living of a Persian prince had clearly added flesh to Themistokles' once slim and angular figure but the way he moved suggested he had kept himself fit as a good Athenian should.

As the poor sat down, Lysanias could see the next speaker. Great Zeus, it was his cousin Boiotos who had leapt onto the stand.

"Cowards!" he yelled. "Cowards! You don't know a great man when you see one! Worn out, are you? Tired of fighting? Afraid to battle the great enemy of all the Greeks!" He taunted the crowd, who shouted and jeered back in fierce indignation. Even near Lysanias, voices expressed outrage. "Arrogant young pup. How many battles has he ever fought in?" "The man's drunk, look at him!"

Then he was gone. The guards had escorted him back to a safe place in the crowd, and everyone slowly quietened down, though there were murmurs and individuals muttering with their neighbours, glancing around to identify potential friends and foes. Lysanias sensed the increasing tension and wondered who he should regard as his enemies if a real civil conflict broke out among this mass of assembled citizens and order disappeared. Despite his worry for Athens, he felt strangely detached.

Normally there would have been several individuals put up for ostracism, and citizens would scratch the names of their choice on the sherd of pottery they gripped in their hand. Today, the death of Ephialtes had narrowed it down to one man, Kimon. So a straight yes/no vote was possible and the herald announced: "'Yes' for ostracism in the amphora to the right, 'No' for Kimon to stay in the amphora to the left, at the exit from each tribal section."

Lysanias concealed his piece of potsherd in one hand, so, when he placed his hands into the amphoras, he didn't drop it. He just couldn't bring himself to vote against his long-time hero, though he could see the logic of Kimon being exiled in the current political climate.

As Philia and Glykera emerged from the temple looking for Makaria, the Assembly meeting seemed to be breaking up. Noisy men had started spilling into the rest of the square, still arguing angrily. Philia looked to left and to right but there was no sign of Makaria or of the cart or groom. In fact, there were few vehicles of any sort in sight, though a few other women stood waiting.

As they placed their votes, each citizen passed between the amphoras, through a gap in the rope enclosure. That left everyone mixed up together to an even greater extent, all tensely waiting for the result of the vote. Lysanias noticed arguments in his immediate vicinity.

Evidently in an effort to speed up the count so people would disperse before the simmering hatreds turned to violence, officials produced hammers and the amphoras were smashed, revealing piles of sherds in the Yes jars far bigger than those in the No jars and cumulatively far more than the total required. Tribe by tribe in turn, each official called out "Majority for Yes" and only Kimon's own tribe and one other returned a firm vote of No. The crowd was hushed until it became clear that the vote was against the great man and the herald shouted it for all to hear. A cheer went up and then a roar from the disappointed supporters of Kimon.

They had done it, they had really done it, thought Lysanias. How could they ignore all Kimon had done for the city. How would they replace their great war-leader. But, then, in a time of peace, maybe they wouldn't need a war-leader. Letting his arm drop to full length, he relaxed his fist, letting the potsherd fall to the ground. He pressed it into the dust with his sandal.

Suddenly Olinthios was up on the podium of the tribal heroes, hoisting himself up to be seen. "I say, make 'em pay for Ephialtes," he shouted. A small group round him took up the cry.

Then a bright red cloak with a yellow border stood out above the heads of the crowd, on the other end of the tribal heroes' podium, topped by a familiar head with the henna-stained hair. Lysanias recognised him as the sculptor. "Sculptors and artists! Citizens! They killed Ephialtes! Let the Hammer strike!" he yelled at the top of his voice. And an answering cheer went up.

Almost at the same time from a plane tree on the other side, a burly Kimon supporter called out, "They've won the vote. We don't have to accept it!"

For all his declaration of loyalty in front of Stephanos, Lysanias still wasn't sure he could fight with his full spirit for either side. He felt real grief at seeing his great hero brought low, even though his sympathies now were with Kimon's opponents. Was there some way out of this? All round him hand-to-hand fights had started.

On the official dais, he could make out the chief magistrate calling for order, gesturing to the officials responsible for law and order to deploy their guards, though there didn't seem to be enough to have much effect. If they couldn't restore order, there was no telling where this might lead.

Suddenly the thought came to Lysanias that his women had been planning to visit the temples today. What if they were at temples on the market square? His eyes swept along the side of the square, the Painted Colonnade, the Sanctuary of Zeus, the remains of the Temple of Apollo, the Temple of The Mother, that strange ugly primitive construction, women in front of that, and there, that slight figure in black dwarfed by the giant stones, could that be Philia? And then she was gone, whoever it was.

Lysanias knew he had to be sure and he started running, forcing his way through already fighting masses of men, himself pushed and punched and stumbling and righting himself. His running seemed to start a wave, possibly a panic, and other men were turning and running ahead of him, older men trying to get out of the fighting, younger men chasing them, thinking they must have guilt to hide. He could hear heralds shouting for order but no-one paid any heed. Knives and other weapons had appeared and were being used.

A throwing spear whistled past his ear and buried itself in the arm of a man ahead of him, who yelled in pain. Another followed, hitting the ground to his side. Lysanias turned. Had those been meant for him? A red, ferociously grinning face, only a short throwing distance away, that looked like Boiotos. Then the face took a buffet from the side and was that a hammer striking the head? Then it was lost from view, but there was Stephanos, making a gesture that could only mean, 'Now you owe me one.' Then something seemed to pull him down and Stephanos disappeared in the affray. No time to go back, Lysanias decided.

Remembering Philia, Lysanias turned and ran on. A foot reached out to trip him, he dodged it, a flailing arm caught the side of his face, a falling man barged against him, he stumbled sideways. There were already people on the ground, being trampled on, he must stay on his feet, find Philia.

"He's probably down one side or other of the Temple," Philia said to Glykera, who she felt she now saw more as a woman and less as a slave. "You look that side, I'll do this one." The shouting from the centre of the market place was even louder now, and, from her raised position in the entranceway, it looked as though a fight had started. Oh, well, that was the men's business, not hers.

Just as she reached the corner, a tide of running men dashed into the alleyway. They swept her along, and she had to run with them, run and run, her feet hardly touching the ground. She was buffeted round and round, like a leaf on a stream. And then she was tripping, falling, falling to one side, grazing her arm and her cheek against the rough giant stones of the Temple, and had enough sense left to squeeze in tight against the wall of stones for protection against the running, thumping feet. Two thumps or kicks in the back and they were gone. Sounds of fighting now came from the square and from the other end of the lane, and her face hurt and her left leg. What should she do now? Try to crawl back into the sanctuary of the Temple? Why did she ever leave that safe haven for women and re-enter the world of violent men?

As Sindron and his companion edged their way out of the watching crowd and stood on the fringes near the Painted Colonnade, it became clear that things could get nasty. There was already shouting. Then, as citizens left the central area, fighting started.

"Quick, in here," hissed Sindron. He had noticed a pile of cloths the painters had used to protect the decorative floor tiles. "You can hide under these till the riot blows over."

"You too, old man. If you can recognise this is a riot starting, you know they are no respecters of status or opinions. If it's the start of something worse, only the gods can help us." As he spoke, Themistokles had nonetheless taken Sindron's advice. This man had long experience of hiding, Sindron remembered, and not a little of running from violence.

Suddenly fearful for his own life and that of Lysanias who was somewhere in among that crowd, Sindron glanced out at the increasing turmoil in the square and, his heart thumping, decided it was his turn to take Themistokles' advice, though he raised his head sufficiently to be able to see any threats coming their way. He knew Lysanias had the fighting skills to defend himself but this was starting to look really nasty. The sounds of shouts and screams, loud and angry, now seemed to come from all sides and to grow in volume.

As he followed the running crowd down the lane beside the temple, Lysanias could see no sign of Philia. Then, there, that bundle of black, beside the wall. Could that be her? As he came close, he saw it was a girl, shivering, shaking, sobbing. It was Philia. Thank the gods, she was all right.

"Come on, Philia! We have to get you away from here. Can you walk?"

"I'm not sure. I seem to hurt all over."

Lysanias helped Philia to her feet and, with his arm round her and her arm over his shoulders, he supported her while she tested if she could put weight on her legs. "Yes, seems all right, nothing broken. It hurts, but not too much."

He started them walking away from the square, still supporting her as much as he could. He could feel her body still shaking, as it pressed against his, warm and frightened, soft and delicate. He wanted to kiss her to try to comfort her, make her unafraid again. She had stopped crying but an occasional whimper escaped her bruised lips.

"There's a building site up here. The new Temple of Hephaistos. There should be places there we can conceal you, while I check if it's safe to venture home."

She accepted this without question, though he really didn't feel very sure what was the best thing to do. There was shouting from the direction they were going as well.

"Why were you alone?" Lysanias asked. "Wasn't Makaria with you? Or any of the slaves?"

At that, Philia burst out crying again and hung on his shoulder sobbing, so he picked her up and hurried as fast as he could up the slope.

Getting there was easier said than done. Along the alleyways behind the Temple of The Mother were shops and workshops, and running in and out of them were ragged urchins and women who looked equally thin and poor, all shouting in elation at the armfuls of goods they were piling onto cloths and sacking laid on the street for others to pick up and carry away. Lysanias felt he should tell someone in authority, but Philia groaned and whimpered. Must get her to safety first. Fortunately, the looters were too pre-occupied to bother them.

"What do you think they'll do to restore order?" Sindron asked in a low voice.

"Nearly all the generals are here today. They're all scared of civil war. They'll just demand military discipline. After all, we're all soldiers."

"What, do a deal between them, you mean?" Sindron looked at Themistokles and saw that the old man was suddenly confused, concerned. In the euphoria of the vote against Kimon, he must have forgotten that the Board of Generals was still divided politically. "Oh, no! They might at that. The idiots could sell out all we've gained. Better fight it out than that. We must outnumber them today. We'd win."

But at what cost thought Sindron, astonished at the old statesman's reckless attitude.

Then the herald's cry reached them. For his voice to be that loud, he must be speaking through a bull-roarer, used to amplify the voices of the gods in dramatic presentations.

"Military discipline. Military discipline. All citizens twenty to fifty years old to assemble in military units. Looting will be severely dealt with. By order of all the generals."

It was certainly effective. The sounds of fighting in the market square stopped, though they could still hear shouting from further away, and, as Sindron propped himself up higher to look out, he could see the generals, Kimon and Myronides, Ariston and Perikles, and the others, standing shoulder to shoulder on the platform with the senior magistrates, all stern-faced. Themistokles sat up beside him. "By the gods, they have done a deal. That's why they took so long." Themistokles looked depressed, almost defeated. And old.

The sky began to darken outside, and those who could still walk made their way to the assembly points. There were people out there lying on the square, some completely still, others writhing and moaning, but they didn't venture out to see if they could help. They both knew what can happen in a violent riot to people who are too helpful or too inquisitive, and this might just be a lull in the storm.

Having passed through danger together, it felt almost as though they were old friends, comrades in adversity, and Sindron started to recall his memories of the great days of Salamis and Plataea. "I offered to take an oar, you know," he said, "but they turned me down."

"Ah yes, we were too proud to let slaves row for us in those days," replied Themistokles reminiscently.

Sindron knew he would never have this opportunity again, so he took the opportunity to ask Themistokles his side of the story and was surprised the great man was so open. Of course he had been dealing with the Persians, he said. Someone had to explore the possibility of a truce but the rich men of the Areopagos, prompted by Kimon and his allies, had used it as an excuse to hound him out of the city and, with their agents after him, where else could he find safe refuge but in Persia? With Perikles too young, he'd left Ephialtes in charge of the radical element but the man had proved too weak to stand up to Kimon's party until Themistokles' machinations, using Persian money to foment rebellion in Sparta, had paid off. Sindron was amazed how much Themistokles claimed to have been behind, even from exile.

Could he really have engineered all this, calculated in advance the outcome of all these wily manoeuvres? This riot, clearly he hadn't anticipated that. Sindron doubted that one old man, forced into disguise and to scuttle from one hiding place to another, could really change history, however cunning he might be. But then he had done it before in his life and Sindron recalled his long-standing admiration for the man's achievements at the time of the Persian invasion.

The politician evidently had dreams too. He appeared to hope that, now in power, the radicals could clear his name, revoke the death sentence on him, and restore him to leadership. Sindron felt a little sad that this old man of well into his sixties, older than himself, however great he once was, still dreamed of a comeback, could not give up and let a new generation get on with it.

"This riot. What if Kimon's men now have the upper hand and take over again?"

"No risk of that. Kimon's hoplites won't be here till tomorrow at the earliest." He actually giggled at his own cleverness in delaying them. "Without them, we've got enough able men to handle things. Don't worry."

Could he really be that confident? What would happen when four thousand fully-armed hoplites did reach the city and discovered that their hero had been exiled in their absence? What then? But Sindron left the old man to his dreams. The fighting seemed to have quietened down and he hoped that Lysanias had managed to keep out of trouble. It would be too ridiculous, after all that had happened, if the boy got himself killed in a street riot.

At the temple site, Lysanias discovered that the workers had placed a canvas over two piles of building stones to form a shaded area for their meal breaks. As luck would have it, no-one else was using it as a hiding place. He lowered the gently-crying girl to the ground, and knelt over her, smoothing her hair back from her brow. She stopped crying and tried a smile.

"Philia, show me where it hurts most." He must find out if she had any serious injuries. He could see a nasty scratch and grazes on her left arm that ought to be washed and dressed but nothing serious. Lost in the worry and pain, she pulled up her gown to reveal her legs. Her knees were bloody, as was the whole side of her left leg, but no deep cuts. He felt her thigh delicately to check for broken bones. Only then did he realise what he was doing, and he was sure she realised too. He blushed, and pulled her gown down to cover her legs again.

"Philia, you must tell me why you were alone." She told him that Makaria and the groom and cart had disappeared, and she had no idea where. That Glykera had been with her but they had been separated. She hoped Glykera was alright but fear for herself and for Lysanias pushed that concern aside.

"I'll try to see if Glykera has taken refuge in the Temple," Lysanias said. "You'll be safe here. I won't be long."

Terror gave the girl strength. He couldn't desert her. She couldn't face being alone again with all those violent men. She suddenly lifted herself, threw her arms round his neck, pulled him down and clung to him fiercely. He heard running feet, and the shouts of men. He thought he heard, "I'm sure he ran up this way." Then another voice, shouting, "Order is being restored. Anyone in hiding, it is safe to come out now." Somehow it didn't sound like a herald's announcement and the voice sounded strangely familiar. It was followed by a laugh. Could it be that someone was hunting him? After those spears came so close, he could believe anything.

He put his hand over Philia's mouth, in case she said something. They crouched low, hearts beating, tense, aware of their closeness, not daring to utter a sound till the men had passed. This was cowardly, hiding from the fight. He whispered, insistently, "Philia, I must see if Glykera's safe." He kissed Philia's grazed forehead to try to calm her.

"You could be killed. We could both be killed." It came out slurred from lips she couldn't fully control. He knew it was true. If this was civil war, everyone was at risk.

She turned her face to his, her eyes still wet with tears, sad, desperate, lonely. He kissed those poor bruised lips. She winced slightly, then returned the kiss. The comfort and the release that at least beautiful Philia was safe and in his arms was so great, that Lysanias relaxed as her hands stroked his hair and his shoulders, and he felt the sexual attraction grow.

"No, we mustn't do this, Philia. We'll be married soon." But he found that his hand was fondling her soft round buttocks and then her thigh where her gown had rucked up and then inside her gown and over the buttocks again, and her hand was exploring similar regions on his body. The stress and tension they had just been through lent fire to their ardour and all thought of other people and the outside world was lost in the careless, all-excluding twoness of sexual passion.

Philia looked up at him and smiled contentedly, though one eye was puffed up and her mouth was very much awry with bruising. "Mmm, Lysanias."

"Yes, beautiful Philia," he murmured back, dreamily.

"Don't kiss me again. It hurts." She tried to laugh, but her bruises wouldn't let her.

More running feet, but again they passed by. Then, in the distance, they heard the herald calling for men over twenty to assemble. He made to rise but she gripped him tight. "That's not you. You're only eighteen."

"Order is being restored. Please return to your homes. Looters will be arrested. This is a joint decision of all factions."

Looking out, Sindron could see that groups of men had started marching in different directions away from the assembly area. They were in ordinary clothes but they were armed. The leader of each shouted the message as he went and it seemed to echo from all over the square.

A group was approaching. The gruff voice boomed the message. "I think I know that voice," Sindron said. Leaving his companion, he slipped over to look out between the columns. Yes, it was that awful young stonemason. Still, from what Lysanias said, this man was well in with the radicals. It could be the only chance of getting Themistokles away to safety. He stepped out and beckoned Stephanos over and whispered to him. Stephanos halted his squad and came into the colonnade.

"Is that Lysanias' slave? Good fight, eh? Gave them a bloody nose. Made up for last night."

"Looks like they weren't the only ones hurt."

"Yes, well, we got a few injured as well, but we still outnumber them." When Sindron indicated Themistokles, his tone changed to fear for the aged politician. "Silly old fool," he muttered to himself angrily, and to Themistokles, "Why didn't you stay hidden, sir?"

Themistokles' hood was pushed back enough to make out his face, though in the gathering dusk that didn't reveal much. "I couldn't stay away when Kimon was getting what he deserves, could I?" he grinned and giggled, he actually giggled.

Stephanos quickly told them what had happened. The rioting had scared the leaders on both sides, and the poor had been looting shops and homes during the meeting.

"They made a deal. Both sides work together to stop the chaos, end the violence and looting. Didn't want to call a curfew and admit order had broken down. So joint patrols, workers and aristos..."

Themistokles became more and more agitated. "What concessions have they made? The fools! Have they given it all away? All we gained? This is terrible! You must take me to them!"

Stephanos looked concerned now. "Lower your voice, sir," he said, his sense of respect returning. "And please pull that hood over. My deputy is one of them. If they recognise you..." The sound of running feet told them that his deputy, coming into the colonnade to see what the delay was, had indeed recognised Themistokles and gone to report it.

"Quick, I'll try to get you to Perikles' house, but we'll have to run." He called to someone else to take over the squad and set off at a trot, that, surprisingly for a man of his age, the old politician managed to keep up with.

Sindron breathed a sigh of relief. At least the problem was off his hands now.

He slipped into the shadows and made his way in the direction of Inner Kermeikos and home, hoping he wouldn't meet any looters or young men eager to take their anger out on someone.

Sindron came across Glykera wandering, staggering, turning first this way, then that. As he approached her she seemed dazed. Her eyes looked right through him.

Sindron called out, "Glykera, are you all right?" He knew she wasn't. Her gown was dirty and torn, she limped with only one sandal, and now it was clear that her pendant and its chain were missing. Up close now, he said, as gently as he could. "What happened to you?"

He still wasn't sure if she recognised him. "Don't worry about me. Look for my mistress. Oh, my poor mistress," she wailed. "She's so pretty and so young. Oh..."

It didn't take much imagination to guess what had happened to Glykera, or, from that, to imagine the fate that might have befallen Philia. But the fact that all Glykera could worry about was Philia said something about the woman's loyalty, or something about the way slavery and subservience can totally erase a slave's own self-awareness.

Sindron took Glykera in his arms, there on the street, amazing himself. He felt her shaking gradually subside and he said, "Glykera, think of yourself for once. The mistress will be safe and sound. You're here now. You're the one that matters." Glykera looked up into his eyes, with wonder more than gratitude, suddenly aware that he was expressing concern and care – for her! Somehow Sindron knew he had taken on responsibility for protecting this woman, who he discovered he did care for quite deeply.

When Lysanias and Philia recognised the very different shapes of Sindron and Glykera silhouetted against the walls of houses in the evening light, they called out.

Relief that all were safe was tangible. The women forgot all about the men to sympathise and croon over one another's hurts, as though they were mother and daughter rather than slave and mistress.

Lysanias and Sindron didn't show their feelings so openly, hiding it in mutual concern for the women, worry about the chances of the fragile truce holding and about how far the looting had stretched beyond the square. From there, however agitated still, it took everyone's mind off things to recount their adventures and discoveries of the day.

Philia found a way of letting them know of Makaria's insistence that she would do nothing to hurt her son, though, for Lysanias, that had a strange ring, knowing the way his grandmother had forced his own father, her younger son, to leave Athens. Philia told, too, her own belief that Makaria had been trying to win her support for whatever underhand activity she might have been involved in. The pieces still didn't fit together and there were many more of them now.

On top of all that, he told Sindron of his promise to Stephanos. The old slave felt very uncomfortable about that degree of commitment to one side in the political turmoil and said so, but, as a loyal slave, he accepted it and agreed to give it thought.

CHAPTER 16

The arguments started as soon as they met Otanes coming down the main street through Inner Kermeikos to look for them with the cart and the groom. They hardly allowed him time to report that looting had not extended as far as the house and that the rest of the household were safe with only one slave injured at all.

Lysanias berated the groom for deserting his young mistress. The groom wailed that he had only obeyed orders from his old mistress. With all the crowds in the streets, and the panic, there was no way they could have driven the cart around looking for Philia and Glykera. All he could do was get Makaria and the cart home as fast as he could.

"So why did none of the men venture out again to search?"

It was Otanes who pleaded now, offended at the slur on his courage. "Master, you were there, you saw what it was like! I'd have needed full armour and a sword to fight my way through."

So it emerged that Otanes had been in the city centre. With that, Sindron remembered where he had last seen Makaria and Otanes and, back at the house, challenged them with the fact. Both master and slave, Lysanias and Sindron, were engaged emotionally now, protecting their women, and their anger was up. It was difficult not to let their suspicion, even dislike, of Otanes as a Persian fuel their anger.

Dismissing the groom, Lysanias ordered Makaria and Otanes to accompany them to Otanes' room, where they made him take out all the scrolls, open them up on his bed, and turn round the picture so that the lease was visible.

"And where is Philia's dowry?" It was a demand rather than a question. Makaria's eyes flicked from side to side like a trapped rat, but Otanes, realising he couldn't conceal any more, put a bold front on it.

"It's here, master. All here." From another small chest, Otanes produced a large leather bag of silver coin. In the chest could be seen gold and silver statuettes and trinkets, and a small pile of precious jewellery.

"So that's why you were in such a hurry to get back! To protect all that!" The contempt in Sindron's voice was sharp and clear. They must have used the cart to return from the bank with the dowry and then found it impossible to get back into the centre because of the riot.

The expressions on Makaria's and Otanes' faces confirmed Sindron's guess. They would have to tell the truth. Lysanias and Sindron hounded for explanations and at last they got them.

It appeared that Klereides had left Philia's dowry in Makaria's safekeeping, because legally it remained Philia's and went with her, if she ever returned to her father's custody. After her husband's death during the Persian invasion, and with Klereides off with the army, Makaria had kept the family going by building up the trade from the weaving room, making cloaks and blankets to aid the war effort, and running the farm through the steward there.

Then Klereides' had the good luck to meet up with Hermon and become his patron. With the income from the business, there was no need any more for the weaving room to do more than supply household needs, but Klereides had not objected when she had kept it up. The proceeds had built up and Makaria had looked for ways to invest as a safeguard against her son's extravagance.

Klereides had brought Otanes back from the war. She and the Persian had struck up a friendship, and he had helped her find methods of obtaining interest on the money she was saving.

Then the opportunity to acquire the lease of the foundry had arisen, which offered profits sufficient to secure her old age and even save the family, if Klereides lost all their money. There wasn't enough cash immediately available, so they had persuaded Phraston to accept Philia's dowry as security against a loan to make up the difference. They had been close to redeeming it when Klereides had died.

Makaria hadn't meant any harm, she declared. Why were women expected to slave and toil to keep a household going and never allowed to enjoy any of the benefits, always totally dependent on men? During the war, women had shown what they could do and, now it was over, they were forced to be appendages and ornaments, worse than slaves.

A whole store of bitterness spilled out. Lysanias couldn't help seeing the justice of her viewpoint, but he didn't feel able to excuse her behaviour. Philia, who had crept closer after her scratches and bruises were cleaned and dressed, found herself experiencing a degree of sympathy for the old woman that she would never have expected. She remembered the lessons about women's status, about her own status, she had learned earlier that day.

"You vouch for all this, Otanes?" In a way, Lysanias felt relieved. It looked as though he might not have to accuse Makaria of complicity in Klereides' murder.

"Yes, master. The mistress awarded me a percentage of profits. I assure you there was never any ill intent."

Sindron could see that the only difference from his own embezzlement in using Lysanias funds to invest in cargo without permission was one of scale, though he still could not forgive himself for what he had done. It was still wrong.

Lysanias knew he could not let it rest there.

"What about the false accounts?"

"No false accounts, master." Otanes was standing on his dignity now. He might have embezzled but he had done it in an honest and businesslike way. Sindron smiled wryly to himself at the hypocrisy. "Every obol is recorded here, except for the value of the dowry. That is shown only in the bank's accounts."

"No, the false account at the bank. Klereides' main account," Lysanias insisted. "It has been completely re-written and recently. Sindron is sure."

Both culprits looked genuinely shocked to be accused of what must be a major fraud. They glanced at one another, to assure themselves that the other wasn't involved. Then Makaria answered, modulating the normal harshness out of her voice.

"No, Lysanias, I'm sure you're wrong. Phraston would never do a thing like that. Why should he, a man in his position?"

Otanes spoke, more to Makaria than to Lysanias. "Do you think they could want to cover up Klereides' losses for some reason?"

"No, why should they, it's none of their business," she retorted.

"Unless what they told us about his debts wasn't true!"

"But I've been contributing money to cover those, when Lydos said it was particularly bad!" Whatever the truth of that, this argument between the two did seem to show that they really didn't know about any falsified accounts and it did do Makaria some credit that she had been prepared to make sacrifices to keep the family afloat. But the opulence of Klereides' possessions and the size of the household belied the whole idea of Klereides being seriously in debt, as did Hermon's evident great respect for the man.

Sindron jumped in. "So you dealt with Lydos more than Phraston? Took his word?"

"Of course, he handles all the bank's day-to-day business." Makaria answered, sounding herself like a woman of business. "You can never get hold of Phraston. Too busy with politics."

Lysanias and Sindron exchanged a significant glance. It felt as though they were narrowing down on someone who had been doing wrong, who might have a motive for killing Klereides.

Lysanias challenged, "Do you think either of them would have a reason to have uncle killed?"

"Is that what this is all about? You still think he was murdered?" A tone of ridicule crept into Makaria's voice.

Sindron answered, before Lysanias anger could take him. "I assure you, mistress, that we have found quite enough proof that his death was not an accident, that it was deliberate and that a human agent caused it."

"And I would point out that, in a case of unnatural death, it is the duty of all close family members to seek revenge, or the vengeful spirits will pursue them as fiercely as they do the murderer," Lysanias added firmly, conviction blazing from his eyes.

Their faces froze. Makaria sat like a statue, white-faced. The silence lengthened. Philia, looking on from the doorway, wondered at the drama of it all, a bit like that play Curly took her to where she hadn't understood the meaning but had felt the tension of the conflicts.

Sindron continued. "We have even wondered why you took such pains to try to ensure that the bloodstained cloak was destroyed, if you weren't afraid it might provide evidence."

"Nonsense!" It was an instinctive response from Makaria, but it wasn't an answer. Before Sindron could respond, another voice slipped in.

"She was expecting a messenger with bad news that morning. She kept looking towards the door." Now Philia had said it, she suddenly felt all eyes on her and shrank back a little but then, remembering her new status, stepped forward again.

Otanes jumped in, perhaps to protect Makaria. "I think I can answer that. The mistress was expecting Klereides back with bad news about the state of the family's finances. Lydos had told us that things were getting bad. She thought the message in the night must have been from a man Klereides used to gamble heavily with demanding payment."

It sounded plausible but how could they verify it?

"What about the cloak, then?" Philia was determined to help to put the old gorgon in her place even if she too felt she was an oppressed woman.

Makaria nearly burst into tears. "I just had to get rid of the horrible thing! How could he? Spend all our money and then get himself killed. Landing everything on me again! I couldn't stand it!" Great sobs came out and her shoulders shook. It seemed real.

There was an embarrassed silence. Then, more gently, Lysanias said, "You haven't answered my question. About Phraston and Lydos having any reason to kill your son."

Otanes stood with a comforting hand on her shoulder, but left Makaria to answer, as she recovered herself. "No, I don't think so," she sniffed.

"I concur with the mistress," Otanes agreed. "If they can create false accounts and keep whatever they were doing from Klereides, why would they need to resort to violence?"

"What if Klereides had found out?" Lysanias threw it at them.

"Or was on the point of finding out, master." Sindron suggested.

"Precisely."

Lysanias looked at Makaria and Otanes as though somehow they could supply the answer to the riddle of Klereides' death, but neither of them could envisage that either Phraston or Lydos would even consider such a deed. Lysanias had become more cynical in his short stay in Athens. He found he could believe it, but, in his general disillusionment at the deceit and deception he had encountered in Athens, he could believe almost anything. He asked why Otanes had been visiting the harbour recently. Merely trying to obtain news of his family, the Persian assured them, on his own initiative, though Sindron was not sure whether this was believable, and Makaria looked surprised.

Lysanias recalled fleetingly that he should be seeking news of his own family but they had to push on. He wondered why they were going down these lines at all. Lysanias knew from Philebos that it was the naval officials, the Men of Poseidon, who had set up the events that had resulted in Klereides' death.

Then Otanes asked, "Master, may I contribute? The old master's last dinner party, the one for government officials, I overheard heated conversations at one point. From outside the door, you understand. The words weren't clear."

"The naval officials were there, is that correct?"

"Among others, yes."

That confirmed it. When had Hermon said he would be seeing them? At the dining club, the Golden Trident, at Ariston's place, and tonight! Well, Ariston had suggested Lysanias should attend the dining club as soon as his mourning commitments allowed, so why not go? This was a vengeance commitment and it over-rode all others, mourning included. He would go. The golden trident connection didn't escape him. Perhaps some of the anonymous plotters would be there as well.

"Otanes, when Klereides went to dining club meetings, who did he take with him?"

"Myself, master, as personal slave and the messenger boy to serve. That is normal for a gentleman of status."

"Right, Sindron. We're going to that dinner party. We'd better get ready."

Then Philia spoke up. "You can't take the messenger boy, Lysanias. His leg is broken. I've just been tending him." She stared at Makaria as she said it, daring her to challenge Philia's right to take charge of a household matter. Makaria stayed silent. "The porter sent the boy to look for us, and he got caught in the riot. He only just made his way back using a stick he found," Philia explained.

They decided that the kitchen boy was too old and too ugly to offer an alternative. Philia knew this was her opportunity, even if the idea both excited and frightened her. "I could dress up as a boy, Lysanias."

"Don't be ridiculous, girl!"

Philia cringed at the old, commanding voice of her mother-in-law. But Lysanias reacted to the impertinence of the woman. How dare she imagine she still had any authority in this household!

"I suggest you keep your own counsel, from now on, Makaria. I will decide what to do with you and Otanes tomorrow." He turned, ignoring them, and went into a huddle with Sindron and Philia. He was obliged to take Philia's suggestion seriously, now he had said that.

Philia saw the men looking at her breasts. "I could strap my bosom in tight, and wear a boy's tunic loose! No-one will recognise me with my face like this." She gestured at her swollen lip and eye and grazed nose. The swelling was enough to fool anyone who had seen Philia before, especially if they darkened Philia's skin with walnut oil as Nubis suggested and slicked her spikey hair flat with grease the way Egyptian slaves do.

The two young people seemed so locked in their conspiracy, so eager to stay near one another, that all the discouragement Sindron could offer carried no weight. It was decided.

Otanes was persuaded to provide a quick course for Sindron and Philia on what their duties would be, and explained to all three what the club procedures normally were, at least for the portions he had ever been present at. It appeared that personal slaves were excluded for some of the time. Lysanias took the opportunity, as he changed clothes, to strap to his body inside his tunic a small dagger he had found among Klereides' possessions, only too aware that this would be seen as a serious insult to his host if revealed.

Hasdrubal, the bulbous Phoenician steward, greeted Lysanias at the door, as though he had been expected all along. He clearly didn't recognise him as the journeyman carpenter he had hired recently. He directed Philiako, as they had decided to call Philia in her disguise, to the kitchen with the other serving slaves, and acknowledged Sindron as a fellow steward, pointing out a room where he might wait.

Then he showed Lysanias, dressed in his smartest cloak, into the entertaining room.

About sixteen men lounged on elegant couches arranged around the edges of the large room and reached down to select morsels from cooked dishes of fish and meat on the tables beside them. The succulent smells immediately made Lysanias aware of how hungry he was. Most of the diners had their slave-boy squatting beside the table to help them, while a personal slave stood behind the couch. In Ariston's case, this was the pretty-boy slave he had seen before.

Heads had glanced nervously as Lysanias entered, as though worried who might arrive next, then turned back to their foods or conversation. There was a sense of fear in the room and slight relief that it was no-one more threatening than a clean-shaven young man. These men huddled together here, speaking in whispers, they must know about the golden trident used to assassinate Ephialtes. Even if they weren't all involved in that plot, the trident clearly implicated them all. Then Ariston pounced on him.

"Ah, our new member! You decided to join us. Thought you might. Excellent!" Ariston rose from his couch at the head of the room to welcome him, though Lysanias noticed a meaningful glace across at where Phraston lounged that sent a chill through him. Well, he had come looking for confrontation…

Before Lysanias could respond, Ariston had already turned to the assembled dining club members, putting his arm round Lysanias' shoulders in what Lysanias was sure was an unusual gesture.

"Gentlemen, introduction, another new member, cadet member rather." Turning to Lysanias he explained that they didn't normally admit men of his age to membership, but in view of his uncle's long association they would make an exception. "If you all agree. Klereides' heir, Lysanias, son of Leokhares, to whom we all extend our sympathies for the recent tragic death of his uncle."

Lysanias looked around at the now watching faces, trying to look as serious and adult as he could. He had hoped that his mere entrance might reveal a disconcerted look on someone's face, which could indicate a conspirator. However, the Athenian art of dissembling was too strongly entrenched. There seemed to be guests as well as members, for there was Hermon, who did look surprised to see Lysanias.

Ariston called for a vote by acclaim and Lysanias was startled by the cry, "Hai-ai, attack! The Golden Trident," sounding like a regimental cry.

There was a scurry of activity, and someone had vacated a couch for him by moving across to double up with someone else. Then he realised the two men were Inaros and Amynias, the naval officials. Was that so there was no danger he might be asked to share one of their couches and so be able to question them? Lysanias was embarrassingly aware of the dagger he had secreted inside his tunic, hopeful that it would not be apparent and that he would be able to get at it if needed, and scared that the gods would frown on this affront to his host's hospitality.

As Ariston guided him to the empty couch, he indicated and named other members. Lysanias thought he recognised one who might have been at the clandestine meeting at Aspasia's, but couldn't be sure. There was that plaited hairstyle, though it didn't seem as dark brown as he remembered, but there was no time to ask Ariston to repeat the name from the list of new names he had just heard. Most were unknown to Lysanias.

He knew Phraston, of course. No room for a second person on that giant's couch, he thought with amusement. He knew Hierokles.

And Strynises over there, sharing a couch with that tough-looking man who had been in the tavern with him. The news-teller must be a guest, surely.

"Ah, Lysanias, my boy," Hierokles greeted as he passed. The man sounded desperately tired and defeated. The vein still throbbed but not so distractingly, with bruises on arms as well as face. "Boiotos isn't well. Badly wounded. Doctor hopes for the best. Thought you'd like to know." Serves the brute right, thought Lysanias, but gave the appropriate sympathies.

As he sat on the couch, he could feel the tension in the room, a sense that people were watching him surreptitiously, yet when he looked everyone seemed pre-occupied. Was this because of his uncle? They couldn't know he was also looking for the killers of Ephialtes. Were they all conspirators in murder and assassination? These dinner parties were ideal gatherings to plot underhand deeds by a closed group.

To identify any more of the plotters by voice he would have to hear them speak, his only memory of them, but that was impossible as voices blurred in a murmur of private conversations.

Otanes had explained the routines, so Lysanias knew to sit on the edge of the couch allocated to him when Philia, no Philiako, must remember, appeared with bowl and jug to wash his feet with rose-scented water. He wished she wouldn't dry them so delicately, not like a boy he was sure. Then he imitated the position adopted by the other diners, reclining back, propped up by an elbow and cushions.

With another slave-boy, Philiako removed the table Inaros had been eating from and brought another, and stayed crouching to move dishes closer to his reach or offer bread. Sindron appeared and stood behind his couch at the same time. Hasdrubal or the chef must have briefed him on the dishes on offer, for he advised Lysanias on the best order to taste them to avoid killing the milder flavours with the spicier ones. At least, Lysanias didn't feel so alone. It didn't escape him that Ariston's pretty slave had surreptitiously circulated the gathering, head in air almost as though acting as host, halting briefly at the couches of Phraston and Hierokles and one or two others, he had to assume with some message. Phraston clearly sent a reply.

Now Phraston, his forehead glistening with sweat, called across, "Ah, Lysanias. Calm seas, I hear, young man. Good weather for cargoes."

Lysanias was looking puzzled, when Sindron said from behind him, "Look puzzled, master. I think that was intended to warn and embarrass me."

No, it goes further than that, Lysanias thought. Phraston had said it loud enough for others to hear. He's telling them I'm his concern, not to worry, he'll deal with me. Well, we'll see about that.

"Fine weather in Athens too, Phraston!" Lysanias called back. Let him interpret that as meaning I am near a solution, if he wishes, thought Lysanias. He noticed an uncertainty flicker across Ariston's face and the pretty personal slave who had accompanied the general before made a casual and elegant circuit to whisper to Phraston and return.

As quantities on the tables diminished, the boy-slaves, including Philiako, left the room.

Hermon sent his personal slave across with a message, which he gave to Sindron, who gave it to Lysanias. Apparently there had been looting in Peiraieos as well. A lot of stock materials had been stolen. That must be why Hermon had been looking so worried. Lysanias looked over with an appropriate expression but, with everyone seated on separate couches, he was more concerned with how he was going to find a chance to confront anyone.

Philia was just beginning to think that this was easy work compared to a day on the loom, when Hasdrubal, with a clap of his hands in the Asian manner, summoned the boys back to the entertaining room at the end of the main course.

Rose-scented water again, to allow their masters to rinse their greasy fingers. Floral wreaths for their heads. Serve cups of neat wine for the traditional toast to good fortune. Then it was all rush, grab a table, two by two, follow those in front out and place the tables in line in the courtyard by the kitchen. Tibios, one of Ariston's boys, teamed up with her to carry the tables, so she followed what he did, but they moved so fast, these experienced slaves. Next, remove the leftovers to plain and functional tables, while the chefs and their helpers lay out the fruit and sweetmeats on the same tables. Go back, with birch brooms and buckets to sweep up all the bones and bread balls and other debris discarded by the diners. She was too busy to feel frightened surrounded by all these males and her disguise gave her a strange freedom, as though she had become someone else.

As she knelt, she felt a stray hand pat her bottom outside her tunic. She had seen it happen to another slave-boy, so she kept her nerve enough not to react. She thanked the gods that wealthy families dressed their slave-boys in knee length tunics these days.

Then back with the small amphoras for the gentlemen to relieve themselves. It was embarrassing but most of the diners were discreet, holding the amphora under their cloak.

At this stage all the diners were standing and walking around, greeting one another, as the slaves continued tidying before bringing in the second tables.

As Philia moved around, she tried to overhear snatches of conversations, as Lysanias had urged her. For a brief moment, she heard a stammer, something Lysanias had especially mentioned, but the speaker didn't continue. Mostly it was meaningless chat, or business matters she didn't understand, but not all.

"Why did Ariston invite that beardless youngster? Don't care if he is Klereides' heir, too damned young to be trusted in the sort of discussions we have!" "What I hear, he's been making a nuisance of himself all over town." "You've been listening to that Strynises again." "That's another thing. Why's *he* here? Damned scoundrel!"

"Don't you see? If Kimon could find some way of getting the hoplites into the city without the radicals knowing, then we'd have enough strength to take over." "Come on! They'll have all the gates closed and guarded as soon as they hear the troops are approaching. Wouldn't you in their position?" Was that Hierokles' voice? Better keep her head down and move away.

"Phraston, see Phraston!" The voice sounded frightened. Then an angry and confused one. "But Philebos distinctly named you two." Sounded like... Philia glanced up. Yes, it was Hermon. "No, Phraston, Phraston dealt with it. He's over there talking with Ariston." "I can't interrupt him there. This is ridiculous..."

Then the other boys were leaving to fetch the tables with fruit and sweetmeats and she had to go with them.

As the diners started getting to their feet, Lysanias thought this might give him an opportunity to talk with Amynias and maybe hear other voices, but, no, he was cornered by another guest, who made small talk about his uncle and how Lysanias was finding life in the big city.

Lysanias realised he couldn't break away to tackle the naval officials. Over the man's shoulder, he saw that Hermon had managed to confront Amynias and Inaros and the conversation looked animated. I must say something to be polite, he thought.

Then Thoukydides, the young man who had spoken at the Assembly meeting, joined in. "Don't you think we young men could organise things so much better," he said, confidingly, grasping Lysanias forearm. The voice was high and sharp, like one he recalled at Aspasia's, but was it the same? He had heard so little of it and the man seemed too rational to be an assassin. "If we'd made sure our supporters were all together in solid blocks, that would have encouraged them, maybe frightened our opponents ..."

Lysanias first reaction to the hand gently kneading the muscle of his forearm was to pull away in distaste but he wasn't sure if that would be regarded as rude and, anyway, the touch wasn't at all unpleasant and the man was personable. Perhaps in Athens one should be prepared to experiment as the Athenians seemed to.

Then the second tables had arrived, and he was able to break away prior to returning to his couch. "Would master like some fruit?" Philiako said softly, brushing her hand lightly against his, and Lysanias immediately felt guilty. Perhaps she had seen his discomfiture. Or his indecisiveness. He turned to look at her, but she avoided his gaze.

He found the sight of her strangely disturbing, half girl, half boy, and realised rather late that he shouldn't have allowed her to do this, bringing her into the groping reach of other men, exposing her to yet more danger. She seemed to be carrying it off, though. Brave girl.

"Ah, now I see why you're not interested in us! A well-formed slave!" Thoukydides interrupted his thoughts. "But what did he do to make you beat him so?" The tone implied that it was perfectly acceptable to beat a slave, but one should ideally have a good reason. Lysanias decided it was better, in this gathering, to appear a little brutal.

"My slaves obey me, no earnings on the side." He said it as though it were a joke, but then realised that it could be heard as a warning to keep away from his slave-boy. Philia looked shocked, and scurried off without another word.

When all were back on their couches, Hasdrubal called for silence, and Ariston raised himself to a sitting position. Sounds of activity, voices of new arrivals permeating through from the front door and vestibule seemed to be making people both expectant and worried.

"For our new members and guests, hah, should say, this stage in the evening, normally discuss matters of common interest regarding political future, our great city, hah, and so on." Lysanias felt sure this would have included how to apply influence on behalf of club members to obtain public offices they wanted or to win contracts. Maybe it was at a dinner similar to this that the naval officials and overseers had discussed Klereides' behaviour and, in effect, condemned him to death. Ephialtes too, if that golden trident meant what it implied. The thought sickened him for a moment.

"Today, special situation, special guest of honour who will be king of our feast."

With that, Hasdrubal threw open the doors, and in marched General Kimon, tall and impressive as ever, appearing to have regained his old confidence and self-assertion despite his ostracism.

Instinctively, Lysanias slid from his couch and sprang to his feet, at attention. He saw that most of the others had done the same, offering a salute Lysanias did not know. Cries that must be regimental rang out from many mouths. Lysanias felt caught up in the wave of admiration and, it could only be, pity, for the great man rejected by his native city. Even Ariston's eyes looked moist.

Kimon stood for a moment, still an imposing figure, and acknowledged their salute, but no tears in his eyes. Sharp as ever, they swept round the gathering, registering familiar and unfamiliar, settling on Lysanias himself, who tried to look nonchalant to cover his sense of guilt at his role in the great general's downfall. A quick word with Ariston appeared to satisfy him, though his eyes narrowed a little before moving on. His manner suggested that, exhausted by his campaigns over the years, he was grateful that it was over, that he no longer had to feel responsible for the city and its fate.

Behind him entered two women. This is unusual, thought Lysanias, for Sindron had told him that it was men only at such dinners, except for maybe dancing girls and 'companions'. That explained one of the women, Aspasia, looking radiant in her usual colours of pale blue and green. Stunning but a little frightening. He felt more comfortable with Philia, he realised. Aspasia's eyes met his for an instant, twinkled in amusement, and moved on.

Was the slim older woman Kimon's wife? No, Ariston welcomed both women by name. It was Elpinike, Kimon's sister. A still beautiful woman, she had the elegance and self-assurance that comes from birth and money, her expensive-looking gown embroidered over-elaborately with small flowers and butterflies that Lysanias did not find at all appealing, brought up as he was to simplicity.

Couches were quickly made available for these guests. In the general re-shuffle, Hermon took the opportunity to slip over to share Lysanias' couch. Across the room, he saw a look pass between Inaros and Amynias that showed they had noticed. Amynias glanced back at Phraston, for some reason, and received a slight answering nod in reply.

A hearty voice called out, "Hey, king of the feast, get on with it, we're dying of thirst!" Evidently, this club liked its wine. Kimon retaliated by naming the stronger mix of wine, three of water to two of wine, rather than the weaker blend that was more usual.

Even now, Kimon did not take his couch. Obviously he had come with a purpose – to put heart back into his defeated supporters.

Having paced rapidly across the floor to thank his closest supporters, including Phraston and Hierokles, Kimon strode to a prominent position. No longer in uniform, he had chosen a plain but regal-looking purple gown, as though he no longer cared that people might consider he was getting above his station – after all, he would shortly have no station, no status at all in Athens.

"Gentlemen, all is not lost." The great voice boomed out, as though he were addressing the troops lined up before a battle. Lysanias was genuinely surprised. Something must have happened since this afternoon that he didn't know about. "The future looks brighter than it did this afternoon, but we must all use our utmost tact and delicacy in the coming months."

Everyone listened intently, admiration in their eyes. It was shared, he noticed, by Aspasia, who he had regarded as a cynic, while it was on Elpinike's face that cynicism, superciliousness and a trace of a satisfied smirk could be detected.

While he spoke, the mixing bowls had been brought in and the first cups served, then the slaves had all left the room to allow the gentlemen privacy of conversation. Lysanias felt uncomfortably aware that his only ally here was Hermon, who whispered, "They claim it was nothing to do with them. Say they didn't know how to go about hiring someone who would frighten Klereides for them, so they asked Phraston and he said he was sure his slave Lydos would be able to arrange it. So they left it to them."

"This is ridiculous! Everyone's blaming everyone else," Lysanias whispered back. A dirty look from the host obliged them to stop talking and listen to Kimon.

Philia was glad of a chance to loll in the courtyard with the other boys, picking at the leftovers from the main course. She had forgotten how little she had eaten today and now realised she was famished. It felt peculiar being so close to so many boys of her own age or younger but she had no trouble with them. One glance at her scars and bruises, and they concluded this strangely unmuscular boy was a scrapper.

"They'll all be drunk tonight," laughed one of the slave-boys, "after what happened today."

"And last night," rejoined another.

"Shh, we're not supposed to talk about that."

Then a voice close by, talking to her. "We'll miss your old master." It was Tibios next to her, and as she turned he winked knowingly. "His fault it ended," he said, indicating Ariston's personal slave, delicately helping himself to the best bits.

"Whadja mean?" Philia grunted, in as deep a voice as she could manage. "Come on! You know! His affairs with other people's wives. Used to come here secretly, when the general was away. Generous tips." Philia nearly burst into tears and had to turn her head before she gave herself away. She was horrified. Curly had been deceiving her! Not just with whores but with Ariston's wife. The adulterer deserved to die. No, Demeter, Kore, Aphrodite, Mother, I didn't mean that. Rest his soul. But she was badly shaken. That must be why Ariston's wife was always crying, for her dead lover, my Curly, but did it mean Ariston had killed him?

With an effort, Philia blinked and turned back. "Oh that! All masters are the same, aren't they?" She did her best to grin and wink, but her swollen lips and eye made it difficult. It hurt too.

Kimon went on to outline the details of the accommodation he had reached with the leaders of the people's party, who he referred to as the radicals.

"What have we gained? Clipped the wings of young Perikles for a start…" That drew cheers. "Stopped them building that eyesore Temple to Hephaistos. One in the eye for Arkhestratos and his damned rowers." With a gesture, he quieted the shouts of support. In return, Ariston and he had agreed to civic spending on new housing for the poor in both Athens and Peiraieos, because, after the looting and Olinthios' threats, they had no choice. There were hisses at the news that Ephialtes would be given a state funeral but Kimon went on.

"That scoundrel Themistokles, he's to be shipped back to Persia straight away on pain of death." There were mixed reactions to this but again Kimon silenced them. "I know you'd all like to see him dead but he's an old man, he'll be dead soon anyway. With their best speaker eliminated and their sharpest mind out of the way … I'll say no more."

Lysanias had registered that, if he kept drinking at the pace the others seemed to be setting, he would never be able to keep his wits about him enough to confront Phraston. If the opportunity occurred! He discovered that, while everyone's attention was on Kimon, it was just possible to tip some of his wine into Hermon's cup without him noticing. He rationalised that, being more accustomed to wine, Hermon could probably take it better.

Sindron found Hasdrubal eager to be friendly and especially keen to show off the house, presumably to demonstrate his able management. In the entertaining room, he had found himself restricted by procedures. There was no way he could help further any of Lysanias' objectives but maybe this was an opportunity.

As Hasdrubal took Sindron into the stable, he commented, "I persuaded the master to buy these Arabian mares too, much faster and sleeker animals than your Scythian breeds." They were fine animals, Sindron had to admit, two blacks, a fine chestnut, and a silver-grey. A bell clanged in Sindron's head. The watchman had remembered a silver-grey horse pulling the chariot that brought Klereides.

"Magnificent, isn't she?" crowed Hasdrubal. "Very rare these, only one in Athens, I imagine. Master lent her to some fool recently who must have raced her over rough ground, judging by the state of her fetlocks."

It could be the one, thought Sindron. He felt it was appropriate to reach out a hand to stroke the horse, but the mare shied away from his touch, as though frightened of a strange hand. "See what I mean? Someone must have ill-treated her!"

"Does your master race, then?"

"Used to, I believe. There's an old racing chariot somewhere around. No, a cavalry general needs good mounts, both for battle and for ceremonial parades."

There was no way Sindron could break away to look for the old chariot, but he could make out an area at the end of the stable where something bulky was covered with large cloths.

"One word before we go back in. Your young master. Not making himself very popular, going round asking questions. Perhaps you could point it out to him? My master could do him a lot of good. Entry to one of the best regiments. Swift promotion as an officer. You know how it goes."

Sindron was taken by surprise. Another one! The phrasing clearly was Ariston's not Hasdrubal's. The slave must have been instructed to speak to him. This and the horse clearly moved Ariston higher up the list of suspects.

"Quite," Sindron said, stalling. "Finding his feet, you understand. Not sure what's acceptable. But he's learning. I'll see what I can do." This disjointed Ariston phrasing is catching, he thought to himself. The steward seemed satisfied. Then, as they passed by a display of war trophies, Hasdrubal added, "The master thought your master might like to have this," and held out a fine medallion cast in gold, celebrating Kimon's conquest of Eion. Very clever. They couldn't have thought of anything that Lysanias would value more, and, for that reason, Sindron couldn't refuse. "Just a small guest-gift, you understand."

Lysanias was getting worried. Hermon was already tipsy and muttering to himself that all these arrogant idlers had conspired together to kill his partner and loot his factory. What if the shipbuilder revealed all they knew? They could be in real danger. His own fault too, he really shouldn't have given the man that extra wine.

"Of course, I do have to go into exile," Kimon was saying. "Like all citizens I must obey the laws of our land, and I have no wish to see our great city descend into chaos." Lysanias sensed that Kimon was determined to do all he could to avoid the civil conflict that could destroy all his achievements.

"So, I have agreed to ride out tomorrow with the generals who support the radicals to persuade our hoplites to accept the situation."

From one of the couches came the rather plaintive cry, "But they're our last hope!"

"Were! If they had arrived in time!" Kimon answered. "They didn't! We must all accept. For the time being. We all know what damage civil conflict has done to other cities – we can't allow that to happen to Athens!"

"But you could …," came back, though Kimon forestalled any mention of making himself tyrant by, "No, I haven't spent all these years bringing independence and democracy to the Ionian Greeks to destroy it here. Not my way." His stern expression closed that avenue firmly. Lysanias could almost feel the relief radiate from Hermon's body that the aristocrats had not discovered the delay had been a plot.

"Even in exile, across the border in Tanagra, I will be close enough to receive information, and give advice. It will not be forever. I have a secret assurance that, at the first opportunity, when the city needs me, I will be recalled."

Was the man deceiving himself, or could the radicals really have said that? It had happened before with other exiles, Lysanias knew, but only in real crises like the Persian invasion and Kimon himself had ensured that wouldn't happen again. Kimon clearly seemed to think he could continue to control the aristocratic faction from outside Attika, guide them back to power, and maybe he could – there seemed to be no-one here willing to challenge his authority and take charge. But once he was gone, in only a few days, the situation would be different.

"Philiako!" Philia alerted on the 'Phil' and recognised Sindron's voice, albeit in an unfamiliar commanding tone. He beckoned her over and bent down to whisper. He wanted her to slip away and look at something in the stables. He almost seemed to have forgotten she wasn't a slave-boy. It felt good to be trusted with something important, but she wasn't sure now if she really wanted to do anything to help Curly's soul rest in peace.

Kimon concluded by thanking Ariston for his support. He clearly saw the General as his successor among the aristocrats and, from the way he preened, so did Ariston. His face darkened, though, when Kimon also praised Thoukydides for the leadership promise his speech revealed, even including Lysanias in the hand gestures that accompanied his trust in the younger generation, which made Lysanias feel even guiltier.

"It only remains for me to thank you all for your support and to assure you that I will return to serve our great city."

No trace of the bitterness the great general must be feeling at this rejection by the city he had served so well for so long. Lysanias was amazed at his resilience. Was it sensible to have ambition in Athens if this was the reward one could end up with? However, he knew that he, too, was keen to serve this great city and to try to emulate this great man, whatever the consequences.

"Hermon, pull yourself together," Lysanias said quietly, applauding like the others. It seemed as though the businessman was grieving for his looted goods and wanted to drown his sorrows.

A horse whinnied as Philia entered the stables. She had taken a small shell lamp and Sindron's directions were clear but that didn't make it less scary, with no telling what might be in the darkness beyond the lamp's small circle of light.

If she lifted back these cloths, she should be able to see if it was a racing chariot painted to look like an ordinary chariot. It was definitely painted. A green colour, she thought, and feeling with her hand revealed mouldings one wouldn't expect on an ordinary chariot. Bending down she could see where the dark paint was flaking off, gilding showed through. Sindron had said look for bloodstains on the floor of the chariot, but, as she bent in, holding the lamp before her...

"Now that's a nice little arse!"

The voice was close, but not loud. Philia froze. "How about a quick one, boy? They won't miss us for a while." She felt her heart pounding. In a way, it was a relief that whoever it was didn't seem to suspect she was doing anything she shouldn't.

Philia straightened up slowly as he spoke, and turned. Horrified, she saw it was Ariston's pretty personal slave who stood, blocking the way she would have to take to run out. She was sure to be discovered now.

Philiako. I'm Philiako. I'm a boy. A tough boy. A fighter. She clenched her free fist, raised the lamp to show the mangled side of her face and growled as deeply as she could. The lustful expression on his soft, smooth face, changed dramatically. Without another word, he turned and went.

Her hands were shaking but she knew she had to hurry back now. No chance that Ariston had sent this slave to topple the amphora on top of Klereides – he'd never have had the nerve for it, she thought, pleased with her own courage, but worried at what the slave might report to his master

"I'll take that grin off your big fat face, you conniving..." Hermon had started aggressively towards Phraston's couch. No help for it, thought Lysanias, and tripped him with his foot. The drunken businessman fell with a great thud.

Lysanias leant down to help him up. "This isn't the way, Hermon. Everyone can hear."

"Whatya do that for?" slurred Hermon, shaking his head to try to clear it.

"I'll deal with it, Hermon. Now why don't I get your slave to take you home?"

"Don't wanna go. Job to do." Lysanias managed to steer him back to their couch. He felt that all eyes were on his back, that he and Hermon must now be inextricably linked as enemies of the group, but, when he looked round, everyone was looking at Strynises.

So that was why Strynises was here – to entertain. Amazing after all the things the man had uttered about Kimon and Elpinike, and here they were sitting smiling in front of him. This time his satire was at the expense of the radicals. How crafty Themistokles, the grey fox with the mantle of Persian gold, had tricked timid Ephialtes into acting against the Areopagos by pretending they were coming to arrest him. He knew how to pander to his audience this man.

When Philiako got back the last boy was just going into the entertaining room. What were they taking? Fresh garlands. She grabbed one from a table by the door. As she put it on Lysanias head, she tried to tell him about the chariot but he was pre-occupied and didn't hear her.

Lysanias was worried. The poem had hinted at a shipbuilder helping the radicals. One or two members had glanced at him at that point, so he guessed they were thinking it was his uncle. Then mention had been made of whores in Corinth. Hermon seemed too drunk to notice and laughed when everyone else did, but the man could be in danger if he stayed. And here he had been thinking that Strynises wanted to help him but the man seemed to enjoy causing trouble and upsetting people whichever side they might be on. Thank the gods, here was Philiako, carrying a fresh garland. He, no she, could fetch Hermon's personal slave to take him home and to safety.

Philiako tore the old garlands up, as the other boys did, and strewed the petals on the floor. Then she went for Hermon's slave. In the process, she found Sindron and told him what she had discovered, but, busy ensuring that Hermon got away safely in his chariot, he had no chance to inform Lysanias either. Now it was Philiako's turn to refill the wine cups. Everything was happening so fast but it was exciting.

The members had been playing the riddle game. Someone had started it off with an old favourite,
        "I am the dark offspring of a light mother;
        Though without wings, I soar to the heavens;
        As soon as I am born, I disappear into the air;
        Who am I?"
and, of course, the answer is smoke. Now Strynises, looking mischievous, aimed one directly at Lysanias.

"Who wields a hammer in the morning, consorts with craftsmen in the afternoon, and beds Aphrodite in the evening?"

Lysanias was startled. How did Strynises know he had been with Aspasia. Did everybody know? At the name Aphrodite, he couldn't help glancing across at Aspasia. She looked totally unconcerned, wasn't even looking at him, but her hands were together in a way like the salute for... Oh, Yes.

"Hephaistos," burst triumphantly from Lysanias' mouth. What a relief the answer wasn't him.

Instead of applause, the name of the worker's god, the god called on so recently by Kimon's opponents at the ostracism meeting, had produced a shocked silence. Before another riddle could be asked, Ariston demanded in a loud voice. "Tell us, young man. What do you know about Hephaistos?" Now he was aware that all eyes were on him and that an air of hostility had developed. Had that been some sort of trap? Strynises had really landed him in it. Even Kimon looked intrigued. How did he get out of this?

"Just that he freed Athene from the head of Zeus with his hammer." That clearly hadn't been the right way to put it. It sounded too much like a political slogan of the radicals. He put on an innocent air. "That's what the poet Hesiod says, isn't it?"

"Not like that, no."

"Nothing more?" That was Phraston, smoothly, sneakily. This was like an interrogation, hounding him to confess to something. How much could they know? Had Strynises given him away? No, they'd have challenged him directly, if he had. He felt very isolated. Try to appear naive, casual, Lysanias told himself.

"You're building a new temple to him by the market place."

"I'm not building a temple," blustered Ariston. "Radicals got the Assembly to vote for it. Disgraceful!"

"Enough of this depressing talk," roared Kimon. "As king of the feast I demand more laughter. A toast to our friends on the road from Corinth!" He raised his wine cup and drank, though the bleakness now in his eyes did not echo the joviality of his manner. The frosty atmosphere eased a little. Lysanias was pleased that Kimon seemed not to share the suspicion that had focussed on himself and even seemed irritated at grown men picking on a youngster, for he smiled encouragingly across at him.

The tension prompted Strynises to divert attention or try to ingratiate himself, or both, for his next riddle, though amusingly phrased, ended up comparing Kimon to the sun god Apollo, who was banished from the home of the gods on Mount Olympos and returned in triumph. Or was he just mocking the great man?

At least one member decided to retaliate. Calm, detached Phraston of all people.

"I am a weasel who snuffles and digs,
To find stories and gossip to sell for cheap laughs,
To pour scorn on great heroes
And belittle their lives
Make fun of their lovers and even their wives."

Kimon guffawed at that, as did most of the other members, but Strynises cut short any escalation of abuse by acknowledging that he was the answer, even giving a victor's salute. Phraston seemed pleased to have defended his colleagues but Strynises had been challenged.

He started another verse. There was a glint in his eyes, an excitement perhaps at having found a worthy opponent, as they swept round the gathering, pausing briefly at Amynias and Inaros then turning to face Phraston.

"When mighty Zeus, in human form,
A shipbuilder espies,
Carousing round the forge,
Deserting kin and friends alike,
While following Midas' urge,
A monstrous thunderbolt he takes
And, under blackest night,
A lure he sets
And down it hurls
To squash the scoundrel quite."

Lysanias sat up straight, astonished, like many of the other diners, some of whom glanced across at him surreptitiously. Nothing there that wasn't public knowledge, except maybe the fact that the victim had been lured, but why at Phraston? Was Strynises trying to tell him something?

Coldly, and confidently, instead of naming Klereides, Phraston answered with a verse. This wasn't a game any more. Phraston clearly regarded it as a challenge and was making his response,

"When the slave of finance
Is in the house of colours
Who can tell when orders may change?
From scare to maim, from maim to kill."

That was it! He was denying the accusation. It was Lydos, 'the slave of finance', who had changed the instructions to whoever killed his uncle. And that was where he was now. The emphasis Phraston had put on those words, the look straight at Lysanias confirmed it. 'House of colours' could only be the dye works Sindron had told him the slave had bought. Lysanias had to confront the man, and now! All he needed was an excuse to leave.

Strynises had, surprisingly, conceded defeat on that one. "Hardly fair," he had said, "to use one's own property as answer, when everyone might not know their name." His eyes met Lysanias' knowingly and he nodded as though in confirmation of Lysanias' own conclusions. Other people looked confused or tense and seemed pleased to move on to other subjects. Kimon was looking irritated at the obscurity and lack of laughter in the game and seemed about to intervene again. Then Strynises was back in full flow, apparently determined to demonstrate his claim to satirise all parties without fear or favour. Standing in the centre of the room, he spun on his heels with arm outstretched, leaving everyone wondering if they could be the next target. He drew in his arm but, when the verse ended, he halted looking straight at Kimon. There was a blank, innocent expression on his face but his eyes said he was enjoying this chance to humiliate the great man.

"A present from a sister,
A present from a wife,
A present from the Thasian,
That's my portrait on a madman.
Who am I?"

Everyone seemed to hold their breath. Kimon wasn't slow, even when he'd been drinking. In Elpinike's eyes, a hint of fear had taken the place of the bored expression. Aspasia's face held cynical amusement, but she looked away from the great general. Kimon's face turned purple, his eyes blazed fire. "You scoundrel. How dare you malign my wife and my sister? Ariston, our gratitude for your hospitality, but we're off to somewhere where we won't be insulted. Come, ladies!"

Ariston looked appalled. The entertainment triumph of capturing Strynises had backfired. He had offended the leader whose patronage Ariston still needed to take over the party. He rushed to try to placate Kimon but without success. Strynises had backed to where his companion was now standing beside the couch, in case anyone decided to resort to the violence the angry faces implied. He clearly was used to taking risks with his revelations but this was pushing to the extreme the license that satirists seemed to be allowed in Athens and the respect due an invited guest.

Lysanias realised he was missing his opportunity – Kimon and the two women had reached the door. He slipped to his feet and paced rapidly across the floor, nodding a quick farewell to Ariston as he passed him. He must act while the fury was on him. Lysanias located Sindron and Philiako, and rushed them out into the street. Sindron insisted on going back to retrieve his knobbly stick and claim two shell lamps to light their way home. Voices in angry argument followed him as he came out again.

A quick question established what Sindron knew of the name and street of the dye works. It should be adequate for Lysanias to find it.

"Take Philia home, Sindron. See she stays there."

"But why, master? Are you sure...?" said Sindron.

"But, master, uh, Lysanias..." said Philia.

"Don't worry about me. I can handle this on my own." Lysanias knew that, if he let them speak, they would tell him he shouldn't go on his own, that it was too dangerous. He already knew that, but he couldn't put Philia at risk again, and she would need Sindron with her to get home safely. "Don't argue. I'm in a hurry." This might be his only opportunity to confront Lydos on his own.

"Master." Sindron held out his stick and one of the lamps. Lysanias took them gratefully. He turned and left quickly to avoid seeing the concern in their eyes.

CHAPTER 17

Lysanias had no trouble finding the dye works. Once in the right area, he just followed the powerful and repugnant smell. He had avoided the one joint patrol he saw. They might think it odd for a gentleman to be out alone without a slave to light his way. Now he pushed carefully the big doors that allowed mule-loads of fabric to come and go, and they yielded. They were not locked or barred. The thought crossed his mind that this might be a trap, that Phraston had misled him, that Lydos wouldn't be here at all so late at night but he felt he had no choice, he had to know. Family honour, his own honour, was at stake here, but his anger was under control. He was calm, calculating, thinking clearly, pleased he had managed to control his wine intake earlier, ears straining to catch any sound, eyes used to the dark now and staring. Even if his sense of smell was flooded by the foul odours, they had helped to clear his head.

Lysanias blew out his lamp and placed it by the wall. He slipped through the opening between the doors, but failed to stop them creaking as they swung to again. He stood still, trying to get a picture of the layout of the place. A long flight of steps to his left led up to a high platform, where lamplight from an un-shuttered window and an open door, in what must be an office, threw enough light together with the waning moon for Lysanias to make out a large number of tall vats and tubs, presumably each containing a different colour dye. The light glinted on the puddles of wet on the stone-paved courtyard. A stream babbled somewhere, which must supply the water constantly needed.

If Lydos was here, he must be where that light came from. Lysanias trod carefully. The steps were as wet and slippery as the courtyard below. Wouldn't want to slip into one of those vats and swallow that foul-smelling liquid! He was glad of Sindron's knobbly stick to steady himself.

As Lysanias looked down, he could see the circles and squares of the tops of the vats with the dye liquid glinting dully within them, and the black spaces yawning in between. For a moment, Lysanias wondered why he had come here alone, why he hadn't laid charges and had the Scythian guard arrest Lydos. Because the physical evidence still isn't adequate for the courts, he answered himself. Because this is a personal matter now. A matter of vengeance. Lysanias had heard that, in the province of Rhamnous, they worshipped the goddess of vengeance, Nemesis, alongside Themis, the goddess of justice. May Nemesis walk with me tonight, he prayed, as he stepped upwards silently, carefully.

As his head rose higher above the top step, he could see more and more through the window and partly-open door. A man. At a table. It was Lydos. Head bowed over scrolls. He appeared to be alone. Good. Despite himself, Lysanias felt his heart beat faster, his anger start to rise again. He stopped and calmed himself. Nemesis must strike calmly in the cause of Justice. He re-assured himself that the dagger was still resting there within his tunic in a position where he could grasp it easily. His left hand clutched Sindron's knobbly stick more tightly.

The door was open. Lydos may be expecting someone. Strike while he is alone. Lysanias took a long step forward, pushed the door fully open, and stepped inside. "Lydos, I have come to settle accounts." As he said it, he realised what an awful pun it was, given the man's occupation, but it was said with the due degree of menace, he hoped.

"Ah, young Lysanias. Come in, we've been expecting you."

We? So Lydos wasn't alone. Lysanias turned rapidly as he heard the door swing closed behind him and saw a slim, lithe figure, tightly swathed in black with bare feet. That face! The barber! And the ruthless wrestler at the training ground! This must be the man who had been paid to kill his uncle! At last! Lysanias instinctively raised Sindron's stick as a club.

"I don't think there will be any need for violence, Lysanias. Not yet anyway. Relieve him of his weapon, would you, Aristodikos?"

The black figure's right hand held a military thrusting spear. Strange weapon for close combat, thought Lysanias, but now he saw its purpose as the man turned it, placed the point firmly to Lysanias' chest and backed him the few steps to the nearby wall.

Lysanias was powerless.

"Drop the club!" The order was grunted in a deep, surly voice. It was a purely functional room, not large, with no furniture other than the table and chair, nothing for Lysanias to duck behind in an attempt to escape from the killer holding the spear. Lysanias had no choice. He dropped Sindron's stick. Just as long as they didn't find the knife, he might still have a chance.

"That's better," said Lydos, with a friendly smile. "Now we'll just wait a while. May I introduce Aristodikos of Tanagra in Boeotia. An acolyte and expert of the goddess Nemesis." Lysanias knew what that must mean. And the very goddess he had been praying to!

The silence lengthened. The assassin's bare foot tapped softly with impatience. Lydos appeared to carry on writing on a scroll. Then sounds came from outside. The big doors creaked, as they had when Lysanias entered. Someone was heaving themselves up the stairs, puffing and panting. The other two appeared to be expecting this. Phraston finally lurched through the doorway. This must have been his plan, but he looked none too pleased at having to leave the dinner party and climb steep stairs in the dark.

So it wasn't Lydos acting alone! Lysanias realised now he should never have allowed himself to believe that story. It needed something big to persuade a citizen such as Phraston to offer a bribe to a slave like Sindron.

"Sorry to keep you waiting ... young Lysanias..." He leant against the doorframe getting his breath back and sweating more than ever. "Just wanted to make sure ... you know ... the excellent reasons ... why you have to die so young."

Lysanias did not react. If they were hoping he would show fear, he would make sure they were disappointed. He had realised some time ago that they must intend that he shouldn't leave this place alive. His worry was that he hadn't yet come up with any scheme to make sure they were wrong.

Phraston looked only slightly disappointed at the lack of reaction, but Aristodikos seemed to want to take physical steps to evince terror in their victim, if the snarl on his face was anything to go by.

"I'm afraid it has to look like an accident, so it must be death by drowning." This did alarm Lysanias, but he did his best not to show it. He had long come to terms with the possibility of death in battle by the sword or javelin. A slower death by drowning, that had always worried him, ever since he'd heard tales of shipwrecks from seamen down by the harbour back home. "Sadly, you came here to see Lydos, you slipped on the wet steps and fell into a vat of dye. Most unfortunate. Lydos was shut in the office, heard a splash, but, when he looked out, couldn't see anything. Your body was discovered by the workmen the next day. Tragic end to a young life."

The man was actually enjoying this, but Aristodikos wasn't.

"Let me get on with it, you old fool! Then I'll take my money and go. The goddess demands action." The man of action from Tanagra was impatient. How on earth had this man ever put up with working at the boring craft of barber, even if it did give him a good disguise and easy communication with the conspirators?

Lydos tried to prevent a row and to protect his master. "Now, Aristodikos, let's not argue among ourselves..."

Phraston had enough wine on him to react angrily. "Shut up, man! You're being paid well to do a job. You'll do it when I say! Nemesis can wait a little longer!"

Something seemed to change in the assassin. Something akin to religious dedication came into his eyes. "I am the servant of Nemesis, a fellow of the League of Nemesis. I act in accordance with the dictates of the goddess, not of man." The deep voice croaked out the oath-like incantation and Aristodikos twirled his spear in a dramatic, almost ritual gesture, swinging it around his head and his body. He and Phraston were standing either side of the approach to the still-open door. Lydos was still seated behind the table and unable to move fast. Lysanias decided this might be his last opportunity, while their attention was off him.

Lysanias let his cloak slip to the floor, leaving only his tunic, and dived under the spear, aiming for Aristodikos' legs, to throw him off balance. If he could knock him to the ground, he might have a chance to use his dagger. The killer turned his head in surprise as Lysanias rushed at him. Then, losing his balance, he pushed out and down with the spear to try to stabilise himself. The sharp point went straight into Phraston's huge chest and in and in and through. The big man went down with the force of the spear and ended pinned to the floorboards. He uttered hardly a sound, only a great long sigh escaping from his lungs, and then a gurgle, as the killer lost his grip and tumbled on top of him.

"What have you done, what have you done?" Lydos was up and running round from the desk, almost crying. Lysanias was up and leaping for the door, hoping they would be too distracted to follow quickly, but Aristodikos was a killer, a hunter, and his prey was escaping. He grasped for Lysanias' ankle as he flew past. He didn't succeed, but it was enough to throw Lysanias off balance. He slithered across the wet platform outside, just managing to stop himself going over the edge.

Looking back as he tried to scramble to his feet, Lysanias saw the assassin complete the spring that took him upright and through the door in one lithe movement. But the man was now weaponless, and, in his own fall, Lysanias' dagger had dropped from his tunic and clattered across the platform in the darkness. It would be settled hand to hand, and the man was a skilled wrestler, and a wrestler not bound by the rules. Equally, he had shown at the wrestling ground that he lost his temper easily and, with it, his edge. Lydos seemed totally pre-occupied with trying to find any glimmer of life in his old master, too pre-occupied to join the fight or provide Aristodikos with a weapon, Lysanias hoped.

The tension had neutralised any effects of wine in Lysanias' body. He was thinking clearly, but knew he hadn't the strength or the experience to defeat this man, if he once let him get a firm grip. How had his instructor in Eion put it? Let the force of your opponent's movements provide the impetus to throw him. It had always worked in training, but could he make it work against an experienced fighter like this?

They were both on their feet now. Aristodikos was circling, trying to spot his opponent's weaknesses, looking for an advantage. Lysanias was trying to edge round, sensing how vulnerable he was with his back to the edge of the platform, the dye-filled vats waiting with gaping mouths below. Suddenly the man rushed, arms wide to grasp him. Lysanias jumped aside. His opponent managed to catch a handful of Lysanias' tunic, but, as his stride took him on and he swivelled to turn, the tunic tore, and Lysanias wrenched more to make sure his opponent was left with only a handful of fabric.

The assassin looked as though he was already annoyed that a mere youth should have upset his plans so much.

"Regard it as an offering to Nemesis," called out Lysanias, teasing Aristodikos to charge again, dancing first to one side then the other. He appreciated the risk of using the goddess's name in that way, but it was obviously the thing the assassin treasured most, what would anger him most speedily.

"How dare you call on the name of the goddess?" It was working but the killer still had it under control. This time he advanced slowly towards Lysanias, legs wide, arms spread, to minimise the chance that Lysanias could rush past him along the narrow platform. Lysanias realised he could back no further. Dare he risk it? It was his only option. He couldn't dive through the open door. Lydos now stood there watching, a grim smirk on his face. The slave really wanted to see revenge taken for his master but must be savouring the thought of the banking enterprise he would now inherit – provided Lysanias did not escape.

Lysanias ducked down from the waist and then launched himself between the assassin's legs. Aristodikos reacted quickly. He sat, hoping to sit down onto Lysanias back and pin him there. He was a breath too late. Lysanias was through and heard the bone-crunching thud as Aristodikos' rear end hit the hard boards. The disciplined assassin let out an involuntary howl. Then he was on his feet again and spinning round. An angry scowl on his face, a growl and then a roar on his lips. He charged.

This is it, thought Lysanias, crouching ready, feet braced. If he doesn't carry me over with him, I should be able to deflect him off the edge of the platform. Suddenly a long stick shot out from the shadows in the space at the end of the small office building, just in front of the assassin's charging feet. Aristodikos tripped, tried to right himself, fell to the side, his feet failing to find a grip on the wet boards, and he was gone, down, down, a howl of his goddess's name curtailed by a mighty splash.

Damn that Sindron! I could have handled him! But Lysanias didn't give himself time to think. He was rushing for the stairs and down to the bottom. Don't slip now, Lysanias, he told himself. Which vat was he in? There, two bare feet sticking up, black-clothed ankles, waving and slightly rising as the man tried to push himself up to get out. Lysanias grabbed hold of the ankles and pushed down. Not an approved wrestling hold, he thought grimly. The legs struggled, kicked, flailed, fluttered and were still, but Lysanias waited to be sure, catching his breath, before he dared let go.

"Let me go, you idiots. There's an important man needs attention here. Can't you see? I must get help!" Lydos' voice drifted down to him from above. Lysanias' breathing was back to normal and the sweat on his body was cooling in the night air as he made his way, triumphant, up the steps. He had avenged his uncle, whose spirit could now rest in peace, whatever the authorities might say about the death of a prominent citizen like Phraston. If Aristodikos really had been an acolyte of Nemesis, the goddess must have felt that it was he, Lysanias, who had the strongest case for vengeance. She had given him the victory. His prayer had been answered.

At the top, Sindron was using his pedagogue's staff to force Lydos back into a corner of the office, while Philia had obviously found Lysanias' dagger and was holding it out awkwardly, stiff-armed in front of her. No, it wasn't his dagger! It was a kitchen knife! Whatever it was, its wavering blade was enough to put real fear into Lydos' eyes, though the fear in Philia's looked nearly as great. Brave girl, thought Lysanias, revising the opinion of her defencelessness he had formed that afternoon.

"I told you to take Philia home," Lysanias hissed at Sindron, as he nodded to indicate that the assassin was dead. He tried to sound angry, but the relief and gratitude were too great and he smiled his thanks.

"I did, master, but she got that knife and followed me back here. We crept up here behind Phraston." Lysanias didn't remind Sindron his orders were to take the girl home and stay there himself. Sindron didn't point out that, by not thinking it through, Lysanias had allowed himself to be led into a trap. He had overheard enough of the riddles to deduce that Strynises could have been paid to help lead Lysanias down this path, and knew that he couldn't have allowed the boy to leap into this on his own, even if it did mean bringing the girl. And just when his master seemed to be starting to act rationally.

"Shall I kill him, master?" It was Philia. He almost laughed. The way she was holding the knife it would be difficult to kill anyone, but he was amazed she could keep up the slave-boy act after all that had happened. "No, not yet," he answered.

Philia felt a secret joy that two of the men responsible for Curly's death were now dead themselves and she had been here to see it. A third was snivelling in front of her. But she had been terrified and, even gripping her right wrist with her left hand, it was difficult to keep the knife steady. She was glad when Lysanias stepped forward and took it from her.

Lydos was wailing at Lysanias now. "Don't let them torture me, master! You won't let them torture me, will you? They torture slaves. Phraston didn't put his seal to my freedom documents yet. I'm still a slave. He was toying with me, making me do things I didn't agree with. He was like that. He made me go to Tanagra and hire an assassin. I never wanted to have people killed." The man was quaking, grovelling.

"Sit down Lydos. Now I want the truth. That man. He's the one who killed my uncle, correct?"

"Yes, master."

"Did he also kill Ephialtes?"

"Yes, master. That's what he was hired for. Klereides was an extra. The brute boasted he climbed over the rooftops, even while the workers were on guard outside, got in through the courtyard and killed Ephialtes while he slept. With a golden sacrificial trident he stole from the Temple of Theseos, he said. We didn't want that! It points straight at the dining club and Kimon. Thank goodness they've hushed that up. He said he could make it look like an accident and then this! He was mad. He says Nemesis tells him what to do, whatever instructions mere mortals give him. Nobody wanted Klereides to die, just to frighten him. He says Nemesis told him to kill your uncle, and he was threatening to inform on us, if we didn't pay him more – in tribute to the goddess for her assistance he said. It's a great relief he's dead. You won't let them torture me, will you?"

Tears streamed down the man's face as he lifted his head fully and turned his mournful face and questioning eyes on Lysanias.

Sindron had stopped using his staff as a weapon, and now stood leaning on it for support. He felt suddenly old and weak. He was sick and disgusted that he had once regarded this man as his friend, and on top of that came shame that he had gone to him for advice, trusting that he would be more honest and truthful than anyone else in Athens. How could he have been such a fool? Before Lysanias came back in, Lydos had tried an appeal to their past friendship, which Sindron had dismissed with the contempt it deserved.

Now Sindron registered that he had just killed a man, something that, as a domestic slave, he had never expected to have cause to do. He was surprised how little it disturbed him, and to find that there was a calm sense of satisfaction under the shaking in his hands and limbs that he decided must be his reaction to the danger his master had been in. Somehow he found it more and more difficult to envisage life not as a slave, even when he looked down at the skewered body of the man who had offered to buy him his freedom.

As Lysanias had her knife, Philia grabbed up Sindron's knobbly stick from the floor as a weapon, but the anti-climax, the release of tension, was too much. She slumped to a cross-legged sitting position on the floor, where she shivered, head bowed, amazed at her own bravado and wishing she was tucked up warm in her bed. Now that the tension was gone, she could feel her swollen eye throbbing, and the dull ache of other bruises. Aware of his own bruises, Lysanias felt an urge to take her in his arms and comfort her, tell her how brave she had been, but now was not the time.

One of the oil-lamps was burning out of oil and the flame was guttering, so that their shadows danced on the walls. It was suddenly cold and very, very quiet. In the distance, a cock crowed. By the gods, could it really be that late?

"Why, Lydos? Why?"

"Phraston thought the radical party would collapse if Ephialtes was dead, or there would be riots and Kimon would be forced to make himself tyrant and reverse all those reforms."

"Not Ephialtes! My uncle! Why kill my uncle? Or even frighten him?"

"He was giving financial support to the radicals, and to the Fellowship of Hephaistos," Lydos shouted back, as though it justified everything, then, realising he was in no position to be shouting, he toned down. "He gave them the land for that shrine to Hephaistos in Peiraieos, and he teamed up with a building contractor to bid for the contract to put up that Temple of Hephaistos, even though my master leaned on everyone not to, even the foreigners. Yet he was assuring the dining club he was a loyal supporter of Kimon, giving statues to the Temple of Theseos. When they found out, Phraston, Ariston, they were all furious."

"So Ariston was in on it too. And he claimed to be a loyal friend of Klereides!"

Sindron joined in. "I didn't have time to tell you, master. We discovered the chariot and horse that the assassin must have used that night to take your uncle to the shipyard. In Ariston's stables. And this worm organised it all..."

If looks could kill, Lydos would have been dead from Sindron's stare alone. Philia had been agitatedly trying to speak. Now she blurted out.

"He'd been having an affair with General Ariston's wife. My Curly. Ariston's slave told me. My Curly." She crumpled into tears.

Lysanias managed to step over to her, where he could stroke her head in sympathy without taking his eyes off Lydos. So Ariston did have a personal motive. Lysanias was worn out by all the revelations. He wanted it all to be over, but he was sure there was more to come.

"What else haven't you told us, Lydos?"

Sindron could see his master was tiring rapidly.

"That's it, master," said Lydos. "That's why they did it, I'm sure. But they just wanted to scare him," he insisted, despite this new evidence that made the claim seem improbable. "Aristodikos went too far. I'm just a slave, master. Doing what I'm told."

Sindron was amazed. Lydos really seemed to think he could just pass the blame onto the others and dismiss his own involvement as obedience to orders.

"He hasn't told us about the falsified accounts, master. They must have something to do with it."

"Well, Lydos?"

"What falsified accounts is that, master?" Great Zeus, Sindron realised the man was going to try to bluff it out. After all that had happened! He felt like hurling him off the platform himself and into the dye vats. He spoke in icy daggers.

"Lydos, I thought you said you didn't want to be tortured. You're not going about it very sensibly. Now, Klereides' main account. I saw for myself it has been re-written in one hand, one ink, so let's not pretend any more."

Lydos' eyes flicked between the faces of the two men facing him. He gave a deep sigh. A gentle snore came from Philia's curled up body where she had slumped against Lysanias leg and slipped to the floor.

"Phraston knew that Kimon's visible contributions to the city had to be hurried forward and made more obvious, if Kimon was to avoid the ostracism vote which we could all see coming. And the propaganda, Mikon's paintings in the Temple of Theseos, in the Painted Colonnade. Except they didn't want it to look like propaganda, so they paid Mikon and others unofficially to enable them to claim to be working at their own expense. It cost a lot of money. He took some out of Kimon's profits from sales of war trophies and slaves. Kallias put up some, before he was sent as envoy to Persia. Phraston spent a lot of his own money. The others all chipped in, including Klereides, but it wasn't enough. Kimon was away. He didn't know.

"Phraston could see time was running out. Klereides was very lax about checking his accounts, lots of spare profits uninvested that he wouldn't miss. So Phraston took it and used it. He intended to replace it. If Hierokles had inherited, it would have been no problem. He knew, he approved. As long as Phraston gave the money back. After all, Kimon and Phraston had helped him pay his fine.

"Then you turned up as the heir not Hierokles. We had to do something. We had a truthful set of accounts to keep track of everything for ourselves. We had a fake set to show Otanes and Makaria showing the high gambling debts and failed investments and less than truthful returns on his main investments to cover our withdrawals – they were bound to tell you about those. But Hermon was likely to reveal the true level of his payments to Klereides and you might seek to verify the return on other investments. So Phraston told me to create a third set with truthful figures for those verifiable items and rather less false withdrawals for gambling and uncheckable investments that would give us time to pay back. He always said it was just a loan. Risky if we hadn't been able to distract Otanes attention at the time we showed them to you but we managed that."

Lydos looked pleased for a moment before he registered that they had actually failed and that he had just confessed to another serious crime.

He was trying to place all the blame on Phraston, when Sindron knew that Lydos' old master had treated the slave as a full partner, involving him in all decisions, even if he was not yet a freedman. Could this be the friend who had saved him when Sindron got into difficulties as they were swimming, the friend he had defended against that group of youngsters who had accused him of being a Persian spy because of his skin colour? He felt a bitter taste in his mouth.

Lydos started pouring it all out as though this would somehow improve his situation.

"It all went wrong. You started asking questions instead of accepting it as an accident. Philebos panicked, didn't claim credit for the meeting as planned, so it was more difficult to blame him. He kept running to Amynias who threatened to involve Phraston. He hadn't done enough to implicate Hermon, so we couldn't do a citizen's arrest and set him up for trial. It was all a mess."

Lysanias stepped in again. "And Hierokles? Was he in on the plot to 'frighten' Klereides?"

"No, master, just the accounts." Was that the truth? Lydos was looking even more uncomfortable now.

"Then why did he set off for Athens before he could have heard of Klereides' death?" asked Sindron. Lydos looked startled, but he had an answer.

"According to Phraston, he and Ariston summoned their key men to Athens as soon as they heard Kimon was on his way back, that the Spartans had humiliated him." It sounded plausible. Kimon would probably have sent a runner.

"Kimon, was he involved in all this?" Lysanias hated to ask it about his hero.

"Great gods, no. He'd have been horrified."

"What by? The inefficiency?" Lysanias new cynicism took over but he was pleased to hear the reassurance, even if he couldn't be sure it was true or that Lydos, as a slave, would have been trusted with that knowledge.

"The tomb carving, what about that?" Sindron asked but it seemed they had reached the limit of Lydos' knowledge or what he was prepared to talk about.

"Surely, n-no-one w-would be that stupid, would they?" Lydos was shivering now in the chill of the morning.

"Boiotos might be," came in a sleepy voice from the slight figure curled up on the floor. They'd forgotten Philia. Lysanias realised he should look after her, see she was warm enough, but no time now.

"That foolish man! I should never have trusted..." In his sudden anger at Boiotos, Lydos blurted it out, and then pulled himself to a halt as he realised he had done exactly what he had been trying to avoid. Now it was out, strangely Lydos looked less frightened.

"Thank you, Lydos. I think we get the picture." Sindron glanced across at Lysanias and their eyes met. He felt sure they had come to the same conclusion. That it sounded as though Lydos had joined forces with Boiotos to pay the assassin extra to kill Klereides instead of frightening him, Boiotos probably in the hope of gaining the inheritance for his father. Lydos to please his master or to cover his own embezzlements but the reason didn't really matter now. Come to think of it, the conspirators would have needed someone not in the public eye like Boiotos to get messages between them and to the assassin and to organise things. Why had they always dismissed Boiotos as a stupid bully instead of checking on him more? There seemed to be an unspoken agreement between them not to try to spell it out. It could come out when Lydos was tortured. Lysanias was coming to like that idea.

"And the stories of Klereides' gambling debts, bad investments? Where did that idea come from?"

"Well, we had to have some cover, something to tell Otanes and Makaria, in case they got suspicious." Lydos even seemed to recover a degree of confidence, now he had confessed. "Just so long as Klereides didn't hear about it. Lucky Klereides, they called him. Always picking good investments, hardly ever losing a bet, knew how to pick a winner, whether it was a fighting cock or a runner."

"Well, you and your master made sure his luck ran out, didn't you!" Lysanias tone was grim. It almost sounded like a threat, and Lydos shrank back. Or was that from the knife that Lysanias had raised threateningly? Lysanias did feel like having his revenge on one more person, but he couldn't do it, not in cold blood.

Then he remembered his promise to Stephanos. Lysanias' uncle wasn't the only victim.

"So what about Ephialtes? Who was in on that plot?"

"I don't know, master. I'm a slave. They knew I could be tortured, so I wasn't in on their meetings, so that I wouldn't know names."

"But you were about to be given freedom, the running of a bank!" interjected Sindron.

"Even so, even so. They're sticklers for propriety," Lydos rejoined with a tinge of bitterness.

"But you found the assassin. You were briefed. Who did that? Phraston? Hierokles? Ariston?"

"Yes, master. Yes, master. Those three. And someone whose name I don't know. Red hair, a stutter..." Lydos was abject, cringing. "And strong hints from them that they'd like Klereides dead as well, were there?" Sindron interjected and, to Lysanias, "There's more than one way a master can give an instruction, master."

Lydos didn't answer. He seemed to clamp his mouth shut, as though he knew he had said too much already.

"Master, I suggest we hand this miserable creature over to the authorities." Sindron could guess that some of the money Makaria had supplied to make good Klereides' so-called gambling debts had found its way into Lydos' own account, but that seemed too unimportant after all the other things they had discovered. He felt sure they had extracted all the substantial information they were going to get. Sindron found he could feel no sympathy, no further friendship towards someone who had so totally abandoned all those principles he once thought they shared. The friendship was dead. He felt no regrets about the torture that would extract the full truth from the man.

"I think we should hand him over to the Fellowship of Hephaistos, Sindron, and see how much they leave of him when they find out he organised the assassination of Ephialtes." Lysanias gave Sindron a slight wink. Lets make the evil worm suffer a little more, it said.

Suffer he did. "No, master, please, not the Fellowship. Let the Scythian guard arrest me!"

Sindron joined in. "Maybe the radicals would be better, master, after all they are the dominant faction now and Ephialtes was their leader."

"No, please, the magistrate in charge of the Scythian guard, he supports the radicals but he's a fair man, he'll lock me up safe in the prison." The panic-stricken words poured out, and, when he stopped, the sound of his teeth chattering filled the silent room, over-riding the regular breathing and occasional whimpers from Philia where she had fallen asleep again on the floor.

With the new agreement between the radicals and the aristocrats, they weren't sure exactly who was in charge, so, in the end, they decided to take Lydos to Perikles' house. They knew it was relatively near and dawn was breaking.

"... I still think it's a terrible deal. We gave away too much!" Arkhestratos great, coarse voice boomed out as they were shown into Perikles' entertaining room. The rowers' champion stood angrily, as Perikles and Themistokles beside him lounged, breaking their fast. Themistokles seemed very subdued.

"I agree entirely, but it's done now..." Themistokles broke off as he saw Sindron. "Ah, my slave friend." He rose, looking genuinely pleased. Lysanias looked quizzically at Sindron, who mouthed "later". He and Sindron had been gripping Lydos by the arms. They now released him, though Lysanias kept his hand on the knife concealed in the folds of his cloak. Philia had followed behind, Sindron's stick on her shoulder like Herakles with his club. The discolouration round her eye showed purple and red even through the brown of the walnut oil, and her lips were swollen. He knew she must have aches and pains – he had quite a few of his own – but she hadn't complained. Now she stood blearily just behind him. Lysanias could almost feel her weariness.

Themistokles came towards them and drew Sindron to one side, as Lysanias explained to Perikles the need to have Lydos arrested and gaoled as quickly as possible for both murders. He spoke confidentially, not wanting to risk Lydos being killed by a mob before he went through the whole process of torture, trial and execution. Lydos seemed to sense the danger and stayed quiet, though his eyes remained alert. He had dropped the guilty and humble slave pose, Lysanias registered, and seemed to be presenting more as the dignified and possibly wronged banker. Well, that won't do him any good, he thought.

"As you see, I am safe, thanks to you," Themistokles told Sindron, gratitude in his eyes. "But they've reached an agreement that I'm to leave Athens for good." Sindron looked sympathetic, but wasn't sure what to say. Perikles had overheard.

"It was the only way to save you from execution. I've told you," he said.

"We could have taken full power, got rid of the aristocrats!"

"That's right," Arkhestratos joined in, from where he had crouched to help himself to some bread and herring. "That's what we should have done! That attempted takeover gave us good enough reason."

Perikles sounded tired of explaining the reasons as he enunciated carefully and clearly, "You both saw the situation yesterday, and there are four thousand fully-armed battle-ready pro-Kimon hoplites approaching the city at this moment, with many inside eager to join with them in any struggle. Without Kimon's co-operation we can't hope to contain them. We had no choice. I just thank the gods we have avoided the civil conflict that could have torn the city apart. We're still on a knife's edge. Don't you see that?"

The other two politicians didn't respond. Clearly they did see it but had just needed to protest at something they knew had to be. Themistokles broke the silence. "Anyway, you're rid of Kimon for ten years. At least I achieved that for you – one promise kept. They've no leader now. Perikles has proved a most able pupil, able enough to outmanoeuvre the master," he said with a slight wry smile. "Make the most of it. Hang onto that majority and you can do what we always wanted."

Suddenly it struck Sindron that maybe this could have been the deal Themistokles had made with the Great King. In return for a princedom, he would damage Sparta and get rid of the Greeks' leading general, disabling the Greeks as a fighting force. Blatant treachery if one didn't understand his motive of giving power to the ordinary people. Knowing what he was capable of, how could the radicals risk letting him stay, even if that were feasible? But what chance would the old schemer have back in Persia once the Great King realised he had been tricked? Or had he?

Sparta was crippled. Athens teetering on the brink of civil war, its great war-leader exiled. The Great King had what he wanted but what had Themistokles really intended to achieve?

The defeated look in the elderly politician's eyes revealed his awareness that he would never again be top dog in his native city. Stop the romancing, Sindron, he thought. This man's a tough politician. He knows the rules of the game. That the crafty newcomer will always seek to oust the crafty oldster. His day was over and he knew it.

Themistokles turned to Sindron again, a slight twinkle in his eye now. "At least, they say I'm to be re-instated when I'm dead and have the honour of a tomb on the harbour side at Peiraieos," he said with a rueful smile. "So I'll be back some day, maybe fairly soon." Despite the smile, he looked much older than yesterday, less firmly erect. "You win and you lose. Have to be going now. The ship is waiting, I'm told."

They all wished him well, even Lydos. Philia felt awed and tired and didn't really understand who these people were, but she felt the emotion in the air. She would ask Lysanias to explain when they got home, she decided. She felt she had proved herself and that it would be difficult for people not to give her more respect in future and hopefully the control of the household that was her due. She had learned a lot in the last few days about the world of women and the world of men. She was determined to make use of that knowledge.

Arkhestratos went with Themistokles to be sure he reached the ship safely. He had a few of his boys waiting nearby as escort and bodyguard.

Perikles moved into action. He called the Scythian guard to arrest Lydos and imprison him awaiting trial. He arranged a chariot, so that Sindron could take Philia home, and they went, though Sindron would have liked to see this through. At least the boy's future now seemed secure, he thought, as Hierokles would now surely be unable to challenge Lysanias' inheritance. His own future looked safe too, especially now Lysanias could see where Otanes' loyalties lay.

Then Perikles sat Lysanias down to break his fast, and the young man discovered he was starving, despite the full dinner the night before. Between mouthfuls, Lysanias told the politician the whole story. Perikles looked surprised, appalled, intrigued, and pleased at appropriate points.

He immediately took steps to have the bodies removed from the dye works before the workers there could spread too many rumours and sent messages to Lydos' family and to other political leaders. Then he surprised Lysanias in his turn.

As Lysanias sat, pleased to relax, Perikles paced before him.

"Lysanias, you are new to Athenian politics, though I can see you have learnt a lot in your brief time here. We have a very delicate political situation at the moment." Lysanias signified that he realised this. "Because of that, to have all this exposed to the public gaze would do more harm than good. Clearly, the aristocrats will not wish it known that some of their leading figures could behave in this way. And I think I can persuade the radical leaders to moderate their desire for revenge for the killing of Ephialtes, as you have exacted it for us. It really is down to you."

"I don't think I know what you mean," Lysanias murmured, confused.

"You have to decide if you will have Lydos charged with complicity to murder, and with embezzlement of your uncle's money. If you do, as a slave, he will be tortured to establish the truth in a way acceptable to the courts and, I'm sure, found guilty and executed by nailing to a board in the usual way. You have that right and he deserves the punishment. But, in the process, everything else will be in the public gaze as well. As for your own killing of a man, that was clearly in self-defence as well as righteous vengeance, so you should have no problem there."

"I think I was aware of most of that," Lysanias responded when the politician paused, "but I'm still not sure what you're trying to tell me." He was surprised, too, at the new authority in this Perikles. His leader only recently assassinated, Themistokles only just despatched to permanent exile, and now here was Perikles, young for a politician, until yesterday only one of a group of men behind Ephialtes, talking as though the fate of Athens were in his hands. Was this presumption or did politics work like that? Was he just taking advantage of good fortune, even though it was the bad fortune of his friends? Or was it possible he had been using Themistokles and Ephialtes to engineer the series of events leading to the exiling of Kimon and had now taken the opportunity to get Themistokles out of the way to clear his own path to leadership?

Could Perikles really have planned all this to end up to his advantage? Down that avenue of thinking, Lysanias realised, lay total cynicism. He dismissed the thought. But still...

"If you do, we risk major civil unrest, calls for the trial of Ariston and Hierokles, Amynias and Inaros, if not of others."

Lysanias began to see what was being asked of him. To give up all further desire for vengeance in the cause of peace in the body politic. After the riots and looting of the previous day, narrowly brought under control, he could see why Perikles was concerned, though he found the man's cool, detached way of regarding everything as slightly alien.

He sighed to himself. "What do you suggest?"

"I will send a message to the leaders of the aristocrats, indicating what has happened. I'm sure General Ariston will choose exile with Kimon, as soon as he hears what you've discovered. Hierokles appears to be implicated for certain only in the embezzlement of funds. I'm sure he will choose to return to his estate and stay there, keeping out of politics for a long time."

Lysanias had to say it. "I think he is implicated in the murder as well, and definitely in the murder of Ephialtes."

"Yes, well, he's not young. Maybe I can see that Boiotos is sent to a military outpost a long way away. Possibly Hierokles too." He paused to see how Lysanias had taken this, but the young man was waiting for more blurring of the clear issues of guilt and innocence. But no! He had to assert himself. After all he had done, he couldn't give in to tiredness. "I'd want a guarantee of that. For both of them. They must feel it as punishment for their crime not just political retribution." Had he really said that? Talking to Perikles as an equal? He kept his expression severe.

"That should be possible."

It didn't sound much of a guarantee but he had to trust this man who was talking as though he had authority.

Perikles continued, "We were planning to round up the members of the Golden Trident and question them about the assassination of Ephialtes, but we couldn't do that till after this business with the troops is settled and Kimon is out of the way. We didn't really believe they would leave such a blatant clue, so we were trying to think of other suspects. Now you've cleared it up for us, and you have my thanks and, I'm sure, those of the city, which will doubtless be given more fulsome expression at some future date."

"Surely you want to see them punished?" Lysanias found all this disturbing. Where was Nemesis now? Or Apollo or Athene, guardians of justice? He wondered what Stephanos or Glaukon would think, if they knew the conspirators were to escape retribution. He found himself agitatedly picking at bits of food, half eating them and putting them down.

"In politics, there are other considerations, Lysanias. The city has need of men with the skills of Amynias and Inaros, for instance," Perikles continued. "I suggest a spell of preventive detention in the prison alongside Lydos will put sufficient fear into them to make them good citizens in future. Does that sound acceptable?"

"Not very, but I suspect I have no choice."

"I hoped you would realise that." Was that a friendly smile, as though Perikles were accepting Lysanias into his club of conniving politicians? If so, Lysanias wasn't sure he wanted it.

"You promise you'll make that hard for them?" He tried to shout it but his voice blurted through the bite of bread he had just taken.

"Very hard."

"And explain that I may take action against them at a future date. So they have something hanging over them?"

"I will interview them myself."

Was that the promise he wanted? Or a politician being evasive?

"If it makes it easier, I have had to take a step back myself," Perikles confided. "The whole deal is on condition that General Myronides takes over Kimon's leadership of the army, the city and the confederacy."

"But why? You're the obvious…"

"Too young. Too exposed. Too hated. The aristocrats and the allies are more likely to trust a general of Myronides' age and experience. They think he can control the hotheads."

Perikles paused, cutting off the note of bitterness in his voice, and for a moment the mask seemed to drop and Lysanias could see that this man was vulnerable too and that he knew how vulnerable he was. Lysanias could sense the politician's deep disappointment and appreciated his struggle not to let it show as his face snapped back to firm self-assurance. So much for his theory that Perikles had manoeuvred events to win the leadership for himself. Or, if he had, he hadn't succeeded.

Not yet, Lysanias told himself. For this man was clearly ambitious. Perhaps he thought General Myronides would be easy to manipulate. And then, looking inward, Lysanias wondered how he himself had become this cynical. Was this what it meant to be an Athenian? Could he really *like* himself as someone who saw the world through these jaundiced eyes?

After that, Lysanias dreaded to ask his next question.

"And what about Lydos?" The completion of his vengeance, which had seemed so assured, was slipping out of his hands.

Perikles' personal slave had come in and started dressing Perikles in his dress uniform as a general, breastplate, greaves, scarlet shoulder cape. It made no difference to their conversation. The slave might have been invisible, a non-man, but with each addition, the politician seemed to transform more and more into the statesman, the man who, whatever had been agreed about the nominal leader, knew his would be the intelligence behind the new regime.

"Ah. Well, I don't think you will like this either. The collapse of a major bank at this time could have serious repercussions on much of the city's trade and business. From what you say, Lydos was due to inherit the bank from Phraston, along with his freedom. We know that depositors will accept him, and that he is the only person available who could run it efficiently."

"You're suggesting we let the villain off! Reward him with his freedom!" Lysanias was genuinely astounded.

"After we have let him stew in prison for a few days with some of the criminals and looters we arrested yesterday, yes, I'm afraid so. I said you wouldn't like it. I realise it may not help, but I'm sure he will be only too willing to offer financial compensation to you for the wrong he has done your family." Lysanias bristled at the suggestion that he might regard money as adequate compensation but tried not to show it.

"It means covering up the real cause of Phraston's death, maybe presenting it as an accident or natural causes," Perikles continued. "That's why I've sent someone to remove Phraston's body. I think we can display the body of Aristodikos of Tanagra as the assassin of Ephialtes. Apprehended and killed by a responsible citizen who prefers to remain unnamed."

"You mean I don't get any credit for all this? I can't tell anyone?" Lysanias wasn't sure he had wanted credit, but it did seem an inadequate outcome for all the worry, stress and sheer effort of uncovering his uncle's killer and Ephialtes'. Was this adequate revenge for brutal murder?

"I assure you a lot of important people will be told, but they will never mention it. That can only rebound to your credit, when you decide to take a role in politics yourself."

These Athenians were all the same. It was a gentle bribe but it was a bribe, Lysanias was sure. His pay-off for keeping his mouth shut. But, as he had said, he had no choice, if he didn't want to be driven out of the city himself. But it wouldn't do. It wasn't enough.

"No," he blurted out. "No. It won't do. I want revenge. Klereides' spirit demands revenge. These men are tainted with the miasma of murder. The city cannot allow them to wander freely into public places and temples, polluting all they meet, the whole city, drawing down the wrath of the gods on us all. Surely you can't allow that!"

The politician seemed to be drawn up short by Lysanias' righteous anger. Perhaps he didn't have the faith in the gods that someone in his position should have. Lysanias had heard that there were doubters, new philosophies.

"Ah yes, maybe I was forgetting the religious angle," Perikles responded after a brief pause. "If you don't mind my saying so, as you grow older, you may find it necessary to question whether some of these ancient beliefs, the ill-matched divinities are really an adequate explanation of why the world is as it is, but I would agree that a large proportion of the populace do share your fears, so we must pay attention to that."

Lysanias' own father had occasionally laughed at superstitions and the more implausible of the stories surrounding the gods but this was much more disturbing. However the politician went on before Lysanias could think about it further. Now he suggested, "Voluntary exile. They will be, ah, 'encouraged' to take a period of voluntary exile to cleanse the city and themselves. After we have ensured competent successors to handle their duties, of course."

"No, now! And Lydos. You won't do that with Lydos, will you? The man has no real remorse yet you want to reward him with his freedom. He could kill again. Do you want that?" He was overstepping the mark, as a very young man he knew he was overstepping the mark. But Perikles took it – and had an answer.

"I was coming to that. We can arrange a course of scourging and starvation and physical labour, which you can have a hand in approving and that I'm sure you will see as suitable punishment and expiation. After all, he is a slave and was possibly acting under instruction and will doubtless say so. It will be assumed by the court anyway. So action would have to be taken against his owner, to whom any pollution would presumably attach, but he is dead. If he acted on his own account, his master would still be liable for any penalty. So we have a clear problem here.

"If he stays, he clearly has to be under close control. With his master dead and no heirs we are aware of, his ownership now falls to the city as does that of the bank. We can refuse Phraston's posthumous manumission and give Lydos and the bank to a responsible citizen who will exercise the necessary control."

Lysanias didn't like where this was leading.

"Me, you mean me," he cried out, his voice coming out as a shriek. "You ask me to associate on a daily basis with the agent of my uncle's murder?"

"I'm sure you could delegate that task to that very capable slave of yours. Sindron was it?"

"But Sindron would…"

"I'm sure you will be able to find ways of ensuring that Lydos does not enjoy the fruits of his crimes." The now fully-uniformed general paused, turning away to enjoy a final olive, as though to give Lysanias time to think. Lysanias felt penned into a corner, as though he had asked for this. It was unbelievable. Could Perikles really offer this? To give one of the city's largest banks to an inexperienced young man of eighteen who has been in the city for only a few days? He felt flattered but doubtful. How much power would this man really have now?

"You really think you could … I could…?"

"I wouldn't suggest it if I didn't. We have time. Think it over for a few days."

Lysanias expressed the one thought that tormented him. "But, if he isn't tortured, we'll never know the whole truth, who was and wasn't involved."

"Ah well, our experience is that slaves confess to anything and everything under torture. Truth doesn't really come into it."

"But…."

After the cynicism, a softer, more avuncular tone came into Perikles' voice as he advised, "Sometimes it may be better not to know, Lysanias."

Lysanias realised that meant he might in the future have to meet and talk and do business with citizens who had had a hand in his uncle's murder or that of Ephialtes. Could he live with that?

"But think it over."

"Very well. I have come to appreciate that politics entails compromise." That's putting it mildly, Lysanias thought to himself. It entails conniving, deceit, conspiracy, deception, self-seeking, bribery, blackmail, pressurising – where did the list end?

"Good man!" A look in his eyes betrayed that the leader felt genuinely relieved. "Believe me, this is the best solution. Great Athene will approve." His slave placed Perikles' great bronze crested helmet on his head, the helmet that was shaped like the one depicted on statues of great Athene, the helmet that hid completely the peculiar shape of Perikles' cranium. This man is a leader, thought Lysanias, even if he is obliged to stay in the background for a while. Though, whether he himself would feel comfortable being led by someone who could think and manipulate the way that Perikles did, he wasn't sure.

Lysanias said no more. He didn't like what he had agreed to, but, in its roundabout way, it did resolve matters. And he had proved his manhood. If Perikles wasn't lying, important people would hear about what he had done and that should mean they would pay him more respect than they had so far, more respect than they normally gave to men of his age.

As Perikles set off on horseback to meet up with Myronides and the other generals to talk with the troops returning from Sparta, Lysanias followed as far as the Sacred Gate from which ran the road to Eleusis, Megara and Corinth. They were joined by an increasing number of curious and still worried citizens, unsure, he imagined, whether they would be called on to welcome or resist the hoplites reported by the lookout on the gate tower above as now visible in the far distance.

Lysanias noted that, as the generals made the necessary libations to Hermes of Travellers at his shrine by the inner gate, for their short but very important journey, Myronides insisted on taking the precedence that was now his due, with Kimon alongside him and Perikles quite low in the ranking. It looked as though Perikles wouldn't have it all his own way in future. He mused that this might be the last time that Kimon would ever wear the full panoply of an Athenian general and couldn't help feeling sympathy for the deposed hero, though not without a tinge of guilt.

As the generals advanced to meet the troops away from the city, Lysanias opted to walk home through the bustling early morning streets, surprised that life seemed to be going on normally. He felt at peace with himself but wasn't sure why. He had achieved something against the odds. He had unearthed the killers of his uncle but failed to achieve the full revenge the gods and his uncle's soul demanded, though the actual killer was dead, the man who would have paid the killer was dead, those who had most supported him would shortly be exiled or as good as. The others involved would be punished, if not as much as he would have liked. That was a lot. He hoped the gods would accept it as all that an 18-year-old novice could be expected to achieve and forgive him for the shortfalls. More important that they would grant Klereides' soul the rest it craved.

Then, with something like elation, he realised he had also survived in the vipers' nest of Athenian politics, kept his household intact and earned respect at least in some quarters. Was that enough? At 18, it felt enough. At least now he could devote himself to the mourning due his dead uncle and the rites of purification for his own infringements of his religious duties.

He allowed himself to think forward to his marriage to beautiful Philia, and, beyond that, to having nothing more to do with his time than be master of the household, manage his investments, exercise his body in the gymnasium and his mind in the Akademeia gardens, and do whatever military training was required of him.

And his mother, his family in Eion, why did he keep forgetting them? He must see they were alright, maybe bring them to Athens out of harm's way. Now he could even use his money to fund a proper search to find out if his father really was dead or still alive somewhere, though he was finding it easier to accept now that he might be dead. And he really must make contact with his mother's parents, even if they were from a class different from the one of which he was now so firmly a part.

Lysanias thought over the compromises he would have to make in his personal life. Now, on Perikles' logic, maybe Makaria and Otanes had been punished enough, but he really wanted them out of the way. If he sent them to look after the farm, that would achieve that, and there would be less chance that Makaria would disgrace the family by her affair being discovered.

That left him without a steward in the house in Athens. Would that post be a sufficient bribe to persuade Sindron not to ask for his freedom yet? Lysanias didn't feel he could do without Sindron around and the old man really had proved himself a great friend as well as a loyal servant. He'd need him even more if he did become owner of Phraston's bank. Maybe, if he were to encourage the relationship that seemed to be developing between Sindron and Glykera, his slave would feel bound to the house? He realised he was thinking like an Athenian politician but, perhaps, living in Athens, one had to, merely to survive. After all, he had promised freedom, but that would mean Sindron would be free to leave him, go away.

Rounding a corner, Lysanias saw Sindron coming to meet him, though it took a second look to be sure it was really his slave. The tidy hair and beard and neatly-draped cloak bore little resemblance to the straggly unkempt style he had known all his youth. Gone too was the slight stoop and shuffling gait. Although, at his age, Sindron must be even more exhausted than Lysanias felt, this Sindron strode confidently ahead, back straight, head erect, with a sprightly step, with no staff or stick to support him, though the slight limp was still there as he stepped carefully to avoid horse, mule and oxen dung. True there was also a wariness in the way he looked at his surroundings but he seemed alert, eager. The assurance was more that of a citizen rather than a slave, of which the only sign was the slightly subservient way he stood aside in deference to any oncoming citizens.

How could anyone change that much in a few days? But, then, he knew that he himself was no longer that eager and innocent youth who trotted down the gangplank at Peiraieos seven long days ago. It seemed a lifetime, so much had happened.

He hoped Sindron felt that the changes were for the better. That his master had become more mature, better able to deal with the challenges that lay ahead but recalled ruefully the impetuosity with which he had rushed alone into the trap at the dye works. He still had a lot to learn, as Sindron would doubtless remind him. And he still had to tell Sindron what had passed with Perikles. The old man's sense of rightness, of justice would be outraged he knew. But Sindron seemed to be coming to appreciate the ways of this world, so he would see through to aspects Lysanias had missed and give his usual sound advice. It was good to have him close.

Then Lysanias remembered Perikles' parting words.

"I must say I admired the way you went about investigating your uncle's death. Very impressive. The city needs concerned citizens determined to seek out evidence and bring charges against wrongdoers who have offended against the common good..."

The politician had left the words hanging, but his implication was clear. Well, it won't be me, thought Lysanias, I've done enough investigating for a lifetime.

HISTORICAL NOTE

Something very like a revolution happened in Athens in 461 BC, taking power out of the hands of the aristocrats. It made possible the development of the radical democracy in Athens, the growth of the Athenian Empire and all the artistic, architectural and intellectual achievements we associate with the Golden Age of Athens, which has played such a vital part in Western civilisation generally. Yet very little is actually known about it.

Most of what we do know about events at this time comes from writers who lived somewhat later, who are not regarded as entirely reliable – primarily Aristotle in his "Constitution of Athens", 130 or more years later, (which may have been written by one of his pupils) and Plutarch's "Greek Lives", about 550 years later (who relied heavily on gossip and anecdote). Otherwise it is mainly deduction from inscriptions and from surviving fragments of artefacts. So, in trying to rebuild this fascinating society and its events, I am speculating no more than the historians. In fact, it proved a complex detective work in itself piecing together likely events and attitudes from snippets of evidence.

Of the major events, we know that, in this year, instigated by Ephialtes, the Assembly voted to reduce drastically the powers of the Areopagos and create real direct democracy of all citizen males over 18, that Kimon was sent home humiliated by the Spartans, that his elite troops (all citizens) were held up at Corinth, that he tried to get the reforms reversed, failed, and was ostracised (banished for ten years), that Ephialtes was assassinated, that Perikles was associated with him in some way, and that a man from Tanagra named Aristodikos was blamed for the assassination. There is no record of an attempted coup, though it seems highly probable, nor of a riot after the ostracism vote, though not unlikely.

How long this took or the precise order of events we don't know.

Was Themistokles in Athens? Aristotle thinks he was and that he tricked an indecisive Ephialtes into finally putting the motion that abolished most of the powers of the Areopagos. However, historians tend not to believe him. After all, though Themistokles' ten year ostracism was up, he had been condemned to death in his absence. Surely he wouldn't dare come back. Yet many happenings at this time bear the mark of his type of cunning and, if you'd been founder of the radical party that now looked like gaining power in a bloodless revolution, could you stay away any more than Lenin could have stayed away from St. Petersburg in 1917?

It is stretching plausibility a little to have Aspasia in Athens in 461 BC but just possible – she had a child by Lysikles after Perikles death in 429, which would put her at about the limit of childbearing age. I have gone along with the tradition that she was a courtesan, though some dispute this.

Historians also dispute whether there was a truce in the war with Persia but the fact that no military actions are reported around this time and Kimon felt free to take a large force to help Sparta implies there was one. Herodotos confirms that Kallias was in Persia on a mission about this time.

Very little is known about Ephialtes apart from his leadership role in the reforms, his suing of members of the Areopagos for corruption, his opposition to sending troops to help Sparta, and his assassination ("under cover of darkness"). And not a lot about Perikles' role, other than that he supported Ephialtes, or whether he was a general at this point.

The League of Hephaistos is my creation but a plausible one. Ephialtes evidently had some way of organising the popular vote, the building of a Temple to Hephaistos was started, implying a wave of new adherents to his worship, but was then postponed and only completed some years later, political groupings and religious sects were not uncommon.

So too is the news-teller Strynises, yet fragments of scurrilous satirical verse have been found that would be just his meat (I have used one or two of them), news and gossip did get around very quickly, and we know individuals did earn money from being the first with news from other cities.

Were women disaffected? Some years later, there was pressure for greater participation of women, as Aristophanes' comedies attest. This is a logical time for such ideas to have started. Is there an element of guesswork? Yes, of course. It will be interesting to see if future discoveries support my deductions.

No foundations have been uncovered for the Temple of The Mother, so I have assumed it must have been something like the ancient temples in Malta and Gozo made from giant blocks of un-hewn stone. And I have no evidence for dispensations from mourning responsibilities but then the Athenians were very practical people.

To aid in creating or re-creating this world, I have done what historians don't and maybe can't do. I have been aware of similarities with, for instance, Britain after World War II (democratic rejection of upper class war leader Churchill and of his party; adoption of policies favouring the poorer classes; extensive war damage and rebuilding; new social relationships), with Russia at the time of the October Revolution (factions battling for power in a time of unprecedented social shake-up; the arts used for propaganda; the wealthy scared for their fortunes), and with Victorian England (a democracy with imperial attitudes; bureaucracy; hypocrisy).

This has allowed me to escape from the upper class bias of the ancient historical writings on which modern historians base their accounts and to go on to explore a multi-faceted society at a time of rapid change as well as, more important, spinning what I hope is an exciting yarn.

Printed in the United Kingdom
by Lightning Source UK Ltd.
127691UK00001B/74/A